Ignis Internum

K. J. Warden

Dedication

To all those individuals who ever tried to put me
down, don't worry. You are too insignificant even to
eviscerate in fiction.

Acknowledgements

To my wife Jacqui; thank you for your patience and
tenacity for sticking with it throughout all the rants,
raves and rewrites. Your love and support is
incomparable and irreplaceable.

Ignis Internum

Chapter 1

Dirk's feet fell heavily on the stone steps as he descended into the dimly lit, windowless, cellar. It closed off the world outside and provided the calm he desperately craved. Having opened just before Christmas the previous year, the quirky little bar offered an eclectic choice of food and stocked a great selection of imported beers including De Koninck, his favourite Belgian brew. Also on the menu was a lovely little barmaid by the name of Melissa. The first beer had no effect and neither did the second, but the third kicked in and his mood began to lift. It was a Tuesday evening in March and he had left work early on the instruction of his boss, urged on by colleagues terrified he was about to do something that he would profoundly regret. Punching someone at work is never the best career move and neither is calling your boss an incompetent prick, at the top of your voice, in the middle of a busy office. Heeding the advice, he was now self-medicating into a more sedate state of mind. He hadn't actually punched anyone or even threatened to, although he'd come close and it was obvious that he'd wanted to. He suspected more than a few others had secretly wanted him to do it, maybe even wanted to do it themselves, although they hardly ever raised their heads let alone their voices or their fists.

After about an hour, sitting at the bar drinking and quietly cursing his stupidity in rising to the bastard's bait, he ordered another beer. Melissa could see something was bugging him and asked if he was ok. Not wanting to relive the moment again and turn off such a sweet young thing, he just said that it had been hard day at the office.

'I get off at eight' she said, 'you can buy *me* a drink then too if you like, or maybe even dinner; how about it handsome?'

Melissa was a tonic. When she smiled, cute dimples enchantingly appeared on either side of her lovely full mouth. Dirk had taken her out a couple of times before and she always cheered him up, however tonight he wanted to call it a night. He wasn't drunk, but he was still smarting and in the mood to get drunk and what purpose would being drunk and angry be? An angry drunk achieves nothing and he'd need to be ready to perform the next day. He knew it would be best to go home and lick his wounds, have a shower and get an early night. But that Melissa!

Before he could say "Let's take a shower together" he realized that he'd left his cellphone in his desk drawer. 'Shit!' He spat.

'Oh, how romantic' said Melissa.

Dirk quickly explained 'Sorry Mel, I just realised something. Hold that thought. I've got to nip out, but I'll be back soon and we'll have that drink, ok?' Standing up to leave, he leaned over the bar to kiss her on the cheek, but she turned and planted the softest kiss on his lips. He almost sat back down immediately.

'I'll be waiting handsome!' said Melissa, giving him a look that contained such promise.

Dirk finished his beer in a single gulp and headed upstairs. It was seven twenty and the air had a sharp edge to it. Fortunately his office wasn't too far from the bar, just a short brisk walk to the far end of a landscaped Square surrounded by beautiful Georgian town houses. Dirk worked for a consulting firm, based in Bristol in the West of England, specialising in financial technology. He'd relocated from London, around the time of the credit crunch and had been immediately impressed. Bristol is an old city, full of character and full of characters; past and present. A famous seafaring and trading port, it has a rich history of pirates and smugglers. Robert Louis Stevenson was said to have conceived his famous novel 'Treasure Island' on a visit to the city, basing the main character of Long John Silver on the then Landlord of 'The Hole in the Wall' pub. Dirk smiled as he passed the old pub and entertained the notion of turning up at work tomorrow with a sharp cutlass to make his point.

Arriving at his destination close on seven thirty, the main entrance was closed and he had to cut around the side of the building to sign back in with security.

"Evening Jeff", he said going into the security booth. "Hello Mister Dagger, working late?" enquired the jovial security guard.

"No, nothing so mundane, I forgot my phone that's all. Just a quick in and out."

"You take all the time you need Sir." announced Jeff with his customary cheery aplomb.

Dirk had known Jeff the security guard for a couple of years now and yet he still insisted on calling him Mister Dagger, even though he'd told him his name was 'Dirk'. Dirk's first name was actually Kirk, but due to the permutation of his first and last names his Grandfather had dubbed him Dirk. Like a Dagger. Like his surname. The name stuck and everyone, including his teachers at school, had elected to call him Dirk.

Passing through security, he walked the entire length of the building concourse and used his pass card to open the main door. Each morning he usually walked up the four flights of stairs to his office for the exercise, but tonight the weight he was carrying warranted taking the lift. For the entire ride up he just stared down at his shoes and shook his head, ruefully thinking that his rides on this lift were numbered. Stupid! Stupid! Stupid! An electronic bell pinged and a pleasant female voice announced their destination, then the doors slid open. Security was tight in the building and he had to go through two more key entry points, before he could gain access to the main office where he worked. The final door clicked open with a quick swipe of his card and he stepped inside. The office was empty and the lights had been turned off, but there was enough ambient light coming in through the windows for him to see. His desk was situated at the far end of the office. He walked slowly down towards it, each step seeming to drag longer and deeper into the floor. Dirk sat heavily in his chair and unlocked the top drawer of his desk, where he'd put his cellphone. Picking it up, he checked for messages. Found none and placed it on top of the desk. Realising there was no point in prolonging the inevitable he proceeded to sift through the accumulated junk of old pens, paperclips, mobile phone chargers, mints, gum and condoms. Binning what he no longer had use for, in case some bastard or other went through his personal stuff before he got another chance himself.

No sooner had he started when a noise emanated

from the other end of the office. It came from the room in the corner that doubled as a cloakroom/stationary cupboard and occasionally for private conference calls or one to one meetings. The door was spring hinged and always closed, but its solid construction couldn't mask the sounds coming from within. Dirk stopped what he was doing and listened. He heard it again. Faint, but unmistakable. It was the sound of voices coming from inside the cupboard. Abandoning his spring clean, he pushed himself out of the chair and did a fast tip toe shuffle up to the door and pressed his ear against it. The voices were that of two people, a man and a woman. The voices were intimate, some comments and giggles interspersed with gasps and groans. He continued to listen for a few moments then, with lightning bolt clarity, the penny dropped: 'No way?'

He'd instinctively picked up his cellphone. Now he switched it to video mode and listened intently to the unmistakable happenings on the other side of the door. Waiting just a few more seconds, he then leaned on the handle and slowly, but cautiously opened the door. To his utter astonishment, there was his diminutive boss having a *one to one* with what looked like a giant beanbag. His suit trousers and underpants were around his ankles and his shirt tails were flapping, like they were caught in a stiff breeze, giving a hint of his bare buttocks as he moved gracelessly back and forth. It took Dirk a full two seconds for his brain to register the scene. Fat legs protruded from the *beanbag* as did a head with a reddened face he recognised. It was a member of the administration staff; the oldest member.

Not renowned for her beauty, she had a mug like a robber's dog and a penchant for Rock 'n Roll dancing, to which Dirk would have admittedly paid good money to see her perform. The image of her Gyrating away in a big taffeta frock, reminded Dirk of a dancing hippopotamus in Walt Disney's classic Fantasia.

She was lying on her back, on top of the table in the centre of the small room. He was half standing, half lying on top of her. The table was quite low, but he still had to stand on his toes to increase his impetus. From this angle Dirk could see the cellulite on her thighs rippling as the compact lothario heaved in and out. Surfing USA by the Beach Boys sprang to mind. Her sizeable knickers had been carelessly discarded on the floor and she was speaking words of encouragement to her paramour in a baby girl voice. Dirk couldn't make out what she was saying, but was sure he heard words like *dirty* and *bad boy*. He didn't know whether to laugh or gag. The little man was grunting like a Portobello donkey and Dirk realised a climactic moment was imminent. Raising his cell phone, he uttered his directive. 'Smile please!'

Locked in place in their moment of rapture, like dogs in heat, they hadn't heard him enter. Now his boss, aptly named Roger, tried to turn his head around. Dirk had never witnessed anything like it nor had the desire to again; although in time, he would replay the moment in his head, over and over again, with exquisite pleasure. She shrieked and covered her face with her hands. Roger's mouth opened and shut, like a goldfish caught in the U bend of a flushing toilet, but no sound emitted. His legs and buttocks shuddered with the intensity of

6

the moment and he seemed to spasm, before collapsing onto the now sobbing and humiliated, still spread eagled, old beanbag sprawled on the table. Roger didn't attempt to, or couldn't, push himself off. He looked like he was drowning; drowning in flesh, drowning in shame, drowning in the bile in his throat. His wide, beseeching, eyes conveyed his one thought. Dirk provided the vocals.

'What am I doing here? Same as you it would appear, just a quick in and out.'

Roger's lips were quivering and his eyes filled with shock and utter disbelief, before they clicked shut. Like Dirk's camera lens. He began moaning in a way that sounded like an extractor fan malfunction. She began wailing too and continued to hide her face in her hands. Roger sagged even further and eventually toppled off his perch, his knees buckling and his face coming to rest at eye level. Dirk captured every fluid moment, as the sobbing beanbag and extractor fan continued with their disharmonious and wretched lament.

Abandoning them to their disquiet rumination, Dirk stepped out of the room, letting the door swing slowly shut behind him. He continued to listen to their sorrowful dirge for a few more seconds, a grim satisfactory smirk spreading over his face before he walked, no, skipped back to his desk. He removed some of his more personal items then locked up and went straight out the door, smiling at the imagery of the scene behind the all-knowing cupboard door.

Dirk arrived back at the bar at exactly one minute to eight. Melissa was pouring a glass of red wine and looked up when she saw him. 'Good timing, handsome'

He gave her a big smile and walked around the bar, 'You have no idea' he said, pulling her towards him and giving her a deep, hungry, kiss. 'Wow' she exclaimed, 'What was THAT for?'

'Just sharing the joie de vivre; now, what would you like do tonight? Cocktails, Dinner, Dancing?'

Melissa's dark eyes flashed. 'I'd like to take a shower', she said, plucking a cherry seductively from a cocktail stick between her full and inviting, wine red lips.

Chapter 2

Dirk arrived for work just after ten am the following day and greeted everyone with a big friendly 'Good Morning'. Some of the others in the office looked at him as if he was nuts. One girl giggled and one of the accountants made a seemingly desultory, but very loaded comment, 'Oh, good afternoon Mister Dagger, so nice of you to join us!'

Ignoring the crass remark, Dirk continued towards his desk. Shot a glance at his boss. Roger didn't look up. He was uncharacteristically subdued and busied himself by pretending to be engrossed in the monstrous heap spread over his desk. This time it was only paperwork. Dirk opened the drawer which contained his laptop and began his usual morning ritual of plugging in and logging on. As it booted up he walked the length of the floor. Made himself a coffee and casually strolled back to his desk, whistling all the while. He didn't bother to look around at the faceless, banal, collection of cardboard cut-outs he knew were watching his every move.

Logged on, he checked his email. Nothing much, just the usual junk, but he took his time and savoured each minute keeping them all waiting in limbo for battle to commence. However, one email did catch his interest. It was from Roger at seven o'clock last night, informing him that he would be taking the serious matter of his outburst further. It went on to say that he would hold a formal disciplinary meeting with a secretary present to take the minutes. You've guessed it, a secretary with a penchant for big pants. Dirk could just picture them both last night huddled together like a couple of pigeons, him with his chest all puffed out and her cooing encouragement before sending the email. Getting all turned on at the delicious thought of Dirk reading it and contemplating his glum prospects. He could visualise them waltzing round the office in triumph. Foreplay to their bare bum boogie in the stationary cupboard. What a difference a day makes!

Glancing around, he noted that Marjorie, the beanbag rock 'n' roller, was absent. She was probably taking a 'sick' day and therefore the pending meeting would be quite different to the one she and dirty little Roger had been salivating over the previous evening. Dirk turned slowly in his chair. Roger was still busying himself amongst the mountain of paper that he placed on his desk each morning, to create the illusion of diligence and productivity. Unsuccessfully it must be noted. A prank amongst the office staff was to take the top sheet from the pile on Roger's desk and shred it to see if he would notice anything missing. He never did. Dirk had no problem interrupting his *important work*. 'Roger, I've just replied to your email. When would you like to press on? We could use the little end room couldn't we?' he suggested, nodding towards the scene of last night's sublime revelation.

The illusionist looked up from his paper shield and blinked profusely, his expression was positively Ga-Ga. Dirk donned his best poker face and continued to stare as Roger dithered about his desk, his smug self-assurance completely gone. Everyone was watching now, intrigued. They had, no doubt, been eagerly anticipating the impending fireworks display, but now they were looking up and around at each other with puzzlement and confusion. It was obvious something had changed, but what? They had no way of knowing. This was in complete contrast to Roger's self-righteous and superior attitude after Dirk's departure. This was not what was expected at all.

Roger stood up, although Dirk almost missed it, came over and announced in a hushed tone that he had booked the conference room for the entire morning and that they could go there now, if that was convenient. Without replying, Dirk swivelled on his chair and unhurriedly unplugged his laptop, making Roger wait. Finally, he stood. Ceremoniously placed the laptop under his arm and walked the length of the office at the sombre pace of a death march. He avoided looking at anyone directly, but was aware that all eyes were on them both. Unable to see Roger walking behind, the silence told him all he needed to know.

Dirk opened the outer office door and held it open. Roger dared a quick, bleary eyed, glance up at him. Dirk maintained his poker face. It barely concealed his contempt. The silence in the room grew even more palpable. It was a pivotal moment. He turned his head and looked back in at the stunned blank faces, but gave nothing away. The bean counter who'd made the disparaging remark earlier was regarding him with a scornful expression. Dirk had never liked him. From the open doorway, his unyielding stance and unwavering glare reciprocated a very distinct message. The bastard bristled and looked away, then went back to counting his beans or whatever boring task he was engaged in. As the office door closed behind, Dirk turned his focus on the little bug edging its way along the corridor in front of him.

~

When they entered the conference room, Roger sat at the head of the table and gestured stiffly for Dirk to take a seat; an action that wasn't lost on him. Roger just didn't get it. Even now, he couldn't read the situation. He always had to be the main man, never sitting beside you or adjacent at meetings or appraisals. Always sitting opposite and slightly higher up, always wanting you to know that he was the man in charge, the man at the helm; the *big* man. Dirk sat at the opposite end and looked all the way down the table at Roger, who looked even smaller than usual and very, very, tired.

'About yesterday...' Roger began, his old confidence inexplicably resurfacing.

'Was that before or after your invitation?' Dirk asked with faux confusion.

Roger blinked, not fully understanding the question. A couple of seconds passed before he said, 'Well, yesterday afternoon...your outburst...'

'Roger', Dirk cautioned by raising his hand, 'I think we can overlook that now.'

Roger dithered again. 'What...Well...I...you...'

Dirk snapped at him, totally devoid of any respect, 'Look, let's get down to the nitty-gritty. We're not here to discuss that and you and I both know it, so don't think you're here to dick me around ok?'

Roger's mouth had fallen open. Dirk outlined his

edict. 'Here's the deal Roger. I caught you shagging a zeppelin in knickers last night and filmed the whole show for posterity. That cancels everything else out. So, let's cut to the chase and discuss the generous severance package you're going to give me!'

Roger's face turned crimson and he began to stammer 'I...I...'

Dirk raised his hand again and spoke in a tone of damning finality. 'Roger, you can make this very easy or you can become a porn star on YouTube? It's a simple choice and it's yours to make.'

Roger was blinking a lot now and his mouth was doing the Goldfish thing again. Dirk said nothing more. Just sat there and waited for Roger to process the situation and consider his options. After about thirty seconds of silence Dirk prompted him again.

'Let's look at the facts Roger. You wanted me out the door, well now you're getting your wish. Not the way you would have liked perhaps, but hey life's a bitch then you get divorced and the wife takes the house, the car, the kids and the cat. I know you can swing it for me to go with a more than generous package. You can make all this nasty business disappear with a single throw of the leg. . . I mean dice.'

Roger didn't speak. He just sat there wringing his hands, looking down at the table, taking deep breaths.

'Roger?' Dirk prompted, but got no reply. He prompted again, louder this time. 'ROGER, make the call. Take the only option you have and get me my money.'

Dirk could see Roger was beginning to drown again and threw him a line. 'Look Roger, I've got no real desire to ruin your life, in spite of what you were prepared to do to me, but I don't see a way to avoid that. Not if you think I'm just going to roll over and dry up. Do you? However, I am willing to play along with your little game…up to a point. So let's just sit here and pretend that you're giving me a grilling, for appearances sake, but I suggest you start the ball rolling for me to go with a golden handshake, because there is no fucking way I'll leave empty handed and not make your little '*liaison_dangereuse*' public. Got it?'

Roger still didn't speak, so Dirk persisted. 'It's Wednesday morning, make the call. We can have all the paperwork completed by Friday. Then it's done. Then I'm gone.'

Roger made another attempt to look confident and said. 'How do I know you have a video, without that it would be your word against…'

Dirk didn't let him finish the sentence. From his inside coat pocket, he produced a flash drive and held it up symbolically for Roger to see. Plugged it into the USB port on the laptop and lifted the screen. In seconds the video was set up and ready to go. Dirk moved the mouse and hit the on screen play button. A mountain of flesh appeared, resembling a gigantic pork belly. Roger stared at the grotesque imagery on the screen for an agonizing moment and then closed his eyes. 'Please…' his voice was barely audible.

'What?' Dirk asked.

'Please…turn it off.'

Dirk paused the video nasty, leaving the frozen image on screen as a grim reminder of what this meeting was really all about.

'There you go Roger, proof enough? You wouldn't want this to fall into the wrong hands would you? I backed it up last night. It's safe and sound and ready for publication. I can give you a copy if you want? In fact I can even get you hard copies of all your favourite stills if you'd prefer? I know a great little picture framers just opposite the courts.'

Roger looked up and glared at Dirk, letting his feelings show. Dirk caught it and raised an eyebrow and dipped his head in Roger's direction in warning. Roger quickly got the message and lowered his gaze. A few more seconds passed, with Roger exhaling big sighs and fighting back tears. Dirk let him have his moment and pushed out of his chair. He walked over to the coffee machine and made himself a cappuccino. He didn't offer to make Roger one. Dirk stood with his back turned and looked out of the window, reflecting on his life so far and where it had brought him. He was disappointed with where he was at. He wasn't miserable, but at the same he wasn't amongst the happiest of people in the world. He was in a rut and needed a change. Returning to the conference table, Dirk sipped his cappuccino and stared over the rim of the cup at Roger. 'You got a nice bonus this year, didn't you Roger?'

'Y...Yes, so? I...' replied Roger, bristling with indignation.

'Well, this video must be at least worth the equivalent of your bonus; don't you think?'

'That's blackmail…'

Dirk shrugged unsympathetically 'I suppose it is, but then you were all set to fuck me today if I hadn't caught you with your pants down.'

Roger started in with his weak defence, 'I...I'll call the police…'

Dirk shot it down. 'And tell them what...you're shagging an old dog, but don't tell the wife?'

Roger looked lost for words, but a little bit of anger had begun to creep into his expression. Dirk glared back and Roger backed down again. Neither spoke for a few seconds, but Dirk was done talking and outlined it plainly for him.

'You think it through Roger. Think about what you have to lose and what you have to gain. You've got my number. Call me when you want me to come back in to sign on the dotted line.' Dirk paused to let his words sink in. However, from his body language, it was apparent Roger was all done talking too. Without excusing himself, Dirk walked out of the room and left Roger to his profound deliberations.

Chapter 3

Dirk felt neither anger nor regret at effectively ending his career in the company. He'd wasted too many years toeing the company line, trying to *'raise his profile';* watching one incompetent clown after another rise through the ranks at the expense and hard work of others. He left at the end of the month and invited most of his stiff colleagues to the usual customary leaving drinks party. He ran a tab at the bar and informed his ex-boss that he'd be picking that up too. Roger gave no objections. Dirty little Roger, whatever he'd had to do to get it, had procured a very satisfactory payoff for Dirk. His parting question had been 'What about the video?' Dirk just smiled and said he had nothing more to worry about. Roger said he didn't believe him. Dirk said he didn't give a monkey's what he thought, it was done and that was that.

~

Now, with a new found wealth of sorts and his freedom, Dirk decided to have some personal time. The weather at the end of March was predictably wet and miserable so, like many of the recently unemployed on such a glorious spring day, he imaginatively decided to have a drink. Three weeks later he was still having that drink and the forecast was still no better. It was a Saturday morning and he was in his apartment lounging on his leather sofa, watching his recently purchased forty two inch LCD TV, when his cellphone rang.

'Hello boozy boy', hailed the jovial retort on the end of the line.

There was a second's pause before he recognized the voice. 'Frank, you old pervert!' Dirk affectionately replied. 'What a great surprise, how the devil are you?'

Frank chuckled. 'Devilishly well, how are things with you my boy?'

'Oh, you know, boy meets beer, boy spills beer, boy gets another beer. Where are you calling from? Geneva? Still working in the launderette?'

Frank chuckled again. 'Someone's got to do it. It's a clean living. What about you, still crunching numbers?'

'Nope, not any more, I quit last month. I'm sick of being cooped up in offices, so I'm taking it easy for a while.'

'Well, I never expected to hear that. What made you leave?'

'It's a short story, I'll tell you about it sometime.'

'You can tell me today if you like, I'm in Bristol.'

'Bristol? What are you doing here? When did you get in?'

'Late last night, it was a last minute thing.'

'You should have given me a call, it wouldn't have been a problem; you know that.'

'I know, but it just so happened that I had some free time and I wasn't too far away. I had some business in London this week and everything went smoothly, until I got to the airport yesterday afternoon and they'd cancelled my flight. They couldn't get me booked on another until Monday morning so I thought, if I'm going to be stuck here until Monday, I might as well use the opportunity to come to Bristol and meet up with my old pal for a drink. Maybe have some lunch or dinner? If you've nothing else planned of course?'

Dirk immediately perked up. 'It's been long overdue. I've been tee-total all morning.'

'Then it sounds like I've called at just the right time.'

'It'll be great to see you again Frank. It must be a year at least?'

'I'm sure it'll seem like it was yesterday when we hit the town my boy.'

Dirk grinned at his friend's casual and familiar banter. 'When do you want to meet up? I just have to throw myself in the shower first.'

'I have some business to take care of this morning, but I should be finished before midday. So, if it's alright with you, I'll come and pick you up shortly after then drop the car off and we can head into town.'

'Do you still have the pink Porsche?'

'Yes, but not with me...and it's cherry red you cheeky bugger'!

'Maybe its Maybelline?'

Frank Laughed. 'God, how I've missed your wit!'

'Yeah, right' said Dirk.

'Anyway, listen!' said Frank, 'I've got to go; look forward to seeing you.'

'You too...Frank, wait! Any idea where you want to go for lunch? What about the River Station? Good food and great cocktails in the bar next door.'

'A couple of Martinis *schounds schplendid Mishter Bond*,' replied Frank in a woefully bad impersonation of Sean Connery.

'Ok, I'll book it for around two.' said Dirk.

'Perfect, see you later.' said Frank and hung up.

With plan in place Dirk decided to spring into action, but just then Tom and Jerry came on TV. It was one of the older cartoons; a timeless classic produced by Fred Quimby and a must see. He settled back down to watch it. When T and J had finished beating the living daylights out of each other, he pressed the remote until it reached the music channels. He marvelled at the perfectly formed buttocks of Lady Gaga and her backing dancers. Took a sip of his coffee and put down his cup. Well, you can't marvel and drink coffee at the same time. Three songs and countless pairs of perfect little buttocks later, the commercials broke his catatonic fugue and he hit the shower, came to life, shaved and got dressed.

At twelve forty five, almost *bang on time* to the designated noon pickup time, Frank turned up announcing in his inimitable air of convivial joviality: 'Sorry I'm a wee bit late'.

'I wouldn't have expected anything less.' replied Dirk.

'Sarcasm is the lowest form of wit. Good to see you too.' said Frank, smiling.

They both smiled broadly as they shook hands and gave each other a manly, back-slapping, hug.

'Come in.' said Dirk 'Can I get you a coffee…beer…Champagne?'

Frank's mouth formed an 'O' and he raised his eyebrows in mock anticipation. 'Even better, what are we celebrating?'

'Life! Women! Saturday afternoon; freedom!'

'Yes, of course, your freedom. You've been fed up working in that place for as long as I can remember.

What finally pushed you over the edge?' asked Frank.

'They made me an offer they couldn't refuse. I got a nice little severance package and then some.'

'That's good news. In fact it's bloody incredible actually, especially considering some of the tyrants running that company. Were you still working for that little Napoleon Roger? I wouldn't have expected him to give you as much as a dry bone to go.'

'It was his dry bone that swung it for me to go.' said Dirk, giving him a sly wink and a smile.

Frank gave him a quizzical look.

'Let me get you some fizz first, then I'll fill you in.' said Dirk, disappearing into the kitchen.

He returned with a bottle of Bollinger NV and two glasses. Handed them to Frank and popped the cork.

'Ah, music to my ears.' said Frank.

The Champagne had been a token parting gift from the company, but he hadn't yet found an occasion to open it. This seemed as good a time as any. He filled the glasses with bubbly and said, 'Wait a minute, you'll love this.' He disappeared again and returned moments later with his laptop. Connected it to his flat screen TV and opened a windows media player file. With the cursor hovering over the play icon, he turned and looked at Frank, 'This is a ride you won't forget'. The mouse clicked and the screen was immediately filled with what looked like the dance of the seven whales. Frank looked awestruck. 'What the...?'

'Just wait', said Dirk.

Frank waited and watched and then Dirk's voice could be heard in the video saying, 'Smile please.'

At that moment the man in the video turned his

head. Frank immediately recognized the main character and spluttered on his Champagne.

'Fuck me…! Sorry.' said Frank, wiping his chin.

'That's what she probably said too', remarked Dirk.

Frank was pointing at the screen in utter disbelief. 'It's….'

'Yup, in full Technicolor, special effects and everything.'

'How in hell's name did you manage to get this?'

Dirk waited until the video had ended and then recounted the tale from beginning to both ends. Frank listened open mouthed.

'Jesus, I'm glad you don't any have videos of me!' said Frank.

'When was the last time you looked on YouTube?' joked Dirk.

They both laughed. Frank looked appraisingly at Dirk, 'You could dine out on that for years; very well done.' Then he raised his glass and said. 'To the future'

Dirk raised his and reciprocated. 'To the future'

They clinked glasses and took a long sip.

'Nice drop of bubbly!' exclaimed Frank.

'A parting gift from the company and presented to me in front of the entire office, by none other than…' replied Dirk, nodding towards the screen.

'Really, how poetic.' said Frank appreciatively.

Dirk took another long sip and topped up their glasses.

'Not too much, I'm driving!' said Frank.

'Sure', said Dirk, topping it up to the brim anyway.

'Still smoking your *Big Bob Marley's?*' asked Frank, referring to Dirk's love of fine Cuban cigars.

'You know me Frank, a man of simple tastes!'

'Simple and expensive' replied Frank, opening the leather bag he was carrying. He pulled out a box of 25 Montecristo No.2 cigars and tossed them over to Dirk. 'Here's a little present for you.'

'Jesus Frank, these cost a bomb!'

'Don't mention it. A client gave them to me as a gift. I get gratuities like this all the time and could never smoke them all. Besides, I know those are your favourites.'

Dirk lightly shook the cigar box with both hands and grinned. 'Thanks Frank, much appreciated. These would be nice to have with our *after lunch cocktails*, pity we can't smoke indoors any more. '

'I was in a fabulous cigar shop in Amsterdam recently' said Frank, 'You'd love it; big smoking room, girls walking around with glasses of fizz and hors d'oeuvres.'

'Sounds like my kind of place, you'll have to show it to me sometime.' said Dirk.

Frank was reflective for a moment. 'I could, if you came out for a visit. In fact, I could show you a lot of interesting sights in Amsterdam; if you aren't too busy at the moment.'

'Steady Frank, no need to mock the unemployed' said Dirk, chuckling.

Frank simply smiled. 'I'm serious, come out for a visit. It's Queen's day soon, you'd enjoy that. It's a great day out.'

'Amsterdam, are you serious?'

'Yes, I just said so didn't I?

Dirk gave him a quizzical look. Frank smiled some

more at this, 'Sorry, how could you know. I've been doing some work in The Netherlands for a few months for a particular client and I'm staying in a really nice apartment in Amsterdam; plenty of room for a guest'.

'Are you no longer living in Geneva?'

'Yes, I am, but I go back and forth, when business dictates. Just recently I've been spending more time in the Netherlands.'

'You've got a great lifestyle Frank. Amsterdam, huh? Nice girls?'

Frank rolled his eyes. 'Well, if you like scorching hot, leggy-blondes in short skirts riding around on bikes, then it's the place for you.'

'Better than Geneva and all those French girls?' asked Dirk.

'It's a close thing.' replied Frank.

'Let me be the judge of that.' said Dirk, chuckling and toasting Frank's glass again.

'We'll work it out. Anyway let's have a look at that video again, I could use a good laugh.' said Frank.

Dirk sat beside Frank on the big leather sofa and pressed play again.

'Roger and out!' shouted Frank at the moment of the on-screen demerger and they both cheered.

Chapter 4

Frank, whose actual name is Francois Perrier, has an English mother and a French father. His mother had wanted to name him after her father, but compromised with the name Francois, knowing that she could still call him Frank. Intelligent and likeable he has an endearing, albeit mildly irksome, habit of prefixing rhetorical statements with an unnecessary explanation of them. For example; when he takes a weekend away he would say something like: 'what I'd call a short break' or ordering a coffee and croissant: 'What I'd call a light breakfast'. Dirk had once asked him. 'As opposed to what, two kippers, three rashers of bacon, eggs, sausage, baked beans and pancakes?'

Dirk had met Frank ten years ago in London, when the company he worked for provided some consultancy for Frank's investment bank. They'd worked closely together on several projects and had hit it off immediately. Frank had gone on to work for another large investment bank in Geneva as a financial guru and his career had rocketed since. He and Dirk had remained friends, seeing each other on the occasional weekend and going on skiing holidays together. He enjoyed what he liked to call *"a comfortable lifestyle"*, earning a telephone number salary and even bigger bonuses. On more than one occasion he'd suggested Dirk should move out to Geneva, where he said he could get him a consultancy position at his bank or several positions with different ladies, if he was so inclined. At the time Dirk had commitments in England

and said he would think about it. However, they'd kept in touch and Dirk occasionally visited him in Geneva where he'd introduced him to a different world. Frank was a more than generous friend when it came to the champagne lifestyle and wouldn't allow Dirk to spend a Swiss Franc. Wherever they went they mingled with the wealthy elite of the banking world. Frank seemed to garner a perverse pleasure in pointing out lots of what he called *the scam boys*; other bankers and clients that he dealt with in business. Frank never elaborated, but after encountering someone he would wink at Dirk and mouth SB for *Scam Boy* or BSB for *Big Scam Boy*. Many of his clients appeared to be from the Middle East or North Africa and Frank could play the game very well. He could speak fluent French, was highly convivial and well versed in the latest financial schemes or scams required to move large sums of cash around different hedges, gilts, stocks or holding companies. The real skill was that it was could all be done through his bank, which he sardonically called "My beautiful launderette".

It was on one such visit to Geneva that Frank had introduced Dirk to the lady in his life. Natalie. Frank had met her through business. She was a lawyer specializing in international finance law and like him was half French, but had a Chinese Father. Another trait they had in common was expensive tastes and enjoying the best things life had to offer. Between them, the cash flowed like a tidal surge. It came in and it went out. They drove his and her Porches and wore only expensive designer clothes. Frank had moved into Natalie's home in the exclusive district of Cologny, overlooking the Lake and the famous Jet d'Eau. On that occasion, he'd been hosting a birthday party for what he called 'a few close friends and had invited Dirk to stay for the weekend. The house was spectacular. Oak beams spanned the high ceiling of the stately reception room and a sweeping staircase ascended upwards to other undoubtedly beautiful bedrooms and sumptuous suites.

At the far end of this imposing room, framed by a large elevated panoramic window, was Natalie. Silhouetted by the fading sunlight, brushing her hair, she stood with her legs slightly apart and her body turned around adjacent to the window. Dirk could see she had a terrific figure. She leaned forward and shook her hair, like Rita Hayworth in the classic 1940's movie Gilda. It was a stunning sight to behold and Dirk had been enraptured in the moment. When she straightened up again she became aware of their presence and laughed, slightly embarrassed at being caught off-guard. It was a nice laugh: throaty, but womanly. She tossed the hairbrush onto a leather lounger, came down the three steps to floor level and walked over towards them. She was dressed simply, but elegantly, in a plum coloured sleeveless silk dress that clung to her figure in the devouring way a snake winds itself around its prey. Equally modest, in its own spectacular fashion, was the large solitaire diamond she wore on a chain around her neck. Dirk was betting it cost more than his annual salary. A pair of diamond earrings matched it in size and sophistication. The rest of her jewellery was simple, but chic: a slim platinum and gold watch adorned her left wrist, a platinum and gold bangle her right. She wore no rings on her fingers. Her walk was confidant and slightly sassy. Dirk thought she had a terrific pair of legs. She wasn't tall, but not small either. Dirk guessed around 5' 7". She wore matching plum coloured suede shoes with three inch heels that she worked like a catwalk model. Although her Mother was French, she had inherited her father's oriental looks. Her eyes were darkly made up giving her an even more exotic and smouldering look. Her lips were full and curled into a playful pout. She was a dangerously beautiful woman.

Dirk couldn't help but wonder what had attracted her to Frank, because he was, well, slightly more plain than she. Frank walked over and met her half way. Took hold of her arms and kissed her on both cheeks in a very French manner saying. 'Bonjour ma chérie; m'as-tu manqué?' She didn't take her eyes off Dirk as she replied 'Bien sur, chérie.

Frank turned and said 'let me introduce you to my very, very, good Friend Dirk Dagger. Dirk this is my Natalie.'

Not normally short for words, Dirk found himself speechless. Frank smiled and said 'Yes, she has that effect on people.' Dirk was quick to recover. He put down his bag and smiled, or rather his mouth was hanging open. Taking her hand in both of his he said 'Enchanté Natalie, it's an absolute pleasure to finally meet you. Frank has told me so little about you. I can see now why he's kept you to himself for so long…' His words trailed off and he looked from Frank to Natalie. 'Thank you for inviting me to your lovely home.' He lifted her hand and kissed it. Well, when in Rome…or even Geneva.

She raised her chin slightly and the pout became wryly more mischievous. Her eyes, dark and intelligent, sparkled when the blazing red sunlight hit them. 'Merci, Monsieur Dagger. Francois told me you were quite the charmer, it's so wonderful to finally meet you too.' she purred, 'I am looking forward to hearing more about you and my Francois this weekend.'

'Please, call me Dirk.'

She turned her gaze full on him and her voice purred again. 'Dirk, I like that name.' She closed in and kissed him on both cheeks, very close to his mouth. Her perfume made him twitch. Not at all an unpleasant sensation. Frank could see that his friend was a little overcome and moved things along. 'Ahem, I think Champagne is called for.'

Natalie reacted like the quintessential hostess. 'Please, make yourself at home Monsieur Dirk. Francois, show your friend our beautiful view of Lac Léman. I will bring the Champagne over.'

As they both watched Natalie walk away, Dirk turned to Frank and asked. 'Has she got a sister?'

'She has a twin.' replied Frank tantalizingly.

'Jesus Christ, there's two like her?' gasped Dirk.

'Don't get your hopes up my boy; her twin brother, not her sister.'

Dirk looked crestfallen. 'Fuck!'

'Never mind, you'll be spoiled for choice tomorrow, some of Natalie's friends make Hallé Berry look as plain as paper.' said Frank.

Chapter 5

Frank had hired a *two seater* Merc, for what he called a short stay. He was still laughing as he drove. 'Christ! Little Roger must shit himself every time he looks at that.'

Dirk smiled ruefully. 'That's up to him, but I wouldn't keep something like that lying around. Would you?'

'Oh, I don't know. It might be kind of fun to watch yourself in action from time to time, don't you think?' said Frank.

Dirk grimaced and shot Frank a glance. 'Are you kidding, you saw what he was banging.'

Frank chuckled. 'Did you keep a copy?'

When Dirk didn't answer, Frank picked up on it. 'You did though, didn't you, you bad boy.'

Dirk had to smile at the reference, but remained philosophical. 'He thinks I've deleted it, but…I decided to keep a copy just in case I need cheering up from time to time.'

'Or when you're short of cash?' said Frank, discernibly.

'I did think about that' replied Dirk, 'but….'

Frank narrowed his eyes and glanced sideways at Dirk, 'But what? The things you've told me about him and what he was planning to do to you. In fact, I wouldn't blame you if you were to give him the full thrust of the Dagger and just stuck it on YouTube for the hell of it; serve the bastard right.'

Dirk adopted a more serious tone. 'No, that wouldn't

be right. Not to mention unprofessional. But I *will* keep it though, in case he needs a little prod from the Dagger in the future.' said Dirk, looking straight ahead.

Frank grinned and gunned the accelerator, making it through the traffic lights just before they turned red.

'Nice set of wheels Frank' said Dirk, in admiration of the car.

'Yes, it's what I'd call a nice little runabout.' replied Frank, in his inimitable way. 'Easy to handle, easy to park; Bristol's a nightmare for parking.'

Frank continued with his continental style of driving and they arrived, blessedly unscathed, at Frank's apartment.

'Here we are, Home sweet home.' announced Frank.

Dirk looked up at the apartment building. He'd only ever been here once before. Frank had gone to university in Bristol and his parents had bought him the apartment when he'd commenced his studies. After leaving University he'd kept it on, renting it out for several years to generate a decent income and to help cover his own rental overheads when he'd first moved to London. It had been an excellent investment, buying it for what he called an absolute bargain at the time and a fraction of its current value. Now that he had no need of the rental income, he was having it completely refurbished in order to maintain a permanent base in the city. Dirk was pleased to hear this news and welcomed any notion of seeing his friend more frequently.

Frank opened the door to the apartment and casually tossed his keys into a large antique fruit bowl in the hallway. Leading the way he passed through the lounge and into the open plan kitchen, where he selected a bottle of red wine from a rack built into the stylish units.

'They've done a nice job of the place', observed Dirk, looking around at the plush furnishings and décor.

'Yes, I'm very pleased with it. Do the honours will you?' requested Frank, handing Dirk the bottle and a corkscrew. Dirk looked admiringly around the kitchen, thinking it resembled the command console of a star ship with its gleaming, burnished, steel surfaces. An American styled ice making refrigerator and a range style cooker caught Dirk's eye.

'Plan on cooking much when you're in town Frank?'

'Oh, you know, beans on toast, cheese on toast; the usual gourmet stuff.' replied Frank.

Dirk popped the cork. 'What a lovely sound!' exclaimed Frank, producing two crystal wine goblets from an overhead unit and placing them on the granite worktop of the central island. Dirk filled their glasses and they raised them in a toast. There followed a moment's comfortable silence. Frank glanced around the apartment. 'This takes me back. I've had some good times in this place?'

Dirk glanced around too. 'Yes, I'll bet its seen more action than the western front.'

'And then some.' chuckled Frank, taking a sip of his wine. He put the glass down and announced. 'I'm just going to change my shirt. Sorry to keep you waiting, I won't be long ok?'

'Sure, take your time. It *has* been a while since we last got together. A few more minutes won't hurt.' said Dirk.

Frank disappeared into one of the bedrooms and

came out five minutes later wearing an expensive handmade shirt with double cuffs and gold cufflinks. He was fastening the bracelet of a chunky, solid gold, Rolex watch and caught Dirk looking at it. As if he'd read Dirk's mind Frank said: 'Gift from a client.'

'Nice. What did you do for him, kill his mother-in-law?'

Frank laughed and gave a brief explanation. 'Not quite. This is what I call a perk if you like. I have clients who'll trade in anything that makes or saves them money and they're very generous to those who can help *optimize their assets*.'

Dirk blew a low whistle then asked. 'So what *did* you do to earn such a valued gift?'

'I'll tell you about it during lunch. Could you call a cab?'

'No problem.' replied Dirk, fishing out his phone and dialling a number from memory. He got through to a local taxi company on the second ring and ordered a cab for as soon as possible. When he hung up he informed Frank.

'Cab's on its way.'

'Great.' said Frank.

'Anyway' said Dirk, changing the subject. 'How's the lovely Natalie? You haven't mentioned her since we met up.'

'Still lovely…' replied Frank, '…but like me, spending a lot of time away on business these last few months.'

'You should marry that girl Frank; she'll keep you in your dotage.'

'We'll see.' shrugged Frank, a touch ruefully, a thin

veil of pathos drawing over and pinching his features. Dirk detected somehow that his friend didn't really want to talk about her and pressed no further. Just then his phone rang, announcing the arrival of their cab.

'Perfect timing' said Frank, grabbing a leather jacket off a coat hook. 'I'm starved, let's go eat.'

The Restaurant was one of Dirk's favourites in the city and he was pleased when they were seated at a table by the window, overlooking the River. From the menu, they both ordered seared Scottish scallops to start. Then for the main course Dirk ordered Roast Monkfish, orzo pasta 'paella' with crayfish tails, saffron, mussels and chorizo. Frank ordered the Gressingham duck breast, caramelized chicory, pommes Anna and poached cherries. Their succulent banquet was washed down with two bottles of Canon-Fronsac 2005 Chateau du Pavillon; *a nice little Merlot* as Frank called it. They chatted about things they used to do in London, places they used to go and the people they'd had fun with. It was an excellent lunch and the old camaraderie hadn't dimmed between them. When they had satiated their appetites with their 'little bit of lunch', Dirk gestured to Frank's gleaming Rolex.

'So, you were going to tell me about your *gift* Frank.'

Frank glanced casually at the Rolex and began. 'Well, my business, as you know, is very confidential and so are my clients. Many of them don't want anyone knowing their business or what deals they're involved in; let me give you some background. Not all of my clients' investments involve bank transfers. Some deals are made directly between clients and I can be of service in facilitating these deals while, at the same time, ensuring clients aren't seen together. I get a very nice commission from both parties and sometimes I even get in on the deal.'

Dirk must have looked slightly shocked because Frank said, 'Don't worry, I don't pimp for them. Let me explain. First, you wouldn't believe the cash that people carry around. Nobody wants to pay more tax than they have to, so they carry it into Swiss banks in their Louis Vuitton luggage and make huge deposits. No questions asked. Or, they lock it away in their safe deposit boxes for a rainy day. A lot of my clients are a bit twitchy with their investments, but then again who isn't when it comes to risking their cash in the current climate. They want to put their money into a sure thing and providing you have the cash, it's a buyer's market?'

Dirk was nodding, but still looked slightly confused. Frank picked up on this. 'Let me elaborate. In addition to having pots of cash, rich people have rich assets, right?'

'Right.' Agreed Dirk

'…and some of these assets are better to own than others, right?'

'Right again.'

'…and some of these rich people maybe aren't so rich any more. They need cash, but don't want the embarrassment of going to auction to raise it. So, how do they do it?' They sell off some of their assets to private buyers, right?'

'I guess so…'

'But maybe they don't want cash, maybe they're just tired of owning something and they just want something else instead, but to sell something and to buy something else you usually end up paying for it at both ends and that makes no sense either, right?'

Dirk was just nodding in agreement waiting to see how this threaded out.

Frank continued, 'Now I just said that some assets are better to own than others. For example some rich, or maybe not so rich, guy has a Ferrari and it's costing him an arm and a leg just to run it. If he sells it, he won't get the best price because a dealer will cut it down in order to make his profit in the resell. That's where I come in. I can connect the guy with the Ferrari together with another one of my clients, who I know wants one for his son or daughter or his bitch on the side and is willing to trade, no questions asked, as long as the paperwork is in order.'

'So he hands over a wad of cash and you take a cut for services rendered?' ventured Dirk.

Frank waggled his hand. 'Sometimes, but sometimes the payment is by other means.'

'What other means Frank?' Dirk asked, becoming a little uncomfortable.

'Well, there are lots of things that people hold that can be traded or simply swapped.'

'Such as…?'

'Such as whatever the client wants to trade. Large cash transactions usually attract too much attention, so direct trading between clients maintains anonymity and cuts out the middle man. Clients will trade Bearer Bonds, antiques, classic cars; you name it, anything really. These are all private transactions between clients and it happens all the time.'

Dirk frowned, said nothing. Frank just smiled and then continued.

'It's strictly legal. I have lots of clients involved in deals like this. I just happen to be in a perfect position to facilitate transactions of this sort. They're a bit like eBay, someone has something to trade and someone else wants it.'

Dirk took a deep breath before replying. 'I don't know Frank; it's not exactly eBay is it? '

Frank elaborated further. 'It's exactly like eBay. People are only trying to optimize their assets by shedding and obtaining different assets.'

'And when they eventually decide to liquidate these assets, you put them through your launderette?' said Dirk.

Ignoring the dig at his bank Frank continued. 'But I digress, *the gift*. I recently had two clients swap one apartment in Geneva for an apartment in Paris, with a Bentley turbo thrown in. I arranged it all between the two clients, kept the paperwork and legal admin to a minimum, but legitimate throughout and I was given this beautiful Rolex as a thank you.' Frank said with sparkle in his eyes.

'Not bad, not bad at all.' said Dirk.

Frank took another sip of his wine and paused for a moment, thoughtful.

'I've been thinking and I have a proposition for you.'

'Oh?' replied Dirk.

Frank smiled 'Well, since you have some free time at present, instead of coming over to Amsterdam just for Queen's day, why don't you come out and stay for a couple of weeks?

'A couple of weeks, won't I be in your way Frank?' asked Dirk, incredulous.

'Not at all, I have a few of small things to deal with next week, before Queen's day, then I have a couple of days to chill out before I go back to Geneva on Tuesday, the third of May. Apart from those days, you'll have the apartment all to yourself. I won't be back until at least the weekend after that.'

As Dirk turned the proposition over in his mind, Frank sat back in his chair and grinned.

'What are you grinning at you old bugger?' asked Dirk.

'You, let loose in Amsterdam for two weeks on your own; doesn't bear thinking about does it?' chuckled Frank.

Dirk grinned back at him. 'But seriously, two weeks? Are you kidding me?'

'No, of course not, why would I? You said it yourself, you can't face another office at the moment and sitting here in dreary old Blighty doing nothing is a pretty crap prospect. So, why not seize the opportunity and have a nice break, in a beautiful city with free accommodation. That can't be bad can it?'

Before Dirk could respond, the waitress brought over the cheque. Frank immediately snatched it up and said. 'My treat.'

'We'll go Dutch!' offered Dirk.

'We can do that in Amsterdam.' said Frank with a wink.

Chapter 6

Frank flew back to Amsterdam on Monday morning, leaving Dirk the rest of the week to organise himself for the forthcoming trip. Having booked his flight with KLM for the coming Friday, April twenty ninth, he spent the next couple of days cleaning his flat and organising his affairs; dealing with any outstanding bills and informing neighbours that he'd be away for a couple of weeks. On Wednesday evening, his arrangements complete, Dirk took Melissa out for dinner. She was excited at the prospect of him going to Amsterdam, saying that she'd never been and asked when he would be taking her. He laughed at her enthusiasm and said "Next time."

After dinner and two bottles of wine, they went back to his apartment and fell into bed. Their hot and tangled alcohol induced lust appeared to have had little effect on Mel, because she talked non-stop about Amsterdam and other European cities she was "dying to see". Dirk was amused by her excitement and glad of her warm and bountiful companionship, therefore the lack of sleep didn't bother him.

The following day, when Melissa had gone, he made his final preparations and packed his battered old Samsonite travel case with a selection of clothes he deemed appropriate for most eventualities. Then, in the evening, he sat back with a glass of wine intending to watch TV and relax before his flight the next day. However, as oft with the best laid plans, they went straight out the window when Melissa turned up on his doorstep at eight thirty, with two bottles of Champagne she had *procured* from her bar. 'I wanted to see you off in style.' she gushed, perched on high heels and wearing the shortest, tightest, mini dress he'd ever seen her in. Her bag and coat were lying on the floor and she was just standing there holding, a bottle of Veuve Clicquot in each hand, awaiting his invitation, the hint of stocking tops peeking out from underneath her skimpy little pelmet. Dirk stood there momentarily gaping in disbelief, before a grin split his face and he pulled her inside.

He didn't get a lot of sleep that night either and felt a little bit woozy after the bubbly and the extra bottle they opened at one am. Melissa had to leave for work at ten thirty on the Friday morning and had brought with her a change of clothes. He called her a sly little minx. She squirmed in his arms as they lay in bed and said 'But I'm your little minx', then rolled on top, engulfing his head and face in her embrace; devouring him with her lush, moist lips. Sensing his approval, she squirmed around some more and locked him in place.

Later, after they'd showered together, he made coffee while she dressed. He was still only wearing his dressing gown when he kissed her goodbye at the front door, promising to call next week and tell her all about Amsterdam. She said she couldn't wait, licked her lips and moved in close and kissed him on the mouth. As she did, she slid her hand under his dressing gown and massaged his ego, making him jump. She giggled at his reaction then promptly turned and descended the stairs with jaunty little skips. Dirk watched her go, admiring her perky bum and lovely legs as she went. As though she had eyes in the back of her head she stopped, half turned and looked back at him. Her lips parted in a breathy smile and she winked.

~

Four large glasses of water and three cups of coffee later, Dirk made his way to the airport. His flight was on time and he boarded the aircraft, buckled in to his chosen window seat and closed his eyes. He was asleep before the plane taxied down the runway.

Chapter 7

Forty winks and fifty-five minutes later, the plane touched down at Schiphol airport. Amsterdam. Dirk was still tired, but relaxed and looking forward to a new adventure in a new city with his old friend. He sped swiftly through arrivals and headed for the train ticket office. On Frank's advice he bought a plastic travel chip card that he could use for the train, trams and buses, putting thirty euros credit on it to allow for the train ride into the city. He didn't have long to wait for his train and exactly twelve and a half minutes later he was pulling into Amsterdam Centraal Station. Frank was there to meet him with his customary jovial greeting.

'Welcome to Amsterdam, boozy boy'.

They shook hands and Frank put an arm around Dirk's shoulder.

'Good to see you too Frank.' replied Dirk a little shakily.

Picking up on this Frank asked 'Good flight, no problems?'

'It all went very smoothly, straight through at every stage of the journey, no problems at all. I'm just feeling a wee bit fragile though.'

'Oh really, someone give you a good *send-off* last night did they?'

'I can't complain.'

'The little barmaid?'

'Well...'

'This is getting serious my boy.' said Frank, giving him an appraising look.

'Not at all, we're really just great pals.'

'...great pals with benefits...'

Dirk shrugged, trying to be casual but not cavalier about it. Frank didn't give up. 'You can't fool me my boy, there's a look that comes over you when you talk about her.'

'I like her, she's a nice girl, but that's it. We're not in love or anything like that.'

'Yes, yes, I'll buy that.'

Dirk was about to make another comment when Frank changed the subject 'Come on, I'll bet you could use a cold one; hair of the dog and all that eh?'

'Oh! If you insist.' grinned Dirk.

They crossed over the tramlines outside the station and walked past a plethora of fast food kiosks. Dirk took in the imposing architecture of Centraal station as they skirted around the stalls and over a bridge onto the main street: Damrak. They'd only gotten about twenty metres when the heavens opened and tipped what seemed like a tidal wave over the city. 'Shit!' they both exclaimed in unison with about fifty thousand others. 'Come on, this way, run' said Frank.

Another thirty or forty metres up the street, Frank dived through a large, open, glass door. Dirk was right behind him, bedraggled and laughing. Glancing around, he realised that they were standing in a large sports bar, with multiple screens and loud music. Great, just what he needed. Dirk was just about to suggest they brave the rain and find somewhere quieter, when one of the barmaids jumped up onto the bar and started doing a pole dance; much to the raucous delight of the sodden clientele. It turned out that all the bar staff took turns performing a little shimmy as part of their job description. Dirk forgot all about his suggestion of leaving. Frank ordered two small Heineken beers and was amused by the expression on Dirk's face, positioned no more than a foot from the gyrating buttocks of the fit barmaid. 'This is nothing' said Frank 'just whetting your appetite my boy!'

'Consider it whetted' replied Dirk, clinking Frank's glass. Smiling, they both turned their gaze to the limber girl on the bar who was now upside down, hanging onto the pole one handed, her legs seemingly rotating like a windmill in a thunder storm. Two hot numbers and two cold beers later the girl was replaced on the bar with another girl, oriental and hot as hell. The beers went down quickly.

'Frank, loath as I am to drag myself away from all this' said Dirk, 'can we go to somewhere a bit more subdued? I still have a bit of a head on from last night.'

Frank shot a glance outside at the awful weather and said 'Sure, but we'll have to run again. It's still chucking it down.'

Outside, Frank gestured with a nod of his head and cut up a side street to the right of the sports bar, with Dirk following close behind. They ran across a busy shopping street and into another side street where there was an older, less touristy, bar called the Wyldeman. It had a draught tap with De Koninck. Dirk nodded in approval. Frank ordered two beers and some traditional Dutch grub, consisting of a selection of Bitteballen, blood sausage and crusty bread.

Looking out at the miserable weather Dirk said. 'Sorry Frank, I seem to have brought the weather with me.'

Frank was unconcerned. 'It's just the same here really, rains just about as much as in the UK. It *is* a terrific place to be when the sun's shining though. The little cafes, the architecture, the ambience…'

'…the girls on their bikes!' Dirk finished for him.

'I was going to say museums, but let's not forget the important things eh?' Frank glanced out the door at the weather. 'I think it's dying down to a mere hurricane.'

'Who cares?' said Dirk, 'I can be stuck here for an hour or so.'

'Well, let's make tracks before then, the beers here are stronger than you're used to and we don't want to get you pissed right off the plane, now do we?'

'It wouldn't be the first time!' Laughed Dirk, beckoning the barman for two more.

Frank put on his sensible hat for a second. 'I thought we'd relax and take it easy tonight, get some food and talk about your bright future young man'. Frank was only a few years older than Dirk, not more than five, but he still liked to play the elder statesman or big brother.

'Whatever you want to do Frank, I'm just happy to be here.'

'I know this great Indo-Thai restaurant for tonight' said Frank.

Dirk made a face. 'I'd prefer a nice big steak. Thai food goes though me like shit though a goose.'

Frank looked a little disappointed before saying. 'Ok, let's compromise, Chinese then!'

When the rain eventually died down, they finished their beers and walked back through the alleyway towards Damrak. Frank stopped at the entrance and pointed out the direction of the red light district and then further over to the left, in the direction of a fabulous floating Chinese restaurant called The Sea Palace, announcing: 'That's where we'll eat tonight.'

'The red light district or the Chinese restaurant?' queried Dirk.

'Depends what you want to eat?' asked Frank.

'I'll go with Chinese for tonight.' replied Dirk.

Frank grinned and asked 'Fancy a Cigar?'

'Right now?' asked Dirk, raising his eyebrows in a manner of anticipation.

'Sure, why not? The big cigar shop I told you about is just up here on the right.'

'You've twisted my arm Frank, but I've brought ten with me in my travel humidor. We can have a couple of those if you really want one.'

'Montecristos?'

'Yes, the ones you gave me in Bristol.'

'Save them for later, we'll have a couple of big Cohibas for now. Besides, you've got to see this place.'

Frank wasn't really a cigar aficionado. He simply liked to create the illusion of being one. Cigars were merely another prop he could exploit to impress clients. Image was everything. However, this time he hadn't exaggerated. The cigar shop was indeed magnificent. A big glass frontage with overhanging red canopies dominated the street. Inside the entrance, long sales counters with polished wood and brass fittings on either side drew you in. Two large chandeliers illuminated the room with their golden orbs and reflected off the glass display cases housing the many and varied accoutrements employed for smoking. Dirk experienced the sensation of stepping back in time; such was the

46

ambience of the place. The wonderful aroma of cigars and *tobacco* filled the air and he breathed deeply in appreciation. Further inside the large room, a promotion of some sort was taking place. It was busy. In attendance was a heterogeneous mix of people: male and female, young and old, well dressed and casual alike; all smoking cigars. Some old guy in a rumpled cream coloured suit was signing autographs. He was sun darkened and grizzled, but had a perfect set of white teeth. No doubt some Cuban plantation owner promoting his wares. As they stood inside the entrance admiring their surroundings, an attractive blonde in her mid-twenties, dressed smartly in a tailored black skirt split to her thigh and snug white shirt that showed great affection for her shape, came over to them with a tray filled with glasses of fizz. Another, equally attractive, brunette dressed in similar attire, complete with cufflinks and bow tie, appeared with a tray of oysters. Both girls had the most beautiful smiles. Dirk was mesmerized. 'You are fickle, old boy, I thought you only had eyes for the last barmaid.' said Frank.

Fortified with a glass of fizz each they were escorted into the humidor room by another assistant, a good looking young guy in a terrific suit, where Frank picked out two Cohiba Siglo VI Cuban cigars. After paying for them, Frank led Dirk away from the crowd and into the smoking room at the back of the shop, passing on the way what looked like cigar safes or private stashes for the rich and ostentatious. The smoking room was comfortably furnished with leather club chairs and solid mahogany tables, on which sat big chunky ashtrays containing boxes of matches and glass containers with cedar tapers. Making full use of the facilities, the friends lit up and sat in silence as their cigars breathed fire. Dirk looked around the room and noticed there was a cigar museum on the upstairs balcony.

'What do you think, nice place isn't it?' asked Frank.

'Very nice, very nice indeed', replied Dirk, nodding his approval and puffing on his cigar. 'I think I'm going to like it here Frank'.

'Hmmm, I can see that.' said Frank, continuing to smile and survey Dirk through a plumb of smoke, savouring the moment.

Frank seemed extremely pleased, both with himself and to see his friend. Business, as he liked to call it, was good and getting better every day. However, the smoking room was too busy for Frank to talk business, so they made small talk about the city, the bars, the restaurants and the girls on their bikes. After about an hour, their cigars were almost at an end and the rain had ceased battering the city. Frank suggested they head straight back to the apartment. As they were leaving, Dirk soaked up the dazzling smiles of the two lovely assistants one more time and kissed their hands like a latter day Don Juan. Frank looked on and shook his head at his friend's antics. 'You're incorrigible!'

'Old habits die hard!' replied Dirk.

Frank's apartment was no more than twenty minutes from their current location. On the way, they passed a couple of famous landmarks: the Mint tower and the flower market. Despite the damp weather, Dirk wanted to stop and spend time at each of them, but Frank hurried him along. When they finally turned into Frank's street, Dirk was struck by the beauty of the surrounding area. A canal split the street, but strategically placed hump backed bridges reconnected it. Nestled on one corner of the bridge they crossed over was a café bar, which Dirk had no doubt would be graced by their presence in the foreseeable future. Antique shops and private art galleries seemed to be everywhere he looked. It was an affluent area. It was perfect. In the immediate distance, only two or three bridges away, loomed the imposing twin towers of the Rijksmuseum. Dirk was suitably impressed.

The building where Frank lived was a magnificent old town house that had been converted into apartments. A short flight of steps led up to a solid oak door adorned with brass fixtures. Dirk noted there were two buzzers on the intercom. Neither had names displayed on the nameplates. Frank opened the front door and stepped into the entrance hallway. It was wider than Dirk had expected, as Dutch houses tended to be traditionally narrow. Straight ahead and flush against the wall was a steep flight of stairs. Frank turned to his right and opened another grand door that had a burnished tone resembling old mahogany.

'Jesus Christ, how big is that?' Dirk asked, on entering the lounge. The large sumptuous living room was filled with tasteful and luxurious furnishings and one of the biggest flat TV screens he had seen outside of a cinema.

'I don't actually know. It looks about three hundred, but I think it's around the fifty inch mark. Great for the Grand Prix, the surround sound makes you think you're actually at the track.' announced Frank.

Dirk was turning full circle in awe of his

surroundings. 'Wow, this is some place Frank!'

'Glad you like it.'

'What's not to like? It's out of this world. Must cost you a few bob though?'

Frank smiled, but proffered nothing more. 'Let me show you where you'll be staying.'

The apartment was in fact a duplex consisting of the ground and first floors. Frank escorted Dirk up to the first floor and into what could be construed as a separate and self-contained apartment. The bedroom overlooked the back courtyard. It was a good sized room, cosy but not confining. It had a Queen sized bed, a built in wardrobe along one wall and an en-suite bathroom with a shower. The view from the rear window was pleasant, looking out over well maintained private patios and verandas. The sitting room was smaller than the downstairs lounge and not quite so plush, though tastefully decorated nonetheless. It had a little balcony that he thought would be ideal for drinking wine and smoking cigars of an evening, or any time. 'This is perfect!' he said before Frank had the chance to ask.

'Good. I'm pleased you like it. Let me know if there's anything else you need ok?'

'Well…those girls in the cigar shop….' Dirk trailed off and smiled.

'Steady my boy, all in good time. Anyway, dump your gear, you can get settled in later. Come and take the weight off.'

Dirk followed Frank back downstairs to the main lounge. Walked over to the window and looked out at the picturesque street. Frank went into the large open plan kitchen, shouting over his shoulder. 'I don't have any De Koninck, but I do have a few Leffe Blonds.'

'You know me Frank, I'll take anything and whatever beer you've got is good too.' quipped Dirk, coming into the kitchen area and taking in its high end gleaming appliances. It was much like Frank's apartment in Bristol, only more spacious and more expensive. Fine wines filled the large wine rack, taking up almost half of one of the kitchen walls.

'Did the all these bottles of wine come with the apartment Frank?' asked Dirk jokingly.

Frank opened a top unit and retrieved two goblet styled glasses for their biers. He turned around and looked at the wines and surprised Dirk with his answer. 'Yes, they did actually. My client arranged the apartment and everything in it for my convenience, all business cost are covered by him. This is what I would call "*a nice little perk*"' declared Frank in his inimitable way.

Dirk whistled, 'Some little perk. You bankers have a tough time of it, don't you?'

Frank smiled at Dirk's dig at the banking community yet again and handed him the glasses.

'Who else lives in the building, Frank?'

'There's another apartment on the top floor, but I haven't seen anyone else coming or going and I've been here for just over four months. So, I suppose I have it all to myself. Anyway, grab yourself a seat and I'll get a couple of cold ones.'

Dirk sat at the table by the window. Frank came over and joined him with two ice cold bottles of Leffe bier. When they'd poured, Frank raised his glass and said,

'Cheers Dirk. Great to have you here, it really is.'

'Cheers. Glad to be here Frank.' was all Dirk could really think of saying, realizing it was the first time since they'd met today that Frank had called him by name. As he pondered upon it Frank used it again.

'Anyway, first things first, I want you to feel at home and relaxed here Dirk. We'll have dinner tonight at that restaurant I pointed out earlier, but we won't have a heavy night. I want us both to be match fit for Queen's day tomorrow.'

'That sounds good to me Frank. I'm looking forward to tomorrow.'

'You won't be disappointed. To the future.' said Frank raising his glass.

Dirk reciprocated and smiled inwardly. He was indescribably contented and more relaxed than he'd been in months. His immediate financial future was secure, thanks to his recent demerger settlement from dirty little Roger. A good friend was magnanimously granting him a free holiday in a beautiful apartment in this magnificent city. It felt like an entirely new beginning. The future looked very good indeed.

Chapter 8

Dirk spent half an hour unpacking and looking around his room, hanging up his clothes and putting his toiletries into the en-suite's mirrored cabinet above the sink. There was a desk in front of the bedroom window with an internet connection and a power point, giving him unlimited access to the world outside. After he'd showered, he went back downstairs. It was now seven thirty. They had both changed into what Frank called smart casual attire. Frank with a yellow Ralph Lauren shirt, stone coloured chinos and a pair of loafers. Dirk with boot cut Levi jeans, Timberland Earth Keeper boots and an Abercrombie and Fitch distressed pale blue polo shirt. They were smart and casual respectively.

Standing at the large front window, Frank pointed out the surrounding area where they were staying. He described the main square, Leidseplein, that wasn't too far from the apartment, with its numerous bars and restaurants. It was one of the many pulsating hearts of the city and in Frank's inimitable words, "*a livelier part of Amsterdam*". They walked up to get a cab and to let Dirk see it. He loved it, but Frank wanted to eat and promised they would stop off on the way back home. There was a taxi rank on the opposite side of the square, so they jumped in a cab and headed for the Sea Palace.

The floating Chinese restaurant was a spectacular sight. A three tiered pagoda, stretching out into the water and lit up like a Christmas tree. They were greeted at the entrance by two beautiful hostesses dressed in

Cheongsam silk dresses split to the thigh. One girl was Chinese the other black. This surprised Dirk, although he didn't quite know why. There was a large fountain to the left of the entrance on the lower deck and a huge staircase leading to the upper deck, beside which was a huge wooden carving of what looked like a giant mythical bird of prey. It was Friday evening and the restaurant was busy. The black hostess escorted them to the upstairs dining area, where she led them to a table by the window overlooking the beautifully illuminated city, giving them a warm smile as they were seated. Dirk smiled back at her with equal warmth and Frank shook his head at his friend's easy charm. However, when she left Frank mused. 'I wonder if she's on the menu?'

'How hungry are you Frank?' asked Dirk.

'Ravenous my boy, ravenous.'

Dirk glanced around the huge restaurant. He had no idea how many people the restaurant seated, but estimated it could seat about a thousand.

'Seats seven hundred' said Frank, as if he'd read Dirk's thoughts. 'This is one of my favourite restaurants in Amsterdam; fabulous food, great views and...' His voice trailed off as a lovely young Chinese waitress silently materialized at the table.

'Would you like to order something to drink?' chirped the soft voice.

'I'll have a Tsingtao, please?' requested Dirk.

'Make that two.' said Frank.

As the waitress floated off to fetch their drinks, they both watched her go.

'Ahem! You were saying…' said Dirk

'…and the service is second to none.'

The girl returned almost immediately with two Tsingtao beers and swiftly filled their glasses. Frank raised his and proposed his familiar salutation. 'To the future!'

The dull clunk of their glasses sounded hollow.

'You ready to order now?' asked the waitress.

Frank ventured, 'I'm pretty much a creature of habit when it comes to food. Could you go for the Crispy Aromatic Duck and pancakes; you know, the one with the spring onions and hoi sin sauce? I know you said you fancied a steak, but what about duck? That's as good as a steak, isn't it?'

'That sounds good, let's go for that. Half or a whole duck?'

'You want a starter?'

'Get the whole duck and we won't need one.'

'Good idea, sorted.'

They ordered a whole duck and two more Tsingtao beers. The girl nodded politely and glided away again. Their feast took less than fifteen minutes to prepare and they watched in amazement at the dexterous skill of the waiter shredding the duck at the table. Dirk tucked in like he hadn't eaten all week. He and Frank both *umm'd* and *aah'd* with each bite, commenting on how delicious it was.

'You know, they do a great Dim Sum lunch here on Sundays' said Frank, between mouthfuls.

'I love Dim Sum. Let's come back here on Sunday, I could eat that stuff every day.' enthused Dirk.

'Excellent idea, let's do that', agreed Frank, 'you *are* on holiday after all.'

They ate and continued with their small talk,

relaxing and soaking up the wonderful atmosphere of their surroundings.

'Amsterdam's a terrific place' said Frank, 'people really let their hair down. You'd think it was Saturday night every night in some of the bars here. It's a fun place, that's why so many tourists come here.'

'Well, let's avoid the stag and hen bars ok?'

'Absolutely, I tend to avoid the tourist traps, once you live in a place long enough you find little gems all over. No tourists at all, just the locals.'

'Leidseplein looked kind of touristy!' noted Dirk.

'Well, yes, it can be, but most of the big groups quickly move on to the Red light district. Besides there are lots of bars in the streets just off Leidseplein that look dark enough to put tourists off. They wouldn't venture down at night for fear of getting lost. We'll head back there and move around a few little, non-tourist, hot spots ok?'

'Just so long as they have something to quench our thirst Frank!' said Dirk.

When they'd paid the bill, Frank said, with a glimmer in his eyes, 'Let's take a little detour. See some hot spots of a different kind first. You did say you wanted to quench your thirst.'

'I knew you couldn't resist it, you old pervert. I thought we were taking it easy tonight?' Dirk reminded him.

'Well, like you said earlier, old habits die hard.' replied Frank.

~

As they left the restaurant, an impeccably dressed gentleman excused himself from the exquisite woman with whom he was dining and went downstairs. Going outside, he watched the two friends strolling up the walkway. Frank was animatedly describing something to Dirk. The gentleman speed dialled the single contact number on his cellphone. It was answered on the first ring. He conveyed a brief message to the recipient and listened until the voice on the other end acknowledged then hung up. Removing the SIM card from the cellphone, he snapped it in two between his thumb and forefinger and casually dropped it into the water. Then, with a last look up the walkway, he turned and walked back into the restaurant to re-join his lovely dinner companion.

Chapter 9

They hadn't stayed out late in the end, getting back to the apartment well before midnight. Frank had only wanted to have a laugh and a look at the naughty ladies in the windows, as he liked to call them. After leaving the floating restaurant, they'd walked over a bridge then across a wide open road, cutting up a side street that took them into the edge of the Red light district. Frank seemed very familiar with the area. Several windows contained all shapes and sizes of semi-naked women, although some barely qualified in that category and others didn't qualify at all. Frank seemed hell bent on shocking and entertaining Dirk, with his antics of mixing it with the prostitutes in the windows, making cringe worthy comments and asking them how much they charged for a good time; as if he didn't already know. At that stage in the evening, Dirk was feeling the effects of his long day and wanted to call it a night, but hadn't wanted to be a party pooper and piss on his friend's parade. Fortunately, Frank seemed to wane after about forty-five minutes and suggested they head back to the apartment for a nightcap.

~

The following day was the last day of April; Queen's day. Dirk lay staring at the ceiling of his new surroundings, slowly coming around, until the street sounds became too seductive to ignore. He glanced at his watch. It was just after ten. With a big stretch and a loud yawn, he threw back the duvet. Got up and walked naked out of his bedroom and into the lounge. He had a lean, toned, physique and kept himself in trim by exercising at the gym three nights a week. On weekends Melissa augmented his fitness regime.

Protecting his modesty as best he could, he dared to look out of the window. On the far side of the canal bank, vendors were busily setting up their stalls and the street below was beginning to fill up with all sorts of people dressed in every shade of orange apparel. There was also some nautical activity on the canal. Queen's day was coming alive. Some revellers were already well into the festival spirit and had begun drinking. Dirk's stomach lurched. Just beyond the first bridge, people were sitting outside the little corner café reading newspapers, smoking cigarettes and drinking coffee. Nice.

Pulling on his jeans and shirt from the previous evening, Dirk headed downstairs hoping that Frank had brewed some coffee or something equally stimulating. His luck was out. There were no aromatic smells, only the sickly sweet tang of stale beer permeated the air. Dirk rummaged around in the kitchen cupboards looking for coffee or even tea, but couldn't find any. There was nothing to indicate that Frank had even been up yet and it was now well after ten. He knocked once on the closed bedroom door and called his friend's name then waited. No answer, nothing, not a sound. Tentatively opening the door, he popped his head in. The bed had been slept in, but Frank wasn't in it. There were no discernible sounds coming from the en-suite either. He called his friend's name again. Still nothing.

Going all the way in, he looked into the shower area. Steam clung to the glass doors and there was water and towels on the floor, but no sign of Frank. He was gone.

Puzzled but not unduly concerned, Dirk exited the unoccupied bedroom and went back in to the kitchen to check out the refrigerator, hoping to find some orange juice or something other than beer. There was no juice of any kind, but plenty of Red Bulls. He helped himself to one of those and sat at the table by the large window. The view from the window overlooked the intersection of four streets, two of which had a canal running down the middle of them. The buildings all around were beautifully constructed and seemed somehow to come alive in the morning sunlight. They were tall and narrow and he loved the way they leaned and settled and sank into the canals in a seemingly laconic slouch. No two adjacent buildings were the same. The effect of this, together with the varied and vibrant stalls of the street vendors, created a canvas of spectacular colour found only in a Van Gogh painting. At that moment Dirk understood a little of the painter's frantic passion to capture the beauty of a moment, before it vanished forever.

The sun was climbing higher in the sky and it looked to be progressing into a lovely spring day. He sighed, gave himself a shake and stood up. He walked into the kitchen and dropped the empty Red Bull can into the bin, then headed upstairs and stripped off. There were a number of small towels hanging on a rack just inside the door of the en-suite. The one he selected just about wrapped around his waist. The shower unit was easy to use, an on/off button and two more for adjusting the water temperature. He leaned in and pushed the *on* button and stood with his hand under the spray waiting for it to warm up. When it appeared to be taking its time, he pushed the red button three times until the temperature suited him. Dropping the towel onto the floor, he ducked under the hot water and let out a luxuriant sigh, turning around to let it flow over his back and shoulders. He spent a good fifteen minutes under the therapeutic jet, letting the water regenerate his senses and soothe his tired limbs. When he'd had enough he hit the off switch, opened the cubicle door and picked up the towel. After he'd given himself a brisk rub down, he felt hot and thirsty. Wrapping the small towel around his waist again, he headed downstairs to get another Red Bull. There was still no sign of Frank.

Passing the front door on his way back upstairs, he heard movement and the jangle of keys in the hallway. With his free hand, he reached for the handle and pulled the door open, 'Good Morning Fra...' He stopped mid-sentence. There, just outside the doorway, he came face to face with the most strikingly beautiful, ice cool, blue eyes he had ever seen. Casually dressed in a denim jacket, combat cargo pants and trainers, she was somewhere in her mid to late twenties with short, stylishly cut and fashionably dishevelled, blonde hair. Slung over her left shoulder was a large sports holdall and in her right hand was a large wad of keys, the sound of which he'd mistaken for Frank. Both she and Dirk froze in their respective spots. Her eyes seemed to penetrate his like laser beams. Neither spoke, neither moved. She scanned him up and down and a smile began to spread across her face. It wasn't just any smile, but a coquettish, Marilyn Monroe type of smile. It was the smile of appreciation. Dirk could only stand there in stunned silence with his Red Bull in his hand just below his gaping mouth. Beautiful women can have that effect. However, he quickly managed to recover some of his composure.

'Oh! I'm sorry. I thought you were someone else...' He spluttered, excruciatingly aware that he was inappropriately dressed for greeting strangers at the door, especially one as beautiful as she.

Never the shy one, Dirk introduced himself. '...I'm a friend of Frank Perrier. That's who I thought you were. He, uh, lives here and I'm a friend of his, visiting from the UK; Dirk Dagger.' Passing his Red Bull to his left hand, he offered his right in introduction. However, in performing this simple but sudden movement, he extended a greeting of a different kind as the towel slipped off his waist, falling to the floor and exposing all of his short comings. Before he could say or do anything else to extend his embarrassment further, Frank pushed in through the open front door carrying a Starbuck's bag in one hand and an orange plastic bag in the other.

Standing in the open doorway, Frank's jaw dropped at this astonishing and perplexing scene, his head moving left to right like a spectator at the Wimbledon ladies singles final. Dirk, in an attempt to assuage his dilemma, simply said. 'Good morning Frank, I'm just introducing myself to your lovely new neighbour.' Then, without another word of explanation, he abruptly turned and dashed smartly back upstairs, double quick, not stopping to pick up the towel. He was fully and painfully aware that her eyes were on what, he prayed, was an end and a beginning of which she approved. Behind him he could hear delicious female laughter and Frank's dulcet tones conveying his profound apologies. He didn't know which was worse.

Dirk emerged from his bedroom twenty minutes later, dried and dressed but a little shrivelled. Downstairs in the main lounge, Frank was sitting on the large sofa reading the financial papers and finishing off a croissant. He looked up from behind his broadsheet and gave Dirk the stern glare a displeased Victorian father would give his wayward son. They both regarded each other for a moment, before erupting into fits of laughter.

'Still haven't lost your touch with the ladies I see.' said Frank, trying to catch his breath.

Dirk had to see the funny side and soon he too was laughing so hard he had to sit down.

Wiping his eyes, Frank said 'I think you made a solid impression, just as well I left the central heating turned on last night stumpy.'

'Cheeky bastard! I could see she warmed to me too, what a smile and those eyes…'

When their laughter died down, Frank said, 'Never a dull moment with you my boy, another classic.'

'Who is she?' Dirk asked, wiping his eyes.

'She said her name was Helena. She's just moved in.'

Frank suddenly looked serious and a little stricken. 'Fuck…and the first time I meet her I have to apologise for the naked man in my apartment. I'll never live this down. We'd better bring a couple of naughty ladies back tonight to save face. Maybe we'll see her out tonight, or we could just knock on her door and say hi.'

'…and say what, remember us, little and large?'

They both laughed again at this and Frank said 'Think she'll know who's who? Hey, that's not a bad idea my boy, maybe she's got a friend? You should go ask, what have you got to lose?'

'What remains of my dignity.' said Dirk. 'Any coffee left?'

'Over there by the microwave. It'll be cold by now, same as the croissants. You'll have to zap them in the microwave, if you still want them.' Frank Replied.

'What's it like out?' enquired Dirk.

'Well it looked a little small…'

'Fuck off, the weather you idiot.'

Frank smirked, 'Oh, yes, of course. It's very nice out, but there's a bit of a stiff breeze. It's ok though, generally speaking. Anyway, how do you feel? Ready to head out and embrace the spirit of Queen's day? Check this out!'

Frank stood up and pulled on the hem of the baggy, garish, orange T-shirt that he was wearing. Emblazoned across the front in large purple lettering was: *I'M WITH STUPID.*

'Yours is in the bag over there.' said Frank.

Dirk looked in the direction he was pointing and saw the orange bag that Frank had brought in this morning. 'Everyone has to wear something orange and I assumed that, like me, you don't own an orange T-shirt. So, when I nipped out for the coffees, I stopped off and bought these two at a vendor's stall up in Leidseplein.' said Frank proudly.

Dirk pulled out an orange T-shirt. It had *STUPID* written on it. 'Gee whizz, thanks pal.'

Frank was nodding and grinning like an idiot. 'Right,

put it on and let's go get a big breakfast that'll set us up for the day.'

The appeal of more appetising sustenance on the horizon won him over. Dirk passed on the cold coffee and croissants. One of the nearby corner cafes provided a hearty breakfast called a bouncer, comprising toasted bread, topped with ham, three fried eggs and melted cheese. Washed down with freshly squeezed orange juice and two double espressos each, they were ready to join in the festive fun of the giant street party.

Leidseplein seemed like the natural choice to kick off, but to their disgust the effluent hoses on the men's public urinals had become detached, spilling raw urine onto a large surrounding area. The warm sunshine was fermenting it quickly into a revolting stench, prompting their sharp exit from the square. They headed up a side street and discovered a bar blaring out 1970s disco music. The atmosphere was lively and they stopped for an hour, enjoying old classics from the Jacksons, Gloria Gaynor and Earth, Wind & Fire, until too many of what seemed like the Village People turned up and the friends decided it wasn't their scene any more.

A number five tram took them over to Dam Square, where their next stop was the cigar shop. Much to Dirk's disappointment, the two alluring female assistants from the previous day were absent, but another pretty girl provided the charm and escorted them into the humidor room. It was too nice to stay inside, so they just paid for the cigars and headed back into the fray. As they left the shop Dirk turned to Frank. 'Aren't there any ugly girls in Amsterdam?'

'She's about the ugliest I've seen.' He replied.

'I think I'll retire here.' said Dirk.

'I can think of worse places.' said Frank.

Diagonally across the road from the cigar shop was a wholesale jewellers called the Diamond Factory and behind that a side street with a bar overlooking a canal, offering seclusion from the main drag. They sat outside smoking their cigars, drinking beer and laughing at some of the more colourful characters; both in and out of the water. One party amongst the flotilla were standing on what looked like an old barn door fitted with an outboard motor. The *crew* were up to their ankles, but at least it kept their beer cool. Most participants had donned orange attire of some description and an assortment of wigs and hats. Some even had orange painted faces, whilst others wearing the wrong colours looked a little left out. All in all, it was quite a spectacle; the whole atmosphere was extremely buoyant, albeit raucous in places.

The day progressed well and around five in the evening they had wandered over to the edge of the red light district to another bar that brewed its own beer. The interior was dominated by a huge copper still and was extremely busy with revellers. However, there was outside seating overlooking another beautiful square. Frank decided it was time for another cigar or a *Big Bob Marley* as he jokingly referred to it. Dirk said he'd stick with the cigars. As they drank in the atmosphere, Frank pointed down to their left. 'There's a little place around the corner from here where the girls get up and dance on the bar buck naked.' said Frank, with an all knowing grin.

'That's got to be worth a visit?' said Dirk enthusiastically.

'I call it the outrageous bar' said Frank, 'we'll check it out after we finish these, then grab a bite to eat. Ok?'

'Sounds good to me.' said Dirk.

Smoking and sampling the fine brewery beer, they sat there for another hour enjoying the last of the sunshine, while the party revellers danced and staggered all around them. When it was time to move on, Dirk followed behind as Frank walked purposefully up and down a series of tight alleyways lined with near nude women on either side, flaunting their hot promises to all who passed their narrow doorways.

'See anything you like my boy?' asked Frank.

'What's not to like?' replied Dirk.

They eventually exited the labyrinth of temptation just behind an imposing Gothic church. A touch ironic mused Dirk. Frank led them down to the end of another tight alleyway that terminated at what appeared to be a go-go bar. The large neon sign of a girl pole dancing *was* a bit of a giveaway.

A huge doorman, with an eastern European accent, confronted them at the entrance. He charged them an admission fee of just five euros each and stamped the back of their hands with an inky blob, as a form of receipt and rite of passage. Dirk followed Frank through a thick, opaque, plastic curtain concealing the inner entrance to the club. The air inside was just as opaque, although it was supposed to be a non-smoking establishment. The interior was small, but had two separate bar areas. TV screens mounted above both bars were showing hard core porn. On top of the larger of the two bars a lithe girl, in high heels and a micro thong, strutted her funky stuff while a group of gentlemen from the Asian subcontinent stood rigidly debating her charms.

Frank and Dirk approached the main bar. A topless barmaid came over and pointedly asked what their pleasure was. They ordered two beers. There were several stools around the bar, providing a grandstand view. All of them were empty. Dirk sat down. The instant he did, the girl dancing on the bar whipped off her tiny G-string and dropped smack bang on his lap, wrapping her legs around his waist and locking him in place. Stunned by this sudden invasion of his personal and most private space he turned to his friend for guidance, but Frank was no longer standing beside him. He hadn't sat down and now Dirk was finding out why, the hard way. Frank continued to remain at a safe distance and grinned at the expression on his friend's face. The naked girl's groin ground into Dirk's and she pressed his face into what could only be described as deployed airbags. He was scandalized at how quickly he was becoming aroused and felt over exposed for the second time that day.

Five dubiously gratifying minutes later, feeling somewhat emotive from the experience, Dirk was rooted to the spot. Frank came to his rescue and pressed twenty euros between the girl's ample charms in appreciation of her performance. She hugged Dirk's face into her overwhelming frontage again. Planted a kiss on his check then lifted her legs up and over his head, giving him a lovely big smile as she did so. She sprang back onto the bar to strut her stuff in search of another eager face, leaving Dirk to slide off the stool. He remained upright for the remainder of their stay.

'Now I know why you didn't sit down you sly bastard.' Dirk growled to a grinning Frank.

'Knowledge is power my friend. Here, have a beer.'

The beers they served in the place were very small, less than half pints. Homos as they were discourteously termed by the locals. Dirk ordered another two almost immediately after the first. When the girl came back with his change from a twenty, she placed a two euro piece on each nipple. Flipped forward and caught them in her hands. Tossed him one and blew him a kiss. When he returned from the bar he said. 'I see now why you call it the outrageous bar, these two crap beers almost cost me twenty euros.'

'Including tips.' said Frank, smiling at Dirk standing there with his forlorn and lonely looking two euro coin in his hand.

'We'll have one more and I'll get a dance from the big dark thing that's just jumped up on the bar, then we'll head off.' announced Frank.

Dirk looked up and saw a fabulous looking, tall and athletic, black girl with fantastic long legs and a sexy Naomi Campbell strut start her thing on the bar. Frank handed Dirk a twenty, 'Get them in my boy, I'm in love', then plonked himself down on a bar stool and beckoned to the big black stunner. She flashed him a dazzling smile and snapped her thong.

Satiated and slightly merry, the two friends headed out of the red light district and back in the general direction of the apartment, grabbing a couple of pizza slices on the way. They finished off in the little corner bar on the rise overlooking the hump backed bridge, a mere stone's throw from the apartment. It was a lot quieter than it had been a few hours before, when it had been surrounded on all sides by a seething mass of orange clad revellers. Frank referred to it as the hovel, but it was actually a charming little place called Café Heuvel. As they headed into the bar Dirk spotted Frank's beautiful new neighbour Helena on the opposite side of the canal. She looked like she was on her way back to the apartment building. Tapping Frank on the shoulder he said, 'I'll be right back' and shot off across the bridge towards her. She was walking quickly, but not too fast. 'Helena?' Dirk shouted. She didn't immediately turn around until he had almost caught up. 'Helena?' he said again. At this she turned around and with recognition, stopped and smiled.

'It is Helena, yes?' asked Dirk.

She nodded and continued to smile at him. A good sign he thought. 'Hello again, we, uh, *met* earlier today and I…well…I wanted to apologise. I hope you can forgive my…how can I put it..?' He suddenly realised he couldn't and his words trailed off. She continued to regard him with those eyes and that smile. Swallowing hard he found his voice. 'I just wanted to apologise for my lack of etiquette this morning…I hope I didn't offend or embarrass you.'

She said nothing, but continued to smile and look him up and down. At first he thought she was trying to imagine him naked again, until he remembered the T-shirt he was wearing had the word *STUPID* written across it. At least it wouldn't fall off. Thrusting out his hand, he extended a more appropriate greeting. 'I'd like to start over, if you'd let me? Please? My name's Dirk. I'm here to visit my friend Frank for a couple of weeks and I'll be staying in the apartment below yours. So, we'll be sort of neighbours.'

Still smiling, she stepped forward and grasped his hand. It was a nice hand, strong but feminine. She introduced herself formally. 'Helena. I like your T-shirt.' Dirk tugged on it and shrugged. Then, still holding onto her hand, he gave a silent sigh of relief and decided to venture a little bit further. 'Would you like to join us for a drink Helena? My friend Frank and I are just about to have a glass of wine across in that little bar over there and we...well, that is, I, really would like to buy you a drink to make up for this morning'.

She didn't pull her hand away, but her eyes flashed and a little dimple appeared on the right side of her lips as her smile widened. 'There is no need to apologise, it was...amusing.'

Dirk didn't feel any better at having his naked form being described as amusing. He let go of her hand and extended his invitation again. 'I *would* feel much better if you'd let me buy you a drink Helena. Please?'

Her smile broadened further at his awkwardness and another dimple appeared on the other side. 'Thank you, but no. I am going home now to sleep', then she paused momentarily, 'another evening perhaps?'

Deciding to snatch a small victory Dirk said. 'Great, I'll knock you up one night next week.' He immediately regretted his choice of words and cringed. They were lost in translation. Thank God.

She began walking away, but maintained eye contact. 'Have a good evening Dick.'

'uh...Dirk! My name, it's Dirk' He spluttered, quickly correcting her pronunciation.

She smiled that smile again and Dirk was sure he caught a mischievous sparkle of fire within her ice cool, azure blue, captivating eyes. When he reached the brow of the hump backed bridge, he stopped and watched her until she was out of sight.

Chapter 10

Dirk entered the bar to find Frank wearing a frown and in conversation with an impeccably dressed young man of about thirty. Frank caught sight of him and broke off by acknowledging his arrival. The well-groomed stranger turned around and regarded Dirk with a slightly cool, but not entirely unfriendly gaze. Dirk matched his gaze momentarily and then looked to Frank questioningly. Frank started in with the introductions, but before he had the chance the young stranger introduced himself with a flamboyant swivel of his upper body. Transferring the cigarette in his right hand to his left, he extended his right like a gunfighter drawing a colt forty five in a single, well-rehearsed, mellifluous movement. 'Jason Sinclair, my pleasure...'

'Hello, Dirk Dagger, pleased to meet you.' Dirk replied stiffly, glancing back at Frank, unsure of the situation or the relationship between him and this indefinable, but somewhat unctuous individual. Frank brokered the missing pieces. 'Jason is a client of mine.'

'Just a client Perrier?' said Jason in mock indignation, 'I thought we were the best of chums, what with all the business I've thrown your way?' Turning back to Dirk he issued a bizarre statement, 'Isn't it always the way with these financial types Mister Dagger. They couldn't care less for anyone else's sensibilities. They're only after one thing, like a rapist in a convent.'

Dirk raised his eyes at this curious analogy. 'I didn't realise Frank was so religious.'

Jason threw back his head and laughed at this

73

remark, a little too readily and a little too loudly Dirk noted. Frank leaned on the bar in an attempt to look nonchalant, but couldn't conceal his discomfort. His thin smile gave him away.

'Excellent, Mister Dagger, excellent.' gushed Jason.

'Please, call me Dirk.'

'Indeed I shall. You have very charming friends Perrier, too nice for an avaricious old bugger like you I'm sure.' Jason beckoned the barman and requested another wine glass with the confident self-assuredness of a quasi-aristocrat. When the glass arrived he poured Dirk some wine, filling the glass two thirds full. 'I apologise if the wine is not to your palette Mister Dirk, stingy old Frank chose it. So, it's probably the cheapest plonk in the whole fucking place.'

A couple of locals had stopped talking and were glancing over. Jason tut-tutted. 'You'd think these bloody foreigners had never heard anyone swear before, but they love our swearing. It's so much better than theirs, more expressive...and such fun. Don't you think?'

Frank interjected. 'Jason, please behave. This is a nice place and I would like to be able to come back here again, so don't offend the locals eh? Try to remember that we're the foreigners.'

'Oh very well Mother,' said Jason, rolling his eyes at Dirk. 'I need to take a piss anyway'. He pushed himself off the bar and strode away in the direction of the loo. In spite of the swearing, Dirk was mildly amused by the aloof and flamboyant mannerisms of Frank's bar buddy. Frank caught the quizzical expression in Dirk's smile and said. 'I'm sorry about that, I had no idea he was here.'

Dirk continued to smile, 'Why? Is it a problem for him to be here? He seems harmless enough.'

Frank gave a slight grimace before answering. 'He comes from money, a lot of money.'

'I sense a "but" in that sentence.' said Dirk.

'But...he has none. Rumour has it he's been cut off...or is about to be.'

'Is he one of the ones selling Ferraris or Lamborghinis and shit?' asked Dirk.

Frank looked at the toilet door before answering, 'Something like that.'

~

With Jason in the loo, Frank told Dirk a little more about him. He had met Jason last year, when he contacted his bank to trade off some bearer bond certificates. Frank was assigned the task of handling the bonds and reinvesting the money. However, Jason was an impatient investor and sold off most of his investments way before their maturity or at a loss. Not that Frank or his bank were unduly concerned, they'd been paid their fees and were only too happy to continue to do so for more advice; whether the client followed it or not. On another occasion Jason had made an offhand remark about selling his old stamp collection to raise funds. Frank had informed him that it wasn't such a joke. Unique collections such as stamps, rare books and coins made up large parts of many of his clients' portfolios and that if he had something of that nature he wished to sell or trade, then he could make enquiries on his behalf of any parties that might be interested. This proposition intrigued Jason and he had asked Frank to enlighten him further. On their next meeting Jason brought with him a collection of King Edward VII gold sovereigns. Frank, being an avid collector of coins himself, immediately took them off Jason's hands for a knock down price. He'd then gone on to broker other trades between Jason and other clients who traded anything of singular value. Jason had since become a *prolific trader*.

~

'What brings him over here, now?' asked Dirk.

'That's what worries me, I don't know. Last week, when I was in London, he got in touch and said he had something I might be interested in, so I met him for lunch.' said Frank.

Dirk said nothing and waited for Frank to continue. 'Well, you know I've always collected coins since I was a boy and I've bought a few from Jason in the past; nothing out of the ordinary, just a few gold sovereigns. He has a fondness for the good life…and cocaine too. Constantly needs cash and I can't resist a bargain…'

Dirk shrugged, as if to say "so what's new?"

'…So this time he produces, right there in the restaurant, a solid gold, King Charles II, two guinea coin.' said Frank, eyes wide open, like a schoolboy who's just seen his first playboy centrefold.

'Is that good?' Asked Dirk.

Frank almost choked. 'Good? They're worth about five grand each and he informs me he's got four more back at his apartment.'

'Did you get a buyer for him?' asked Dirk.

Frank hesitated and looked slightly sheepish before replying. 'Yes…me.'

'You?' balked Dirk, doing a quick calculation in his head of the total value of the coins.

'They were absolutely exquisite and in pristine condition. He wanted money desperately and was offering them to me for a price too good to turn down.' rationalised Frank.

'What did you pay for them, if you don't mind me asking?'

Frank glanced ruefully at the closed toilet door again before answering. 'Too much I think.'

Keeping watch on the toilet door in case Jason suddenly reappeared, Frank continued.

'When I paid Jason what I paid him for the coins, he got very excited. Said he had something of even greater value and that he could get it for me next week. I told him I was busy for the next two weeks, but would see him when it was next convenient. However, he didn't want to wait that long and insisted I introduce him to the clients who'd traded his stuff in the past. I told it was out of the question. Maintaining anonymity between clients is paramount to the continued success of such trades.'

'What'd he say to that?'

'He got a bit stroppy and accused me of holding out for a better price or a bigger commission. I managed to calm him down, but left him sulking in his apartment. That was just before I came down to Bristol.'

'So, how did he know you'd be here?'

Frank grimaced slightly, 'My fault I suppose, me and

my big mouth. I mentioned I was looking forward to Queens's day in Amsterdam…just idle small talk over lunch but…'

'But what?'

'But…I spoke about where I was living, how beautiful it was with all the antique shops and art galleries. You see, the problem is, he knows Amsterdam very well…and maybe…probably…when I mentioned where I was staying and…well, I might have mentioned a few of my favourite places to eat and drink, including this place…' Frank trailed off, looking pensive.

'So what if you did, what's the worry?' Dirk asked.

'The worry is that it's a little too close for comfort, he keeps pressing for an introduction to my clients.'

'So you think he's here now to try to force an introduction with your client here in Holland?'

Frank shook his head. 'He couldn't make that happen, but it could be a pain in the arse if he was to try something stupid. What if the bastard's been following me? It's no coincidence he's turned up here.'

'Ask him.'

'Ask him what?'

'Just ask him what he's doing here, straight out, it's a fair question.'

Before Frank could answer, Jason returned from what Dirk now suspected was a tactical disappearance and sat down. He lit up another cigarette and asked the very question Dirk had suggested Frank ask of him.

'So, tell me Mister Dirk, what brings you to Amsterdam?'

Before Dirk could answer, Frank jumped in. 'He's just visiting me for a few days.'

Jason gave Frank a look like he'd just perpetrated something vile and then focused back on Dirk. 'Oh, so you're not working together or anything so droll, just two old mates on the razz eh?'

Dirk could see Frank was beginning to get wound up by the situation and deflected any conflict by reciprocating Jason's question. 'What about you Jason, what brings you to Amsterdam? Queen's day?'

'Absolutely spot on; you know, last week this old bugger Perrier talked it up so convincingly, that I thought I'd have to see it for myself. I've been here on many occasions, but never for Queen's day. And I must say I'm having a stimulating experience, even though my *friend* here didn't invite me.' Jason looked at Frank in a mock huffed manner. 'Anyway, I intend to stay for a week or so and peruse the lovely antique shops. Any dealers in particular you can recommend or introduce me to Frank?'

'I told you Jason, I don't really have time next week.'

'What about you Mister Dirk, do you know any good dealers in town?'

'Dirk doesn't have time next week either.' blurted out Frank.

Jason casually lit another cigarette and blew an 'O' with the smoke. Rolled his tongue around in his cheek and looked between the two friends.

'I thought you said you two weren't in business together?' asked Jason coyly.

'Nobody mentioned anything about business Jason.' rebuked Frank.

'Oh come now Perrier, I know you love your little…what do you like to call them…murders and executions. Who doesn't like to make a killing? What are you up to next week that you don't want to share?'

Frank was beginning to lose his temper. 'I think you mean mergers and acquisitions and for God's sake keep your voice down Jason, people are staring and starting to get pissed off. Here, have some more wine.'

'Why, thank you kind Sir.' said Jason.

An uncomfortable moment of silence followed until Jason raised his glass and offered a curious salutation.

'Gentlemen, may I propose a toast? Wealth is health and health is wealth, if you don't have wealth then to hell with health.'

Jason downed his wine in one and slammed the empty glass down on the bar.

'Well then Frank? If you aren't going to tell me where all the good dealers are, you can at least tell me where the good whore houses are.'

It took forty five minutes and another bottle of the bar's most expensive wine before Jason bade them farewell, threatened to get in touch, then left in search of paradise.

The two friends remained in Café Heuvel until one thirty am. Frank's tension over his unexpected encounter with Jason Sinclair seemed to dissipate with the wine and convivial atmosphere in the bar. When they finally tottered back to the apartment, Dirk downed about a litre and a half of water in Frank's kitchen, before clawing his way up the steep stairs to collapse into bed. He lay on his back and thought of Helena. She was somewhere above him in the upstairs apartment and he wondered if she was alone. It disturbed him to think she might not be. Her lovely smile drifted into his dreamy thoughts and he remained like this for a few more minutes staring at the ceiling, entertaining lustful fantasies, until exhaustion finally overcame him and he drifted into a deep and contented sleep.

Chapter 11

Dirk was awakened the next morning by the sound of a radio playing loudly through an open window from somewhere in the courtyard at the rear of the building. The artist was Lil' Wayne and the music had a lively, rhythmic, beat. He could just about make out the lyrics of the song. It was about some guy's chick's pussy having changed; charming. Just as lustful fantasies began to creep into his thoughts again, the sound of church bells rang out and tried in vain to compete for dominance over the amorous rapper. Slowly raising himself up on his elbows, he looked out through the open curtains at another fine day.

Not wanting to waste it lying in bed, he rolled himself off into a standing position and stumbled into the en-suite bathroom. He groaned in disgust at his reflection in the mirror. His complexion was the colour of cat shit and his mouth tasted like it too. Turning on the shower he absentmindedly stepped into the cubicle only to jump straight back out, breathless with shock, as the ice cold spray stung his body. It did have the immediate effect of jump-starting his numbed senses. Cursing, he hit the red button and the water soon got to a satisfactory temperature that warmed him up again.

Thirty minutes after he'd risen from the dead, dressed in fresh jeans and a T-shirt and feeling slightly more alive, Dirk descended the stairs to the main lounge where he found Frank in a bright and chipper mood. He looked none the worse from their all day drinking binge and seemed to have put behind him his woes over Jason Sinclair.

'Good morning my boy, are you ready for some brunch and a hair of the dog that bit your arse?' Asked Frank, with annoying joviality.

Dirk looked at him through bloodshot blue eyes. 'What's your secret Frank? Got a morning after pill or something?'

'Or something: two Nurofen and two Red Bulls.' declared Frank.

'Gimme!' implored Dirk.

'Bulls are in the fridge, I'll get your drugs. Go and sit down.' Said Frank.

Dirk retrieved an ice cold can of Red Bull from the fridge. He sat down on the large settee and rubbed his eyes, still sensitive to the bright sunlight. Frank brought over two pain killers and Dirk sank them with a single gulp that drained the bull. This was swiftly followed by a loud belch.

'House in the lounge.' shouted Frank.

With a satisfactory big sigh, Dirk requested another Red Bull. Frank removed one from the now almost depleted stock and tossed it over to him, announcing: 'You'll feel as right as rain in no time. However, if you still fancy a Dim Sum lunch we'd better head over there soon. It's gone past eleven thirty and it gets very busy very quickly.'

'Yup, I'm up for that. A couple of Tsingtaos will be just the thing to set me straight again.'

Dirk swiftly downed his second Red Bull and they headed out into the bright sunshine of Sunday, the first of May.

Chapter 12

It had just gone past midday when they arrived at the Sea Palace and it was already filling up. They were once again escorted upstairs, this time by an older Chinese lady dressed smartly in a black business trouser suit. A bustling waiter immediately beckoned them forward and escorted them over to the same table at which they'd sat on Friday evening. Dirk was pleased by this, he liked the familiarity. Scanning around the diners in the large room, he couldn't pick out another non-oriental face in the busy restaurant. This pleased him too. It was always a sign of good food to come.

'I could eat a dead horse right now.' Said Dirk.

'I'm sure they would oblige with your request, but it does seem rather a pity to miss out on the lovely dim sum on offer.' remarked Frank.

'I'm sure it'll be equally as good. I *am* starved though, we should have eaten more than just the crap junk food we had last night.' bemoaned Dirk.

'It was good though, wasn't it?' said Frank.

'Fabulous, it really was. Queen's day was brilliant. It was everything you said it was and more. I had a great time Frank. Thanks again for inviting me over.'

'You're welcome my boy.' replied Frank with his usual cheerful aplomb.

Just then a waiter came over and they requested two Tsingtao Chinese beers. The waiter left them menus and a card with which to cross off their dim sum selections.

'I like the little pork and beef dumplings' said Dirk

'Me too' said Frank, 'they're called Siu Mai. Want one of those?'

'For starters at least and Wan Tan soup, I always like the soup.' said Dirk.

'Sounds good.' said Frank picking up the card. 'Let's just order a mix, two of each. Do you like squid and prawns?' asked Frank.

'Does Dolly Parton sleep on her back?' replied Dirk.

Frank grinned at the intriguing analogy. When the waiter returned with their beers they selected two Siu Mai, two Wan Tan Soup, two Sa Cha Tai Yaun Squid and two Ching Yeung Deng deep fried Prawn and Beef Dumplings. Their last dish of choice was mandatory, according to Frank pointing out Dirk's heritage, 'No Scotsman should go without something deep fried for breakfast on a Sunday.'

'I'll drink to that.' said Dirk, raising his glass.

Dirk was again impressed by the efficiency of the staff. Although the restaurant was filled almost to capacity, their first serving of food arrived inside ten minutes. Soon after that, the little portions of dumplings piled up. They both ate ravenously. Dirk's hangover abated and his appetite was satiated. Taking a moment's respite from their banquet, Dirk sat back in his chair and relaxed. 'What are your plans for tomorrow Frank?'

'I have a meeting in the morning, with my client in Den Haag…or as it is better known to you tourists: *The Hague*.'

Dirk smiled at Frank's pseudointellectual pretention. 'What's it like? I've never been.'

'It's a lovely city. The Queen lives there. The seat of Dutch Government resides there too; the Binnenhof parliament building is quite something to see. They also have the International criminal court of justice, so you'd better be on your best behaviour if you decide to pay a visit my boy. It's not quite as touristy as Amsterdam, but it does have some terrific bars and restaurants…not to mention your favourite and mine, girls on bikes.'

'Sounds like my kind of place.'

A waitress appeared and enquired if everything was ok. They said yes and ordered two more pork and prawn dumplings and one more squid. They also ordered a pot of Jasmine tea and two more beers. However, their eyes proved to be larger than their appetites and they were defeated by a single remaining dumpling. As they sat there nursing their swollen stomachs, savouring the flavours and contemplating coffee, a familiar voice interrupted their thoughts.

'Well hello there, isn't this a cosy coincidence?'

They both looked up and into the dazzling, but vaguely leering smile of Jason Sinclair. Hanging onto his arm was a lovely young oriental girl of no more than, what Dirk estimated to be, nineteen and could have easily passed for fourteen. He didn't want to consider the possibility. Frank proffered nothing in the manner of a greeting, but Dirk could see immediately by the sudden change in his demeanour that this was yet another inappropriate encounter bordering on the ominous. Unperturbed by the lack of warmth forthcoming Jason introduced his dining partner, Mei Lei, ungallantly pronouncing her name *"My Lay"*. The girl put her hand to her mouth in a girlishly shy manner and giggled. Dirk winced at Jason's crassness, but reacted well by courteously acknowledging her. 'Lovely to meet you, my name is Dirk and this is Frank.'

Frank nodded stiffly and acknowledged her graciously. The girl giggled again at all the unaccustomed chivalrous attention she was receiving and squeezed Jason's arm tighter. Dirk wondered where he'd scooped her up from. Glancing around the restaurant, Jason made a discernibly obvious observation. 'It's rather busy isn't it?' then, notably, he glanced back at Dirk and not Frank, 'May we join your table?'

Frank answered the question with bland indifference. 'We were just about to leave Jason. You can *have* our table.'

'Oh, I'm sure you have time for a glass of Champagne.' said Jason.

'Champagne? Are we celebrating something?' asked Frank.

Jason didn't reply. He turned to the waiter at his elbow. 'A bottle of Moet et Chandon and four glasses; we'll join our friends here...and make sure it's well chilled!'

The waiter disregarded the insult to his professionalism and nodded politely. Dirk rose up to offer Mei Lei a chair. She was a delicate little thing, very petite, very pretty and very, very, young was all he could think of. She was squeezed into snake skin jeans and a black chiffon blouse with nothing on underneath; thus, inadvertently providing an accurate gauge of the wind chill factor outside. Frank was looking at Jason with unconcealed displeasure. Dirk tactfully tried to lighten the mood by engaging Mei Lei in some banal small talk. 'Do you live in Amsterdam?'

Mei Lei just smiled coyly and blinked at him. Dirk was about to persevere, but Jason intervened and spoke for her. 'Mei Lei's English is not so good Mister Dirk. She's from Shanghai and hasn't lived here very long. But you are learning aren't you my little sushi doll?'

Mei Lei giggled again and nestled her face against Jason's neck. Dirk was aware of the attention she was receiving from other nearby tables. Male and female alike were scrutinising her, disapprovingly he noted. When one of the women at an adjacent table said something in Mandarin to her group of fellow diners, Mei Lei cocked her head towards the direction of the remark and lowered her eyes. She appeared to conducting a detailed analysis of the comment. Next, she did something quite unexpected but remarkable. Picking up one of Dirk's discarded chopsticks, she twirled it around in her nimble little fingers like a miniature majorette's baton. Then, with her head still cocked in the direction of the catty wife, she muttered something in mandarin. Dirk could see that the woman and her fellow diners at the other table clearly understood, because they took on a look of undisguised alarm. The mesmerising windmill motion of the chopstick abruptly stopped and Mei Lei skewered the sad remaining dumpling in the centre of the plate with deadly dexterity. Turning her head fully in the direction of the frozen wife, she fixed her with a cold menacing glare. Plucked at the chopstick with delicate finesse, blinked once and popped the dumpling into her mouth. When she turned her attention away from the stricken group, she casually placed the chopstick onto the plate and licked her lips. Dirk was amazed at her transformation back into that of a seemingly innocent, but tarty little schoolgirl façade. It had all happened in such a blinding moment that he reassessed his initial opinion of her, re-categorising her more Jet Li than Mei Lei. She wasn't so delicate after all.

'Isn't she the most adorable creature?' effused Jason disingenuously, breaking the stunned silence.

'Indeed.' said Dirk, taking a swig of his beer.

Frank didn't appear to be impressed or even fazed by Mei Lei's striking display of dining etiquette. Dismissing it out of hand, he turned to Jason. 'So, another remarkable coincidence in two days, if I was paranoid I'd say you were following us.'

Jason snorted derisively. 'I'd say you were more delusional Frank. I'm just here having a bit of fun, that's all.' He patted Mei Lei's hand resting on his lap. She raised her left shoulder coquettishly to her cheek and looked up into his eyes and blinked twice. 'But, since I am here Frank and well, you're here too. I don't see why we can't include a little business with our pleasure. Wouldn't you agree?'

Frank took a deep breath and let it out slowly. 'Jason, this is neither the time nor the place. I can and I shall, if you wish, see you in London in a couple of weeks, but not before. I have other commitments at present.'

'What about your friend here? Are you abandoning him during his vacation? Some friend, I must say!' Jason declared, with indignation.

Frank said nothing. Jason turned towards Dirk. 'Well, if he's ditching you and going off gallivanting on his business quests next week, perhaps you and I can get together for some fun? Mei Lei has some delicious friends. What do you say Mister Dirk?'

Before Dirk could reply, Frank cut in. 'I'm sure Dirk will be much too busy next week Jason.'

Jason sneered at this. Frank was about to give him directions for perdition when the waiter arrived with an ice bucket and their Champagne. Dirk caught Frank's eye and gave him a look that intimated he should *chillax* and go with the flow, for now. The waiter popped the cork and filled all four glasses, beginning with Mei Lei. She giggled when the bubbles tickled her nose.

'A toast gentlemen and My Lay', Jason said, with a faux noble bow of his head towards his squeeze, before proceeding with another bizarre salute.

'Excessive excesses and successive successes…in equal measures.'

'We'll drink to that, won't we Frank?' said Dirk, in another vain attempt to lighten the mood.

Frank dignified it with silence. Mei Lei got up from the table to look for the ladies room. Dirk respectfully rose up with her. She giggled again at his eccentric display of chivalry before sashaying off, heads turning as she went. As she moved suitably out of range, Jason leaned closer to Frank. 'I really do have something you'll be interested in. It's something I know you wouldn't want to miss out on, believe me.'

Frank tried to remain aloof and indifferent in his reply, 'I'd love to see what you've got Jason, but I simply don't have time. I have an early morning meeting tomorrow and then I'm away on business all next week.'

Jason fixed Frank with a look that conveyed a tangible irresistibility. 'Are you sure? It won't take long. What about later this evening, at your apartment? You wouldn't mind would you Mister Dirk?' asked Jason.

Dirk shrugged dispassionately. 'It's not my call.'

Frank shot him a glance and sighed, 'You'd better not be wasting my time Jason.'

Jason raised an eyebrow and gave Frank a look that said *would I*.

'Alright, do you remember the little bar where we met you last night, Café Heuvel?' asked Frank.

'Yes, of course.' Replied Jason

'You can meet us back there later today...' said Frank. Then, fixing Jason with a stare, he nodded in the direction of Mei Lei's chair. '...and don't bring any *friends* with you.'

'Why, don't you like girls Frank?' Jason teased.

'I like to keep business and pleasure in different rooms.' replied Frank.

Jason feigned a shocked expression. 'Well, Amsterdam is the wrong place for you to be then isn't it?'

Dirk had to smile at that. Frank caught it and said 'Don't encourage him.'

Jason grinned at Dirk and then turned back to Frank, 'What time shall we say? Six o'clock this evening?'

Frank looked at his watch. 'Let's make it five.'

Jason toyed with his glass and smirked. 'I look forward to seeing you Frank; I can't wait to give you the heads up.'

Frank frowned at the remark, but before he could comment, Mei Lei returned. A few moments of awkward silence followed, making Dirk feel slightly uncomfortable. He made an excuse about spending a penny, nodded stiffly at Mei Lei and wished her "bon appetite". This elicited another giggle. Frank exchanged a final disconcerting look with a grinning Jason, before he too got up and followed his friend.

~

At another table, just out of sight, behind a large rosewood carving of Buddha, sat an elegant non-Chinese couple. The gentleman picked up a cheap cellphone from the table in front of him and dialled the sole number programmed.

Chapter 13

Outside the restaurant, the warm spring sunshine was a welcome contrast to their encounter with Jason. A refreshing breeze coming off the water felt cool on their faces. Dirk deeply inhaled the air and absentmindedly remarked on it and how good it made him feel. When no response came back, he perceived a change in his friend's normally verbose disposition.

'Everything ok Frank? You seem a bit edgy.'

Frank looked pensive, 'I'm fine. It's that bastard Jason, I'm never completely at ease in his company.'

'Don't you trust him?'

'Less and less each time we meet.'

'You must be used to dealing with less than trustworthy characters in your business by now Frank?'

'Well, private transactions like this have to be handled differently and with the utmost discretion.'

'Do you think he's got some more coins to show you?'

'More than likely; it's no big deal, if they're any good I'll take them off his hands or maybe offer them to my client here. He's a big coin collector too.'

'Is that how you got to be closely involved with him?' asked Dirk.

'Which one? Jason or my client?'

'The client you're working for here. Is it because of your mutual interest in coins that you happen to represent him so personally?'

'Not essentially. I am his banker, but he likes the work I've done for him and yes the coin thing has created an affinity between us. I've accompanied him to auctions and the more I've got to know him, the more I've got involved with his more *private transactions.*'

'So, he's one of the principal characters involved in the kind of private transactions between clients you told me about?' asked Dirk.

'Yes, he's the main one I represent for that sort of thing, but like I said, he lets me in on some of his dealings.'

'Sounds like you can't lose on a deal like this. You either get what you want or you get a commission from your client or maybe even another Rolex?'

Frank looked at Dirk and smiled. 'That's always acceptable.'

'Was he the one who swapped the apartments you told me about?' Dirk asked.

Frank nodded. 'Yes, he'll trade almost anything. Scoops up all sorts of art and antiques. The Netherlands is a fabulous place for both.'

'Is he Dutch?'

'Why do you ask?'

'He's got you working here for starters.'

'I think he just likes it here because of the art and antiques shops. He has a home in Den Haag.'

'Well, if he does give you another Rolex and you don't want it, you could always give it to your best mate, right?' Dirk was nodding eagerly.

'Sure, no problem.' replied Frank, smiling.

'What's his name by the way?' asked Dirk.

'Sadim Maudasi' Replied Frank.

'Doesn't sound Dutch, does it?'

Before Frank could answer, their conversation was

interrupted by a motorcycle roaring deafeningly past causing them both to grimace. Frank waited until the noise had abated then, unexpectedly, suggested they go for a massage.

'Does that include a happy ending?' asked Dirk, raising an eyebrow.

'That would be nice, but no, there's a bona fide place not far from the bar that brews its own beer. What do you say? It'll do you the world of good and it'll help me unwind a bit before we meet up with that jumped up little prick Jason.'

'It does sound good, but you're not stitching me up again like you did in that outrageous bar are you?'

Frank gave no reply. Just smiled an enigmatic smile and crossed the road towards a destination known only to him. Dirk decided not to rise to the bait by asking anything more about where they were going, because it would only fuel Frank's delight in tormenting and teasing him. He figured there wasn't a down side to getting a massage, only up.

When they arrived at their destination, Dirk was pleasantly surprised and relieved to discover that Frank hadn't lied. It was indeed a respectable establishment. The staff wore traditional dress and greeted them in the Thai manner of putting their hands together as if in prayer and bowing courteously. They were led downstairs to a tastefully decorated basement that smelled of incense, where they were separated by their respective female masseuses and taken into private rooms. The girl assigned to Dirk did a wonderful job with her strong and skilful hands. He experienced both pain and soothing in muscles he didn't know he had.

There were rails fixed to the ceiling for her to hold on to and keep her balance. She walked up and down his back and legs, massaging his muscles with the balls of her feet, providing a genteel combined musculature torture and relaxation. A full stress busting hour later, Dirk felt like he was walking on air. The entire experience cost thirty five euros. He gave the girl fifty. She smiled and gave him the same courteous gesture he had received on arrival. He smiled back and reciprocated the gesture, making her laugh. Frank was finished around the same time and suggested they stop for one beer in the small brewery, before heading back to meet with Jason Sinclair. He also suggested they stop on the way to pick up a couple of Cohibas in the cigar shop. Dirk gave no objections.

~

Café Heuvel was busy, as it usually was on Sunday afternoons and the sunshine had tempted even more people out. All the outside seating was taken.

'Not the best place to be flashing your valuables around, is it Frank?'

'No, it isn't.' said Frank, looking around, 'but I'm reluctant to take Jason back to the apartment.'

Before Dirk could offer a suggestion, Frank succinctly announced that he *needed a piss* and briskly walked away in the direction of the toilet, leaving Dirk at the bar alone. From the in house music system, Rihanna was tunefully telling someone to shut up and drive. Frank hadn't said what he wanted to drink, so Dirk ordered himself a small Palm beer and sat down on a bar stool; this time without fear of being jumped upon. The beer was excellent, dark and sweet. A bit like Rihanna he mused. It went down a treat and he drained the glass almost in one. He was just about to order another when a voice behind him said. 'Ah, timing is everything.' Turning around, he found the onerous Jason Sinclair standing behind him.

'Hello Jason, want one of these?' said Dirk, holding up his glass.

Jason completely ignored the offer. 'Where's Perrier? Isn't he here?'

'Don't worry, he'll back in a minute, he's just popped to the loo. Do you want a beer or not?'

Jason looked down his nose at Dirk's empty beer glass and appeared to take umbrage at the very suggestion he would entertain the notion of drinking such a common beverage. He gave Dirk a frosty look before turning to the bar and requesting a bottle of red wine. Turning back to Dirk again, with his two fingers sticking up in a V sign, he asked, 'Two glasses or three, or are you sticking with that?'

'I'll stick with beer, just get two.' Dirk replied nonchalantly, returning the V sign. Jason favoured him with a thin lizard smile and told the barman to put it on the same tab. 'You don't mind do you Mister Dirk?'

Dirk replied with a cavalier wave of his hand. As Jason was trying to puzzle him out, Frank returned from the loo and unwittingly paraphrased what Jason had said when he'd arrived.

'Ah, timing is everything.'

'Yes it is Frank, you've got a tab going already.' announced Dirk.

Frank shot Dirk a disparaging look then glanced around the small bar. All the seats were taken and there was nowhere all three of them could stand together to conduct a private conversation. 'Let's go outside,' he said, 'we can have a cigar while we talk.'

'Celebrating your good fortune in meeting me Frank?' asked Jason.

'You've convinced me Jason, perhaps business and pleasure *can* mix sometimes?' Quipped Frank.

Outside, they found a recently vacated table with enough chairs to accommodate them. The sun had dipped behind the buildings opposite and there was now a distinct chill in the air, sending the thin blooded smokers indoors. Jason poured some wine into both glasses, while Frank checked to his left and right and behind for open windows. Satisfied no one could eavesdrop on their conversation, he got straight down to business.

'Ok Jason, let's see what you've got?'

'Don't beat about the bush Frank, get to the point why don't you!' huffed Jason.

Frank exchanged a frustrated glance with Dirk, who remained reticently silent. Jason lifted his glass and took a long sip, drawing the moment out and delighting in Frank's visible impatience. He put his glass down and topped it up before producing, from his inside jacket pocket, a small wooden box no thicker than a mobile phone. He ceremoniously placed the box on the table and slid it towards the centre. Frank looked down at it then back at Jason.

'Well, aren't you going to open it?' asked Jason.

Dirk found all their secrecy amusing and tried hard

not to laugh at the seriousness of their actions and reactions. However, when Frank opened the little wooden box and regarded the object within, the sight of it had a profound impact and he seemed to shrink back into his seat. Dirk caught the expression on his friend's face and he too was suddenly, acutely, more than intrigued.

'You're very pleased to see me now, aren't you Frank?' announced Jason conceitedly.

'Is this...genuine?' Frank stammered.

Jason lifted his wine glass and smiled smugly, 'As genuine as Charles!'

Dirk didn't have a clue what they were on about, but he could see by Frank's reaction that it had a dramatic effect on him. He was utterly spellbound by the object in his hand.

'Can I see what it is?' asked Dirk.

Frank closed the box and immediately handed it back to Jason. 'Put it away.'

Jason was still smiling. 'So, you're not interested then?' he asked with a thick slice of sarcasm.

'We won't discuss it any more here' said Frank in a hushed voice. 'Let's go back to the apartment. I want to get a better look at it.'

'Oh, and I was so looking forward to having a cigar too.' bemoaned Jason.

Jason topped up their glasses and offered a toast to the Queen, whatever the hell that meant. Maybe he was still celebrating Queen's day. Frank looked like he was in shock and downed his wine in one, then announced he had to go to the men's room again, giving further rise to Dirk's concern. Jason stood up too and walked over to the edge of the canal taking his wine with him, making it blatantly obvious that he considered Dirk to be inconsequential. Dirk couldn't have cared less, although he was concerned by his friend's reaction and subsequent flustered behaviour.

Frank returned a couple of minutes later with a slight flush to his face. Jason took his turn to go too. When he was out of earshot, Dirk asked if everything was ok. Frank leaned in close so no one could hear what he had to say.

'He's got another coin to sell.'

'I guessed that, so what's the big deal?'

Frank rubbed his hands together and gave the impression he was about to start bouncing up and down in his seat with glee.

'The suspense is killing me here Frank, what the hell is it and what did he mean by "*as genuine as Charles*".'

'Ok. If it *is* what I think it is, then it's very rare and very valuable.'

'It must be. I don't think I've ever seen you in this much state of excitement since happy hour at the Mint Leaf Lounge.'

'Sorry, it's just…I love coins…and this…this is…' he trailed off looking introspective.

Dirk had alarm bells going off in his head, 'I thought you said you paid too much for the last set of coins you bought from him, remember? Are you sure you can trust this guy Frank?'

Frank didn't seem to be listening and Dirk didn't get the opportunity to press him further. Jason had returned and haughtily asked if someone had paid the tab. Frank's thoughts were somewhere else, so Dirk offered to pay and said he would catch them up. However, he made no attempt and kept his distance all the way back, puzzling over Frank's body language and what kind of coin could have stirred him up so much. As they entered the apartment building, he got to the top of the front steps just as the door was about to close. Once inside, Frank didn't mess about. He disappeared into his bedroom and reappeared almost immediately with what looked like a magnifying glass in his hand.

'Ok, Jason, let me see it again. Put it on the table at the window, in the light.'

They all sat down at the table. Frank opened up the wooden box and removed the object within. Dirk could see it was indeed a coin, encased inside some kind of plastic protective casing. Frank was poring over it, totally engrossed. When he'd finished his study of the coin he placed it back into the box and leaned back in his chair, adopting an air of casual contemplation. Dirk assumed no such air. 'Can I see it now?' he asked.

Jason replied dryly, 'Go ahead. Just don't break the plastic casing.'

Dirk picked up the wooden box and removed the coin. He looked through the magnifying glass at an old coin; a very old, gold, coin. It was dated 1703 and adorned with four coats of arms representing England, Scotland, Ireland and France. Turning it over, he read the words '*ANNA.DEI.GRATIA*' around the monarch's head. Underneath was a single word '*VIGO*'. None of it had meaning for him. Carefully placing it back in its box, he put it down on the table and waited for the punchline. Frank was looking at Jason who looked like the cat who had just cornered the market for cream.

'What do you want for it Jason?' asked Frank straight out.

'What do you want to give me for it?' teased Jason.

'Do you have a certificate of validation?' asked Frank.

'Yes, all the relevant paperwork is available, if you really want it, but I'm sure you know its value without it. However, I think we can agree on a price that's fair to both of us, say…around forty thousand.' proffered Jason, with an air of conceit that eluded Dirk.

'In which currency would you prefer payment?' asked Frank again, straight out, no haggling over the price.

'Oh, the same currency as before will be more than satisfactory. I think we can both profit from this.'

Dirk couldn't believe how casually they were discussing such a huge sum of money over a single coin.

'Let me make a call, I'm sure I can find you a buyer.' said Frank, excusing himself and going into his bedroom for privacy. Dirk remained seated with Jason, not quite knowing what to think of it all. Sensing his discomfort, Jason began drumming his fingers on the table.

'Are you interested in coins Mister Dirk?' asked Jason, keeping the rhythm going.

'I used to collect old pennies when I was a boy.' was all that Dirk could think of to say.

'Not worth much then?' said Jason derisively.

Before Dirk's irritation began to grow, Frank reappeared. 'You have a deal Jason. Can you meet us in Den Haag tomorrow afternoon at four o'clock, outside a bar called La Grenouille in Molenstraat? Do you know it?

'I'm sure I can find it.' replied Jason.

'And bring the coin with you.' said Frank.

'We can't really have a deal without it can we?' said Jason sardonically.

'Quite' replied Frank.

'And the asking currency is agreeable?' asked Jason.

'It is.' Replied Frank flatly.

'Excellent.' said Jason, 'I'll look forward to seeing you tomorrow.'

With that Jason stood up to leave then paused. He turned to Frank and asked with an air of certainty. 'May I have one those cigars now?'

Frank took a Cohiba Siglo VI tube from his jacket pocket, removed the cigar from within and held it upright and out in front of him. Dirk wondered if Jason grasped the object symbolism of the gesture. Whether he did or not, Jason accepted it without a shred of gratitude and then sidled towards the door and let himself out. On hearing the outside door close, Frank looked out of the window to make sure Jason had indeed left the building. He watched him walk away in the opposite direction from where they had just been. Once he was out of sight, Frank turned back to Dirk with urgency in his voice. 'I'll need your help tomorrow.'

Chapter 14

Frank continued to stare out of the large front window, even though Jason had long since disappeared. Dirk hadn't refused his request, because not helping wasn't in the equation. He waited for his friend to ascertain what he required of him, but when the moments passed the minute mark he broke the silence. 'I could use one of those cigars myself now Frank.'

Frank snapped back to reality, 'Sure, let's head back to the bar, I could use some air.'

'That'd be good, but first could you enlighten me some more about what just went on?' asked Dirk.

'Of course, you must be totally confused by now; my apologies, really.'

Dirk shrugged and said, 'Just a bit.'

Frank nodded ruefully. 'Do you know anything about coins?'

Dirk repeated the answer he had given Jason earlier, but added the observation that some are obviously very valuable, like the one he had just seen. Frank confirmed that the coin was indeed very valuable and worth a lot more than Jason was asking for it.

'What exactly did he mean by "*as genuine as Charles*" Frank?' asked Dirk.

Frank stood and walked across the room, 'Do you remember I told you I bought some coins from him in London?'

'Yes, five very expensive coins, I can recall you mentioning.'

'Correct! They were King Charles II two guinea

pieces, worth approximately five thousand pounds each. Well, the one he just showed me is just as genuine.'

'Did you doubt it?' Dirk asked.

'No, I just couldn't believe I was actually looking at it. Did you see the date?'

'Yes.'

'...and the word *VIGO* written on the bottom of the coin?'

Dirk nodded and Frank continued. 'Ok, that's what makes it special. It's a Queen Anne five guinea gold piece from 1703. The word *VIGO* commemorates the destruction of the Franco-Spanish bullion fleet in Vigo bay off the north-eastern coast of Spain the previous year. The coins are said to be minted from the bullion that was recovered and only about twenty of these particular coins from 1703 with the word VIGO exist.'

'That's rare' acknowledged Dirk.

'Indeed, now there are different categories of a coin's condition that determine its actual value: fine, very fine and extra fine. In fact, here, let me show you.'

Frank fetched his laptop. Placed it on the table and powered it up. First, he *googled* Charles II two guinea coins; the ones he'd bought earlier from Jason. This showed an example from the year 1677 and in very good condition. It was valued at over four thousand pounds sterling. Next, he searched for the Queen Anne five guinea gold coin Jason had just shown them. The result threw up an extract from the Spink Auction catalogue for the Samuel King collection, 2005. The article explained that on October 12th 1702 an Anglo-Dutch fleet destroyed the Franco-Spanish fleet in VIGO bay. Only a small amount of booty was recovered:

4500lbs of silver and a mere 7lb 8oz of gold. Noted in this extract was that Sir Isaac Newton, no less, was master of the mint at the time. A royal warrant was commissioned for the bullion to be turned into commemorative coins for Queen Anne, with the word VIGO under the monarch's head. Most notable within the extract was the price it fetched at auction: £130,000. When Dirk saw the auction price he understood Frank's enthusiasm.

'Now, I don't know if the coin Jason has is worth as much as that, not without a full and thorough examination of it by someone more qualified than I am, but it *is* a real bargain for what he's asking.' said Frank.

'If you consider spending forty grand on a single coin to be a bargain.' said Dirk. Frank smiled enigmatically. Dirk's eyes narrowed. 'What am I missing here Frank?'

Frank shrugged and continued to smile. Dirk knew he was waiting for him to figure it out. He remembered the conversation between Frank and Jason earlier. 'Jason asked for *the same currency as before* didn't he? That lost me completely at the time, but I think I get it now; you're not going to give him cash are you? You're going to trade something for it.'

Frank favoured him with a wry nod. Dirk looked at him questioningly and lost a little bit of colour. Frank saw the dread on his friend's face and quickly interjected. 'Oh? No. *NO! NO! NO!* It's got nothing to do with drugs if that's what you're thinking, God no, don't panic.'

Dirk still said nothing, so Frank prompted him again. 'What else is The Netherlands famous for?'

'I don't know; tulips?'

Frank rolled his eyes at his friend's glib remark, 'Apart from tulips?'

Dirk tried to come up with an answer, but after the hectic weekend they'd just had, his brain couldn't connect the dots. Frank enlightened him.

'Diamonds!'

'Diamonds?'

'Yes, they're one of the best fixed assets to hold. Easy to move around, hard to trace and much more safe and reliable than the world's currencies today.' announced Frank.

'Are you saying what I think you're saying? You're going to give Jason forty grand worth of diamonds for his coin?' asked Dirk.

'In a manner of speaking, yes.' replied Frank.

'I don't quite follow you Frank.'

'Ok, let me simplify it. A business associate of mine recently gave his wife a four carat diamond engagement ring. De Beers valued it at more than fifty thousand pounds Sterling. However, he bought it for only fifteen thousand and that was after his source made a two grand profit on commission. It all goes through a trade chain, with each link in the chain marking it up accordingly. So, what I'll give Jason tomorrow will be maybe four or five one carat diamonds valued at around a total of forty thousand pounds, but they won't have cost anywhere close to that. These will have a trade value of around three or four thousand each from the source. Jason will still get a good deal, more than what he's asked for in terms of retail value. He'll be happy and he can sell them on or trade them with someone else and maybe make a decent profit too. It's a very convenient form of currency and that's why we refer to it as such.'

'Won't he have to explain them at airport customs Frank?'

'They're small and made of carbon. The X-ray machines at the airport won't pick them up, providing he's not stupid.' said Frank without a hint of immorality.

'Isn't that called smuggling Frank?'

'Depends on your point of view; jewellers, wholesale and retail alike, procure their diamonds in Amsterdam and Antwerp in pretty much the same way.'

'But they pay tax Frank.'

'Only on what they choose to declare.' announced Frank, as if they were talking about one too many litres of duty free booze.

Dirk continued to look sceptical. Frank continued to elaborate.

'As I've already told you, I make trades like this between clients all the time. My client here in Den Haag buys diamonds at trade price. That's what I meant by getting in on the deal. Through his source and business contacts I can buy a few diamonds myself.'

Dirk was wide eyed. 'Are we talking blood diamonds Frank?'

Frank was incensed, 'No, of course not! Why do you think I'm here in Amsterdam? It's one of the world's biggest diamond centres. Antwerp is only a couple of hours away by train. Diamonds can be bought wholesale at huge discount prices and sold on for huge profits, or traded in the just way I've described.'

'So, what you're saying is you can get your hands on forty grand worth of diamonds by four pm tomorrow?'

Frank gave him a confident smile that bordered on arrogance, 'Yes, I'm meeting with my client tomorrow morning.'

'Why are you risking meeting Jason in Den Haag tomorrow? I thought you didn't want Jason to meet your client, what's his name, Maudasi?'

'He won't, we're the only people Jason will meet. It's just simpler to have him come to Den Haag, rather than me having to transport diamonds all over Holland. We can kill all the birds with a few stones.' announced Frank sanctimoniously.

Dirk's concern was growing at Frank's reference to the collective. '*We* Frank?'

Frank respected his friend's scepticism. 'Look, I'm not involved in anything illegal and I'm not asking you to do anything illegal either, but I could use your help tomorrow.' said Frank.

Dirk thought about it for a moment before answering and rationalised that his friend wouldn't intentionally put him in harm's way. 'Ok, how exactly do you want me to help you?'

'Thanks Dirk, I knew I could count on you, but let's agree to refer to it as currency from now on and not diamonds ok?'

'Fine, so who else will we be meeting tomorrow?'

'No one; just Jason.'

'Just Jason and you'll *just* hand over forty grand worth of diamonds? Sorry, currency.'

Appreciating that his friend was still a bit twitchy, Frank outlined the agenda for tomorrow: He would leave first thing in the morning for his business meeting and pick up *the currency*. Dirk would catch a later train. After lunch, they would meet with Jason to trade the coin and then they would return home; job done. All Dirk would have to do is accompany him all the way through to the conclusion of the trade. It sounded too easy. Dirk still wasn't fully convinced.

'There's one thing that concerns me Frank, the location for the trade. A bar doesn't sound like a wise place for something like this.'

'Don't worry, we'll just be meeting him there, there's a cigar shop across from it with a private smoking room in a converted cellar that we can use for privacy. It should be empty at that time on a Monday afternoon.'

'In what capacity shall I be accompanying you tomorrow Frank?' asked Dirk in a mock serious tone of voice.

Frank answered him in an equally sincere voice. 'Do you wish an official title? Confidential advisor…Personal assistant….'

'… bodyguard?' Dirk finished for him.

Frank smiled and sat back in his chair. 'Well, I was going to say trusted friend, but now that you mention it, I've seen that you can handle yourself, remember?'

~

A few years earlier, before Natalie came on the scene, Frank and Dirk were in a nightclub in Geneva chatting with a couple of beautiful girls. Frank was his usual ostentatious self, splashing out on champagne and cocktails and flashing his cash. This didn't go unnoticed by the ladies or their would-be suitors. At the end of the night, as they were leaving the club, girls on tow, four surly looking guys followed them out. Frank hadn't really seen this building up, but Dirk had noticed two of the guys in the club glaring and had been alert for possible trouble. However, he hadn't expected four of them.

'English assholes!' shouted an aggressive voice from behind. At first Dirk tried to ignore them and continued walking, but the four guys drew too close for comfort. He stopped and turned around to face them. Frank had drunk too much for it all to register. Without hesitating Dirk kicked the one closest to him in the balls, dropping him to the hard pavement. Next, he jumped back and smashed an elbow into one of the guys trying to get round behind him, breaking his nose. As he hit the ground, Dirk put the boot into him; he saw no point in just pissing him off and made sure he was out of the fight for good. Frank, still holding a bottle of champagne, reawakened and smashed it over the head of the guy kneeling on the ground clutching his balls. Seeing this, one of the other two still standing turned and bolted like a Roe deer on skates. This left only one. However, this one looked determined and was probably the instigator that had shouted *English assholes*. Now, this insult probably hadn't bothered Frank as much as it bothered Dirk, which he pointed out at a later date: *'Frank, as much as I like you, you can be a asshole sometimes and you are half English, but me, I'm a Scottish asshole and proud of it'*. Frank had laughed loudly at his friend's acute observation and said *'Fair point, old boy!'*

Dirk took a step forward with a mind to giving the remaining thug a lesson from the school of hard kicks, when he unexpectedly turned and sprinted off. The doormen outside the club had seen the events taking place and as Frank is a generous tipper they came, albeit a little late, to the rescue. Both "corpses" on the ground were rolling and groaning, but not much else. The doormen said they would *"clean up the mess"*.

Not wanting to attract further unwanted attention the *partie carrée* quickly left the scene, jumped into a cab and headed back to Frank's pad.

That evening had obviously left an impression on Frank who, incidentally, passed out half an hour after arriving back at his apartment, leaving Dirk alone with the two girls and a fridge full of champagne to share with them. As the champagne continued to flow, one of the girls asked Dirk if he'd like to share something else with them. Being the magnanimous kind of guy he was, he did the right thing.

Chapter 15

Café Heuvel allowed smoking indoors and was still fairly busy inside. The early evening air was surprisingly less chilly than before, so they ordered two small palm beers and sat back outside to smoke their cigars. There was no more talk about the following day's events or Jason Sinclair. Instead their thoughts turned inwards, to their stomachs.

'Have you thought about what you want to eat tonight?' asked Frank.

'Let's go to one of those Argentinian steak houses up towards Leidseplein.'

'Good idea, a high protein meal for a high protein task. Let's see, what's the time now? Six thirty, how hungry are you?' asked Frank.

'Not too bad, we can head off once we finish the cigars. Are you ready for another?' Dirk asked, indicating the evaporating beer. Frank replied with a laconic nod. Dirk went to the bar and returned with two more beers and a large glass of water.

'Water, are you unwell?' asked Frank playfully.

'No, but I don't want to overdo it, we've had a fair bit to drink in the past couple of days.'

'We'll take it easy then and stick to beer tonight and maybe have a small glass of port after dinner.'

Dirk smiled at Frank's idea of taking it easy and changed the subject. 'Where and when will you pick up your *currency* Frank?'

'Don't worry about that, it'll be good to go before we meet with our friend Jason.'

Dirk puffed on his cigar and tried to imagine what it must be like to have such wealth to play with. As the thought struck him, he decided to ask about Frank's mysterious client.

'Tell me about Maudasi.'

'Sure, what do you want to know?'

'Anything really, what's he like? I mean, what does he do apart from spend money?'

'Well, he's about your height, but looks taller somehow, stands very erect and noble. He's an extremely fit-looking fifty something; deeply suntanned, weathered complexion and a shock of thick grey hair. Well educated. Speaks with a refined English diction and has a trace of an accent. I think one of the eastern European dialects, but not Russian. He's rich, obviously and it shows, but not in an ostentatious way. Sure, he's got all the trappings you'd expect of a guy like him. Wears expensive, tailored, suits and rides around in a chauffeured Bentley. He's a very successful businessman'.

'Sounds like your archetypal megalomaniac billionaire; you know, like a Bond baddie or something?' said Dirk.

Frank gave a little laugh, 'No, he's nothing at all like that, but make no mistake though, he's a tough, no nonsense, guy and very determined. He conducts his business with ruthless precision and can be extremely uncompromising. Just last month, for instance, he and I were having dinner and his driver turned up late. It wasn't the guy's fault, the weather and the traffic were abysmal, but Maudasi just up and fired him on the spot. Took the keys off him and told him to fuck off, just like that.'

'He sounds like a real Prince.'

'Well, I don't know if his driver had pissed him off before and this was just an excuse to fire him, but I do know that if he requests something and you work for him, he wants it done when he wants it done. Not ten minutes later.'

'What's his main business Frank?'

'He made a fortune in oil during the first gulf war, but he makes a lot of cash through a wide and diverse variety of very smart investments. He's well versed in all the markets, especially commodities. Loves gold, can't buy enough of it.'

'I thought you said he wasn't a Bond baddie? He sounds just like Goldfinger.'

Frank shook his head and laughed, 'You've got too much of a vivid imagination my boy.'

After that they sat in comfortable silence and enjoyed their cigars. Relaxing as it was sitting by the cool ambience of the canal side café, Dirk couldn't shake the feeling of pending doom that had descended or maybe it was just the hectic weekend catching up, he couldn't tell. Before the melancholy took hold, he shrugged it off and ordered another two beers and some more water. Frank had the good sense to join him this time. They remained until just after seven thirty then headed off in anticipation of their steak dinner.

The choice of eating places in Leidseplein was overwhelming. There were at least four steakhouses within spitting distance of where they stood. Frank asked Dirk which one took his fancy. It was an impossible choice, they all looked good. Suddenly the door to the one closest opened and some people came out, the aroma of steaks sizzling on the grill following in their wake. That clinched it.

A smiling waiter escorted them to a booth covered in cowhide and brought them two Desperado beers. Dirk opened the menu on the table and instantly spotted a 500 gram fillet steak. Closed it again and put it down.

'Decision made?' asked Frank, without looking up from his menu.

'Easy choice really.' replied Dirk.

Frank chose the 400 gram sirloin with Chimichurri sauce. Dirk ordered the sauce too. Both came with French fries, but Dirk passed on those.

'Watching your figure?' Frank asked.

'Well, yes, if I'm honest, all these beers are bad enough without a couple of hundred more grams of carbs on top.'

Frank shrugged and ate his fries and then ate Dirk's too. 'You ok about tomorrow? Any questions you want to ask? Anything you're not comfortable with?

Dirk shook his head. 'No, not really, it seems straight forward enough. I just can't get my head around the amount of money that's changing hands so casually and in such a public place.'

Frank chuckled. 'It'll be a good experience for you, see how the other half live.'

When they'd finished wolfing down their carnivorous banquet, the waiter offered them dessert and coffee. They both declined and requested the bill. Fifteen minutes later, they were back at the apartment building. Dirk noticed Helena had put her name into the brass nameplate. *Helena Vos.* He ran his finger over it and wondered if she was home. There were no lights on. Before his thoughts ran away with themselves, they were back inside the apartment. Frank immediately suggested having a port.

'Jesus Frank, I don't know if I can handle any more? Port's a bit heavy.'

'Ok, a glass of wine then, it'll do you good my boy; help you get a good night's sleep. I want you to be on top form tomorrow.'

'Then give me some water…and make sure the Red Bulls are chilled for the morning.'

Frank responded with a silly grin and disappeared into his bedroom, leaving Dirk to make the selection. In the kitchen he scanned the wine rack and decided to work his way along the bottom, starting at the far side. Taking hold of the neck of the first bottle, he pulled on it. As it slipped out, something else slipped out with it and caught his eye. He momentarily lost sight of the elusive glint of metal, but tracked it again as it tinkled to the tiled kitchen floor. Still clutching the bottle, he bent down and picked up the small object that had fallen out. It was a little gold key. Turning it over in his hand, he pondered the possibilities for such a key. It was too small for a house door key and it didn't look like part of a charm bracelet. He looked around the kitchen at each of the cupboards in turn. None had locks. Maybe it was the key to a desk drawer or a cupboard in another part of the house. Not wanting to appear like a snoop, he slid the key back into the slot along with the bottle of wine and continued with his selection.

Frank reappeared and asked facetiously, 'Found any you *don't* like yet?'

'Any preference?' asked Dirk.

Frank walked over and pointed, ''Red top, third on the left, just there.'

Dirk plucked the bottle out and looked at the label. It was a Château Langoa-Barton, 2005, Saint-Julien.

'Looks good.'

'It should be at fifty quid a bottle.' announced Frank.

Dirk almost dropped it, 'Christ on a bike, your joking?'

'It's only money my boy. It's only money.' declared Frank.

'Where are the good glasses Frank? We can't drink this from the bottle.'

'Just open it and let it breathe for a bit, I'll sort out the fine crystal in a minute.'

Dirk did as Frank suggested and opened the bottle, then went over and switched on the TV. He skimmed through the movie channels and saw that *Apocalypse Now* had just started. "Excellent" he thought. Frank returned a short time later and saw what was showing on TV, 'Oh, great, just the thing to help when you're having trouble sleeping.'

'Want me to change it?' asked Dirk.

'No, leave it on, maybe it'll give me some ideas how to handle Jason tomorrow.'

Frank poured two large glasses of wine and brought them over to where Dirk was sitting.

'Actually, would you mind switching the TV off, I'm not in the mood for this right now.' said Frank.

'Sure.' Dirk hit the button on the remote and sent the TV images into their own apocalypse.

Frank took a long sip of his wine. Dirk did the same

and licked his lips. 'That's a fifty quid bottle of wine Frank, no doubt about it.'

'Delicious, isn't it. By the way, did you bring a suit with you?' asked Frank.

'Yes, I did. Why?'

'Good, wear it tomorrow, I'll be wearing mine and I want us to look the part. We're having lunch at a very special place and as it's business, it's on me.'

'Great, I'm looking forward to it.'

'Anyway, I appreciate you helping me out. It'll be worth your while I assure you.'

'Christ's sake Frank, we're pals, I don't need payment. You're giving me a free holiday in this magnificent apartment.' Dirk gestured around with his free hand, taking care not to spill his wine. 'I'm pleased that I'm able to help you out any way I can.'

Frank held up his hand. 'It's *way* more than helping me out, believe me. It certainly boosts my confidence having you with me, rather than walking around on my own with a pocket full of diamonds. Making money is what my business is all about and I stand to make a potential killing with this, so don't argue and take what comes your way ok?'

Dirk was about to protest, but knew his friend too well. 'Well, if you insist, who I am to refuse a shiny gold Rolex?'

'That's the Dirk I know and admire. To the future.' said Frank, raising his glass.

Frank called it a night around ten and insisted Dirk take the bottle with him, telling him he didn't want to see such a fine wine go to waste. Respecting his friend's wishes to have his own space to get organised for his early morning meeting, Dirk dutifully obliged.

Upstairs in his own self-contained apartment, he switched on the not so large TV and polished off the remainder of the delicate wine, whilst watching the remainder of the indelicate *Apocalypse Now*. He appreciated having a more relaxed evening, as it had been a hectic three nights on the trot. When Sheen finally killed Brando, Dirk killed the lights and went to bed.

Sleep, however, didn't come easy. He was restless. Staring up at the ceiling again, it wasn't the lovely image of Helena that was keeping him awake, but that of another; Queen Anne. He suspected Jason hadn't procured the gold coin through honest means, but so what. Everyone at some time or another has bought something that fell off the back of a truck. Frank was a grown up and a businessman. However, this wasn't just a cheap pair of gold earrings. He was still uncertain about his role tomorrow or what to expect. Something was gnawing at him; he just couldn't put his finger on it.

Chapter 16

Lying in bed, sleep was the last thing on Jason's mind and his time was almost up. At the foot of the dishevelled bed lay a distraught girl, curled into a foetal position. But what did he care, that was what he'd paid for. He freshened up with a shower and got dressed. Checked his image in the tarnished mirror on the wall and made a face. The lingering smell of cheap shampoo offended his sensibilities and he looked upon the reflected image of the sobbing wretch with contempt. Then he smiled and unlocked the door.

As he stepped out into the corridor, an older lady was waiting with a basin of warm water and a towel. She avoided eye contact and slipped past, gently closing the door behind her. The experience had almost depleted the last of his funds, but he wasn't too worried. There was always more where that came from.

~

Jason Sinclair had never wanted for anything. His education had been the best money could buy: a public school education followed by a degree in Art History at St. Andrews University in Scotland. On graduating, he'd been given a position with a prestigious firm in the city. This hadn't lasted long. He had no talent for making money, only spending it.

Since losing his job, several years ago now, he had spiralled in a continuous descent and was living off his parents. His father had, on many occasions, tried to set his son straight; even paying off his frequent gambling debts. Then, there was a hefty fee for drug rehabilitation when Jason acquired a taste for cocaine and finally, a date rape charge. This was eventually dropped, but only down to the skills of a clever and expensive barrister, who managed to sully the girl's reputation by petitioning images from her own Facebook page, showing her in various states of drunkenness and undress with a variety of equally drunk young men and women. It was hardly the image of a demure debutant or of one who would say no; the perils of the social network.

Jason had consistently proven himself to be a useless and thankless arrogant bastard, out of control and a menace to those with whom he came into contact. His mother always made excuses for him. His father, however, seriously doubted if his son possessed any integrity at all.

He stood to gain a massive trust fund when he turned thirty later this year, but couldn't wait that long. His lifestyle of Champagne, women, gambling and the occasional snort of white powder demanded much more than his annual allowance allowed. Now he needed cash again, badly. His Porsche, a present from his parents two years ago when he came out of rehab, was now the property of a London wide boy to whom he'd lost large on the Cheltenham Gold cup. As a consequence, his father was in the process of disinheriting him and cutting him off from any further access to the family wealth, including his trust fund.

~

Prior to arriving in Amsterdam, Jason had gone to his parent's home in London to pick up a few *trinkets* that could further fund his vacuous lifestyle. He'd known the house would be empty because his parents had left for a short golfing vacation in Perth, Scotland. The family wealth included large collections of valuable paintings and prints, rare first edition books, stamp collections and coins. An investor rather than a collector, his father spent little time admiring the family heirlooms except for the books, which remained in full view in the library and were always a point of conversation amongst his father's dinner guests. Jason never touched those as there were less conspicuous rich pickings he could procure for someone who, like himself, appreciated the finer things in life and was prepared to pay the price.

Chapter 17

Dirk awakened at 07:45 and deliberated whether or not he should disturb his comfort by answering the urge to pee. Unable to prolong it any longer, he hauled himself upright and into the en-suite. Then, still not fully awake, he shuffled through to his small lounge and over to the window. Raising his hand against the sunlight scything in through the open curtains, he glanced down at the street below and saw a black Mercedes. It was just sitting there, outside the front door, engine ticking over patiently. Before he could begin to speculate if this was Frank's ride, the front door opened and banged shut. This was quickly followed by the familiar, suited, figure of Frank descending the front steps. He continued to watch, while Frank said something to the driver and then got in. When the luxury saloon moved off, he yawned and stretched up on his toes. He considered returning to his comfortable bed, but gave himself a shake and headed back to the en-suite to shower and prepare for the curious day ahead.

The 09:19 train from Amsterdam Centraal was on time and quickly filled up with commuters and students travelling to Leiden University. Looking around the carriage at his fellow passengers Dirk couldn't help but notice that, apart from him, everyone else was totally absorbed in their smartphones with games, music or texting. A teenage girl sat down opposite him and immediately did the same; plugged in and switched off. No one opened a newspaper, a book or a magazine. No one spoke. He mourned the death of conversation.

When the train pulled out of the station, he turned his attention to what was happening in the real world outside. The vibrant colours of springtime were everywhere and they captivated him, as did the flat Dutch landscape and its many canals and houseboats. It surprised him how much he was taken by it, considering his own upbringing was amongst the contrasting mountainous scenery of Scotland. As the train sped along, he was enchanted by the occasional old fashioned windmill and smiled, then scowled at the *progressive* wind turbines that blotted the beautiful landscape. The journey took exactly forty eight minutes and he was quite disappointed when it ended.

Stepping outside Den Haag Centraal Station, he followed Frank's directions and caught the number 17 tram just opposite the entrance. Two stops later he alighted across the street from the Binnenhof parliament building. It was an inspiring sight and appeared to rise majestically out of a large central man-made lake. Dirk could have stood there admiring the architecture and splendour of the building for hours, if it hadn't been for the aroma of coffee in the warm morning air. His stomach rumbled and he decided it would be a good idea to *fill up his tank* before he did anything else. Following his nose, he spotted a lovely square to the right of the lake. He sat outside a charming café called Juliana's and ordered what Frank would have called 'a light breakfast', comprising a bread roll filled with warm goat's cheese, walnut, honey and Aceto Balsamico accompanied by an Americano coffee.

His refuelling complete, Dirk sat back in the wicker chair and soaked up the glorious sunshine. Den Haag was quiet at this hour of the day and time seemed to have little meaning. Closing his eyes, he tilted his head back in worship of the sun's rays and breathed deeply. He was contemplating having a cigar to accompany the moment, when the waitress interrupted his rapture and asked if he would like anything else. Feeling satiated and reawakened, he simply requested the bill. He also asked for directions to the Mauritshuis museum. She recommended he walk through the courtyard of the Binnenhof, which was only around the first corner and across the street.

Passing through the grand archway entrance to the Binnenhof, he entered a magnificent courtyard with a spectacularly ornate gold fountain bathed in glorious morning sunshine. He could have spent all day in awe of this splendid sight, within the grandeur of its surrounding architecture, but it was now almost eleven o'clock and he'd promised himself a date with the Girl with the Pearl Earring.

The Mauritshuis museum was quiet and he enjoyed the cool silence amidst the priceless artworks. There were many self-portraits on display of that great Dutch master, Rembrandt, at various stages of his life. Dirk experienced a profound sadness when he viewed them, as it seemed to underline the tragic brevity of life and the great loss when someone of such genius and talent dies. However, he also ruefully reflected on what can be achieved in such a short time and what can be left behind to inspire others. He also reflected on the fact that he was beginning to crave a beer.

The famous painting of *The Girl with the Pearl Earring,* by the artist Johannes Vermeer, was housed on the top floor of the museum and was what he'd mainly come to see. He'd seen it in magazines and knew there was a movie about it starring the very lovely Scarlett Johansen, but he'd never seen the real thing before. He'd seen the Mona Lisa in the Louvre and had been distinctly underwhelmed; while still a beautiful painting, its size and celebrated charisma were somewhat lacking, it just didn't really do it for him.

When he stood in front of the Girl with the Pearl Earring however, he had to sit down such was its effect on him. She was beautiful. She was mesmerising. She was Helena, the girl upstairs.

~

At precisely that same moment Frank was also admiring a beautiful woman. He was having a glass of Armagnac in the hotel's cigar lounge and watching the news on the large TV screen when she walked in. It immediately felt like déjà vu. He'd seen her before. It had been this morning in fact, shortly after his arrival, in this very room, while he'd been making preparations for his imminent meeting. She had entered on her own then too.

Frank politely said good afternoon and she acknowledged him with a slight movement of her head, causing her long dark hair to shimmer and shine. It told you she was worth it. Her astonishing figure was accentuated superbly by her style. She wore a navy coloured silk dress, adorned with medium sized cream coloured polka dots. It clung to her figure and wasn't something just any woman could pull off, but then it was hard to imagine anything *she* wouldn't look good in. Her matching navy shoes looked as expensive as the dress, as did the large red leather bag she held up and slightly away from her body. She had the carriage and stature of a fashion model and as she walked past, Frank's eyes were drawn all the way down the length of her long legs and all the way back up. His imagination extended under the hem of her tight dress with thoughts of unconditional impurity and he gently bit his bottom lip. God he loved beautiful women!

She sat down at the opposite end of the room and crossed her legs with the utmost feminine grace. He continued to regard her with less than subtle awe. She was aware of him watching and smiled imperceptibly to herself.

The waiter arrived with a bottle of mineral water, which she had obviously requested. He too was stricken. As he performed the simple task of filling her glass, he tried desperately to maintain an air of indifference, but her perfume was beating him down. He successfully managed to complete the task, but let his mask of discretion slip on departure, giving Frank a subtle but evocative smile. Frank tried to remain focused on the news, but his eyes were drawn to the movement of her foot. It was gently bouncing up and down as she nonchalantly leafed through a copy of Vogue magazine on the table in front of her. Her heel had slipped out and her shoe was perched on the tips of her toes, making it dance in an almost erotic rhythmic cycle. Frank found it inexplicably mesmerising and couldn't look away. Suddenly, she looked up and held him in her gaze. He was unnerved by her and she knew it; she was acutely aware of how men reacted to her and the power she possessed.

Then, like an invitation, her lips parted slightly and she licked her forefinger before using it to turn a page. Frank gasped and almost dropped his glass. However, before he had a seizure, a tall, elegantly dressed, gentlemen entered the lounge and she greeted him with affection. Frank took his cue and turned his attention swiftly back to the news.

Chapter 18

It was almost one o'clock and he still hadn't heard from Frank. Dirk stepped into the bright sunshine and looked around the vicinity. Adjacent to the museum was a large main square, edged on two sides with café bars. There were so many, he was spoiled for choice. He walked diagonally across and sat outside the first café he came to. As luck would have it, they sold De Koninck beer. Just as his drink arrived, Frank called. Dirk told him where he was and the name of the café. Frank told him to stay put and that he would come get him. Mere minutes later, Dirk saw him walk past the solitary, but occupied, open urinal that stood on the edge of the square. He felt as relived as its occupant that they weren't having lunch here. Frank wagged an admonishing finger when he saw the beer.

'Want one?' Dirk asked when Frank got within earshot.

'No thanks, I've just had a drink with a beautiful woman.' replied Frank.

'Really, does she have a friend?'

Frank smiled, 'I'm sure we can sort something out for you later my boy. Let's have lunch first!'

As they walked back across the square Frank posed an odd question. 'Do you know what this place is called?'

Dirk frowned. 'I think it said Plein on the street sign, why?'

'You'll never guess what that means?' said Frank, in the form of a question.

Dirk shrugged.

'It means square. I mean what the hell possesses someone to name a square SQUARE?' said Frank.

Dirk could see the irony at the lack of imagination that had gone into naming such a beautiful place.

Exiting the square, they walked past the Mauritshuis museum then through a tree lined park strewn with the dismantled remnants of a market. A brisk five minutes later, they arrived at a colonial styled building of grandeur. The name above the entrance said *Hotel des Indes*. A uniformed concierge doffed his top hat and greeted them courteously, ushering them through revolving doors and into the impeccable foyer of the hotel. Frank led the way up the stairs to the restaurant, where the waiting Maître d'Hotel greeted him like a minor celebrity.

'Good afternoon M'sieur Perrier, so nice to see you again.'

'Always a pleasure.' replied Frank.

The Maître d' favoured them with an appraising smile and escorted them to their table in the spacious and ornately decorated restaurant. He flamboyantly recited the choices of the "*wonderful luncheon menu*" and "*took the liberty*" of recommending a bottle of 2010 vintage Château Lafite Rothschild, Bordeaux red, at 600 euros a bottle. However, Frank's keen business eye spotted the non-vintage 2011. *A bargain at 420 euros a bottle*, he informed Dirk when the Maître d' had departed. Dirk noted the price and decided against making comment. He raised his eyebrows and mimicked the Maître d', "*Good afternoon M'sieur Perrier?*" You seem to be well known here Frank. What are you, *the graduate*? Do you come here often with older women for a little bit of nookie or something?' asked Dirk, obviously impressed.

Frank rolled his eyes, 'I've been here on a few occasions, mainly for business, sometimes staying overnight and having dinner. I had my meeting here this morning.'

A waitress, dressed in black and white serving attire, politely interrupted their conversation and asked if they were ready to order. For starters Frank ordered North Sea Crab with three preparations of avocado and ginger beer and a caviar supplement. Dirk ordered Roasted scallops on sushi of Riso Venere in curry, coconut and lemongrass soup. For the main course Dirk had Confit of Sea Bass on a ragout of fennel with light Kalamata olive juice, while Frank opted for Maigret de canard with cashew nut crumble and dumpling of duck rillettes.

As they waited for their lunch Dirk enquired about the *currency*. Frank was surprisingly reticent. Dirk pressed him a bit more. 'Are you meeting someone here to pick them up?'

'Question, questions, questions.' said Frank.

'I'm only asking what I consider to be a pertinent question. If I don't know where they are, how am I going to keep an eye on things for you?' said Dirk.

'It's all arranged, don't worry.' replied Frank, with an air of casual indifference.

Dirk was a little bit mystified by Frank's evasive behaviour. 'Did you pick them up earlier? Have you got them on you now?'

'Question, questions, questions.' Frank teased.

'You're not going to tell me are you?'

'Maybe, maybe not?'

Dirk's mildly mounting irritation was stemmed by the arrival of the Maitre d' with their wine.

'Would you care to taste the wine Mister Dirk?' asked Frank.

Dirk fixed Frank with a reproachful eye at his use of the irritating moniker Jason had used with him, then turned his attention to the Maitre d' indicating that he *would* like to taste the wine. Frank continued to wear a silly smile while Dirk performed the ritual like a connoisseur, giving his approval with exaggerated indifference.

As the Maitre d' filled their glasses, Dirk mirrored his friend's smile. But once they were alone, he chided him. 'Don't you start with that Mister Dirk crap Jason comes out with; what the hell is that all about?'

Frank chuckled. 'I could see he really got under your skin with that. Personally I thought it was quite entertaining.'

'Well, just leave it to that clown ok pal?' said Dirk, in mock annoyance.

Frank raised his glass, 'Proost, my friend. Here's to our success today.'

'Chickens Frank, too soon to count them.'

Frank waived his hand dismissively and sipped his wine. Then, placing the glass on the table in front of him, he outlined his plan for this afternoon; like it was nothing at all.

'After this delicious lunch we'll head across and do the deal with Jason.'

'And after that?' asked Dirk.

'After that, we say *adieu* and go on our merry way. We could come back here, they have a wonderful cigar lounge right here in the hotel.'

'However you want to play it Frank. I'm just the help remember?'

Frank gave Dirk a serious look. 'I appreciate your help on this one, I really do. Thanks for this. I mean it.'

Dirk hadn't expected Frank to be so Frank and was quite taken aback by his statement, but before he could respond their lunch was served. Their conversation was light throughout. Neither currency nor coins were mentioned again.

At the end of their succulent feast, the waitress returned and asked if they would like to see the dessert menu. Frank immediately said yes and requested the Gateaux Chaud. The waitress informed him that his choice of dessert would take fifteen minutes to prepare. Frank looked at his watch. It was only two o'clock, plenty of time. Dirk ordered the cheese board. When the waitress departed, Dirk decided to press Frank again about the diamonds. 'Did your client give you some more *currency* Frank?'

'Maybe, maybe not?' replied Frank, taking the same infuriating stance as before.

'Do you have them with you?'

'Maybe, maybe not?' repeated Frank.

'You're enjoying this aren't you?'

'Yes!'

Dirk shook his head 'You're such a child!'

'High praise indeed.' said Frank.

Dirk could see it was pointless to continue, Frank wasn't going to reveal anything. Shrugging it off, he gave himself up to the sophistication of fine dining. At three o'clock Frank glanced at his watch again and announced. 'I have to spend a penny.'

'I'll join you, just to be sociable.' said Dirk.

Inside the men's room, Dirk checked the cubicles one by one. They were all unoccupied. When he had finished looking round the empty space, he gave Frank an inquisitorial look. Frank regarded him with a puzzled expression, then with one of revulsion. 'What, surely you didn't think I'd conduct business in a public toilet did you?' asked Frank in a haughty manner. 'I'm very disappointed in you my boy.'

Dirk gave a sigh of resignation and entered one of the toilet cubicles. 'I have to see a friend off to the coast.' He said, referring to the scientific disposal of domestic waste in Den Haag. 'Don't do anything stupid without me.' He shouted from behind the door.

'I can't promise anything.' replied Frank.

When Dirk returned to the restaurant, the Maitre d' was recharging their glasses with the last of the wine. Glancing around, he was glad he'd worn his suit. The opulent room generated a sophisticated ambience that made him feel as though he'd been transported back in time, to an era when the world celebrated style and good taste. From the way in which they presented themselves and their mannerisms, it was obvious many of the diners were of affluent means. One couple, however, stood out above the rest. Dirk couldn't really see much of the woman, only the back of her head, but the gentleman had presence and was a stylish dresser. He was wearing a beautifully tailored taupe coloured suit and a pale blue shirt, matched with a pale blue handkerchief that protruded neatly from his left breast pocket. His tie was something of a surprise. It was midnight blue silk, decorated with what was a very subtle, but altogether stylish pattern of flame red dragonflies. His outfit was complimented further by a pair of tan loafers made of the finest leather. Sunlight from the overhead domed glass caught and illuminated a magnificent solitaire diamond ring on the little finger of his big right hand. He had broad shoulders and strong features. The man exuded wealth and power.

Chapter 19

At precisely three thirty, Frank announced they'd better make tracks and requested the bill. The concierge opened the door for them and touched the brim of his hat again in reverence. Dirk spoke to Frank without looking at him, 'You've had the currency on you the whole time haven't you?'

Frank smirked and did a Roger Moore thing with his eyebrows, but remained tight lipped.

'You do have them though, don't you?' pressed Dirk.

Frank's expression changed to one of consternation. He shot Dirk a sideways glance. Dirk took the hint. 'Right.' he said, straightening up and glancing around their environment. 'How far is this place Frank?'

'Not too far, less than ten minutes away.'

Pausing to look for traffic, Frank crossed the road and turned right; back into the tree lined park. Dirk tagged along. This side of the park was quite different to the route they had come before. Perpendicular to the other side, the architecture of the surrounding buildings mirrored the level of grandiosity of the hotel. Many of the walls were adorned with large bronze plaques, whilst various national flags flew outside embassies. On display in the central promenade was an art exhibit of unusual and eclectic bronze sculptures. Some tourists were snapping away at them with their cameras. The first statue they encountered was that of an ominous, hooded, hollow figure without a face, followed by more hooded figures and dinosaurs of varying size and description. Last of all, was an enormous kneeling giant large enough to walk under. These oddities together with the tall, spreading, trees gave the park and the surrounding area a portentous air to it; even though it was a bright and sunny day. Dirk shuddered with the sensation attributed to someone walking over his grave.

At the end of the park, they crossed over some tram lines at the bend in the road. Frank pointed to a restaurant on the near corner of the street they were headed.

'That's the oldest Indonesian restaurant in Den Haag. We should check it out sometime, maybe tonight?'

'Jesus Christ Frank, we just ate. I can't even contemplate food right now.'

Frank grinned and continued with his purposeful stride. At the far corner, he turned left onto a busy main shopping street then cut across and turned sharply right into a narrow cobbled street. About fifteen metres in on the right hand side was their arranged meeting place.

La Grenouille was a dingy little bar with about half a dozen drinkers, workmanlike in appearance, all smoking rolled up cigarettes. Heads turned as they entered. Dirk was acutely aware that their appearance was in direct contrast to the clientele, making him slightly uncomfortable. There was a heavy plume of smoke and no women present, apart from the barmaid who was so small that she could barely be seen over the bar. She welcomed them warmly and they ordered two small glasses of house red. Frank put ten euros on top of the bar. In return he received a friendly smile and four euros in change.

Outside, the solitary table and two chairs that

belonged to the bar were vacant. Dirk nudged Frank and indicated they seize the opportunity. They picked up their drinks and headed outside. Frank left his change on the bar. He never carried coins, claiming they ruined the line of his suit. While they waited for Jason to arrive, Dirk could see why Frank chose this place. It was an ideal vantage point, covering both ends of the street. No one could sneak up on them. Frank pointed across to the cigar shop with the downstairs smoking cellar. Dirk acknowledged with a nod of his head then turned his face skywards. The sun could just about hit this spot at this time of day and it felt good upon his face. The minutes passed quickly. Dirk checked his watch. 'Think there's a chance he might not show?'

Frank shook his head slowly, 'Jason has a propensity for the dramatic. He'll turn up bang on time. In fact, I wouldn't be surprised if he watched us arrive.'

Frank looked at his Rolex and glanced to his right. 'Look. Here he comes now.' It was one minute to four exactly.

Dirk followed Frank's gaze and saw Jason strolling out of a side street, twenty meters or so further down from the cigar shop.

'Good afternoon gentlemen, what a glorious day.' he pronounced, 'I see you're both dressed for business, excellent.'

Jason had dressed for business too. He was wearing a beautifully cut, pale grey, Armani suit complimented with faultlessly tasteful tan shoes and a pale pink shirt with gold cufflinks that glinted in the sunlight. Dirk felt distinctly underclass in his off the peg suit, even though it was Hugo Boss. Jason glanced cynically at the choice of venue and then at Frank. Dirk could see what he was thinking, being dressed in what looked like a three grand outfit. Frank also read his thoughts but said nothing, taking his time to finish his wine. Dirk could see the game Frank was playing, but so too could Jason. He was unmoved.

Finally, at Frank's discretion, they trouped across the street, en masse, towards the cigar shop. A bell above the door chimed their arrival. They were warmly greeted by two friendly women and a little Pug dog that wagged its short curly tail at Dirk, but barked at Jason. After some convivial exchanges of dialogue with the proprietors, Frank went into the humidor room alone and selected three Cohiba Siglo VI cigars. Dirk selected three small 25cl bottles of red wine to accompany them.

When Frank finished paying for it all they were escorted downstairs, by one of the ladies, to a cellar with a low arched ceiling and no windows. Small but not confining, it was perfect for the business in hand. Cuban posters adorned the walls, together with other paraphernalia, in an attempt at creating a Latin American setting. There was even a hi-fi system playing Flamenco music. Dirk was relieved to discover it was vacant, because they hadn't discussed any contingencies in the event there were others present to witness their inexplicable transaction. The room was comfortably furnished with a single sofa and half a dozen club chairs encircling low tables. While they went and sat down, their hostess fetched some wine glasses from the small bar-cum-kitchen area provided. As she poured their wine, the dysfunctional triumvirate proceeded with the ritual of lighting up their cigars. A façade had to be maintained. When she left them to their pleasure, as she politely put it, they were all smiles and thanked her courteously for her kind hospitality. The moment the door closed behind her at the top of the steep stairs, Frank rounded on Jason. 'OK Jason, let me see it?'

Jason didn't respond in the slightest and puffed away dreamily on his cigar. 'These really are quite wonderful aren't they?'

Dirk and Frank exchanged an uneasy glance. Frank repeated the request. 'The coin Jason, let me see it?'

Jason still didn't answer. Dirk moved uneasily in his club chair. Frank asked again, this time in a more demanding and authoritative tone. 'Jason. The coin, if you please. You do have it with you, don't you?'

Jason turned and looked languidly at Frank. 'Well, I've been giving it a lot of thought and I don't want to sell myself short; like I did last time. This particular coin is worth a great deal of money you know.'

'What are you saying Jason?' asked Frank.

'I'm saying I've decided to hold out for the right offer to present itself.' replied Jason, turning his cigar around to blow on its fired end.

Frank couldn't believe what he was hearing. Dirk almost swallowed his cigar.

'We have an agreement Jason, now stop wasting my time and give me the damned coin.' demanded Frank.

Jason sneered, 'I don't have to *give* you anything. I haven't signed a contract. We didn't shake hands on it. There is no agreement, only a conversation and an intimated price as I recall.'

Frank's face had turned crimson and he was going bug eyed with rage. Dirk interjected before Frank committed murder. 'Frank, sit back, have a drink. Let's hear what Jason has to say.'

Jason's head swivelled in Dirk's direction. 'My, aren't you the cool one Mister Dirk.'

Dirk gave him a wry smile. 'I can afford to be cool, it's not my money and what the fuck is this Mister Dirk crap?'

Jason bristled at the barbed tone, but was smart enough not to say anything further. He warily regarded Dirk, reappraising him. Dirk held his stare until Jason gave a small derisive snort and looked away. Frank took Dirk's advice and sat back and waited. The seconds ticked past. No one said a word.

It was Frank who finally broke the silence. 'Well, Jason, this presents a bit of a dilemma. We've gone to the trouble of arranging a deal for you and turned up here today, in good faith, only to have you turn us down flat; just as we're all set to make good on it. Now that just isn't good business, is it?' Dirk noted the use of the collective "*we*" again in Frank's dialogue.

'All I want is good business Frank.' said Jason.

'And how will you achieve that by reneging on a deal Jason?'

'I haven't reneged. I'm negotiating.' said Jason.

Frank balked. 'Negotiating?'

Jason looked between Frank and Dirk. 'How much can I say in front of him?' he said, indicating Dirk.

Frank shrugged. 'Depends what you have to say?'

'Well, let's talk about diamonds then shall we?'

Dirk was astounded that Jason had come right out with it and looked to Frank for guidance as to whether he should stay or leave. Although Frank appeared to have it together, he was still simmering on the verge of boiling point. He continued to glare at Jason. 'Ok Jason, let's hear it, what do you want?'

Jason crossed his legs and took another long puff on his cigar. Frank waited. Dirk prayed.

'I know why you're here in Holland Frank.' said Jason.

'You do?' said Frank dryly.

'It's obvious. You have a source for diamonds. They can be bought for pennies over here in comparison to Hatton Garden in London; if you have the right contacts of course. How else could you have so casually procured them at such short notice?'

Frank gave nothing away. Jason continued with his pitch.

'Well, I have my source too and I've come to the conclusion that I shouldn't be selling my wares so cheaply; not when I know my buyer can give me a better deal. Wouldn't you agree?'

Frank still said nothing, forcing Jason to prattle on with his ridiculous notions of business negotiation. 'This is simply a business deal Frank. It's all about supply and demand. I have the supply and I demand you give me a better deal. Nothing wrong with that now is there?'

Now it was Frank's turn to play it cool, 'Nothing at all Jason, except you've already made a deal and that's why we're here, but now you say you want more. That's no way to conduct business. A transaction like this has to be based on mutual trust.'

The cracks in Jason's business plan were splitting apart. 'What do you think is a fair price Frank?'

Frank called his bluff. 'What we agreed upon...forty thousand...in diamonds.'

'No, I said *around* forty thousand. I want you to make me an offer.'

'The diamonds I was prepared to give you are worth considerably more than forty thousand which, incidentally, is a better deal than you're likely to get anywhere else; because if you could get a better deal you'd be having this conversation with Sotheby's and not me and certainly not here, in this windowless cellar.'

'So you're saying you're not prepared to give me anything now?' asked Jason, with a touch of petulance in his voice.

Frank had obviously recovered because Dirk noticed, even if Jason hadn't, that Frank had his tough negotiator head firmly screwed on. 'A deal is a deal Jason, you can take it or you can leave it. The choice is entirely yours.' said Frank, letting his words hang. Dirk hadn't thought of Frank as a poker player.

It didn't take long for Jason to crack and he broke into one of his obsequious, trademark, smiles. 'Frank, you're so serious; do you know that?'

Although maintaining a cool façade, Frank's face was still bordering on crimson. Recognising it as a hair trigger moment, Dirk intervened before Frank threw his wine all over Jason's beautiful suit.

'Do you have the coin Jason?' asked Dirk, holding out his hand.

'I have it right here.' said Jason, patting his inside pocket.

Turning to Frank, Dirk asked. 'You still interested?'

Frank was fuming, but managed a slight nod of his

head. Jason fished out the wooden box containing the coin. He notably didn't hand it to Dirk and placed it in the centre of the table, between the three of them. Frank coolly regarded the small box in front of him for a few moments, then leaned in and picked it up. It took him a full five minutes of uninterrupted study before he spoke again, in a low and measured tone of voice.

'The original offer still stands. Do you wish to accept it Jason?'

'Of course I wish to accept it Frank.' replied Jason.

Frank didn't skip a beat. 'Do you wish to examine the diamonds first?'

'Of course not Frank, I trust you. Business partners must have trust. Isn't that what you just said?'

What happened to calling it *currency?* Dirk thought. Frank reached into his jacket pocket and took out a Cohiba Siglo VI cigar tube. He handed it to Jason.

'Another cigar Frank?' puzzled Jason.

'You won't have to light this one, it has its own fire within.' said Frank.

Jason took the tube from Frank and gave it a little shake, making it rattle. He proceeded to open it and out tumbled four sparkling diamonds into his grasping hand. Dirk's eyes grew wide in amazement.

'Very nice Frank, very nice indeed.' remarked Jason.

Frank delivered a brief account of the contents. 'Four diamonds: three just over a single carat and one just over two.'

Jason carefully placed the diamonds back into the cigar tube and slipped it into his inside jacket pocket, all the while smiling to himself. His sudden change in demeanour showed great satisfaction with his recent negotiations. He was clearly a poor poker player.

'Well gentlemen, that concludes our business for today. Now, how about a little pleasure? I think this calls for a toast.' proclaimed Jason, as if they'd just sold him a quality used car.

Neither Frank nor Dirk reached for their wine. Frank closed the wooden box and carefully slipped it inside his jacket. Buttoned down the pocket and patted it as a symbol of ownership.

'Yes, that concludes our business.' said Frank dryly.

'But Frank, we have so much more to talk about?'

Frank was still quietly fuming, 'No Jason, we don't.'

'All business and no pleasure eh Frank?'

Frank glared at him and stood up.

'Going so soon? Another time then?' said Jason. 'Goodbye Mister...' Jason caught Dirk's dour expression and stopped himself, 'sorry...Dirk. Perhaps we can have a drink together in Café Heuvel later this week, when Frank's away on business?'

'Goodbye Jason.' said Dirk, turning towards the stairs. Frank gave Jason one last withering look and pointedly stubbed his cigar out in the ashtray right under Jason's nose, leaving him to celebrate his Pyrrhic victory alone in the gloom of the cellar.

As the door at the top of the stairs clicked shut, Jason took the cigar tube out of his pocket and opened it again, smiling as each one of its glittering contents hit his tacky palm. Elated at his success and thrilled with his own *resourcefulness*, he puffed contentedly on his big cigar. Consulting his Rolex, another gift from his parents, he carefully returned the diamonds to the security of the cigar tube and stood up. He checked his appearance in the large mirror on the back wall and raised his glass to his own reflection. Took a large satisfying swig of his wine and drained the glass. With a final smug glance at himself in the mirror, he turned and slowly ascended the precipitous staircase.

Chapter 20

On the short walk back to the hotel, Frank's diatribe was interspersed by colourful expletives and the phrase *'fucking prick'* several times. Dirk could see there would be no point in trying to placate him. Frank needed to work it off for himself. Although, he did hope his friend's rant would provide sufficient catharsis before they arrived back at the genteel environment of the hotel.

At the end of the tree lined promenade, where the faceless hooded statue stood like a silent custodian to another realm, they stopped walking. Dirk looked around to make sure Jason hadn't tagged along behind them. There was no sign of him. A few people were milling around the statues and surrounding areas, but none had a lurking intent about them. Dirk had held on to his cigar, though it had gone out during their brisk walk. He relit it and waited for Frank to regain his composure. Standing in the warm sunshine, Frank let his breathing slow and he began to calm down.

'Was it worth it?' Asked Dirk.

Frank took the wooden box out of his pocket, opened it and held the coin up to the sunlight. 'I think so.' He said, handing it to Dirk.

Dirk studied it. 'Will Maudasi think so?'

'Only, if I decide to sell it to him.' said Frank abstractedly.

Dirk was knocked sideways by this statement, 'What do you mean? I thought you made the trade on his behalf?'

'Maybe I did, maybe I didn't?'

'Jesus Christ Frank, don't start playing silly buggers again.'

Frank smirked, but didn't elucidate.

'What do you think it's actually worth?' asked Dirk.

Frank adopted an oddly conceited expression when he gave his reply.

'It's not a question of how much it's worth, but having ownership of it; that's what's important. Maudasi would love to get his hands on this. I told you he likes coins, but he loves gold infinitely much more. The combination of the two, augmented by its rarity makes it irresistible to someone like him.'

The coin suddenly seemed tainted somehow. Dirk handed it back. Frank slipped the box back into his pocket and clapped his hands together in a cavalier display of brushing aside the past hour.

'Right, I feel much better now. Throw that old stogie away. Let's have a celebratory drink in more conducive surroundings.' He declared.

Relieved that his friend had seemingly reconciled his recent business transaction, Dirk took a final draw on his cigar and placed it on an old stone sundial to let it to die with dignity.

The same smart concierge ushered them through the revolving door again with his customary flair, as if their return wasn't entirely unexpected. Frank walked straight past reception and turned right, just before the stairs that led up to the restaurant. He passed through a concealed doorway and disappeared between a heavy set of burgundy velvet curtains. Dirk followed him through and discovered himself standing in the cigar lounge.

The large room resembled a gentlemen's club. Ornately framed paintings hung on the walls and elegant lamps adorned rosewood tables. A large mirror towered above a large open stone fireplace with a broad mantle, on top of which stood a great antique glass carriage clock. The window directly opposite the entrance faced into the park. Dirk walked over and looked out. He could see all the way to the end. The Mauritshuis and the Binnenhof were just about visible, but the opposite side of the park was largely obscured by the tree line from this angle.

When the waitress came in to take their drinks order, Frank had no hesitation requesting another bottle of Château Lafite Rothschild Bordeaux. Dirk noted that he requested the 600 euro bottle this time and again, made no comment. Frank seemed to be in a world of his own. Before taking more liquids on board, Dirk excused himself and went to the bathroom. When he returned, the wine had already been opened and there were two fresh cigars balancing on the edges of the ashtray. It would seem a 600 euro bottle of wine prompted first rate service.

'This wine is absolutely delicious,' proffered Frank as Dirk sat down on the large sofa. Needing no further prompting, Dirk picked up his glass. It was indeed a fine bouquet; he just couldn't believe Frank had spent more than a grand on two bottles. Glad he wasn't paying for it Dirk shrugged it off. He fired up his cigar and looked around the room once more. To the left of the entrance, along the back wall, were row upon row of private cigar safes or crypts as they are sometimes incongruously known. Further to the left, in the corner, by the window, was a large flat TV screen. It was on, but the sound was muted. A grandfather clock stood sentry against the outer wall. Dirk admired the burnished tone of the wood and ornate cherub statuettes atop the old fellow. His eyes continued upwards and he leaned back to look at the high ceiling, taking in its detailed carvings and cornice. Not surprisingly, it was slightly discoloured from all the cigar smoke. As well as sofas and chairs, there were tables situated at both windows for reading or simply sitting and gazing at the world outside. It was a setting of refinement and elegance.

The velvet curtains by the entrance parted and an elegant couple entered. They walked over to the table by the far window and sat down. Dirk recognised them immediately as the striking pair from the restaurant earlier. The man was aged around forty and the woman at least ten years younger. Both exuded the confidence that affluence generates, but with understated chic. Dirk got a better look at the woman this time. She looked like a supermodel. He admired her legs as she walked past; he was a leg man and she had a terrific pair of legs. Turning to share his feelings with Frank, he saw that he was regarding her with a frown. Dirk kicked him and mouthed "*what?*" Frank mouthed back "*later*". Up to this moment they hadn't paid much attention to her companion, but as his bull neck swivelled in their direction, atop his massive shoulders, the friends quickly averted their eyes and resumed their conversation with renewed gusto.

The waitress re-appeared and the man requested a glass of port, the woman a mineral water. Without a single word passing between them, the woman opened her bag and placed a large Cohiba Siglo VI cigar tube on the table. From his inside coat pocket, the man produced a mahogany covered cigar cutter, the shape and size of an American silver dollar, which he placed beside the cigar. From another pocket, he pulled out what looked like an old, single shot, derringer pistol. This turned out to be his cigar lighter. When all his accoutrements were laid out in front of him, he opened the cigar tube and retrieved his prize. He gazed at it adoringly. Dirk had to smile. He fully understood the ritualism of cigar smoking. It begins with the caressing touch of smooth skin followed by an anticipation of its unique seductive scent, then taste when first contact is made with your lips and tongue. When you ignite the flame, the experience is incomparable.

In a bizarre twist, the man held it out and handed it to the woman. Taking the cutter she expertly snipped a small piece off the closed end of the cigar. Replacing the cutter with the *Derringer,* she pulled the trigger and fired the open end, turning the cigar around in a slow semi-circular motion. When it began to glow she blew on it, making it glow even more. Satisfied with its fiery radiance she parted her full, flame red, lips and placed the perfectly snipped end of the cigar between them, drawing on the cool aromatic smoke; her mouth forming an oval pout.

Leaning back, she let her glossy tresses cascade over the back of her chair as she exhaled to the carved ceiling and the heavens beyond. It was a breath-taking sight. Both Dirk and Frank were transfixed. She took two or three more short puffs before handing it back to her imperious gentleman companion. The big man took it from her and thrust it into his mouth like an all American five star General.

'Nothing like a fine cigar.' ventured Frank, blighting the moment. Dirk drew on his own cigar and blew out a large plume of mutual appreciation. The man's mouth twitched into a wicked smirk. When the waitress returned with their drinks, Frank toasted their health. The man acknowledged graciously, but his face said something entirely different. Respecting the couple's obvious desire to be left alone, Dirk refocused Frank's attention by changing the subject.

'When are we catching the train back Frank?'

Frank consulted his Rolex. 'We should probably leave within the hour, but certainly not before we finish this fine wine.'

With others in the room, no discussion was made of Jason or the coin. Instead, they made small talk about Queen's day and what Dirk was proposing to do with his time when Frank was away. The stylish couple didn't really say much to each other, but when they did, it was in a language Dirk didn't recognise. They intrigued him, but he didn't want to appear rude and offend them by staring.

The friends remained in the cigar lounge until they'd finished their wine, but left with their cigars still burning. When they got up to leave, they said goodbye to the elegant gentleman and his luscious partner. The man acknowledged them with curt a nod, but his eyes exhibited cold contempt. The woman didn't bother to look up.

Walking out of the hotel, it was obvious by their silence that they were both thinking the same thing.

Dirk was first to comment once they got outside. 'Now that's what I call a woman!'

'I concur.' said Frank.

'Too dangerous for my taste, did you get a good look at her husband or whatever he is.' said Dirk.

'I'm sure you could handle him my boy.'

'I doubt it. Anyway, why were you scowling when you saw her?'

'It's nothing really. I've seen her before that's all. I saw her here at the hotel this morning. She was in the cigar lounge of all places. I saw her again just before I met you for lunch...with him. They must be guests of the hotel. She's quite something isn't she?

Dirk blew a low whistle and thrust the remainder of his cigar into his mouth in the manner displayed by her daunting companion, making Frank laugh. The route to the station was almost a straight walk from the hotel, through the tree lined park. At the end of the park they walked across some tram lines and past the entrance to the Mauritshuis Museum, where Frank pointed out houses the famous *Girl with the Pearl Earring* painting by Vermeer. Dirk had already told Frank where he'd been that morning, but decided to let Frank be Frank. A few metres further on they were once again walking across *"square"* square and within ten minutes they'd arrived back at Den Haag Centraal train station. Their train was already in and they boarded the first carriage and went upstairs to find a seat.

When the train pulled out of the station and disappeared from sight, Jason Sinclair turned around and headed straight back in the direction they had come.

Chapter 21

Frank wanted to head straight home to get organised for his forthcoming Geneva trip the next day, but it was a nice evening and they decided to walk; this time avoiding the red light district. Frank pointing out that you can have too much of a good thing. Another thirty five tempting minutes later they arrived back at the apartment.

'That wasn't easy', said Dirk, 'most of the bars we passed were lively and just getting warmed up by the look of it.'

'Don't let me stop you, head back out if you're in the mood to party.' replied Frank.

'No, I think I've had enough in the past few days. It *is* only Monday night after all.'

'Suit yourself. Anyway, I'm just going to freshen up. I want to get sorted out for tomorrow. Are you up to going out and grabbing a bite to eat later?' said Frank.

'Sure. I'll just lose this monkey suit first.' replied Dirk.

Dirk went upstairs to his rooms, shrugged out of his suit and hung it up. One minute later he was luxuriating under the soothing jets of a hot shower. He dried himself quickly and pulled on his jeans from the other day and a clean T-shirt. Stole a glance in the mirror and teased his hair into an acceptably tousled state then padded bare footed downstairs. When he entered the lounge he found Frank sitting at the window table. Ashen faced.

Concerned, he asked, 'Everything OK Frank?'

Frank looked up blankly. 'I've just had a call from Maudasi. He'd like to know who my friend is.'

'Doesn't he know I'm staying here?'

'Not you...the one sitting in the cigar lounge of Hotel des Indes...right at this moment.'

Chapter 22

Sadim Maudasi took a small sip from his large glass of aged malt whisky and paused for a moment. 'Tell me Dragan, what are your thoughts?'

The mobile phone had been set to speaker mode allowing them both to hear the voice at the other end. Maudasi's *aide-de-camp*, Dragan, was in the process of removing the SIM card. He casually brushed the leg of his impeccable suit trousers before answering. 'It's difficult to say. I thought they might all just be friends, after their little Champagne party on Sunday, but now when one secretly follows the other two…'

Dragan let his sentence hang and placed the SIM card into an ashtray, where he assiduously flamed it to destruction with his lighter. The smell of the burning plastic made Maudasi turn around. 'Must you do that in here?'

'I'm sorry, but yes. I learned a long time ago that when you no longer have use for something, get rid of it.' He replied, pragmatically.

Maudasi nodded with equal pragmatism, although he sometimes thought Dragan was over cautious, even paranoid. He also thought it ironic that Dragan should walk around Den Haag, of all places, so comfortably and invisibly. Standing six foot two and weighing in at over one hundred kilos, he was an imposing presence. With his close cropped, slightly greying hair and steel-grey blue eyes, he projected an intimidating countenance that, when required, could deliver its promise of cruelty to the recipient. An asset Maudasi had exploited on numerous occasions.

'They do seem to be rather more than mere friends, would you agree?' asked Maudasi.

'It would appear so, yes.' said Dragan.

'And the other one, the one with the female companion, what about him?'

'Not so much of a friend it would appear, if he spies on them; perhaps a business associate or a rival?'

Maudasi raised an eyebrow and commented with a thick sliver of irony, 'A business associate who spies on his partners, how curious?'

'Perrier did sound genuinely confused, when you informed him about the one in the hotel. However, I am inclined to remain sceptical. This can't be dismissed lightly.' said Dragan.

'*Genuinely confused...*' Maudasi was unconvinced, '...or maybe it was just the shock of being caught out?'

'That too is very possible. However, the individual sitting in the cigar lounge didn't join them for lunch today and he didn't return with them to the hotel.' declared Dragan.

'Exactly, maybe they didn't want to be seen in the hotel together? No, I don't think Perrier is telling us everything. If we have picked up any unwelcome interested parties then we must persuade them to become disinterested. I want you to go and collect Perrier tomorrow morning. An hour in your company should influence any forthcoming decisions he's contemplating.' said Maudasi.

Dragan snorted, 'Do you think that wise? We've just had the car valeted.'

Maudasi smiled. 'We can valet them both if the need arises.'

Chapter 23

Frank was bordering on apoplectic, staring at his mobile phone with a deranged look on his face. When he looked up and caught sight of his own reflection in the mirror on the opposite wall, his darkening countenance alerted Dirk to the imminent destruction about to take place. He leapt forward and snatched the phone from Frank's grasp before he did something regrettable. Frank was shaking with what could only be perceived as irrepressible rage. Dirk threw the phone into an armchair out of harm's way and placed a firm hand on each of Frank's tensed up shoulders. Frank was seething. It took Dirk a full five minutes of holding onto him, trying to cajole some sense out of him, before he eventually calmed down and allowed himself to be gently pushed into a chair. As Frank sat there staring at the floor Dirk said. 'That's got to be Jason, he must have followed us, but how does Maudasi know he's there?' Dirk paused when he realised the ramifications of his own words. 'What's going on Frank?'

Frank didn't answer or look up from his quasi fugue state. Dirk gave him a gentle prod. 'Frank, you're freaking me out here, what's going on? Talk to me.'

Frank remained frozen for another minute before he regained control of himself, although he didn't look up when he finally spoke. 'I shouldn't be entirely shocked that he's been watching me.'

'I take it you mean Maudasi; why would he do that Frank?' demanded Dirk.

Frank took a deep breath and sat back in his chair,

but still didn't look up. 'The next few days are crucial. Maudasi has invested a lot of money.'

Dirk was reluctant to know exactly what Frank was involved in, particularly after their clandestine meeting with Jason to buy a questionable coin with questionable diamonds, but this was a new twist and maybe it was in his best interest to find out more.

'Was he really pissed off at you Frank?'

'No, he was very calm and measured in his speech, but…it's disconcerting that he felt the need to call and ask me so directly.' said Frank, reflectively.

'How did the conversation go?' asked Dirk.

Frank sighed deeply again and finally looked up. Dirk tried to read his expression, was it guilt? He couldn't be sure.

'Maudasi simply wanted to know who my friend was, the one sitting in the Hotel des Indes at this moment. I said I didn't know what he was talking about, but then he described him: young, well dressed, drinking brandy and smoking a cigar.'

'That can only be Jason.' said Dirk.

Frank nodded in agreement. 'Has to be, description fits, but what could I say other than I didn't know he was there.'

'Did you say you knew him?' asked Dirk.

'Yes. I couldn't really deny it, if he's been having me watched, could I?'

'I suppose not. So what did you tell him?'

'I told him that, if it is who I think it is, he's an antiques dealer I know in London and that we'd bumped into each other, here in Amsterdam, on Queen's day.'

'What did he say to that?'

'He said he'd be interested to hear all about it tomorrow.'

'Didn't you tell him Jason is the guy you bought the Queen Anne coin from?' asked Dirk.

Frank's face reddened slightly. 'That fucking prick Jason, I knew he was up to something. Bastard!' Frank spat out the last word.

Dirk puzzled over Frank's reaction momentarily then it dawned on him. 'You didn't call Maudasi at all last night did you? That was that all a big charade for Jason's benefit?'

Frank looked sideways at him as if to say *no shit Sherlock*.

'Why didn't you just come clean? Tell him about the other coins you've bought from Jason. If he's a coin aficionado like you then he'll understand.'

Frank's face fell again and he shook his head ruefully.

'What? Are you worried Maudasi will be pissed at you for not telling him about it and keeping it for yourself?' asked Dirk.

'It isn't the coin I'm worried about' said Frank, sounding distant.

Frank's odd behaviour and the root of his concern suddenly became clear.

'I think I'm beginning to understand. It's the diamonds. You said something earlier, something about paying Jason too much before. You paid him in diamonds last week too, didn't you? And now he thinks he's got his hooks into you, sees you as an easy mark. Doesn't he Frank? That's it, isn't it?'

'He can sling his fucking hook after this. I don't care if he comes up with the crown fucking jewels next.' fumed Frank.

'So these diamonds you gave to Jason, were they yours to give away?'

Frank swallowed hard, 'Yes, I didn't steal them if that's what you're thinking?'

Dirk refrained from making any comments about honest bankers. 'So what's the big issue with Maudasi then?'

Frank shifted position in his chair, 'I told you Maudasi lets me in on some of his deals right? Well, when he buys diamonds from his source at rock bottom price, excusing the pun, I get paid in diamonds, not cash, for the private work I do for him. It's something we discussed months ago. He gave me the option of how I would prefer to be paid and we both agreed this was the optimum way. A single transaction from Maudasi to his source for a job lot, shall we call it, and the fee he would normally pay me goes towards the purchase of additional diamonds…at cost price. Thus we both get an excellent selection of diamonds and I do a hell of a lot better than I would simply on commission.'

Sensing there was more, Dirk waited. Frank looked furtively up at him from under his brow, but had enough respect for his friend not to try and deceive him. 'Before I went to Hotel des Indes this morning, I met with Maudasi at his home in Den Haag…' Frank hesitated in his speech. Dirk waited impassively for him to continue.

'…in addition to being his banker, I also arrange for

the transportation of his diamonds back to my bank in Geneva, where they're stored in a safe deposit box...' Frank hesitated again, momentarily, before continuing. 'That's why I was there...to meet with a business associate and hand over...a package.'

Dirk almost had a fit. He rolled his eyes to the ceiling. 'Jesus Christ! Frank! Frank! Frank!'

'What? What? What?' Frank snapped back, sounding irritable.

'For fuck sake Frank, can't you see it, he's got you smuggling diamonds for him and you're being blinded by his charm and the big bucks. I don't care what you or he or anyone says, this isn't legal and you know it. Don't tell me otherwise.'

'Granted, we might be bending the rules slightly.' said Frank, lamely.

'Bending the rules? You're breaking international fucking law Frank.'

'I don't see it like that. We buy the diamonds from a reliable source and then move them somewhere else. Both Maudasi and I have homes in Geneva, what's wrong with keeping your assets close?'

'Ok Frank, you know the legalities more than me, but I don't agree that it's totally legal and I know you don't either. You're turning a blind eye while the going is good.'

Frank continued with his brazen talk, 'Maybe I do and maybe I don't, but the going is so good, you can't begin to imagine.'

Dirk couldn't believe this was his friend talking. 'Let's pull back a bit Frank, we're losing sight of things here, why would Maudasi have you followed?'

'Just being cautious I suppose, it *is* a lot he's entrusting me with.'

'Has he set any rules regarding how you disperse...or dispose of your diamonds?'

'He trusts my discretion and acumen as a broker. So, no is the answer to your question; he hasn't stipulated any rules to me. What I do with them is my business.'

'Well, that's ok then, he won't be angry with you for trading diamonds with Jason. By the way, what are you going to do about him?'

'Nothing, I'm finished doing business with him. He's just proven he's more trouble than his coins are worth.'

'That's another thing; the coin. I suggest you come clean about that with Maudasi and maybe offer it up as a peace offering.' suggested Dirk.

Sitting forward with his elbows on his knees, Frank contemplated his options and chewed on his bottom lip. His hands were set as if in prayer and he pressed them against his lips.

'I've been such a bloody fool, but you're right, of course. I will offer him the coin and he *will* understand, even if he is a little disappointed at my judgement. Alright, so I might get my wrist slapped and he'll want to know all about Jason, but I'm sure all will be forgiven when he sees the Queen Anne and we'll go on with our business as before.'

Frank had taken on the glazed expression of someone conducting a conversation with an imaginary friend. Dirk determined it might be best to change the subject and get him focused on something else. 'Tell you what, why don't you go get yourself sorted out for your trip and then we'll decide where we'll eat.'

Looking up he regarded Dirk with a deranged look of confusion, as if he'd suggested something wholly arcane.

'You ok?' Dirk asked.

Another moment or two passed before Frank's opaque expression came into focus again. 'Look after the place while I'm gone, don't let that bastard Jason back in here ok?'

Before Dirk could reply to these curious instructions, Frank turned and walked into his bedroom. The situation required another drink. Dirk got himself a much needed cold beer from the fridge and listened as Frank banged around in his bedroom muttering to himself. His friend's behaviour was worrying and he felt helpless in the situation. He sat down on the sofa and began leafing through a magazine that was lying around, but it was in Dutch. Tossing it aside, he stood up and walked over to look out of the window. The street was dark and quiet, but just as beautiful with the street lights twinkling in the still canal waters that reflected the colourful buildings. On the opposite bank, the interior of the houses were now visible as they too were lit up. Their high ceilinged rooms looked grand and tastefully decorated. All of the occupants were doing pretty much the same as others do the world over; watching television with their dinner on their laps or surfing the web. It moved Dirk to ponder what life was like here a hundred years ago, without all the electronic technology that locks us indoors today. When he'd finished his beer, he went and got another. As he cracked it open, Frank's bedroom door opened and he reappeared looking slightly more like his old self, but no less stressed.

'That was quick Frank, packing all done?'

He came over and snatched the beer from Dirk's hand, taking a long drink before handing it back. 'Yes, sorry about my behaviour a moment ago. I've got a lot on my mind. That business with Jason was just one thing too many.'

'Do you really think he'll come around here sniffing?'

'I'd be grossly mistaken if he didn't, but don't let him worry you, he's my problem not yours. Just tell him to fuck off if he turns up. You're here on holiday, so concentrate on having a good time and I'll see you again at the weekend when everything comes to a conclusion.'

Dirk didn't like the sound of that somehow. He wasn't convinced at Frank's renewed optimism and felt compelled to ask, 'What exactly is the business deal you're involved in next week Frank?'

'I can't tell you that, client-broker privilege, but I will pay you for helping me out with Jason today.'

'I've told you Frank, there's no need.'

'Well, I shall nonetheless. In fact when I get back, I want to talk to you about maybe helping me on a more regular basis, but we'll talk about that next weekend.'

Dirk didn't respond to his friend's unexpected offer of employment and didn't want to ask or consider what he had in mind. He redirected the conversation again. 'Well, I hope it all goes well for you next week and good luck with Mister Maudasi tomorrow. I'm sure he'll understand when he sees the coin. If it becomes necessary, I can always vouch for your good name Frank.'

Frank smiled fleetingly, 'I know you can, but I'm

sure that won't necessary. I'll simply tell him the truth about Jason and my business dealings with him.'

A thought suddenly struck Dirk. 'Jason doesn't know anything about your business next week, does he?'

'Of course not, but Maudasi will want conclusive testimony and that could be challenging with Jason appearing on the scene so unexpectedly.'

'Well, it could have been a lot worse if he'd popped up and introduced himself.'

'He already has though, hasn't he? The little prick.'

'What time is your flight tomorrow?' asked Dirk, in an attempt to steer the conversation away from Jason.

'17:05' replied Frank.

'Well, that's good. You don't have to catch a train to the airport until around three. Maybe we can have a nice relaxing lunch together before you head off?' suggested Dirk, trying to sound upbeat.

Frank looked a little pensive again. 'Maudasi is sending a car for me.'

Sensing Frank's discomfort, Dirk asked, 'What's wrong with that? You did say he was a cautious man. He's just looking after his business interests by making sure you don't miss your flight.'

Frank winced. 'He's sending a car for me here at eight am.'

~

Dining out was no longer on the cards. Frank was too pre-occupied, checking and rechecking his items for the next day at least six times, such was his disposition. Dirk left him to it and walked up to a pizza takeaway near

Leidseplein, ordering an extra-large pepperoni with cheese to share. When he got back, he managed to persuade Frank to have something to eat before he turned in, but after just one slice Frank had had enough and called time.

Dirk went upstairs to his own living quarters, taking the remainder of the pizza and two more beers with him. He left the lights off and opened the balcony doors. The night air was cool and the sound of laughter coming from the nearby café bar drifted in. It didn't lighten his mood. The questionable ethics of Frank and his business associates bothered him and he couldn't shake it off. But then again, when in the history of banking have bankers been ethical. Knowing there was nothing he could do about Frank or what he'd gotten himself into, he went back inside and switched on the TV. He searched through the channels until he landed on one showing *"The Good, the Bad and the Ugly"*; a classic Clint Eastwood spaghetti western and one of Dirk's all-time favourites. This would take the edge off. Although he'd seen it countless times before, he settled down to watch it and even contemplated getting into character with another cigar; big Clint smoked one in every scene.

When the movie ended he flopped into bed and sank immediately into a deep sleep, with dreamy thoughts of Helena lying in bed directly above him.

Chapter 24

The following morning Dirk was awakened just before eight, by Frank bustling about downstairs preparing to leave for his unscheduled assignation. He rolled himself out of bed and walked naked through to the small lounge. Hiding his modesty behind the curtain he peered out of the open balcony doors at the street below, eager for a glimpse into the world of Frank's mysterious client.

Standing in front of the building, as if in judgment, was an enormous, panther black, Bentley turbo. It looked like a hearse. A shiver ran through him like a current of electricity and he instinctively recoiled. The outside door banged shut and then Frank came into view, slowly walking down the steps like a condemned man on his way to the gallows. Dirk heard the click of the car door as it opened to receive him. The driver was largely hidden from view but the nearside window was down. The driver's right hand dropped to the passenger seat and he placed a cellphone on top of a folded newspaper. The bright morning sunlight caught the movement and danced over the magnificent solitaire diamond ring that he wore on his little finger. Dirk made a mental note to ask Frank, when he got back, if the job he had in mind for him was a chauffeur. When the Bentley rolled away he shuffled back to his bedroom and slumped back into his comfortable bed, intending to sleep until at least midday.

~

Frank was slumped in the back seat of the Bentley and not the front. Having observed the driver's personal paraphernalia lying on the passenger seat, he'd read it as a subtle statement denoting *"up front is my space"*. The box with the gold coin nestled inside his coat pocket and he could feel it against his chest. It felt good and it gave him confidence. All would be smoothed over when he presented it to Maudasi. His real worry was that he'd been followed for some time and his every movement watched and recorded. Nevertheless, he was confident he could explain away and justify any of his actions; the convenience of having Dirk there provided credibility against any wrongdoing. Frank allowed himself a fleeting smile. Seatbelt fastened, he settled into the spacious back seat. He was looking forward to catching a power nap in the luxurious car, while he considered his stratagem. However, when he looked up and recognised the driver as the daunting gentleman from the Hotel des Indes cigar lounge, his confidence evaporated like spit on a steakhouse grill.

He thought he was hallucinating. The driver had welcomed him with a very courteous *good morning*, as he'd gotten into the car. He'd reciprocated the salutation and proceeded to make himself comfortable and safe. Now he felt neither. As the bull necked driver slowly and deliberately negotiated his way around the narrow streets of Amsterdam, Frank's trepidation mounted exponentially with each passing street. Panicked, he looked out of the window in a frantic attempt to project a relaxed and composed façade. He was normally cool under fire, being a seasoned corporate negotiator, but this was something else completely. This was something he couldn't control or even have predicted. Someone else was in the driving seat and that someone was the person whom Maudasi had most certainly assigned to watch him.

When they hit the motorway, the flat landscape flashed past and everything else blurred. He recapitulated the events that had prompted this unanticipated summons. Had he made such a grave miscalculation in giving Jason a few diamonds? *Yes*, a voice echoed in his head. Silently he cursed Jason and his damned coins. The stones he had given him thus far were untraceable and a paper trail didn't exist, therefore it was reasonable to assume that he and Jason couldn't be linked by them. Neither could Maudasi or his source. His further attempts at rationalization reasoned that Jason could easily have gotten the diamonds from several different sources, if challenged. There was no real proof to suggest otherwise. The real problem was Maudasi. How angry was he likely to be with him for flaunting his privilege in such an overt way? Frank's thoughts ran amok and he closed his eyes, his tormented mind considering every torturous scenario imaginable. What if Maudasi had other questions concerning diamonds or worse? No, he couldn't have or else he would have hauled him in a lot sooner than this. Maybe it was just a coincidence that Maudasi's flunky had entered the cigar lounge at that precise moment and reported back what he'd seen. Frank didn't buy that either. *What if, maybe?* He thought he might go out of his mind before they reached their destination. His thoughts were still swirling when they pulled up to the gates of Maudasi's estate.

Chapter 25

Frank reined his imagination back in. He fearfully considered what he was going to say and when he should bring up the subject of coins. His initial plan was to tell Maudasi he'd bought the Queen Anne with him in mind, but dismissed that idea as being too contrived and concluded it would be best to admit the truth: Jason had caught him by surprise and it had been too good an opportunity to pass up. This explanation sounded more plausible, because it was; Jason *had* caught him by surprise.

The large electronic gates swung open and the Bentley continued with its smooth glide through, following a wide gravel pathway up to a large gothic styled mansion set in its own private, beautifully manicured, grounds. When the car came to a stop, right outside the imposing entrance, no members of the household staff were on hand to meet them. Dragan got out first and pointedly didn't open Frank's door, leaving him to let himself out. The front door to the large house was unlocked. Dragan opened it and stepped inside. Turned around and held it open, like GQ's take on the image of a dungeon gatekeeper. Frank slunk past and didn't dare a glance. Dragan issued a single instruction, 'Wait here' then walked over to another large door to the left of the cavernous hallway. He knocked once and entered. The door closed behind him and the house fell silent.

Frank felt like a schoolboy awaiting the headmaster's rebuke. He remained standing and looked around the grand entrance, with its polished marbled floor and lofty ceiling. A central table supported a vase filled with a glorious flower arrangement and beyond that two large Chinese urns stood either side of a wide oak staircase. Stained glass windows framed the front door and streamed a rainbow of colours into his holding cell, providing a mercifully serene setting. His frayed nerves, however, found little comfort in the overall tranquillity and beauty of the opulent surroundings. Dragan was merely seconds, but it felt like several minutes had passed before the door opened again and he reappeared, impassive as ever, his large frame filling the doorway. Without a word, he simply stepped aside to indicate Frank could now enter.

The arena in which he now found himself was an impressive study, surrounded by bookshelves and objects d'art. Maudasi was sitting behind a large desk centred at the gothic bay window, a large broadsheet newspaper spread out in front of him. He was drinking tea from a fine bone china cup.

'Good Morning Frank, I trust you had a pleasant journey?' Maudasi boomed in his deep rich voice.

Frank bristled at the undisguised callousness in Maudasi's rhetoric and he countered facetiously, 'As pleasant as it can be riding in the back of a hearse.'

Maudasi's eyes flashed. 'Let's hope that's not a journey any of us will have to make any time soon. Sit down. Would you like some tea?'

Frank suddenly had the urge to go to the bathroom and excused himself. Maudasi smirked, Frank was sure of it. After purging his anxiety he washed his face and hands with cold water, then carefully dabbed at his face with a towel until it was dry. He didn't want to appear flushed. When he descended the grand staircase and re-entered the study, he noticed Dragan had taken up position standing at the far side of Maudasi's desk. They stopped talking when he entered. Maudasi turned to Frank and said. 'I believe you two have already met, but let me formally introduce you. This is Dragan.'

Frank looked across room at the elegant behemoth and asked with all the confidence he could muster. 'Why didn't you introduce yourself yesterday in the cigar lounge?'

'Should I?' replied Dragan, indifferently.

'Why were you following me?' asked Frank indignantly.

'Was I?' asked Dragan in the same circumspect manner.

Sarcasm noted, Frank saw it would be pointless questioning him further. He turned back to face Maudasi. 'How long have you been having me followed Sadim?'

Maudasi smiled without a hint of warmth or humility. 'That's what I like about you Frank, you always talk straight. Now, let me be straight with you. We have a very important business transaction in the coming days and I do not want anything or anyone interfering. I was sure that you of all people would understand this.'

Frank opened his mouth speak. Maudasi raised a hand to stop him.

'Dragan takes care of all my security and it is of paramount importance that he is kept up to date with any changes regarding anyone in my employ. Yes, I have had you followed; but not simply to see what you do or where you go. It was more to see if someone was following you. You see, you are a creature of habit, which I know you to be. However, others may know it too and attempt to compromise our efforts.'

Frank attempted to speak again, but Maudasi's countenance indicated that he wasn't quite finished.

'Now, tell me which part of this story you don't find strange. Yesterday morning I gave you a package of great value and even greater importance to deliver to our associate. He left the Hotel des Indes at twelve thirty to go to the airport. You remained in the hotel, until one o'clock I believe. You returned a short time later with another gentleman, with whom you had lunch; was the caviar supplement too much with the crab Frank?'

Maudasi had taken him by surprise yet again. Frank attempted to speak once more and once again Maudasi put the brakes on.

'After lunch, you both left Hotel des Indes and met with another *friend,* with whom you all disappear into a secret cellar. Quite some time later, you and your luncheon partner leave, without the third party, but this other, uninvited, friend follows you back to the hotel and then to the train station. Finally and to cap it all, he returns to the hotel alone and sits there smoking a cigar and smiling to himself. Now tell me I am wrong to be a little paranoid Frank.'

Frank was suddenly aware of the cold moisture on his face. A trickle of sweat ran down his neck into his collar and his shirt began to cling to his torso. His head swam and he couldn't speak. His tongue was stuck to the roof of his mouth. Dragan walked over and pulled a chair out for him to sit, then leaned over in an ostensibly magnanimous gesture of pouring him a cup of tea. Frank managed to conceal his unease, or so he thought, drank a mouthful without tipping the contents of the cup over himself and unglued his tongue. 'As I told you last night Sadim, I have a friend visiting me from England. His name is Dirk Dagger and he's staying in the apartment. The other one is Jason Sinclair; he's someone I know from London that I ran into in Amsterdam on Queen's night.'

'And again on Sunday for a Champagne lunch.' interjected Dragan.

Frank refrained from asking again how long he'd been followed and simply offered his best explanation, 'Well, I didn't arrange that, it was just a coincidence that he was there on Sunday. He turned up with a Chinese girl and after all, it was a Chinese restaurant. They do serve an excellent Dim Sum lunch on Sunday.'

Frank's vain attempt to make light of the situation was rebuffed. 'Do you believe it to be a coincidence Frank?' enquired Maudasi.

Frank hesitated momentarily, 'No, I don't think it was. I think he followed us to the restaurant.'

'And why would that be Frank?'

Frank had the good sense not to hesitate and get caught in a lie. 'He's an antiques dealer and he had something to sell.'

'*An antiques dealer*?' questioned Maudasi, raising his eyebrows.

Realising that Maudasi, or more likely Dragan, had done his research Frank decided to come clean.

'Not in the truest sense of the word, no, but he does

sell antiques and rare *coins*.' He finished on the word coins last and let it hang there.

To Frank's immense relief, Maudasi took the bait. 'Coins?'

Frank strived to project a casual confidence, 'Yes, I bought some from him in London; two weeks ago in fact.'

'Are you telling me he came all the way over to Amsterdam just to sell you some coins?' scoffed Maudasi.

'Well, no, I mean yes…what I mean is, he knew I was going to be here for Queen's day and he obviously sought me out because he has another coin to sell.' Frank stammered and cursed his nervousness.

Maudasi was derisive, 'Just the one, it must be a very special coin indeed?'

Frank decided to go for broke. 'Yes, it is…very special!'

Maudasi said nothing more. Just sat there waiting for Frank to elaborate. Realising it was his only option, Frank gave it up.

'It's a Queen Anne five guinea gold piece…1703…VIGO.' announced Frank, his chest swelling with self-gratification. Maudasi didn't even blink.

'And you didn't think to offer it to me. I'm deeply offended Frank.'

Frank was deflated and scrabbled to recover, lapsing into his formerly planned and rejected speech. 'I *was* going to offer it to you Sadim…I bought it with you in mind.'

Maudasi looked unconvinced, but was gracious

enough in his response, 'Don't worry Frank, I'm not angry. After all, why shouldn't you buy it? Is that the only reason why you met with...what was his name, Jason, to buy this coin?'

Frank eagerly explained, 'Yes, we'd agreed a price for the coin on Sunday evening and arranged to meet him on Monday in Den Haag...but only after my business for you was concluded.'

'*We*?' asked Maudasi, as if he didn't know.

'Yes, I asked my friend Dirk to accompany me for support, because of the nature and value of the trade.'

Maudasi frowned. 'I don't quite understand. What do you mean by the nature and value of the trade? How much was he asking?'

Frank hesitated a little too long before answering. Maudasi picked up on it immediately. Frank knew there would be no point in blurting out a fragmented and incoherent explanation. Taking a deep breath, he stepped off the plank. 'It wasn't *how much* he was asking, but *what*.'

Maudasi's eyes flashed with illumination. However, the tidal wave of abuse Frank was expecting didn't materialise.

'You gave him diamonds.' concluded Maudasi.

Dragan smiled in veneration at his master's perception. Maudasi's face exhibited disapproval, but not for the fact Frank had flaunted diamonds. That was his privilege. It was the timing and indiscretion that he had shown. This was a critical period and he should have been focused on the task in hand, not getting a hard on for a coin; albeit a magnificent coin. Maudasi demanded total commitment from anyone who worked for him and their devotion to his affairs.

'Do you have it?' asked Maudasi.

'Yes, I have it with me now Sadim.'

Maudasi paused for a moment's thought then held out his hand.

Frank nervously unbuttoned his inside jacket pocket and retrieved the small wooden box. Leaned forward in his chair and handed it over. Maudasi opened it and removed the coin. He scrutinised it with meticulous attention to detail for several minutes. When he'd finished, he simply asked.

'Would you still like to offer it me?'

'Of course Sadim, it's yours if you want it.'

'What did you pay for it?' asked Maudasi.

'Forty thousand pounds…in diamonds' said Frank, with a trace of guilt in his voice.

Maudasi gave Frank an appraising look, then got up and walked over to the bookshelves and pushed something on the wall. Part of the bookshelf swung out to reveal a wall safe. He took his time opening it and stood for several moments carefully considering its hidden secrets. Then, seemingly satisfied, he closed the safe and pushed the same area on the wall. The bookshelf swung silently back into place. Maudasi came over and sat on the edge of the big desk facing Frank. He didn't appear to be carrying anything, but his fists were clenched. He fixed Frank with an impenetrable stare. Frank felt a sudden urge to go back upstairs again. Maudasi thrust out both his clenched fists. 'Choose one.' He demanded.

Frank looked confused. Maudasi prodded again, 'Go on Frank, choose one; let's have a little fun?'

Frank stared at Maudasi's hands not knowing if this was a game, a gamble or his last act on earth. Regardless, he was being forced to make a decision, whether he wanted to or not. Suddenly, something in his subconscious kicked in. Maudasi was right handed. He'd seen him press something on the wall with his left hand and by his posture, appeared to have been holding something in his right. He'd passed in front with his back turned, concealing his hands, making it impossible to determine if a switch was being made. Certain Maudasi would favour strength over weakness he held his breath and made his choice.

'Are you sure?' Maudasi teased.

'I'm sure', said Frank with a confidence that surprised even himself.

Maudasi opened his right hand and to Frank's horror it was empty. Confused and grappling to comprehend what had just happened, he could only stare in disbelief. Maudasi opened his left hand and revealed the Queen Anne gold coin. 'I guess it belongs to me now.' He said, grinning triumphantly.

Frank looked at him in bewilderment, not sure what to say. *You bastard* came to mind first, but this was swiftly rejected out of good common sense. If this was his punishment then better to accept it and not make matters worse by throwing a fit and insulting his host, who also happened to be his boss and the guy who kept Dragan on a leash. He'd gambled and he'd lost, simple as that. But before Frank could reconcile his loss, Maudasi burst out laughing.

'You should see the look on your face Frank, that's got to be worth at least the price of the coin.'

Dragan was grinning too. Frank could see him in his peripheral vision. He wanted to respond, but couldn't think of a smart quip. He wished Dirk was here, he'd know exactly what to say. Maudasi reached into his coat pocket and pulled out a banded wedge of banknotes and tossed them over. 'Fifty thousand Euros; I think that's a fair price, don't you?'

Frank was staring at the money he'd just caught, he was in the clear and he was in profit. 'More than generous Sadim, I...I don't know what to say'. He spluttered.

'You can say thank you!' said Maudasi contemptuously.

He casually opened a drawer in his desk and dropped the coin in without even giving it a second glance.

'Now, to our business in hand, no more private deals of any kind. Not until our business is concluded in Geneva. Do I make myself understood?'

'Yes Sadim.' Grovelled Frank.

'Dragan will drive you to the airport.' declared Maudasi dismissively.

And with that, Frank was off the hook; just so long as Jason didn't come back to haunt him. Such was the overwhelming wave of relief that flooded over him, he didn't even object to sharing a car with the daunting Dragan again. Frank got up to leave and glanced over expectantly. Dragan just stood there impassively in his immaculate suit, making no attempt to move. Sensing there was a pending conversation he wasn't privy to, Frank bowed out as graciously as circumstance allowed and withdrew from the room of inquisition. There was no benefit to be gained by being aggrieved or even paranoid. They were going to discuss him and that was all there was to it. He profoundly regretted getting involved and cursed his weakness and grave lack of judgement. Then he cursed Jason and his damned coins, repeatedly.

On reaching the Bentley, he noticed the paraphernalia from the front passenger seat had been removed. Frank deliberated this momentarily, then got into the back seat of the large limousine again and smiled. He rather childishly believed he might get something over on Dragan by regarding him as a flunky. Dragan was barely five minutes behind and got into the driving seat without so much as a word or a glance back. Fired up the big car and pulled out of the driveway. Neither spoke for the entire journey. Frank suspected this silent treatment was all part of his punishment. A tactic conveyed by Maudasi to make him feel uncomfortable and keep him on his toes. Well, he could suffer in silence with fifty grand in his pocket and that big arrogant bastard up front having to chauffeur him to the airport. Although, he did want to ask about the stunning beauty who'd accompanied him in the cigar lounge.

The road all the way to the airport was quiet and they arrived at ten thirty five without mishap. Dragan brought the car to a stop just outside departures and remained stoically silent. Frank, however, didn't have the good sense to follow suit, 'Shall I bring you back a nice big cigar from Davidoff's or maybe some Swiss Cheese?'

Dragan's large head swivelled around on his thick

neck, his cold eyes fixing Frank in their penetrating glare. Frank immediately regretted his rash and flippant remark and wished he's kept his mouth shut.

'Take care *Monsieur* Perrier, cigars are like risks; take too many and you may find yourself turning into Swiss cheese.'

Frank attempted a smile, but it came out more as a grimace. Confounded by his own folly, his retreat was swift. He opened the door of the Bentley and got out, closed it gently behind him and walked briskly away without looking back.

Safely inside the airport terminal building, he consulted the time on the departures display screen. It was still only mid-morning. His flight, however, wasn't until early evening. More than six hours away. What the hell could he do in an airport for that length of time? Dumping him here had just been another tactical manoeuvre on Maudasi's part to control his movements. Frank suspected he was probably being watched at this very moment. However, his paranoia was interrupted by the rumbling of his stomach and the aroma of coffee. He came to a snap decision. Staring up at the large departure screen again and looking around like a confused tourist, he surreptitiously scanned the area for any obvious signs of someone watching. Seeing no one or anything obvious, he began strolling around the vast airport concourse, pretending to go through the perfunctory motions of browsing in gift shops and clothes shops. He even went into Victoria's secret, although that didn't count as an imposition. While performing this mundane touristy ritual, he glanced at reflections in shop windows and mirrors for a full thirty minutes before he was sure he wasn't being followed. If someone was watching him then they were bloody good, because he couldn't pick them out. In a souvenir shop he picked out an orange T-shirt with *I love Amsterdam* printed across it and a red baseball cap with what just about passed for an embroidered image of Bob Marley on it. Paid cash then went into a nearby cafe, carrying his new purchases in an orange carrier bag. Now almost eleven thirty, he decided to make his move. He glanced around one more time before taking out his cellphone.

At precisely eleven thirty, still unable to make out anyone observing him, he casually stood. Picked up the bag containing his newly purchased items and headed off in the direction of the toilets. Once inside, he entered one of the cubicles and removed his scarf and jacket. Opened the plastic carrier bag and took out the tacky T-shirt. Slipped it on over his shirt then put his jacket and scarf back on, thus concealing the T-shirt underneath. He flushed the toilet for effect and exited the cubicle. No one suspicious was loitering. He quickly washed and dried his hands and left. Focusing straight ahead, he walked purposefully towards the train station and located the platforms for Den Haag and Amsterdam: five and six respectively. They went in opposite directions and both trains were due to arrive within the next five minutes, about a minute apart. He went over to a nearby newsstand kiosk and pretended to browse among the plethora of magazines on display. Walking all the way around the kiosk, he continued to scan the area as best he could for a tail, while simultaneously and furtively glancing at the announcements boards above the platform escalators. Two minutes until the Den Haag train arrived. Three for the Amsterdam train.

Less than a minute later, a large group of Japanese tourists were heading his way. Deducing they would reach the escalators leading down to his desired platform in about ten seconds, he casually strolled towards them. One minute to go. As the chattering throng marched past, he could hear the rumble of the first train echoing in the tunnel at the bottom of the escalator. Reaching the end of the loud and lively crowd of travellers and their numerous bags and cases, he made a dash around behind them and down the escalator. Running down the moving staircase, two steps at a time, he got to the bottom just as the Den Haag train came out of the tunnel. The moment the doors slid open, he jumped on board and ran down the small flight of stairs to the lower level. Tore open the orange plastic bag and pulled out the Bob Marley baseball cap and put it on, pulling it down low. He threw off his jacket and scarf and stuffed them both into the empty carrier bag. His transformation was complete in ten seconds flat.

As casually as his adrenalin sapped legs would allow, he then proceeded to go through the sliding door and into the next carriage. When he reached the door at the far end, the Amsterdam train arrived on the other platform. Pushing past some commuters getting on, he slipped off the train and walked smartly across to the other side. Swiped his travel card over the electronic reader and got on board. Keeping his head low, he went down to the lower level again and sat down on the first empty seat. The train pulled out less than one minute later.

Chapter 26

Dirk stood at the top of the front steps, taking a moment before setting off. A voice called out. 'Good morning.'

Turning in the direction it came from, he groaned when he saw who it was. Ten metres down the street was Jason Sinclair, walking jauntily towards him.

'Frank's not here Jason.' Dirk said, in a brusque and dismissive manner.

Jason shrugged nonchalantly. 'Actually, it's not Frank I'm here to see, it's you. I thought we could maybe start over. Have some lunch perhaps, build some bridges. What do you say?'

Dirk had to bite his lip to stop from saying what he wanted to say. He politely declined. 'I have to say no. I'm just off…somewhere…another time.'

'Then may I walk with you? Do you have any objections to that?'

'I'm in a bit of a rush. I'm meeting a friend.'

'A friend you say?' mused Jason, arching an eyebrow.

'Yes, a friend. Do you have any objections to that?' said Dirk, with a sliver of sarcasm.

'This *friend* wouldn't happen to be mutual would they?'

Dirk didn't answer. He was looking left and right.

'Are you lost?' enquired Jason.

'Not exactly, I'm just trying to get my bearings, these damn streets all look the same.' He lied.

'Where are you going, perhaps I can be of assistance?'

Dirk wasn't going to give him an exact location, but he knew a couple of landmarks within reasonable walking distance to where he was headed. 'Dam Square, we're thinking of going to Madame Tussauds.'

Jason was no dummy and humoured Dirk by giving him directions. 'Well, you can get a tram from Leidseplein, which is just up here or you can walk in that direction, but it'll take about thirty minutes, maybe more.' Jason pointed both ways as he explained.

The clock was ticking, so Dirk opted for the tram at Leidseplein. 'Ok Jason, you can walk with me as far as the tram.'

Jason shrugged and fell into step. 'Tell me Dirk, is Frank pleased with his purchase?'

'What purchase?'

'Oh, don't be so coy; the coin, what else do you think I meant?'

'I really don't know anything about coins Jason.'

'I didn't ask that, I asked if he was pleased with it.'

'He didn't say if he was or he wasn't, but I suppose he must be, he paid you enough for it.'

Jason replied with an arrogant smirk that tempted Dirk to give him a hard slap across his face and push him into the canal, but he said nothing more and just kept walking. As they neared the square Dirk spotted a tram approaching that displayed *Centraal Station* as its destination and dashed for it, but not before acknowledging Jason's assistance. 'Thanks for your help. Bye.'

Jason shouted after him. 'Give my regards to Frank.'

Dirk got on, swiped his travel card and sat down. He looked back and could see Jason still standing there, waving like a lover saying farewell. It made him cringe with embarrassment. Turning around in his seat, he put all thoughts of Jason out of his mind; in any case, he couldn't run behind the tram could he? However, in a busy city like Amsterdam there are many trams and like all big cities, three usually turn up at the same time.

Less than fifteen minutes later Dirk was walking towards the Sea Palace. He arrived just past midday and went inside. He told the girl at reception he was meeting a friend and requested a table for two. While he waited, he remained standing in the foyer admiring the artefacts they had for sale in a glass cabinet strategically situated by the entrance. He didn't have to wait for long. Five minutes later he looked up to see a garishly dressed tourist walking down the gangplank of the floating restaurant. *"Jesus pal, don't you have any mirrors at home"*, he thought to himself, turning away to conceal his mirth at the dork who was now pushing in through the glass doors of the restaurant.

'Haven't you got us a table yet?' cried a familiar voice.

Dirk whipped his head around when he recognised the voice and stared, open mouthed. The *dorky tourist* on the run from the fashion police was none other than Frank. Dirk opened his arms in a gesture of disbelief and confusion. Frank snorted. 'Yes, very stylish I know. Let's eat, I'm hungry.'

They were shown downstairs to the lower deck of the restaurant this time, where it was dark and more subdued. Dirk supposed this suited Frank if the fashion police were close by. The waitress left them with menus and went off to get the two Tsingtao beers they'd requested.

'So, what's all this Frank, did you wake up this morning and think it was Queen's day all over again?'

'I'm incognito.' replied Frank in a whisper.

'You're in something, that's for sure.' said Dirk.

Frank removed the hat and pulled the T-shirt off. He dropped both on the floor. Patted his hair down and retrieved his jacket and scarf from the carrier bag. When he'd called from the airport he hadn't said much, only that he could make lunch after all and suggested they meet here. He'd said nothing about dress code. Dirk waited for him to get straightened out.

Finally, with the tacky tourist regalia back in the bag and looking considerably more business-like, Frank began his tale. He explained that the driver who'd picked him up this morning, then later drove him to the airport, was none other than the same big scary guy, with the great looking woman in the cigar lounge, who it turns out works for Maudasi; but is no *fucking chauffeur*, as he succinctly put it.

'He's called Dragan, you saw him didn't you?' said Frank.

'He's not someone I'd like to get on the wrong side of that's for sure.' said Dirk.

Frank informed Dirk that Maudasi *has* been having him followed, allegedly for his own protection, but it was Jason who had set the alarm bells clanging by following them back to the Hotel des Indes.

'So, what happened with Maudasi Frank? Did you offer him the coin?'

'I didn't really have much of a choice did I? But he gave me a decent price for it, fifty thousand euros…cash.'

Dirk almost choked on his beer.

Frank shrugged it off, 'Anyway, after I explained who was who and why we were there and what we were there for, he understood.'

'So he wasn't angry with you?'

'Not the way I thought he would be. He *was* angry, I could see that, but I think he just wanted to shock me back into reality.'

Dirk was incredulous. 'I can see it had a profound effect on you? What if you were followed here Frank? Have you considered that?'

Frank didn't answer, because the waitress arrived with their beers and took their lunch order. When she left, Frank immediately turned to Dirk and delivered another mind boggling piece of information. 'The money Maudasi gave me for the coin…I have it with me now.'

Dirk almost swallowed his tongue. 'What? You're kidding right?'

Frank shook his head. 'I think he did it on purpose, he knew it would make me uncomfortable carrying that amount of cash onto a flight.'

'So, what's the big deal? You just put it in a locker at the airport and pick it up again when you get back.'

'No, he knows I wouldn't just leave it in a public locker; he probably expects me to contact someone to come pick it up and wants to see who turns up.

'And you think the best way to avoid further scrutiny is to leave the airport and come here to meet me? For fuck sake Frank!'

Frank shrugged, 'If anyone *was* following me, I'm pretty sure I gave them the slip.'

'Hence the disguise.' said Dirk.

'Brilliant, wasn't it?' said Frank, looking pleased with himself at his own ingenuity, if you could call it that.

Dirk was already calling it something else entirely, but kept it to himself. 'Seriously Frank, do you really think it was wise to come here if he *is* having you followed? It'll only create more suspicion if you're caught sneaking around, deliberately trying to shake off any spies he's got on you.'

Frank smiled again, 'Relax, I'm pretty sure no one followed me here.'

However, his smile didn't last. The expression on Dirk's face gave way to unease. 'Only one problem with that Frank, I think I might have been followed.'

Chapter 27

Jason Sinclair was speaking with the girl at reception. Frank looked like he was about to grab a pair of chopsticks and run across and stick them into Jason's eyeballs. Dirk put a hand on his friend's arm, 'Let me handle this.'

Frank stopped him, 'No, don't cause a scene. I have to get back to the airport after this and I can't miss that flight. Any other time I'd give you this fifty grand just to throw the bastard in the canal.'

To their surprise Jason didn't acknowledge them. He simply went straight upstairs to the other dining area. The friends exchanged a quizzical look. Dirk spoke first.

'He *knows* we're here.' said Dirk. 'He came by the apartment this morning and walked me up to Leidseplein. I jumped on a tram and left him there, but he must have managed to somehow follow it and watched me get off. After that it would have been easy for him to walk behind me in a crowd unseen.'

'Of course he did, he's a slippery shit. He came to the apartment this morning?' asked Frank with some concern.

'Yes, he said he wanted to see me, build some bridges and crap.'

Frank looked up the stairs Jason had just ascended with scepticism.

'What do you want to do?' asked Dirk.

'Nothing; have lunch.' replied Frank.

By the time their lunch arrived, they'd both lost the edge on their appetites and didn't do it the justice it deserved. Even their conversation was a bit stilted, like a first date going badly. Eventually, Frank remembered why he had taken the risk to come here. 'The money; I want you to take it back to the apartment after this.'

Dirk's eyes widened at the incredulity of the request. 'You want me to walk around Amsterdam carrying fifty grand, with Jason and God knows how many other pickpockets are out there?'

Frank was unperturbed. 'We'll walk back to Centraal Station together and you can get a cab straight back to the apartment.'

Realising he didn't have a choice, Dirk asked. 'Where do you want me to stash it?'

'I don't know, put it in a shoe and stick it under your bed or something.'

'Don't you have a safe in the apartment or somewhere secure in case of break-ins?'

'Don't worry about that, it's a pretty safe area; like a neighbourhood watch. But use your imagination and stash it somewhere sensibly.'

Glancing around the restaurant, Frank removed the money from his jacket pocket and passed it under the table. Dirk hefted the thick wad in his hand momentarily, then put it in his inside coat pocket and zipped it up. 'Any good sales on at the moment Frank?' he quipped.

'Take a couple of grand out for yourself.' said Frank, as though it was nothing.

Dirk stared at him incredulously. Frank stared back at him. 'What? It's only money and you're earning it. This is what couriers do, so take it.'

Dirk was shaking his head, 'It's only money when you have lots of it.'

After that, they said no more about. Dirk was extremely relieved that Jason hadn't joined them. He could see Frank had some trepidation regarding what Jason might be planning next and asked if he was going to confront him before he left for the airport.

'No, let's just leave the sleeping dog lie. If he follows us, then you have my blessing to plant one on him the next time you see him.' replied Frank.

'It'll be my pleasure.' said Dirk, glancing upstairs to where Jason lurked.

When their bill arrived, Dirk felt obliged to pay. It was the very least he could do considering what Frank had just handed him. Before embarking on their respective journeys, they went downstairs to the men's room to freshen up. Standing shoulder to shoulder, Frank repeated his instructions. 'Ok, go straight back to the apartment with the money and I'll see you at the end of the week, all things considered. I hope Jason doesn't give you any hassle.'

Right on cue, as Frank spoke those infamous words, the bathroom door pushed open and in strolled the all too familiar sneering figure of Jason Sinclair.

'What's all this? Two men having a confab in a public toilet, how very working class.' pronounced Jason.

What happened next was so sudden that Frank didn't take time to consider his actions. He launched himself forward and raised his right foot like he was taking a penalty shot and kicked Jason smack in the balls. The electrifying shock from the pain throttled Jason's breath. Frank was grateful for this because he couldn't possibly have explained his actions to the restaurant staff, who would've undoubtedly called the police upon hearing an agonised shriek from their restrooms. He stood above the tortured figure of Jason Sinclair writhing on the bathroom floor for a few moments, until realisation of what he'd done kicked in. With Dirk's help, they dragged Jason into one of the toilet cubicles and propped him up against the commode rim.

'Breathe.' encouraged Frank. Jason was embracing the bowl with his head inside it. Frank remained remarkably calm, which surprised even him after what he'd just done. His calm found a voice, 'Don't make a sound Jason, are you listening to me?' Frank snarled. 'Do you have any fucking idea the problems you've caused because of your stupid little games? Do you?'

Jason pressed his eyes tightly shut and cupped a protective hand around his precious jewels. He looked like he was about to start crying. 'Don't you fucking dare cause a scene you miserable little shit.' commanded Frank.

Jason fought back against the tears. Frank waited until he was convinced Jason was dealing with the pain and hopefully the situation, before outlining his ultimatum. 'Listen up very carefully, because this is the only time I'm going say it. You and me have done business for the last time, got it? And another thing, this is the last time you'll follow me or my friend; because if you ever try something like this again, I assure you I will put the matter into the hands of someone who will make your life very uncomfortable. Do you understand me?'

Jason wasn't really up to making any decisions, but

Frank thought he detected a little nod of acknowledgement. The experience had empowered Frank and he was on a roll. Something flashed across his mind. 'One last thing Jason, get out of town!'

With that, Frank stood up and straightened himself out. He regarded the retching form lying before him like he would a pile of rotting fish heads, then turned and walked out of the bathroom; leaving Jason slumped in the stall, with Dirk looking on in disbelief. Moving over to the cubicle, Dirk leaned in and regarded the crumpled heap on the floor. He had to smile. Jason was bellowing for Ralph.

~

At the top of the stairs, Frank was nowhere to be seen. At the reception counter, a girl was in the process of skilfully folding napkins for the evening diners. As Dirk approached, she looked at him nervously and then over at the entrance. Standing by the glass doors, were three more anxious and animated restaurant staff, yammering vociferously and staring out at something with horrified expressions. Upon reaching the glass doors he saw the object of their distress. It was Frank. Bent over a railing, he was grouting the cracks in the walkway with his undigested lunch. Grabbing a bundle of folded paper ducks, or whatever they were, from reception, Dirk went outside to assist his friend.

When Frank had finished throwing up, Dirk handed him a couple of napkins and asked if he was alright and ready to move on. Frank managed a nod and thanked him. As they began walking away from the scene, two

Chinese waiters came out with a bucket of hot water and a brush to remove the negative advertising that Frank had so colourfully displayed across their entrance. Dirk apologised, but the waiters just yammered away in Mandarin with what was, most assuredly, not an invitation to come back again anytime soon.

On their way back to Centraal Station, they stopped at a small shop to buy a large bottle of water for Frank to wash his mouth out and clean the puke off his shoes. Fortunately, he hadn't gotten any of it on his suit. His Cashmere scarf had taken the brunt of the abuse and had to be binned. They made it to the train station without any further calamity and scanned around for signs of Jason Sinclair. Not that he mattered for the moment. As they stood outside the entrance of the station, beside the taxi rank, Dirk chuckled and said to his friend, 'Get out of town? So you're Clint Eastwood now Frank?'

Frank looked a bit sheepish and rolled his eyes, 'Well, it was all I could think of at the time; besides, haven't you always wanted to say that to someone?'

Dirk smiled. 'Well right now I think I should say it to you, but in the nicest possible way of course.'

Frank acknowledged the advice and thanked him again. Standing amidst the busy crowd of commuters, they said goodbye and good luck to each other. Due to Frank's recent gastronomic evacuation, they simply shook hands and went their separate ways. Dirk walked over to a waiting taxi and got in. As it pulled away, he looked back for Frank, but the throng had already swallowed him up.

Chapter 28

The taxi ride back to the apartment took twelve minutes exactly and cost the same amount in euros. Dirk gave the driver fifteen. He bounded up the front steps two at a time. Closed the outside door behind him and leaned against it, relieved to be inside. He still couldn't take in that he was carrying around fifty thousand euros in his pocket. It had an unsettling effect. Not knowing where he should hide it, he went straight upstairs to his own living quarters to consider his options. Walking into the bedroom he came to a dead stop. It looked like it had been ransacked by a herd of buffalo. Most of his wardrobe was piled up in a corner of the room and last night's clothes were scattered at the foot of the bed. Realising he'd been there for the best part of a week, he cringed at the shambolic mess of his own making. It was time to do his own dirty laundry as well as Frank's.

Shrugging off his coat and hat, he threw them onto the unmade bed and grabbed an armful. Took it all downstairs and bundled it into the washing machine. All of his clothes were made of cotton and with no whites to separate, no problem. His mother would have been proud he'd remembered her advice. He presumed domestic trends in Holland were no different from those in the UK and looked under the sink for washing powder and fabric conditioner. He didn't know what surprised him more, the fact that he had guessed correctly or that his friend actually owned some. Figuring out how to use the washing machine was a bit of a challenge at first, all of the text was in Dutch, but the symbols were pretty universal. Loaded up and ready to go, he selected his best guesstimate program and hit the start button. When the machine started making the positive sound of filling with water, he turned his attention to the refrigerator and pulled out the last remaining Red Bull. While he waited for his elixir to give him wings, he considered the money Frank had entrusted him with and where he could safely hide such a big wad of cash. With the eye of a potential burglar he paced around the apartment, considering where the most obvious hiding places would be; such as drawers, sofa cushions and objects that could be easily lifted or removed. On his third turn he saw it. It was perfect. Even he wouldn't think to look there. It looked brand new and unused and he certainly wouldn't be using it any time soon. Without any further consideration, he dashed back upstairs to get the fifty thousand.

Back in the kitchen he found exactly what he needed in one of the cupboards. Taking a casserole dish off the shelf, he lifted the lid and dropped the cash in. Walked over to the pristine cooker and placed it inside the oven. Closed the door and stood back. He scrutinised the dark tinted glass concealing the object within. Everything looked as it should and it didn't advertise expensive nouvelle cuisine.

Satisfied with his ingenuity Dirk switched on the TV and flicked through the channels until he found an English speaking news channel. A group of Muslims somewhere in the Middle East were trying to blow up another group of Muslims; all in the name of Allah. The stock markets were still going south and the bankers were still banking, despite their obvious incompetence.

The internet was expanding more rapidly than the universe and the entire world was plugged into it, yet even more deaf and ignorant than ever. When the news summary ended, a ubiquitous blonde, bubbly, weather girl popped up and announced in her inimitable style that it would be wet and shitty all next week. She did this with great aplomb and a big happy smile then handed over to the studio, where a guest celebrity chef was about to demonstrate how to boil an egg. Dirk sat and watched it all dispassionately.

He necked down the last of his Red Bull and searched through the TV channels again until he found a decent music channel for company, then went upstairs and logged onto his laptop to check his Hotmail account. It was mostly junk, but there was one from Melissa saying *Hi, remember me?* Cursing himself for not calling her sooner, as he'd promised he would, he decided not to put it off any longer. He checked the time. Two fifteen local. It was one hour behind in Bristol and it was lunchtime. Knowing she would be working, he rang her anyway.

She answered almost immediately and pretended to be all hurt and offended that he'd forgotten about her so soon. He told her most of what he and Frank had been doing and that he was presently busy with the glamorous task of doing his laundry. When she reminded him to separate his whites from his colours, he knew they were still cool. She asked if he'd met any nice Dutch girls and Helena crossed his mind, but then he'd only met her on two brief occasions and one time not even in those. He flirted and teased that he only had eyes for her. She giggled. He missed her laugh and had a momentary pang of melancholy. Quickly dismissing it, he said he would see her soon and asked what she would like him to bring her back from Holland. Not backward in coming forward, she said she'd heard they have nice diamonds. Dirk gulped and babbled something incoherent about tulips, made an excuse about the washing machine making strange noises and ended the call. With duty done and no more emails in his inbox, he logged off and went back downstairs to make some coffee. However, the moment he stepped into the kitchen he remembered Frank had none, only beer and Red Bull. All of which had run out. There was nothing in the kitchen units either, just a couple of tins of tomatoes, a few jars of pesto and curry paste. It made old Mother Hubbard look like a hoarder.

When the washing machine came to the end of its spin cycle, he transferred his wet clothes into the tumble drier and set it for one hour. Not relishing the prospect of listening to its rhythmic cycle compete with MTV, he headed out to find a supermarket and stock up with more Red Bulls and coffee and maybe a few more necessities. He found one up near Leidseplein and aimlessly wandered around the aisles with a basket, perusing the stalls for his essentials. At the magazine rack, he thought about maybe buying a TV guide. There were dozens to choose from and many were the same as those he would find in the UK, apart from the fact they were all in Dutch. His eyes inevitably caught sight of the adult magazines and he shook his head in disbelief at their liberal placement and juxtaposition with magazines that could easily be seen and accessed by children. One well known gentleman's magazine caught his eye, with a celebrity nude photo shoot of someone he'd marvelled at before. Furtively glancing around to make sure he was comfortably clear of other shoppers, he reached up and casually took it down from the shelf and opened up her spread. Flicking through the glossy pages of the magazine, he was appreciating the exquisite charms of the naked actress when a voice beside him interposed, making him jump. 'Hello Dick.'

Caught again in another embarrassing situation, he looked up and into the cool blue of Helena's magnificent eyes. Momentarily thrown off guard by her untimely appearance, whilst holding open a magazine of some questionable choice, he swallowed hard and said, 'Oh, Hello…Helena...' *Shit! Shit! Shit!*

She glanced at his empty basket and then the magazine and smiled *that smile*. 'Do you need me to translate?'

Dirk was caught red handed and decided to come clean. He held out the magazine for her to see. 'Lindsay Lohan. I felt compelled to look, sorry.'

'Don't apologise.' Helena said, leaning in close to look at the pictures. 'She looks good, yes?'

'Lovely', said Dirk, quickly closing the magazine and placing it back on the shelf. 'So, what are you doing here?'

Helena frowned and pursed her lips at him then looked around. 'Can't you guess?'

Dirk had to laugh, she was a good sport. 'Maybe you could help me find a few things? This is my first time here. Do you come here often?'

He cringed at how corny that sounded and thought maybe he should be called Dick.

'This is my first time here too. We can help each other.' She declared.

'I'd appreciate that, thanks. It's DIRK, by the way.'

She gave him that playful look again. 'My name' he repeated, 'it's Dirk, not Dick.'

'I like it.' She said.

Resisting the urge to respond by asking the discourteous question she'd just inspired, he bit his lip. Desperate not to blow it he sought to say something more cultured, but nothing immediately sprang to mind. Fuck! However, he couldn't help but notice she was carrying an expensive looking camera case, together with other photographic paraphernalia. Hoping he didn't sound too prying, or worse, boring, he struck up a conversation. 'What do you do here Helena?'

Swinging the camera around on her shoulder, she announced with some pride that she was a freelance photo-journalist. He displayed genuine interest and she was happy to enlighten. As they talked among the aisles, he found out that she was working on an article for a Dutch magazine on the upcoming war trial in Den Haag involving the former Serbian military leader Ratko Mladić.

'So why are you not living in Den Haag, close to the International court?' he asked.

'The magazine I work for is here in Amsterdam. Also the airport is closer, if I have to fly off somewhere in a big hurry, you know?' Helena replied.

Dirk spotted the coffee he was looking for in the aisle they were in. Helena made a face when she saw his choice and selected a roasted Columbian blend for him instead, telling him that it was '*much better than that crap'*. He accepted her recommendation and smiled to himself, noting that when she spoke she used the word crap and other English expletives a lot. It wasn't offensive, but it did make him consider why other Europeans can do everything with just a little more style than the Brits, even making swearing sound classier. Moving into another aisle, they both laughed as they chose the exact same honey granola. Dirk picked up some much needed Red Bulls and Helena chastised him again for *drinking that crap.* He shrugged saying, 'It works for me.'

She tossed a bag of apples into his basket along with a bar of chocolate. This time he gave *her* a scolding look. She made another face and shooed him away. When they got to the checkout, Dirk insisted on paying for everything in appreciation for the help she'd given him. She responded by saying she would allow it only if she could buy the first drink. Dirk was beginning to think he should surprise women with his naked form more often.

They left the supermarket together and headed in the direction of the apartment building, stopping on the way at a charming little canal side café. The weather had brightened up, allowing them to sit outside. Dirk teased Helena by informing the waitress she was a coffee expert and that the coffee they served had better be the best. Both girls exchanged a withering look regarding his comments, making remarks in Dutch and laughing. Dirk didn't know or care what they were saying and just sat there grinning like an idiot.

Their coffees arrived and didn't disappoint. Helena raised an eyebrow at him for his opinion. He conceded it wasn't bad, prompting her to give him another playfully reprimanding look. Seated at the opposite table was a young English couple; students on a break. They were smoking a spliff. '*I love the smell of reefer in the morning*', the boy was saying to his girlfriend. He had obviously watched *Apocalypse Now* the other night too, Dirk thought. The boy passed it to his girlfriend and she promptly took her turn. Within minutes, it became obvious that the young couple had little experience with Dutch dope and they soon descended into a fit of the giggles, generating annoyance amongst the café's patrons. Taking it as a cue to move on, Dirk and Helena decided to go to Café Heuvel and have that drink. For the remainder of their journey, Dirk was thrilled at the ease with which they got along, in spite of their first encounter. He just hoped it wouldn't enter into their small talk.

On arriving at Café Heuvel, they ordered two beers. Helena took out her chocolate bar and announced that she hadn't eaten since breakfast and was starved. Dirk's stomach rumbled with empathy. His lunch with Frank hadn't been quite what he'd anticipated. Deciding to take a chance, he suggested they could maybe go somewhere else and get a bite to eat. She delighted him further by agreeing. Twenty minutes later, having dropped off their shopping at the apartment building, they were on their way back to Leidseplein with keen appetites. They found a Mexican restaurant that appealed to them both, where they could sit outside in the sunshine and view the entire square. The special on the menu was a platter of tortillas with chilli to share and Mexican beer. They went for it.

She'd brought along her camera and constantly pointed out people and anything else that fascinated her. She handled the camera with such ease and proficiency that Dirk couldn't help but be impressed. He learned that she'd studied art and photography at Leiden University; had lived in Paris for five years, but moved back to The Netherlands after a failed relationship. He was amazed at her openness and how comfortable he was in her company. She was great to be with. He was captivated by her.

Afterwards, they went for a walk and ended up in Dam Square. When Dirk realised where they were, he insisted on taking her into the cigar shop. She knocked him sideways by announcing that she loved the smell of a good cigar. He was beginning to believe he'd found the perfect woman. He got himself a Montecristo No 2 and she surprised him even more by selecting a small Joyita for herself. She told him that, when she was younger, her Grandfather smoked a pipe and that she'd always loved the smell of it and was disappointed pipe smoking now seemed to be a dying art. Dirk asked her where she was from originally and she told him Delft, where the artist Vermeer was buried. He said this didn't surprise him at all and told her that he thought she looked a little like the Girl with the Pearl Earring. This made her laugh and she asked him about his strange accent. He told her that he was Scottish and that it wasn't so strange. 'Braveheart, I love that movie!' she announced enthusiastically.

They spoke about other movies they liked and she asked who his favourite actress was, apart from Lindsay Lohan. He tried to play it cool, but she saw through his façade; eliciting laughter instead. She wanted to know what he did when he wasn't visiting his friend and he told her that he was between jobs. At this she said 'So, you're out of work?' and teased him again as he strove to explain why he wasn't working. There was nothing malicious in it, she simply enjoyed laughter and it was infectious. He enjoyed her company and she seemed to be enjoying his. When Helena finished her small cigar, Dirk suggested they move on to another bar that he knew of not far from the cigar shop. She seemed to think about this for a moment and then took him completely by surprise, suggesting they take a walk into the red light district first. 'Lots of good subject matter for my camera.' she said emphatically.

She wasn't wrong. The area houses a bright canvas of colour and contradiction that provides an endless source of subject matter for a photographer, or for those seeking something less inspiring. Dirk had no real objections when she playfully photographed him standing beside the crimson windows of brisk business. She even persuaded him to pose holding a girly magazine, pretending to look at the contents. They exited the red light district close to the brewery bar Frank had taken Dirk on his first night. It was surprisingly busy for a Tuesday evening, but they managed to find a seat inside. They stayed for an hour and shared three different beers.

As day became evening, it was turning into a date and they both knew it. A quaint little sushi restaurant close to home provided the setting for dinner, but before long darkness was closing in and their time together was coming to an end. On the way back, their pace was slow. Dirk felt electrified that she had taken hold of his hand. Their conversation too, had quietened to a slightly awkward, but comfortable silence. Inside the apartment building, Dirk closed the front door then turned to her and said. 'I don't want to spoil such a lovely day, but I have some wonderful Columbian coffee inside; it was recommended by an expert.'

Whether intended as a reply or not, Helena leaned in and kissed him on the mouth. He kissed her back and wanted to be standing naked before her again. He was rock hard and knew she could feel it as she pressed herself against him and kissed him ravenously, her searching tongue finding his. He fumbled to get his key into the lock as he returned her hot kisses. The door opened and they staggered through it and immediately fell to the floor. She was pulling at his belt. He was doing the same to hers. They weren't concerned about closing the apartment door, because there were no neighbours to worry about. Kicking and scrambling to get their jeans off, Helena managed to get one leg free and was immediately on top. Dirk felt himself slide exquisitely inside and they bucked and sweated for four and a half minutes, before she gave a long low moaning sound that almost drowned out his own gasps of gratification.

They lay on the wooden floor panting and kissing and hugging. He was still inside her as she lay on top with her head on his chest. Her hair smelled of lemons. He breathed in her wonderful scent and pressed his lips against her hair. She lifted her face towards his and kissed him again, then moved her lips onto his neck. He felt her tongue in his ear. 'Do you still want coffee?' she purred.

~

From across the street, on the opposite side of the canal, a lone figure standing in the shadow of a tree had watched them enter.

Chapter 29

Wednesday Morning 4th May

He lay breathlessly beside her and smelled her hair. Buried his face in it and kissed her neck. His hands moved over her soft pale skin, tracing the contours of her back and shoulders, slowly moving down her arms and across her flat stomach. He gently squeezed her small but perfect breasts, making her sigh with pleasure at his touch. She arched her neck back, towards his kiss; her hand reaching up, catching the sunlight and creating a spectrum of dazzling colour within the four carat diamond ring on her finger. He'd been mildly concerned that its size might look a little ostentatious, maybe even vulgar on a hand as delicate as hers, but she'd loved it, desired it; her eyes shining like black pearls when he'd presented it. *One of many such trinkets to follow my darling* he'd said to himself. It announced to the entire world how much he cared for her and gave him great satisfaction to see her so thrilled with his gifts.

The trip had been all about business, but he'd made it infinitely more pleasurable by bringing along his wife of six months. She was beautiful and he treasured her more than anything else he possessed. The daughter of a Shanghai fisherman, she'd barely been sixteen years old when he'd met her five years ago. He was twenty years older. Although deemed too young to marry, her family hadn't entirely discouraged his attentions. Money has a way of levelling things. Crowning her Asian beauty was a luxuriously silky mane of long black hair, hanging below her slender waist. She had the grace of a ballerina and when she walked around naked it swished and caressed her perfect little derriere atop her lovely, shapely legs. It gave him the greatest pleasure to watch.

After making love they bathed together. She pampered him, intimately washing every part of his body, sensually kissing his eyes, nose and lips as she performed this erotic ritual. He closed his eyes and settled deeply into the sunken bath, luxuriating with breath-taking pleasure; like an Emperor with his concubine.

~

At one time, Chong had worked for a large global exporting company, managing freight and logistics. He'd been responsible for providing a wide range of shipments and containers, for anything from machine parts to other products requiring specialist handling and storage. He was ambitious and he loved spending money, but his career had been rising far too slowly for his tastes. When he'd paid a visit to one of his largest customers in the Columbian coffee industry, he'd seen an opportunity. Coffee wasn't the only Columbian export and the profit from drugs can provide a huge amount of spending power; more importantly, it can buy silence and blunt pencils. Only a fraction of all containers are checked due to their numbers, so it was easy for him, with his unique knowledge, to provide these specialist services. Both he and his Columbian associates had been very satisfied with this arrangement until his official employers became suspicious and terminated his contract. Since then he had branched out on his own.

Smuggling and trafficking are big business and he was good at scattering the risks. Through his work he'd made many contacts and could still organize container ships for private customers with legitimate goods, thus maintaining a professional façade. However, he still provided services for clients with particular requirements and it was these services that brought him now to Hong Kong. A large amount of gold had come onto the black market from the Middle East and he was perfectly positioned to make this deal pay big for him and his partners.

~

Satiated and relaxed Chong rose from the bath. Dried and put on the complimentary white bath robe and slippers provided. He exited the en-suite and went through to the bedroom, leaving his wife to finish her ablutions with a cool shower. He knelt at the head of the bed and pulled out from under it, a small silver attaché case. It contained the merchandise that had been supplied for the trade. They hadn't left the hotel since their arrival and he'd kept it close by; in the place where they'd spent most of their time.

He carried the attaché case through to the sumptuous lounge. Sat down on the oversized sofa and placed it on top of the oval glass coffee table in front of him. Snapped it open and removed the package he'd been given on Monday morning in Den Haag. Opening it with great care he couldn't resist running his fingers over the contents, pondering the value of each in turn. He planned to make love again after lunch, on top of his priceless possessions, like a Matador flexing his prowess before entering the arena. They would spend the day relaxing and dine again in their suite. Tomorrow, whilst conducting business, his wife would entertain herself in the numerous expensive boutiques Hong Kong had to offer and then they would feast again in the evening in celebration.

Looking out at the dazzling vista that was Hong Kong Harbour, the sunlight creating a billion little sparkles on the surface of the sea, Chong couldn't contain the broad smile that spread across his face. He was feeling extremely pleased with himself, everything was going to plan. The meeting was set for tomorrow afternoon and would bring him the riches he deserved for all his hard work. Well prepared, his meticulous planning had brought him to this glittering finale.

The doorbell rang, interrupting his muse. He closed the package and placed it back in the attaché case and snapped it shut. Getting up, he casually walked across the lounge to answer the door. As he reached it, the doorbell rang again. 'Who is it please?' he asked.

'Room Service Sir' replied the voice from behind the door.

Looking through the spy hole he could see it was a hotel maid, dressed in a service uniform, with a service trolley.

'I didn't order room service.' said Chong, through the door.

'By special request Sir.' replied the maid.

Chong opened the door and the maid brightly said

'Good morning sir'. She handed him a small envelope and waited for him to respond.

Opening it, he retrieved and read the small card inside. The note simply said: "***Success. M.***"

Smiling at the subtle and evocative lettering, he glanced down at the trolley and his smile widened. It looked wonderful. There was a mouth-watering selection of exotic fruits, fruit juice and coffee and, most appealing of all, a bottle of Champagne on ice.

'Please…' said Chong, inviting her in and closing the door.

The maid wheeled the trolley over to the dining table situated near the floor to ceiling windows; all the while taking in the surroundings: the space, the view…the silver attaché case. She glanced towards the closed bedroom door and then back at Chong. He walked over to the coffee table to retrieve a generous tip from his wallet lying there. She didn't take her eyes off him. When he turned around he was still smiling and holding a fistful of Hong Kong dollars. She was holding a sound suppressed automatic pistol. It was aimed at his head. His smile froze for eternity as his brain exploded before he could conceive a single thought. He went down like a felled tree, falling straight back onto the coffee table; smashing it on impact. A scream from behind alerted her to the fact that Chong's wife had emerged from the bedroom, just in time to witness her husband's horrific demise. She whipped the gun around, but the door slammed shut as her prey retreated back inside. Gliding across the room like a spirit, she opened the bedroom door and entered with gun raised in a single mellifluous movement. It was a large room, but there was no place to hide. With three swift strides she was at the en-suite door. She turned the handle. It was locked. This presented no problem. Inside, she discovered a petite robed figure huddled on the bathroom floor, wedged between the sink unit and the commode. Chong's wife was screaming with her head down and her hands covering her ears.

The propulsion of the first bullet made a perfect round hole in the top and centre of her skull, cracking her head against the hard wall tiles with brutal force. She slumped backwards against the bathroom wall. From point blank range the gun fired again, creating another red circle in the centre of her forehead. Blood exploded from the back of her head and splashed up the wall. Her little body shuddered and was still.

Before the blood began to pool, she removed the huge diamond ring from the dead young woman's finger. Smiling, she put it on then went to obtain her main prize. On the floor of the main suite lay Chong, his left foot still twitching. She walked over to where he lay and fired another bullet into his head then turned her attention to the silver attaché case. Opening it, she checked the contents and allowed herself a moment to handle the merchandise. She too marvelled at their value, but resisted the temptation to remove them. Wasting no more time, she closed it and walked over to the service trolley, where she pulled out a leather shoulder bag from underneath. Stripped off the maid's uniform and dropped it onto the floor. Movement to her left caught her eye; it was her own reflection in the large mirror by the door. Wearing nothing but a bra and panties, she stood momentarily to admire her form

215

and smiled in appreciation of herself. It was a pity Chong's wife wasn't her size, but no matter. Hong Kong airport had Victoria's Secret.

In less than three minutes the maid's uniform had been replaced with smart, but nondescript street clothes of Jeans and a white linen shirt. The uniform she'd worn was stuffed into the shoulder bag to be disposed of at a later, more convenient, time and place. She pulled on a little saw tooth patterned cap, set it at a jaunty angle and put on a pair of large dark sunglasses. Stole a last look in the mirror and smiled.

Finally, she slung on the shoulder bag and picked up the silver attaché case. Took a cautious look through the spyhole and checked it was all clear, before stepping into the hallway and closing the door on the gruesome scene. The DO NOT DISTURB sign she hung on the door would provide a buffer. She would be well on her way by the time the ripened pair would be discovered. Waiting for the elevator to arrive, she pulled off the latex gloves she was wearing and placed them into the bag with the other disposable items. It was zipped, fastened, secured.

She boarded the elevator and travelled down to ground level then coolly, but smartly, walked through the hotel lobby out of the main door into the sunshine and was gone.

Chapter 30

Sadim Maudasi was having breakfast in his conservatory, overlooking a sea of green lawn bordered by tall trees. A high wall ringed the entire property, guaranteeing his seclusion. His breakfast consisted of yoghurt and figs with Turkish coffee and a cocktail of fresh tropical fruit juice. Dressed in a silk robe and nothing else, he slowly perused the markets in the financial papers and sipped his coffee. Seemingly satisfied that the markets didn't hold any banking horror stories, he discarded his newspaper and slid his hand into the pocket of his robe and retrieved the object from within. The small wooden box looked inconsequential. It was plain and simple and without markings of any kind. He opened it up and removed the gold coin, held it up to the light and turned it over to examine it. His eyes flashed their approval and he brought his hand down hard on the marble topped table, shattering the protective plastic casing. Then, with almost delicate finesse, he split it like he would a dry cracker; exposing the coin to the elements. Fully aware that handling the coin like this could tarnish and devalue it, should he get marks or scratches on it, he didn't care. He loved the feel of gold. It was different from all other metals. Unlike the coldness of steel, it felt almost warm to the touch. To deny himself this pleasure was unthinkable. It belonged to him and he could do whatever he pleased and at that moment he was very pleased. He'd received a communique from his business associate in Hong Kong, informing him they'd arrived safely. This news had thrilled him tremendously, as it meant the next stage of his plan had moved into position. By this time tomorrow he would have something infinitely more tactile within his grasp. He was elated. Manipulating the exposed coin with effortless dexterity, he danced it across his knuckles and between his fingers like a lucky strike gambler weighing up a bet. Tossed it into the air and caught it with his other hand. Unclenching his fist, he gazed at the coin for a long lingering moment and then pressed it against his lips. He closed his eyes and absorbed its essence.

A servant appeared with the utmost stealth to remove the clutter, including the broken plastic casing and left with the same silent reverence for his master. A few moments later, Maudasi opened his eyes and asked, 'Has my bath been prepared?'

'Yes Sir', Came the reply from another, statue-like, servant standing by the door.

Rising slowly from his chair, still caressing the coin, he abandoned the wooden box and walked upstairs to his luxurious bathroom, where a young Filipino male servant awaited his pleasure.

~

Maudasi descended at ten, looking immaculate in a midnight blue suit and lemon coloured shirt. No tie. To complete his ensemble, he wore gold cufflinks inset with black enamel and large gold lettering embossed with his initials intertwined. Dragan had arrived to take him to the airport. He too was dressed sharply in a pale grey suit and greeted his master with a silent, courteous nod of his head. Maudasi acknowledged him in a similar manner. The previous evening Dragan had joined him for dinner in his palatial residence, where they'd discussed several important issues; not least Frank and his friends. Now he stood before him again, ready to receive his latest instruction.

'I trust you will take care of things with your customary discretion while I'm gone. Arrange a meeting and deal with them both accordingly.' said Maudasi.

Dragan nodded deferentially; he was adept at dealing with people.

Chapter 31

Dirk awoke with the fragrance of Helena's hair on his pillow, stirring his senses. He remembered immediately where he was and why he was there and boy, were those memories good. Outside in the courtyard, a radio was playing again. His eyes came into focus and so did the song. This time it was Lady Gaga and Beyoncé singing *Telephone*. Images of the music video flashed in his mind and he came fully awake. Bouncing female buttocks in your head in the morning can have that effect. Helena heard movement and came into the bedroom, the aroma of good coffee following behind her. 'Ah, you're awake.' she purred in a throaty morning voice.

'What time is it?' he asked.

'Ten o'clock, you sleep late.'

'I think I earned it.' bragged Dirk.

Slightly embarrassed by his saucy comment, she gave a wicked laugh and sat down on the bed. She was wearing a loose fitting T-shirt and he could see she had nothing on under it. When she leaned in to kiss him, he playfully grabbed her and pulled her on top. His hands caressed her bare buttocks and found their way between. She was warm and receptive to his touch. He raised the duvet and she responded to his invitation with a smile and stripped off her T-shirt. The duvet closed around them.

Half an hour later, the room was like a sauna. They threw off the sodden duvet and lay there for several minutes, kissing and caressing each other. Dirk was suddenly struck by a thought, 'Don't you have to work today?' he asked.

'I am working. I have some material I can read here at home for my assignment. I've been awake since eight thirty and working next door on my laptop.'

'Have you had breakfast yet?' Dirk asked.

'Just coffee.' she replied.

'Well, let's get dressed and we'll go out for some breakfast or maybe even lunch.'

She made a face, 'I have to go to Den Haag this afternoon; to the International court.'

Dirk had another idea, 'Why don't I come with you? We can have lunch there and dinner this evening, when you finish work. There's this really old Indonesian restaurant there I've heard is fabulous. What do you think?' He was suddenly aware how eager that sounded. *Shit, maybe I've come on too strong and blown it. Slow down,* said a little voice in his head. She smiled, she had the loveliest smile or was she just humouring him. His paranoia rattled him and he decided to shut up. She kissed him again and said she would think about it, then sprung athletically out of bed and walked naked on her toes out of the bedroom. His eyes followed her pert bum all the way out the door. Dirk got up, pulled on his jockeys and went through to her lounge. It was a good size, about the same as his lounge area downstairs, but without the little balcony. There was a small table by the window where she'd been working. Her laptop was on and there was a large folder and some handwritten notes on a pad beside it.

Helena came out of the kitchen carrying two cups of coffee. She had put on a short kimono styled dressing gown to cover her modesty, but it left little to the imagination. He met her halfway and took one of the cups from her. She indicated they sit at the table. As she made space amidst the clutter, he asked about her assignment. She told him that as well as covering the trial, she was also working on an article on the atrocities committed by the accused, his known associates and their war crimes. She offered to let him see and pointed to the folder. He declined at first, but found it bizarrely compelling when he started leafing through. It was stuffed full of articles, testimonies and horrific graphic images of genocide not shown on CNN or any of the other news channels. Some of the pictures were more horrific than those he'd seen from both World Wars and Vietnam. There were photographs of bodies, lots of them, both human and animal. Bomb blast aftermath shots where the streets were littered with their remains. Worst of all were those of dead children; some were just babies with bullet holes visible in their little romper suits. "*What sick bastard could do that to a baby*" he thought. There was a section on the accused with pictures of him posing in dress uniform and in combat uniform with his troops. Then there were pictures of the troops themselves, mopping up after a battle. In the background, behind the posturing militia, Dirk could see dead civilians lying on the ground. Several of the shots were grainy and shadowy, but clearly depicted groups of soldiers lining up people and shooting them. Helena disclosed she even had film footage of beatings being doled out and worse. Dirk didn't want to imagine it. Another section contained files on known associates of the accused. These had ACTIVE or INACTIVE

222

stencilled across them. He asked her what this meant and she explained that some war criminals had yet to be brought to justice and were classified as active. The accused was classified as inactive because he'd been arrested and was awaiting trial. Dirk continued to leaf through the files and was shocked to see how young some of the wanted war criminals were at the time they'd committed their atrocities. Worse still, most of them appeared to be smiling and laughing in the group shots. The scenes in the photographs almost portrayed a party atmosphere of people eating and drinking and having fun. If it wasn't for the uniforms, tanks, guns, torn up bodies and carnage all around, it might have resembled a country fair. It was a chilling insight into the human psyche.

Depressed by the scenes of human slaughter and depravity, Dirk announced he was going downstairs to shower and stood up to leave. Helena stood up with him, her Kimono falling open and lifting his spirits. His hands slipped inside and it fell to the floor. Thirty minutes later, with his clothes tucked under his arm, jocks included, he entered Frank's apartment. He took his bundle straight over to the washing machine and dumped the lot in. His laundry from yesterday was still in the tumble drier. It was bone dry and somewhat creased. Folding the items as best he could, he took them upstairs to his own living space and placed them at the bottom of the wardrobe out of sight. He stripped the sheets from the bed and replaced them with clean ones, just in case there was a change of venue this evening when they got back from Den Haag. Then, with nothing more to do, he jumped into the shower.

Standing there with the water cascading over him, Melissa flashed across his mind and he experienced a slight pang of guilt. But what the hell, she wasn't his fiancée or even his girlfriend and he was a free agent. He reminded himself that he was on holiday and had done nothing to be reproachful for. It didn't make him feel any better.

Dressed in a clean pair of jeans and a fresh shirt, he went downstairs. Grabbed a Red Bull from the fridge and checked on the *casserole* in the oven. The stack of euros was still present and accounted for. He removed five hundred of the two thousand Frank had told to take and put it in his wallet. Feeling more than pleased with himself, he sat down at the window and waited for Helena to arrive. Gazing out and drinking his Red Bull, his heart came up to meet his bobbing Adams apple. Coming up the front steps was the big mean looking guy from the cigar lounge. The guy Frank had called Dragan.

Dirk thought he was imagining things, but the doorbell rang and told him otherwise. He glanced out of the front window again and sure enough, Dragan was just standing there looking into the street, as cool as you like. Dirk was in a quandary. Should he answer it or ignore it? Why was he here? Had Frank been followed yesterday from the airport after all and he was here to deliver the good news? Does he know about the money Frank had given him to stash? Would he demand Dirk hand it over? The doorbell rang again and his runaway thoughts abruptly ceased. Coming to the conclusion he had nothing to lose in answering it, Dirk opened the door.

Dragan spun around and with a smile said. 'You

must be Mister Dagger.'

Dragan didn't introduce himself or offer his hand. Neither did Dirk. Holding on to his nerve and his Red Bull he played dumb. 'You must be psychic, I don't know you.'

Dragan's smile broadened at Dirk's remark and his head lolled back slightly, 'I believe you are staying in my employer's apartment.'

Dirk continued to feign ignorance, 'I believe this is my friend's apartment. Do you work for Frank Perrier?'

Dragan continued to smile, 'Monsieur Perrier works for my employer.'

Dirk knew the jig was up, 'How can I help you Mister…?'

Dragan still didn't offer his name and simply said. 'It's better if we talk inside.'

Unable to think of a reason why he could say no to the landlord's representative, Dirk allowed him in with the proviso that he had to leave soon to meet a friend. Dragan came in and sat down on the sofa, uninvited, making it clear he didn't consider Dirk to be his host. He wasted no time in starting his inquisition.

'Would that friend be the one from the other day; the one who has something to sell?' asked Dragan, transparently omitting to use Jason's name.

Dirk adopted a blank expression and attempted to get him to say his name again 'I'm not sure I can help you Mister…?'

Dragan parried again. 'I'm sure you can Mister Dagger. You and Monsieur Perrier met with him here in Amsterdam and also in Den Haag. So, tell me, does he have anything of interest to sell?'

Dirk noted that Dragan seemed neither to care about alluding to the fact that he knew where they'd met with Jason, nor did he seem to care about any challenge Dirk might have regarding these facts. Dirk was unsettled by the audacious nature of the questions. He was also getting a little pissed off. But this guy looked like somebody who wouldn't care if he did, so he played along and kept his annoyance under wraps. 'I wouldn't know. I don't know him. I only met him on Saturday, the day after I arrived. You should really be talking to Frank.'

'But Frank isn't here is he?'

Dirk sensed menace in the guy's tone and tried to throw him off, 'Wait a minute, I recognise you now. You were in the cigar lounge in Hotel des Indes on Monday…with a very beautiful woman, as I recall. Why didn't you speak to Frank then?'

Dragan didn't skip a beat, 'Monsieur Perrier and I have never met.'

Dirk knew he was lying. 'But you obviously know who he is.'

Dragan didn't reply, didn't even blink. He was deadpan, daring Dirk to challenge him. The situation was starting to really unnerve Dirk, because he knew who this guy was, but there was no way he was going to reveal that Frank had told him all about the scary Bentley ride yesterday.

'Why don't you call Frank now and ask him?' suggested Dirk.

'Because I am here, now, asking you.' Said Dragan, in a tone that suggested he was used to getting what he wanted. Dirk could feel his temper rising, but knew better than to lose it with guy like this.

'Well, I really can't help you. You'll have to talk to Frank or wait until he gets back, because I wouldn't want to contact him while he's working. I'm sure you can appreciate that, since you both work for the same employer.'

Dragan changed tact again and mentioned Jason by name. 'Then could you tell Mister Sinclair that I am interested in anything he has to sell?'

'But I've just told you, I don't know him. I only just met him. I don't know where he's staying or how to contact him. You'll have to speak with Frank.' Dirk said, with a little too much irritation in his voice.

Dragan suddenly stood up and Dirk almost took a step back, but held his ground. Standing so close, Dragan looked bigger. He was powerfully built and gave off the impression he liked to demonstrate the fact by smashing the occasional face in. He had the look of a classic bully; full of himself. Dirk wanted to smash his face in. He tried not to look intimidated, but Dragan was well practiced in coercion and didn't budge. Lightening his tone Dirk opted to concede, without appearing to back down.

'Look, I can't guarantee I'll run into him, but if I do…whom shall I say wishes to speak with him? Can you leave a contact name or telephone number I can pass on?' he asked, attempting to get Dragan to say his name one last time.

Dragan's head lolled back again and he regarded Dirk contemptuously. 'Tell him to consult a psychic.'

~

227

Helena came down the stairs just as Dirk closed the door on Dragan. Her timing was impeccable. Perish the thought if Dragan had seen her or worse, she him.

'Who was that?' she asked, getting to the bottom of the stairs.

'Just someone looking for Frank, I told him to come back next week.' said Dirk dismissively.

She gave him one of her heart melting smiles, then threw her arms around his neck and kissed him sweetly on the lips. She smelled and tasted so good that Dirk wanted to stay home and have her for lunch, but she was off the menu. Tapping her watch, she reminded him that she had to be at the ICC for two o'clock. He nodded and went back into the apartment. Helena followed him in. Dirk went into the kitchen with his empty can and dropped it in the rubbish bin. When he turned around she was standing by the large window looking out. Caught in the morning sunlight, she appeared to be glowing as it lit up her beautiful face. At that moment Dirk wished he was a Dutch master. Locking the image in his mind, he came back into the lounge, shrugged into his Barbour jacket and put on his hat. 'Ready? He asked.

She turned around and smiled at him, 'Ready, cowboy.'

On the walk up to the tram stop, Helena commented on how strange he was acting. He knew it too, because he was edgy and constantly looking around to see if Dragan was stalking them. He told her that she had just worn him out and that he'd be fine once he'd put some good food inside him. He also suggested a kiss might help in the meantime. She obliged without hesitation.

On the journey to Den Haag he tried to put Dragan out of his mind and focused instead on Helena. She informed him that she was meeting the court administrative staff, together with some of her colleagues to arrange their press passes, but would be free to meet him afterwards. She gave him that smile again. He was spellbound.

They arrived in Den Haag at twenty past one, which didn't leave Helena a lot of time for lunch. She grabbed a sandwich at the supermarket in the station and asked where he would like to meet later. Dirk suggested La Grenouille in Molenstraat, mainly because it was the only bar he knew by name in Den Haag. She said she knew the street and agreed to meet him there around five. She kissed him goodbye and smiled again at his reaction to her kiss, then she was off and running to catch her connection that would take her to the court buildings. He watched her until she disappeared from sight then walked out of the station. Outside, he stood for a minute trying to remember the direction the tram had taken him on Monday. Recognition kicked in and he turned to his right, then left at the bank on the corner and walked on until the street opened up onto Plein. The Square called "Square" was busy with lunchtime diners, but he found a good seat outside a different cafe to the one he'd been to last time and it didn't have a view of the urinal. Better if he was planning to eat. Having only had Red Bull and coffee this morning, his appetite was sharp. He ordered a large Americano and a big all-day breakfast *bouncer*, followed by a De Koninck beer.

After his man-sized brunch, he went for a stroll and

randomly chose a street. His practice in any new city, when trying to find his way around, was to walk in either a clockwise or anticlockwise direction. That way he never got lost. Because by turning around in his chosen rotation, he'd eventually come back to the street in which he started. That was the theory. He walked around the city for an hour, enjoying the architecture and the busy shopping areas, noting buildings and landmarks for points of reference. When it turned three o'clock, he found himself back in Plein; a good time and place to stop for another beer. He also had the urge for a cigar, but hadn't thought to bring any with him. Glancing around his surroundings, he tried to recollect the route back to Cigar shop with the downstairs cellar; where Frank had bought Jason's coin. It was opposite the bar where he was meeting Helena later. Consulting his watch he decided it might be a good idea to go there now and find it again, rather than leaving it to the last minute. Diagonally opposite from where he was seated was the Mauritshuis Museum and beyond that the entrance to the Binnenhof parliament courtyard. Recognition kicked in again and he remembered the direction he should take. He finished his beer and placed five euros under his glass then walked across the square towards the Museum.

Inside the Binnenhof courtyard, a bridal photo shoot was taking place. It was a perfect day for it and the splendid backdrop of the building's magnificent architecture was inspirational. Together with some other tourists he stopped and watched the shoot for a few minutes, sitting on the edge of the gold fountain. In spite of what was going on around him he found it very peaceful and remained for another twenty minutes or so, enjoying the sunshine on his face, before continuing on his cigar quest. He exited the courtyard through the archway and followed the tram tracks until he came to the old Indonesian restaurant on the corner. Now he knew exactly where he was. Turning the corner into the side street, he came to a halt after only a few feet. Nestled within a row of shops was a little tobacconists that he hadn't noticed on Monday, when they'd come this way to meet Jason. A thought struck him. Not far from here was the hotel where he and Frank had eaten lunch on Monday. In fact, it was just about visible at the far end of the tree lined park with the bizarre art display. Considering his options, he decided it would be nicer to have his cigar in the lovely cigar lounge, rather than a windowless cellar. It was a mere five minutes away and an almost straight line back to his rendezvous with Helena. He checked the time again. Three thirty five, plenty of time.

After treating himself to a Montecristo No 2 he came out of the shop and turned right. Then, with a renewed spring in his step, he crossed the road and entered the park. His mood was buoyed up some more when he arrived at the entrance to the hotel. The concierge appeared to recognise him and welcomed him with affable civility. Dirk gave him a big friendly grin and headed straight for the cigar lounge. Pushed through the velvet curtains and stopped dead in his tracks. There, seated at the same far window table as before, was the daunting Dragan and his breathtakingly beautiful lady friend.

Chapter 32

Dirk's gut contracted. It felt as though someone had just stuck a knife into him. He deflated faster than a burst balloon at this second startling confrontation. Dragan's head swivelled in his direction. 'Mister Dagger, what a pleasant surprise to see you again…and so soon?'

Before he could even begin to comprehend the situation and recover his composure, a waitress came into the lounge and asked what he would like to drink. Dragan waived her away, informing her that *his friend* would be joining them. This classification of friendship sent a chill through Dirk, but he could see no choice other than go over and sit at their table.

Sitting down, he realised a third chair had been placed at the table. Whereas, he could only remember seeing two the last time he was here. There was also a third glass. It appeared that he'd been expected. *What the hell is going on?* Once seated, Dirk got a really close look at the woman. She was one of the most beautiful he'd ever seen. Although he'd thought this of many women over the years, she really was in a super league all of her own. She had long, thick, dark hair with dark eyes to match, high cheekbones and a perfectly sculpted nose and chin. Her full red lips were curled up slightly on either side of her mouth and when she pouted, they seemed to reel him in. She belonged in the Mauritshuis too he thought.

Dragan broke the spell. 'Are you having a cigar Mister Dagger…what a stupid question, of course you are, why else would you be here? Do you mind if I call you Dirk?'

Dirk didn't reply, instead he turned to the woman, 'Are you psychic too?'

She looked slightly perplexed at his remark and looked to Dragan who offered an explanation, 'British humour, who can understand it?'

Dragan offered no introductions and poured Dirk some wine. Dirk noted that it was a Château Lafite Rothschild; the same wine he and Frank had shared here the other day. He was sure this too was no coincidence.

'I'm sorry, I've forgotten your name, Mister...' said Dirk in yet another attempt to extract a name. This time it was forthcoming, but without warmth or benevolence. 'Dragan!'

Dragan surprised him further by introducing the woman too. 'This is Ulyana.' said the beast, giving name to beauty. She extended her hand gracefully and Dirk gently grasped it in his, 'It's a pleasure to meet you Ulyana. My name is Dirk.'

'A pleasure to meet you Dirk', she purred, like an Indian tigress; pronouncing his name like a Kalashnikov AK47 on a firing range. He held only the tips of her fingers, but felt slightly aroused when she gently slipped them from his grasp.

'Let Ulyana light your cigar for you Mister Dirk, she is very skilled.'

Dirk removed the cigar from his pocket and held it out to the dark haired beauty. She leaned forward and delicately plucked it from his fingertips. He sat back in his chair and watched, enthralled, as she went through the same ritualistic eroticism she had performed the previous day for her Dragan. It felt like déjà vu. A mesmerising five minutes later she slipped the cigar from her lips and handed it to Dirk. He took it and placed it into his open mouth like an automaton.

'As good as a kiss, no?' teased Dragan.

'I doubt it.' remarked Dirk, audaciously.

Ulyana's eyes flashed with approval. Maybe she wasn't accustomed to men being so bold with her in front of Dragan. She excused herself and rose gracefully from the table. Dirk got up from his chair with her as she did. She seemed to appreciate his courteous chivalry conveying it, imperceptibly, but most definitely, with her dark sparkling eyes. As she sashayed towards the exit Dirk willed himself not to look at her legs and admire her catwalk. Sitting back down, he turned to face his tormentor.

'I think she likes you Mister Dirk.' Dragan said, without a trace of humour in his voice.

'Have you been following me around all day…Mister Dragan.' asked Dirk, equally humourless.

'I suspected you or your friend would show up here at some point. You are…what is the term for it, creatures of habit…predictable?'

'You do realise stalking is a criminal offence, even in a liberally minded country such as Holland?' remarked Dirk, endeavouring to be casual, but not too flippant.

'I am not stalking you Mister Dagger, I am only interested in what Mister Sinclair has to sell. Now, that is not a crime. Is it?'

Dirk knew the bastard was trying to wind him up. It was working.

'Look, how do we resolve this? I don't know Jason Sinclair. I don't know where he lives and I don't know if he has any more coins to sell. I don't even know if he's still in Holland, that's how much I know.'

'Ah, *but* you do know he sells coins don't you?' noted Dragan.

Dirk gritted his teeth at the blunder. 'I saw him with one coin. I was there when he sold it to Frank, but I'm sure you already know that. I don't have any more information to give you. I'm just here to visit a friend.'

Dragan drew on his cigar. He was getting under Dirk's skin and he knew it, he could see the cracks forming and was determined to prise them open, 'A friend who isn't here.'

Dirk tried not to appear exasperated, but struggled in his discomfort. 'Frank invited me over for Queen's day and said I could stay in his apartment while he was away...why am I explaining all this to you?'

Dragan drew on his cigar and looked steadily at Dirk, then played another high card, 'Because, I don't believe you.'

Dirk had the good sense not to react to the provocation. He tried to make light of it and threw his hands up in mock surrender, but Dragan persisted with his exasperating questions, 'Do you know what your friend paid for the coin Mister Dagger?'

'No, I don't, that was between him and Jason.' Dirk lied.

Dragan smiled his cruel smile. It was the first time Dirk noticed the cruelty in it and it provoked an uneasy feeling. He could see how a woman like Ulyana might consider Dragan to be handsome. He exuded a strong alpha male presence, but in a brutal kind of way. Maybe she liked it rough. At first glance his smile looked kind of wry, with a touch of sarcasm. His head seemed animated somehow and his eyes rolled upwards, like he was about to give a hearty laugh. But when he bared his teeth, it was cruel; cruel and evil. Dirk's growing unease swiftly turned to acute wariness.

'Do you know what business your friend is involved in?' asked the beast.

'I assume you mean Frank' said Dirk. 'Banking, that's how I know him.'

The beast continued. 'Do you know why he is here…in Holland?'

'He has a client here, your employer, what's his name? Moondanski.' The moment Dirk spoke the name he knew he'd made another blunder. Dragan hadn't spoken his boss's name before now, had he?

The cruel smile widened and Dragan's eyes exhibited triumph as he corrected Dirk's pronunciation: 'Maudasi.'

'Whatever.' said Dirk, trying to sound casual. He lifted his glass in an attempt to divert his mistake and felt his hand trembling. Quickly, he began swirling the wine around in the pretence of releasing its flavour and prayed Dragan hadn't noticed the chink in his armour. He managed to take a sip of the wine without shaking it all over himself. If Dragan was aware of Dirk's nervousness he didn't let on and coolly continued with his inquisition, 'So, you know what business Monsieur Perrier is involved in and who he works for. What you may not know is that he has a huge responsibility and plays a prominent part in taking care of Mister Maudasi's assets. How much he may have told you, I do not know.' Dragan waived his hand as if he didn't really care. Dirk said nothing. Dragan continued. 'My business, Mister Dagger, is also protecting Mister Maudasi's assets and any unwelcome attention they attract. Do you understand what I am saying?

'Are you saying that Mister Maudasi wants me to leave his apartment?'

Dragan shook his head at Dirk's naive question, 'Mister Maudasi is happy for Monsieur Perrier and his friends to have a good time, as long as it doesn't interfere with his business in any way. I'm sure you can appreciate that Mister Dagger?'

'Perfectly; Mister Maudasi has nothing to worry about with Frank, he's the consummate professional.' proffered Dirk.

'That is good to hear. Who are you meeting here? You mentioned a friend earlier.' he asked, abruptly changing the subject.

'I'm not meeting anyone here. I just wanted to have a cigar and a glass of wine. I am, however, meeting a young lady for dinner later this evening. I'm sure that's something you can appreciate Mister Dragan.' said Dirk with a mischievous smile. Dragan smiled back, but the cruelty in his eyes was still very much in evidence.

Before another word could be spoken, Ulyana padded silently into the cigar lounge with feline grace. She slid into her seat with equal poise, swivelling her long legs under the table with a single fluid and elegant motion. Dirk tried desperately to keep his tongue from lolling, just in case Dragan ripped it out in a display of inflamed manhood and strength. She didn't speak, she didn't have to; a choir of angels did it for her. There followed a few seconds of awkward silence until Dragan

237

turned his attention to Ulyana and by some means of telepathic communication, or whatever, conveyed something to her. She appeared to understand, because they both stood up simultaneously. Dirk stood with them, more as a courtesy to Ulyana. Her eyes flashed her appreciation again and maybe something else too, he was sure of it, or maybe it was the wine. He held his hand out to Dragan as a gesture of good will and immediately wished he hadn't. It was enveloped by a bear paw with the strength to match.

'I hope to see you again soon Mister Dagger…and your friend Mister Sinclair too. Please give him my regards when you next see him.'

Dirk tried not to grimace as his hand disintegrated. 'It's a small world.' He said, grimacing at his corny line.

Dragan's eyes locked onto his, 'Too small Mister Dagger.' And with that he and Ulyana departed, leaving Dirk alone and relieved to get his hand back intact.

He watched them walk around the corner, through the lounge window, until they disappeared out of sight down a fashionable street lined with expensive designer boutiques. No doubt for Ulyana to buy some lingerie to train her Dragan. Dirk was shaken up by the experience. He was angry and considered calling Frank to tell him what had just happened. Brooding over what to do, he drank the some more of the wine. There was plenty left in the bottle, Dragan and Ulyana had barely touched it. Suddenly, a horrible thought struck him. Maybe it was poisoned. Panic crept over him. He couldn't remember either of them drinking. He couldn't believe what he was thinking. They didn't know he'd be here, that was a just a lucky guess. Then he remembered how much the wine cost. Why would they choose the most expensive bottle to poison him with when a cheap one would do? Deception! Panache! A touch of irony! To his relief, he noticed Ulyana's glass had lipstick on it, so it couldn't be poisoned. He was being melodramatic, why would they poison him? What had he done? Still, he didn't drink any more.

Panic over, he puffed nervously on his cigar and looked out at the park. It had clouded over and didn't look so bright any more. The weather reflected the change in his demeanour. No longer comfortable in his present surroundings, he decided to move on.

Chapter 33

By five o'clock, he was sitting in La Grenouille with a small glass of wine, waiting for Helena to show up. His cigar still burned, but was now just a glowing stump. He placed it in the ashtray on the bar to let it die with dignity. When it turned five thirty he considered calling her, but didn't want to appear like an overly keen schoolboy. She had probably just been delayed. When it turned six, his concern was growing. His mind paraded thoughts of her being abducted by a leering Dragan. He glanced at his cellphone lying on the bar and was about to pick it up and call her when, to his enormous relief, she walked through the door. She was all smiles and many heads in the bar turned around to admire her. She greeted him with a big hug and an even bigger kiss, then apologised for being late and said something about a meeting with a colleague who wouldn't stop asking questions. Dirk hardly heard a word she said. The little barmaid came over and Helena requested a cold beer. She asked if Dirk wanted one. He declined, his glass was still full. It had been sitting on the bar in front of him for almost an hour, because he'd been too concerned and too fidgety to touch it. Thankfully she didn't pick up on his trauma. He asked her how it had gone at the court and did she put any bad guys away. She laughed her infectious laugh at his question and said she wished she could put away all the bastards in the world that deserved it. They toasted each other in Dutch and he asked if she was hungry. She said she was and he suggested the old Indonesian restaurant again. She informed him that there were several good eating places near where they were now and suggested they should take a look around, before making a decision. Helena finished her beer in two swift gulps. Dirk was at last in the mood to do the same.

They left the bar and walked around the corner to a street just off Molenstraat called Oude Molestraat, which for a small street had a great choice of bars and restaurants. Helena was in a happy and vivacious mood and suggested they have a drink in each of the bars in turn. Dirk wasn't sure if she was serious or not, but couldn't have cared less, he was just pleased she was here. The first place they went into was too small and too busy, the second: too loud and too empty, but the third was lively without being manic and had De Koninck beer on tap. Perfect. It was a nice bar with the quirky name of Momfer de Mol. There were lots of retro objects and photographs on the walls and the clientele seemed a conducive and likeable bunch. There was an upstairs dining area and the food they were serving looked and smelled great. The house special was Stoofvlees, a rich beef stew with French fries. Dirk was sold and after just one drink, they decided to eat in the bar instead of going to a fancy restaurant. During dinner Helena told him all about her day. She'd had her photograph taken for her security pass and then been given a tour of the building and the main courtroom, where the war crimes trial would take place. Followed by strict instructions on where and when they would be allowed to take photographs and of whom. He listened intently as she spoke. She was a smart girl and didn't hold back on her opinions. She was engaging and witty and loved life and good food too. Once when she was talking, between mouthfuls, she noticed he was just gazing at her and smiling. 'What?' she asked, 'Do I have food on my face? What?'

'No, nothing, I'm just enjoying listening to you and watching you eat, that's all.'

She smiled her Marilyn Monroe smile and leaned across the table and kissed him, then scolded him for not eating and told him to eat some more. He couldn't, he was falling in love with her and it made him sick in the most appetising way. Never before, had a woman had such an effect on him; well not since he was thirteen years old and his high school art teacher, Miss Mellish, had leaned over with one too many buttons loosened on her denim shirt and he'd glimpsed her lacy bra bursting with enthusiasm.

They remained in the bar until eight thirty, when their sensible selves kicked in and they caught the train back to Amsterdam. They held each other like teenagers all the way and got a taxi cab from the station to the apartment. It was a forgone conclusion where they would stay again that night, but Dirk insisted they first stop at his place and pick up a bottle of Frank's expensive wine. Inside the apartment, everything looked exactly the same as he'd left it. However, he couldn't shake the feeling that something wasn't quite right.

He asked Helena to choose a bottle of wine while he had a quick look around. The first thing he did was open the cooker and check the casserole dish. The money was still there. She saw him do it and asked if he was still hungry. He lied when he told her that he thought he saw a crack in the glass door and was just checking it out. Continuing to scan around the room, he couldn't see anything obviously amiss. He walked over to the window and looked out. There was nothing out of the ordinary, no one furtively trying to hide behind a tree or anything else to fuel his paranoia. Helena shouted over to him. 'What about this one?'

He turned around. She was holding up a bottle of wine, 'Great.' He said, barely glancing at it. That was when he saw it. On the table by the window, sitting in the large ashtray, was a partially smoked Cohiba Siglo VI. Someone had been in the apartment.

~

Dirk just stood there, staring vacantly at the spent cigar in the ashtray. Helena noticed his peculiar stance and asked if he was alright. He reacted quickly by saying that he had to bag up some trash before the apartment started to stink; holding up the ashtray with the incriminating cigar as an indicator. He suggested that she go on up to her apartment and that he would be right behind her after he'd locked up. She said fine and kissed him on the cheek and told him not to keep her waiting. He said he'd be so fast he'd be standing at the top of the stairs waiting for her. When she'd gone, Dirk quickly ran upstairs to his own little lounge area. Nothing seemed to be out of place. His bedroom was in exactly the same state he'd left it in that morning and the en-suite bathroom looked to be the same too. But it wasn't. The toilet seat was up and he was sure he'd left it down. In fact, he knew he'd left it down. With the exception of public toilets, Dirk preferred to sit down when he was having a pee, especially at home. Some time ago he'd read an article in a magazine by a Swedish physician who had written an interesting and convincing hypothesis, outlining that when sitting down to pee it put less strain on the prostate gland. Being health conscious, Dirk had adopted this practice; besides he'd found it more relaxing and hygienic than standing up.

This invasion of his very personal private space angered him more than the decaying phallus protruding from the ashtray downstairs. Dirk had no doubt in his mind as to who the culprit was. Pissing in his toilet was just the sort of thing a big alpha dog like Dragan would do to mark his territory. As he thought about it some more, it technically couldn't be considered a break-in. Not if Dragan had a key and permission from Maudasi to check up on the apartment. Still, it wasn't quite kosher without permission from the tenant. But that was another technicality they could throw at him; he wasn't the tenant, Frank was. Shit. It wasn't a pleasant thought, but he knew there was nothing he could do about it if Dragan wanted to come and go when he wasn't in the apartment, or even when he was. Although Dragan rang the doorbell the first time, Dirk doubted he would be so courteous next time. Dirk went back downstairs and switched off all the lights. Then, under cover of the gloom, went over to the cooker and recovered the remainder of the fifty thousand euros from the oven. Tucked it into his inside jacket pocket and zipped it up. It would remain at his side for the rest of the night, even when he and Helena went to bed.

Chapter 34

At that same moment Frank was in Natalie's Geneva home, gazing out at the still darkness of Lake Geneva, admiring the lights reflecting on the water's surface from the opposite bank, contemplating its depths. He tilted his head back and sipped a vintage Delord Freres Armangnac and gazed up at the tranquil night sky. The stars twinkled and blinked at him seductively. He smiled. It was the first time in twenty four hours he'd really felt relaxed.

~

The previous afternoon following his consecutive confrontations, first with Dragan and Maudasi and then with Jason, he'd found it difficult to focus. The events of the past couple of days had unsettled him and he was worried everything was beginning to unravel. He was fearful of losing control and had desperately wanted to call Natalie, but decided against it. She had been very clear about contacting her and would not have appreciated hearing about his self-inflicted dilemma. However, the image of Jason squirming on the bathroom floor clutching his balls, after he'd separated them with a well-placed penalty kick, filled him with feelings of self-satisfaction. Even now, he could still feel the solid impact when his foot had connected with Jason's nuts. On a similarly gratifying level, no one appeared to have followed him from Schiphol airport. He hadn't felt the need to disguise himself on the journey back and had walked confidently through to departures and straight into the executive lounge. The free bar had provided some calm during the remaining three hour wait for his flight. However, he was still keyed up when he touched down in Geneva. Upon arrival, he'd gone directly to his favourite restaurant and ordered a dozen Lac Leman oysters and a bottle of Champagne. It was a charming little place called Au Coin du Bar, not far from Le Jet d'Eau. It was also close to Natalie's. After polishing it all off in less than an hour, he went home and poured himself a large glass of Armagnac, followed by another. This had finally administered the desired effect and he'd slept like a drunken baby.

He had awakened this morning in a heightened mercurial state, with the irresistible urge to go for a drive around the Lake in his Porsche. Frank loved to feel the surge of its awesome power when he stepped on the accelerator; it evoked in him a feeling of empowerment and an artificial sense of being in control again. On his return home from his power drive, he'd spent the remainder of the morning alone regrouping his thoughts and then, in the afternoon, gone to his bank to make final preparations for Maudasi's arrival. Finally, in the evening, Maudasi had requested his company for dinner at his splendid town house in the Old Town. Although more of a summons than a request, it had been an unexpectedly agreeable evening. Maudasi had evidently been in better spirits since their last meeting and appeared to have put behind them the business of Frank's indiscretion with the gold coin. Frank made a supreme effort to relax and enjoy the evening, because he knew that by this time tomorrow, Maudasi would be in another mood entirely.

~

Now, within the peaceful tranquillity of Natalie's home, Frank sipped the last of his Armagnac and admired the bejewelled night sky. His thoughts were not of sleep, but of conquest and power. There would be collateral consequences, that was unfortunate; that was business. But the rewards, he rationalised in his banker's mind, were like the stars: infinitely sublime.

As Frank gazed at the stars, a Singapore Airlines jet was almost touching them somewhere over the Middle East. The small silver attaché case was part of her cabin luggage and stored safely overhead. She had resisted the temptation to remove the contents and examine them, but was growing ever more excited at the prospect of running her fingers over them. She passed the time gazing at the four carat diamond on her finger adoringly; touching it, caressing it, as a lover would an erect nipple.

Chapter 35

Jason Sinclair Jason was having a massage. Not because he wanted to relax, he just needed to see if his balls still functioned. The masseuse oiled and massaged him all over, working wonders with her hands, feet and other parts of her anatomy. He'd insisted she be naked for the entire two hours he'd paid for her time. When it came to the happy ending, he was ecstatically relieved and overcome with Joy which, paradoxically, was the girl's name.

After Frank delivered his succinct message in the Sea Palace's rest room the day before, Jason had gone back to his hotel room and ran a cold bath. Sat down in it, fully clothed with a large glass of Russian vodka and seethed. He'd kill Frank for this, if he ever got the chance. His balls still hurt, but not as much. Everything improves with time, providing you have the patience to accept it. However, patience wasn't something he held in abundance. Yesterday and most of today had been spent massaging his bruised ego, considering what to do next. He'd figured correctly that Frank hadn't carried the diamonds he'd given him on Monday all the way from Amsterdam. If they'd been in his apartment, he'd just have dealt with him on Sunday evening and that would have been that. No, Frank had got them in Den Haag. The question was: where? When he'd followed them back to the Hotel des Indes, after the trade, he'd hoped it would have led him to the source. It had led only to another smoking room.

Now his patience had grown gossamer thin. Frank

was gone and wouldn't be back until the weekend. Jason didn't want to wait that long. However, his friend was still around. He was pretty sure Dirk knew more than he was prepared to let on. That much was obvious. The problem now, was avoiding another kick in the balls.

Earlier this evening he'd gone round to the apartment to see Dirk again. This time, however, he'd taken a different approach. Not wishing to provoke a confrontation, he'd watched from a safe distance. After several hours and two full packs of cigarettes, his patience had finally been rewarded when Dirk bounced happily up the front steps to Frank's apartment with a cute blond; interesting.

Chapter 36

Frank arrived at Maudasi's town house precisely ten minutes to the hour, for his eight am meeting. Parked his red Porsche in the private courtyard beside a Black Mercedes Benz and a racing green Morgan Roadster. Before he reached the front door it was opened by a male servant who bade him good morning and ushered him through to his host. Maudasi was already up and dressed for business. He was wearing a dark blue pinstripe suit and a pale blue shirt matched with a navy coloured tie that had a subtle watermark pattern running through it, making it shimmer slightly. Frank was dressed in a conservative slate grey suit and looked every inch a Banker. A breakfast of cold meats, cheeses, yoghurt and fruit had been prepared, together with a selection of freshly baked bread rolls, croissants, fruit juice and coffee. They breakfasted in a grand high-ceilinged room with three large windows overlooking the old town. Maudasi wasted no time on small talk about how beautiful the view was and got straight down to business.

Their arrangements had been meticulously planned. A business associate had gone to Hong Kong to secure the deal and if all was going according to schedule, another meeting would be well underway. On offer was one metric tonne of gold, valued at almost sixty million US dollars. The asking price of the gold was a bargain at two thirds the current market value. However, there was a catch. It was available for a limited time only and would go to the first buyer who could meet the vendor's demands and come up with forty million dollars...in diamonds. Of course, the field was limited to a handful of buyers in the world and hadn't been advertised in The Wall Street Journal or the Financial Times.

Through their concerted efforts, Maudasi and Frank had secured a deal that involved a two-fold payment of twenty million dollars in the designated *currency*. The first of which would be delivered by their associate and reviewed by experts in Hong Kong, before the next stage of their business transaction could proceed. On successful review and acceptance of this initial payment, a communication from both parties would be made to Geneva to progress the next part of the trade. On receiving this call Frank would go immediately to the Woodrow Wilson hotel, on the other side of Lake Geneva, to meet with two diamond experts representing the vendors and escort them back to his bank. Maudasi would meet them there. After the usual courteous pleasantries they would all enter a high security room within the inner sanctums, where a safe deposit box would be delivered to them. Maudasi held one key to this box. The bank held the other. As Maudasi's personal representative at the bank, Frank would readily be in a position to obtain the second key at his client's behest. This box contained a fortune in diamonds, all of which had been categorised by their cut, carat, colour and clarity and sorted into groups that designated their valuation. Within this room, the experts would review all of the diamonds individually; a painstaking and lengthy process. However, with such amounts involved they were entitled to take all the time they required. Upon conclusion of their assessment, a return call would be made to Hong Kong and the trade could progress immediately to the next stage.

Diamonds were the perfect commodity for trading. Small, light in weight and easy to handle. Even a small quantity equates to a vast amount of money, making them ideal for transporting. Another reason for the vendor requesting diamonds was that money is dirty, in every respect. It can be more readily traced and difficult to put together in large quantities. Moreover, what paper currency is safe in these uncertain economic times, hence the convenience and simplistic genius of timeless currencies such as gold and diamonds.

The real problem was the gold. One metric tonne is a huge amount to move and a tradable commodity of this magnitude would attract unwelcome attention from governments and the stock markets alike. Therefore, arrangements had been made for transporting the gold out of Hong Kong on a container ship bound for Brazil. The ship had been chartered to deliver a cargo of soya beans and return with, among other things, machine parts for the mining industries there. This was a nice touch of irony, because the boxes containing these *parts* would actually be carrying a commodity already mined and refined. Another subtlety in the plan was that similar trips had already been made with genuine mining parts and so, wouldn't be anything new or out of the ordinary to arouse suspicion with customs. But just to be certain, arrangements had been made to safeguard against the shipment being interfered with or subject to scrutiny.

When the gold had been safely stored on board the container ship, the next stage of the trade could go ahead without anyone leaving the bank. Maudasi's key to the safe deposit box would simply be handed over to the vendor's representatives, while the other key would be retained by Frank's bank in Geneva. This second key would then be signed over to the vendor's designated trustee at the bank and all business would be concluded.

~

When the phone call didn't come at nine, Maudasi didn't show any concern. At nine thirty he asked Frank to check his phone for any texts or voicemail messages. At ten he instructed Frank to contact the Woodrow Wilson to apologise for the delay and placate the two waiting representatives. By ten thirty he asked Frank to check again to see if he had received any communication from Hong Kong. Frank dutifully did as he was told and checked his voicemail, email and text messages again. By eleven o'clock Maudasi was pacing the room. He was not a man who liked to be kept waiting. He called the Woodrow Wilson himself and asked to speak directly to the two representatives. When he got through to them, he turned on his mellifluous charm and apologised for their inconvenience. Frank suspected this must have been tying a knot in Maudasi's guts, because he never apologised to anyone for anything. Frank watched Maudasi talk for a few more seconds. Then he knew. He could see the colour draining from his face and his body begin to sag, as he struggled to take in what the person on the other end of the line was telling him. Maudasi didn't say goodbye or anything else when he hung up the phone. Just stood and stared out of the large windows at the cloudy sky. Frank was counting down the seconds until Maudasi exploded in an uncontrollable rage and upended the breakfast table or worse, but nothing of the sort transpired. Maudasi continued to maintain his composure.

Standing with his back to Frank, he announced in a flat tone. 'Chong is dead!'

Chapter 37

The old man smiled his lascivious smile when he opened the door, his all-consuming eyes conveying his debased longings. She smiled back. She had no objections to his lust. It always gave her great satisfaction to see men react to her in this way, even one as loathsome as this. Besides, judging by the state of his health and deathly pallor, he was most certainly incapable of acting upon his desires. He lived in a shabby apartment on Rue de Lausanne, on the right bank of Lake Geneva, not far from the train station. She had come directly from Geneva airport, having breezed through customs without arousing suspicion.

The apartment stank of old sweat and ammonia. Three cats seemed to have the run of the place. Two were lying on a beat up and tattered old sofa, while one surveyed all from a windowsill behind a filthy net curtain. All three regarded her with disdain. The old man beckoned her over to a tall, cluttered, work desk where he had positioned a high stool for her to sit. Very close to his she noted. She placed the silver attaché case on top of it and clicked it open. Inside was the package containing the merchandise: a box of twenty five cigars. When she handed the box to him he grasped it with both hands, reminding her of a Dickensian Fagan. He opened it and looked inside, then reached into a container of small precision tools and gently plucked out a silver hook resembling a crochet needle, as though he was tugging at the string on a lacy negligée. He removed one of the cigars from the box and proceeded to examine it.

After a few seconds of probing it with the needle, something popped out and made a soft clunk as it landed in the petri dish he held it over. With his thumb and forefinger, he reached in and picked up a large sparkling diamond of about three carats. He held it up for her to see it and she rewarded him by licking her lips. At that moment he didn't look so impotent. She offered no further invitation and nodded sternly at him to get on with it. Somewhat disappointed in her response, he picked up his eyeglass and held the rock under a lamp and studied it very carefully. He frowned slightly and removed the eyeglass, rubbed at his eyes for a moment then replaced it and viewed the stone again under another light. Seemingly still not satisfied, he placed it under the glare of an Ultra Violet visible spectrometer and his frown deepened. He spent several more minutes examining and reexamining it until he eventually spoke. 'This stone is synthetic.'

She blinked twice. 'That's not possible.'

~

On the way out to Hong Kong, she was on the same flight as Chong and his wife, sitting six rows behind them in business class. Prior to boarding she had closely shadowed them, intrigued to see how Chong would get the diamonds through the security scanners. Although diamonds are virtually untraceable under airport x-ray inspection, he was carrying a lot of risk. His technique however, was simplicity itself. He let his wife carry them.

Departures had been busy. Many Chinese tourists

were returning to their homeland with too much hand luggage and duty free purchases for the flight. Security remained focused and tight, performing thorough checks on the chaotic and dysfunctional masses. She'd kept her distance and a close eye on Chong and his young wife, as they edged their way closer to the x-ray scanners. She knew the diamonds were in the silver attaché case, because it was the only thing large enough to contain them and there was no way he would have put them in the hold. One thing had puzzled her at the time. Chong and his wife had gone into the duty free shopping area where he had purchased a bottle of Glenlivet single malt whisky and she a bottle of Channel No.5. Nothing odd about that; however, he'd also purchased a box of twenty five Montecristo No. 2 cigars.

On leaving the duty free area, he had gone directly to the gentlemen's rest room carrying the silver attaché case and his newly purchased box of cigars. Sticking with the diamonds, she followed him and waited for him to come out. Within minutes he re-emerged with the silver case, but no cigars. She'd been intrigued by this, because the case seemed too small to hold two boxes of cigars and whatever else he was carrying as a pretence at businessman like legitimacy.

When it was their turn to pass through security, it all became crystal clear. He handed the silver case to his wife and made a call on his cellphone, or at least pretended to. His wife moved forward and began the obligatory process of removing items of clothing and jewellery for the scanners. She appeared to be having difficulty juggling the case, along with her hand handbag and the duty fee bag, while she struggled to get out of her coat. Two young security men, who had been unable to keep their eyes off her, came over and helped her with her wares. One asked if the case contained a laptop computer and any other electronic devices, while the other relieved her of the duty free bag. The two beguiled attendants took their time asking the mundane, but necessary, security questions. Chong's wife answered with charming coyness and rewarded their tenacity and professionalism with cute little smiles all the while.

The silver case was placed on the conveyor and put through the x-ray scanner. The duty free bag containing the whisky and the perfume was passed around without going through the scanner. Security saw no need to risk liquids breaking in the machine. When his wife walked through security, Chong terminated his 'call' and quickly shed his coat and Rolex. Placed them into a plastic tray along with his cellphone then stepped through the body scanner without setting off the alarm.

Keeping a safe distance, but remaining close, she was only one person behind Chong and came through the scanner as the silver case was coming out of the x-ray machine. She noted that the wife had already taken possession of the liquids. Chong busied himself with his coat and Rolex. Another attendant requested the silver case be opened, because its metal skin had restricted the scan to some extent. Chong's wife gave no objection. Inside the case was another duty free bag, the non-sealable kind. It contained one box of cigars. The attendant removed them from the bag and looked at the receipt and then at the other duty free bag Chong's wife was holding. It appeared all had been purchased in the airport. The attendant dropped the cigars back into the bag and moved them along. Chong and his wife dutifully did as they were told and casually stepped to the side. When they'd gathered up their belongings, he helped her with her coat and took possession of the case. They both strolled away in the direction of the coffee lounge.

While watching the entire charade, it dawned on her what Chong had done. The cigars he had purchased in duty free were no more. When he'd gone to the gents they were probably flushed. All he had wanted was the receipt of purchase and the box with the correct bar code and duty free labels on it. The three hundred or so euros he'd paid for them had been an insignificant expense for this simplistic, but highly effective, ploy.

On her return trip back to the Netherlands she had seen no reason to change the method of concealment Chong had used. However, she had been careful to transfer the cigars into the box she purchased in the Hong Kong duty free shop, because Chong's box had Dutch lettering. A simple point, but one she had been careful not to overlook.

~

Now, as she stood in the shabby apartment staring at its shabbier occupant, her mind replayed it all over again. What had she missed? He held a stone up to the light and pointed out the greenish hue surrounding it like an unearthly aura. 'This is called Moissanite. Look at the colour when it catches the light, no true diamond would show this.' he announced authoritatively.

259

She demanded he check another one. He obeyed and put the stone to one side and then proceeded to follow the same process as before with another. Once again he concluded that it was exactly the same as the one before. It was most definitely not a diamond, but something of high quality that looked and felt like a diamond, making it almost impossible for anyone but an expert to authenticate. He attempted to explain, but she had tuned out. She caught some of what he said: "high-pressure"…"high-temperature"…"crystal formation methods"…"a synthetic product…"

She blinked again, only once this time and demanded he check them all. Her caustic tone was beginning to frighten him, but he obeyed nonetheless. One by one the cigars were dissected and the stones examined. When he had completed the arduous task of checking them all, he concluded that all the stones secreted within the cigars were undeniably Moissanite and most definitely not diamonds. She couldn't believe what he was saying and picked up one of the stones to examine it. She even compared it with the diamond ring she was wearing. There seemed to be no difference between them, until she held them both up to the light. The ring on her finger had no greenish hue to it, whereas the other clearly did. He eagerly informed her that he could still get her a good price for them and waited for a response. None was forthcoming. She curtly told him to gather them up and place them back into the box. Motivated by fear, he willingly obliged. When he was done, she placed the box back inside the silver attaché case and snapped it shut. As he proceeded to clean up the debris from the cigars he furtively watched her, silently awaiting her next instruction. When he'd completed his task she smiled at the little man and placed her hand against his cheek as a reward for his services. 'Merci, Monsieur Claude.'

His eyes twinkled with the exquisite pleasure of her touch and then clamped tightly shut, as she thrust the silver hooked crochet needle into his left eyeball…all the way to the back of his brain.

Chapter 38

Frank was bug eyed with disbelief at Maudasi's stark revelation. His mouth had gone bone dry and he could hear his heart beating like a base drum in his ears. He started to hyperventilate and thought he was going to pass out. Reaching into his jacket pocket, he took out a packet of Prozac and fumbled to get one out. Popped it into his gaping mouth and washed it down with cold coffee. He'd started taking them six weeks ago and his dependency was increasing. His endeavours were taking their toll. Wiping his mouth with a napkin he stammered.

'Dead? That…that's not possible.'

Maudasi, still fixated on the gathering storm outside, turned around at Frank's statement and stared at him with a cold hardness. His eyes drilled into him, searching for an answer, looking for someone to blame; demanding retribution. The intensity of his glare was such, that Frank thought it might turn him to stone. He knew he had to say something. Speak for Christ sake.

'Chong's dead? H…how do they know this? What did they say?'

Maudasi continued to glare at him with the intense concentration of a blow torch, processing the information he'd just received and coming to a decision, 'Call Chong.'

Frank looked at him, 'B…but if he's dead?'

Maudasi almost chewed his head off, 'CALL HIM NOW!'

Frank hesitated momentarily then groped for his

cellphone. He speed dialled Chong's number. It rang out for a long time before it went to voicemail. He left a message requesting he contact him as soon as possible and ended the call. As well as being Maudasi's banker he was Chong's too. So, this was an entirely customary, but non incriminating message to leave on his phone. Maudasi was scrutinising his every twitch and gesture. Frank stared back, seeking an explanation, waiting for the punch line. Neither came. Exactly one minute later, Frank's cellphone rang out, making him jump. He stared at the caller display with disbelief and almost had an apoplexy. It continued to ring and Frank continued to stare. His face had turned ashen. Maudasi snapped at him. 'Aren't you going to answer it?'

Frank's mouth was working, but no sounds came forth. Maudasi bellowed at him, 'ANSWER THE DAMN PHONE!'

Frank looked up with a glassy expression and announced, 'It...it's Chong!'

More colour drained from his face at the terrifying, but unlikely possibility of hearing a ghostly voice from beyond the grave. To his indescribable relief it turned out not to be the spectre of death, but a member of the Hong Kong Police. They had listened to the message he'd just left on Chong's cellphone and made the decision to call back. However, they wouldn't say exactly what the situation was. They didn't have to. It confirmed with absolute assuredness Chong was dead. They informed him that they would contact him again in the near future and terminated the call. Frank relayed this information to Maudasi, who appeared to be indifferent to the fact that his deal had gone sour and the guy in charge of millions of dollars of his diamonds, thousands of miles away, was dead and that they were now in the hands of God knows who. Frank fleetingly entertained the notion that Maudasi had stronger Prozac than him.

Chapter 39

Thursday, 5th May. Amsterdam.

Helena left to go to work in her Amsterdam office at 08:30, leaving Dirk with a pot of coffee and a contented smile on his face. Immediately after she'd gone, he got up and routinely checked that the money was still in his jacket pocket. He pulled on his jeans and followed the tantalizing aroma into the kitchen. Helena made great coffee, among other things. Still spooked by the notion of Dragan secretly entering his apartment, he showered in Helena's rather than his own. He didn't relish the idea of standing naked in the shower while Dragan looked on or worse…had a pee. The thought crossed his mind that maybe he should just stay with Helena until Frank got back; she had even left him a key.

When he'd finished drying himself off, he tucked his jacket under the bed then went downstairs to his own apartment for a change of clothes. He was relieved to see it was exactly as he'd left it last night and even more relieved to see there were no more cigars in the ashtray. Upstairs in his bedroom, his wardrobe looked a little depleted. At the bottom lay his laundry from the other day. He regarded the crumpled pile of clothing lying there and groaned. Realising there was no way of avoiding the mundane task of ironing before going out for the day, he took it all downstairs and dumped it on top of the sofa then went in search of an ironing board and an iron. There was neither in the apartment and he hadn't seen one in his own upstairs area. He hadn't noticed one in Helena's apartment either, but then he hadn't been looking. Curiosity kicked in and he opened the apartment door to the communal hallway. Sure enough, there was a utility cupboard built in to the opposite wall. Opening it, he discovered that it not only housed the electrical and gas meters to the building, but was also the storage area for a brush, a bucket with a mop and an ironing board and an iron. He grabbed what he was after and nudged the cupboard door shut with his elbow. When he turned around he noticed a neatly folded piece of paper lying on the carpet by the front outside door. Propping the ironing board up against the wall, he bent down and picked it up. It was a note written in beautiful penmanship. It read: '*Meet me in Café Heuvel at noon today.*' It wasn't signed. At first the possibility that it wasn't intended for him didn't enter his mind. But then he thought, maybe Helena has a secret admirer and it was for her. But if it was for him then it could only have come from a small number of people. Both possibilities caused him concern. He looked at his watch, it wasn't yet ten. Two hours to think about it. He stuffed the note into his jeans pocket, picked up the ironing board and went back into the apartment. Locked the door behind him and put the chain on.

Before embarking on the exhaustive task of ironing that lay before him, he fuelled up with a Red Bull. He switched on the giant TV to scan for some more entertaining MTV buttocks and was more than satisfied when he found a channel showing Madonna's top ten videos. It took him forty five minutes and one more Red Bull to complete his chore. He flopped down on the sofa and flicked through the channels again and stopped at CNN news. Nothing much was new in the world and he was about to switch channels when the newsreader started talking about a double murder in a Hong Kong hotel. It's amazing how the word murder grabs your attention. Dirk sat there and watched as the correspondent *in situ* outlined in detail that a husband and wife had been shot dead in their hotel suite. No motive for the killings had yet been established. Dirk shook his head and said to himself, 'It's a crazy old world out there.'

He flicked back to the music channels and stopped when the gyrating form of J-Lo filled the screen. His stomach rumbled and he got up and went into the kitchen to get something to eat and maybe a coffee. Thoughts of food reminded him of the lunchtime invitation on the note he'd found in the hallway. With some trepidation, he took it out of his pocket and looked at it again. Frowning, he considered the implications intimated by the note. Was it a request or a demand? He considered calling Helena and asking her it if was from her. But what if it wasn't? That could prove to be awkward and embarrassing for them both.

Deciding to bite the bullet, he concluded that since the meeting was in a public place there would be no harm in finding out. He put on a pot of coffee and sat back down. Two cups and several stimulating music videos later, he glanced at his watch. It was creeping closer to noon. He took his newly ironed clothes upstairs, stripped off his clothes from the day before and put on fresh ones, then came back down with another load to wash. As he put his dirty laundry into the washing machine an idea came into his head. He dashed back upstairs to Helena's apartment and retrieved his jacket from under the bed. Back downstairs, he took the remainder of the fifty thousand out of the pocket and walked over to the washing machine. Pulled out a dirty sock and stuffed the money inside. He placed it at the bottom of the pile. 'Now that's how to launder money', he said out loud. Closing the small round glass door he stood up and had a last look around the apartment, before heading out to meet the mystery postman. It was eleven fifty five.

Dirk walked away from the apartment building in the opposite direction from the café and crossed over to the other side of the canal. He intended to approach from a different angle to get an idea of who, or what, he was walking into. He ran through all possibilities as to whom the author of the note could be. It seemed too polite and proper to have come from Dragan. That definitely wasn't his style. It hadn't come from Frank either, because he wasn't here. Maybe it *was* Helena who'd delivered it and she didn't want to disturb him? No, scratch that, she would have slipped a note under the apartment door, not leave it lying in the hallway. Before the fourth and final possibility entered his mind, he saw him sitting outside; nonchalantly having a coffee. Jason Sinclair was alert because he saw him too and waved cheerfully, as if they were old friends just meeting up for a cosy lunch or whatever. What an unbelievable character.

'Good morning Dirk, you're looking extremely well, Amsterdam must agree with you.' Jason said affably.

'Hello Jason, sending love notes now?'

Jason shrugged, 'Well I didn't want to knock you up, just in case you were busy engaging in something similar.' He laughed at his own little witticism.

Dirk didn't react, just looked at him blankly. 'Well, Jason, this better be important because I think Frank made his feelings very clear the other day and I don't think he would warm to the idea of a blossoming friendship between us. Do you?'

Jason invited him to sit down and asked if he wanted a coffee. Dirk accepted. He had to admit he was relieved that it wasn't Dragan who'd sent the note. Even so, Dirk wasted no time starting in. 'Ok, what's this all about?'

'Just like Perrier, straight down to business.' remarked Jason.

'That's the thing Jason. I'm not here on business, I'm here on holiday. Remember?'

'Of course you are, but I'm sure if you had the opportunity to make a little easy money you wouldn't turn it down; now would you?'

'It isn't something I've given any thought to.' answered Dirk, guardedly.

Jason smiled, 'Well, let me see if I can provoke some thoughts?'

'You've already provoked me by disrupting my day.'

Jason ignored the disparaging remark and continued with his agenda, 'Are you a wealthy man Dirk?'

'What?'

'Are you happy with your status in life? What I mean is; do you have enough money never to have to work again?'

Dirk didn't want to tell this condescending piece of

269

shit anything about himself, but he was riled up. 'I've done ok.'

'Ah, but you still have to dance to someone else's tune to earn a living, before the wheels of industry grind you down and the government throws you a pittance of a pension don't you?'

Dirk wanted to smack the spoiled bastard in the face and maybe give him another kick in the balls, but refrained and sipped his coffee before answering. 'Only if I'm unlucky enough to live that long; what about you, has Daddy got the rest of the family silver all polished and ready to join your spoon?'

Jason snorted, 'I can understand why you would think that of me, but no, I don't have an enormous family inheritance to look forward to; I'm just like you really, stumbling through life, looking for a way to earn a simple living.'

Dirk didn't feel insulted by Jason's inference that they were kindred spirits. In fact, he was amused by it. The guy really was more delusional than he'd given him credit. Dirk ruminated that this encounter could be highly entertaining and quite illuminating; not least considering it would make a great story for when Frank returned. Letting himself relax and go with the flow, he decided to have some fun and string Jason along.

'So, Jason, what's this all about, why do you really want to see me?'

Jason regarded him warily before answering. 'Where do you think Frank gets his diamonds from?'

'I've no idea. A diamond dealer would be my guess. They're all around this part of the world.'

'What about the diamonds he gave to me? Where do

270

you think he got them from? Did he just happen to have them on him? You were with him. It was rather a lot to be just carrying around, don't you think?'

Dirk shrugged, 'I haven't given it any thought. He gave you diamonds for your coins in London too, didn't he? Why are you so interested to know where he gets them from all of a sudden?'

Jason's eyes flashed and Dirk, realising that he shouldn't have alluded to having that knowledge, immediately regretted saying what he'd said.

'Aren't you...interested I mean? Your friend gets his hands on forty thousand in diamonds just like that...' Jason snapped his fingers. '...and you don't give it a second thought. Come on, don't treat me like a fool, he's got a source here. Wouldn't you like to get in on that?'

'I couldn't afford to buy diamonds.' said Dirk, indifferently.

Jason was studying him, considering his next move. Dirk waited unwearyingly for him to make it.

'I was in the cigar lounge of Hotel des Indes the other day.' announced Jason.

'Really? No shit, Jason.'

Jason sniffed at this as if to say, so you caught me, big deal.

'Aren't you intrigued to know why Frank asked me to meet him in Den Haag to give me the diamonds and not here in Amsterdam?'

Dirk was reluctant to talk or even speculate about his friend's business practices, but he remembered Frank telling Jason he had a meeting in Den Haag that very day. He saw no harm in pointing it out. 'He had a meeting there on Monday. In fact, I remember him mentioning that to you. I guess he thought he could kill two birds with one stone.'

'Quite a few stones actually. So you agree that he picked the diamonds up in Den Haag? Where was his meeting before you both met with me?'

Dirk gave nothing away, 'I'm not privy to that information. I don't know where his meeting was or with whom and if I did know anything, I wouldn't discuss it with anyone; least of all you.'

Dirk knew he should terminate this conversation, but was smart enough to grasp that if he walked away now, he would only confirm all of Jason's warped, or otherwise, suspicions. He sipped at his coffee.

Jason persisted, 'Aren't you at all interested in finding out? Frank most likely has a few more diamonds stashed away somewhere close, probably along with the coin I sold him and maybe some cash too?'

Dirk looked at Jason in astonishment. 'Are you suggesting we rob Frank and split the proceeds Jason?'

'No, of course not, what do you take me for?' huffed Jason.

Dirk refrained from giving him the answer that immediately sprung to mind. 'So, what are you saying then?'

'I'm saying he's got a source for buying diamonds, at trade price or less, even you can't deny that. I think he's become blasé about it and keeps his working stock stashed somewhere within easy access, in case he needs them in a hurry; like he did on Monday. And if he has become that blasé then there has to be more than enough to go around. Wouldn't you like to have just a little bit of that Mister Dirk?'

Dirk ignored the dig. 'I think you've blown any opportunity to get involved with Frank after you pissed him off.'

'How did I piss him off, just because I sought to get a better deal for myself?'

Jason seemed to be suffering from short term memory loss or amnesia. Maybe the kick in the nuts had given him brain damage. Dirk attempted to point out Jason's shortcomings. 'I think you know you could have handled a lot of things better than you did Jason.'

Jason wasn't listening. 'I can get more coins. He'll talk to me again if you suggest it to him…and if you help me, I'll cut you in on any deals we make. What do you say…Dirk?'

Dirk couldn't believe this character, acting like his best pal and trying to make deals with him against his best pal. Recollecting his conversation with Dragan and the fact he wanted to meet with Jason, to strike a deal for any coins he had to sell, Dirk considered proposing an introduction. Dragan would give him a lesson in business management he'd never forget. But knowing that wouldn't meet with Frank's approval, he decided to withhold this information.

'Are you done Jason, because I am? I don't know what you expected to gain from this little rendezvous, but if it was an attempt to ruin my day then you've failed. I think we should just say goodbye and leave it at that ok?'

Jason wasn't done. He had another impertinent request to make. 'You don't happen to have any more of those wonderful cigars do you? I seem to have misplaced the last one Frank gave me and I'd love another one right now.'

'Why don't you go back to Den Haag for one, that'll give you an excuse to search for Frank's stash won't it?'

'What a good idea. Can you suggest where I begin?'

'Goodbye Jason.'

Jason had one last parting comment to make. 'I'm disappointed in you Mister Dirk Dagger. I thought I saw something of an entrepreneurial streak in you. Frank should show more appreciation and share his good fortune with you. I certainly would, with a loyal partner of your dedication.'

Dirk sardonically wished him good luck and said goodbye once more then watched him flounce across the canal bridge, no doubt in search of a dedicated partner.

With Jason out of his hair, Dirk contemplated lunch. However, the unsavoury nature of the encounter had stemmed his appetite. He was left with a queasy feeling and didn't like the idea of Jason creeping up to his front door to deliver notes or for any other reason. Troubling as it was it brought another problem sharply back into focus, something that made him very uncomfortable. That something was Dragan. He'd been in the apartment and that was way further out of his comfort zone. But on an even more disturbing level, both he and Jason seemed to regard him as the conduit to achieving their goals. He could see it being a serious pain the arse if the two of them somehow did team up. Finishing his coffee, he dropped two euros on the table for a tip. Stood up and returned to the apartment at a brisk pace. He suspected Dragan would be back to pay him a visit and probably Jason too. He didn't want to be home if either of them turned up again.

Prioritising on what he considered to be essential, he threw some clothes into his travel case together with his laptop. Next he went and retrieved the money hidden in his sock in the washing machine. His plan was to stash the cash upstairs in Helena's apartment and keep it close, but not in her washing machine. That carried too much of a risk of her finding it. He hoped his moving in wouldn't freak her out, but he'd play it down by telling her that the landlord has people coming and going while Frank is away and that he's not comfortable with strangers being around his personal stuff. He made the decision not to unpack his case and hang his clothes up in her closet, because that would probably freak her out. When he was packed and ready to leave, he tore off a small strip of paper from a magazine then, mimicking something he had seen in countless movies, placed it in the door jamb and closed the apartment door.

The first thing he did when he got upstairs to Helena's apartment was to head straight for the kitchen with the money. Her cooker looked like it had never been used either. He went into the bedroom and put his case under the bed, in the hope of making his moving in as unobtrusive as possible. Satisfied he'd done the right thing, Dirk decided to get out of the apartment for a while to clear his head.

The weather was fair and he walked for quite a distance around the city, ending up at the bar that brewed its own beer again. This time he sat inside and spent a chilled hour looking out of the window, just watching people. Around three o'clock, he texted

Helena and asked if she'd like to go anywhere nice for dinner this evening. She texted back: *'call later'*. Realising she was probably busy or in a meeting or something, he decided to kill the time by walking around some more.

He cut through the red light district, marvelling and shuddering at the sights both inside and outside the windows. It was grotesquely entertaining, but he didn't linger. Before he knew it, he found himself in Chinatown. The aromas stirred his taste buds and he realised he still hadn't eaten anything yet. It would be hours before he met with Helena. The street was long and full of restaurants, but none of them appealed. Most were too large and touristy for a lone diner. He continued on, amazed at the number of coffee shops there were mingled in amongst them. There seemed to be one every twenty meters and the smell of reefer was overwhelming. Reaching the end of the street, unsuccessful in his search for somewhere suitable to eat, he was about to turn around and go back when he suddenly froze. Parked up in a side street was the big Black Bentley.

Chapter 40

The past few hours had been pure torture. Maudasi had gone off to make enquiries, or whatever it was he was doing in another part of the house. The doors to the breakfast room had been closed, leaving Frank alone and isolated behind them. He endured this snub for an hour before he attempted to open them. However, when he tried to leave the room a servant materialised, as if transported from the USS enterprise, to tell him: *Mister Maudasi had requested he remain where he was for the time being and that all his needs would be catered for, should he require anything.* Frank reluctantly accepted his situation and asked for some more water. An hour after his first attempt to leave the room, he made another. When the same message was conveyed he asked for a pot of strong coffee. At three pm he insisted on speaking with Maudasi. The servant looked at him as if to say *is that wise?* Frank was decisive, *yes damn it*, he demanded to see him. Things had clearly not gone to plan and he was desperate for answers. The servant assured Frank he would see what he could do and closed the doors on him again. Thirty minutes later, the doors were thrown open and two servants came in with a platter of food and a bottle of wine. Frank began to protest, but Maudasi appeared behind them dressed casually in an open necked shirt and a pair of tailored Cashmere slacks and calfskin loafers.

'You must be tired of waiting Frank', was all he said, as if he'd taken too long with his putt on the eighteenth green.

Frank was exhausted with the stress of not knowing.

Maudasi had obviously showered and changed and done God knows what else to make him so relaxed. Maybe he had taken a couple of Prozac and washed them down with a large malt whisky? Frank wanted to do the same. Maudasi gestured that Frank sit and remarked, nonchalantly, 'I'm quite famished; my sudden rise in blood pressure seems to have given me an appetite.'

Maudasi proceeded to select some meat from the food tray, followed by feta cheese and Kalamata olives, while Frank looked on in disbelief. He poured himself some wine and filled Frank's glass too. Frank remained standing, trying to gauge the change in the situation. However, nothing in Maudasi's countenance gave anything away. Maudasi, with his mouth full, gestured for Frank to sit again.

'My God Sadim how can you be so calm? Chong's been murdered.' spluttered Frank.

Maudasi leaned back in his chair and wiped his mouth with a napkin. He looked Frank straight in the eye. 'Who said anything about murder?'

Frank suddenly felt like the mouse to Maudasi's cat, but recovered quickly with a feasible hypothesis. 'Surely with the police being in Chong's hotel suite indicates that it was no accident?'

Maudasi countered with one of his own. 'He could have had a heart attack, a seizure or a stroke; maybe he committed Hara-Kiri. Are none of those possibilities worth a consideration? The hotel would still have an obligation to inform the police about a death on their premises. Why do you assume it was murder?'

Frank was on the back foot. 'If it was anything other

than murder, I don't think the Hong Kong police would have been so quick to answer a call from his banker, do you?' His answer was delivered with such keen logic and confidence that, just for a moment, Maudasi was forced to reconsider. He quickly changed the subject. 'You still haven't asked about the diamonds Frank.'

Frank strived to be the pragmatist in the face of adversity. 'I'm assuming the worst, that he was killed for the diamonds.'

Frank knew Maudasi would have assumed this too and had no doubt deduced and eliminated all probable scenarios. 'But who could have known he had the diamonds?'

Frank considered his answer to Maudasi's rhetoric with great care, 'I only know what you know Sadim, probably less.'

Frank thought he detected the trace of a smile from Maudasi, but he could have been mistaken.

'I know that Chong is dead. But you are correct in your assumption, it *was* murder. He was shot...twice. His wife was shot too.' announced Maudasi, somehow managing to make this sound superfluous and trivial.

Frank shrank some more at this revelation, 'His wife?'

Maudasi didn't skip a beat, 'I know we no longer have a deal for the gold because of this misfortune and I know we have a problem with the diamonds. I also know we can't go to the police. But all of this is academic, because I shall know all there is to know soon.'

Frank was still reeling with the news of Chong's wife, when Maudasi blindsided him again. 'Tell me more about your two friends.'

Chapter 41

Dirk was positive it was the same car. It was too much of a coincidence for it not to be, although he'd need confirmation. Looking around, he saw a coffee shop within spitting distance just opposite where the Bentley was parked. He crossed over and went inside. The room was small and very dark and the pall of smoke was so thick that he couldn't make out any discernible shapes of people in there. The music coming from the overhead speaker sounded like the mournful dirge of lost souls and for a moment he thought he'd stumbled into a witches' coven. His eyes accustomed quickly and he glanced around. Apart from one member of staff there were only two other patrons, both of whom sat with heads bowed swaying hypnotically to the music, their long greasy hair covering their faces. Maybe it was a coven? The barman acknowledged him and didn't seem to object that he obviously wasn't one of their tribe. Dirk ordered a coffee and a diet coke. When he declined the reefer menu, the dreadlocked Dutchman just shrugged. Dirk sat at a corner table out of sight, but with a good enough vantage position to see out.

Forty five minutes, three coffees and two diet cokes later, Dragan emerged from a small Chinese restaurant. Dirk shrank back impulsively although, through the gloom of the coffee shop and the reefer smoke, he couldn't be seen. Dragan didn't even bother to look around and got into the Bentley. The car didn't immediately start up and move off, it just sat there. Several minutes passed. Dirk couldn't see what Dragan was doing behind the tinted glass, but figured he was probably making a call. Dirk took out his cellphone and made a call of his own.

Chapter 42

Maudasi's cellphone rang and he left the room to take the call in private. Frank was desperate to find out exactly what had gone wrong in Hong Kong, but could do nothing from within the gilded cage in which he was confined. Minutes later, he received a text message from Dirk asking him to call whenever it was convenient. With Maudasi out of the room, he saw no time like the present and immediately rang his friend back. Dirk answered on the first ring and sounded very relieved to hear from him. Frank was equally pleased to speak with a friendly voice and asked if he was having a good time. Dirk reciprocated by asking how his business trip was going. Frank said he'd had better. Dirk empathised and said that if he was busy then he could call back another time. Frank said it was alright and that he had a few moments to spare.

Dirk began by apologising for contacting him, but felt that due to recent circumstances it was warranted. He explained what had prompted the call and told him where he was and what he was looking at. He recited the car's number plate and then went on to recount his threatening visit from Dragan, mentioning the fact that he'd let himself into the apartment on at least one occasion. Frank asked if he was sure and Dirk gave him the reasons why he was convinced someone else had been in the apartment. He also mentioned the note he'd received from Jason and their bizarre meeting, but withheld some of the details of their conversation. When he'd finished telling his tale, the silence on the

282

other end of the phone was palpable and he had to ask if Frank was still there. The sound of deep, measured breathing confirmed he was. When Frank finally answered, he tried to sound upbeat and in control, but Dirk could tell by the tone of his friend's voice that he was unnerved and more than a little concerned by everything he'd just been told. Frank ended the call by saying he would take care of it and that Dirk was not to worry. Before Dirk could say goodbye, the line went dead.

Chapter 43

A full fifteen minutes passed before the big car fired up and powered away. Dirk waited another five before he left the wholesome environment of the coffee shop. Feeling a little light headed in the fresh air environment of exhaust fumes and fast food stalls he weaved his way across to the Chinese restaurant and stopped outside the window. While pretending to peruse the menu, a black BMW seven series in mint condition pulled up. Three young Chinese guys wearing dark suits and sunglasses got out and entered the restaurant, each of them giving him a mean look as they walked past. The last one to go inside turned the sign on the door around to 'Closed' and locked it behind him. Dirk looked on as this disturbing triad went straight through the small dining area and into the kitchen at the back. He thought they were the best dressed chefs he had ever seen. Taking the closed sign as a hint he should move on, Dirk headed back in the direction of the brewery bar. As he walked, he reflected on what he'd just witnessed, but the more he considered all the possibilities, the more anxious he became. The thought crossed his mind that maybe he should just leave them all to it and go back to Bristol. However, this notion angered him even to consider it as an option. Why the hell should he leave? He was on holiday. He'd met the most beautiful girl and had done nothing wrong, except stay in a diabolically rich megalomaniac's apartment for God's sake. Helena eventually called and told him she would be finishing work in about an hour or so and would like to be finishing her first beer very soon after that. He told her where he was heading and she agreed to meet him there. He hung up and picked up his pace.

At five thirty Helena appeared looking as fabulous as always. Several male heads turned and gazed at her longingly when she skipped into view. She wore her Marilyn Monroe smile and all his thoughts of Dragan et al dissipated in an instant. She was so lovely that Dirk was reluctant to spoil her exuberance by mentioning the events of his day, so instead asked about hers. She told him that her article was progressing well and that she was looking forward to going back to Den Haag to take some pictures of *that bastard*, as she referred to the Serbian war criminal on trial. Dirk was keen to know more, but she seemed reluctant to expand on it and changed the subject. They talked about food and she offered to cook. He told her that he didn't want her to get dish pan hands and had to explain what he meant by that. She laughed at his quirky British sayings and informed him she was an excellent cook and would prove it tonight. He made a mental note to get the money out of the oven when they got back to her apartment. They had one beer each then went to find a supermarket. She bought the ingredients for a spaghetti Bolognese and selected two bottles of Italian Chianti. Dirk tried to dissuade her from buying wine and reminded her of Frank's limitless stock back in his apartment. She shooed him away, telling him that she was the chef and would decide what wine they were having. He backed off and smiled at how much she was enjoying the process of putting together the ingredients for their supper. He asked her what they were having for dessert and she leaned in, kissed him on the mouth and squeezed his bum; much to the mirth of the elderly couple standing behind them at the checkout.

On the way home Dirk suggested they stop for *just the one* at Café Heuvel. She was amenable to that idea and in a good mood. Deciding now was a good time, he told her he had moved some of his stuff into her apartment and why. She sat and listened to him attentively and then, much to his relief, threw her arms around his neck and said that she hoped the intruders would be in his apartment day and night forever. He tried to play it down by emphasizing Frank would be returning sometime at the weekend and would resolve any issues with the landlord etcetera. He said he hoped it wouldn't be a problem for her. She said *"no problem cowboy"* and kissed him again. After their one drink they walked all the way back holding hands.

Once they were inside, Dirk immediately checked his paper trap in the door jamb of Frank's apartment. To his monumental relief, it was still in place. She shook her head in bewilderment at the depth of his paranoia and told him she could recommend a good psychiatrist. He thanked her for her concern, but declined the offer. Dirk didn't open the door and they continued up to her apartment. When the opportunity presented itself, he retrieved his money from Helena's oven. He saw no point in telling her about it as she might think it was drug money and that would freak her out. He put it back in his coat pocket, zipped it up and casually threw it over a chair.

Helena's spaghetti Bolognese was superb and she was delighted when he requested seconds, but advised him to leave room for dessert. After dinner, they made themselves comfortable for the evening on the sofa. As she kicked off her cowboy boots, her dress fluttered up slightly, giving him a tantalising flash of what looked like expensive lingerie. She got up to close the shutters in the lounge windows and informed him that there were no men outside wearing trench coats. He sarcastically told her how witty she was and they both laughed. When she dimmed the lights he knew it was time for dessert.

Chapter 44

That evening Maudasi insisted upon Frank dining with him again in his town house. Frank suspected the game was to keep him close and in a mental stress position until more information came forth. They both watched the news coverage of the Hong Kong Hotel Killings on CNN. The news reporter stated that a husband and wife had been found shot and killed in their hotel suite, but no further details had been released regarding the exact nature of the shooting. Their identities were being withheld until relatives of the deceased had been notified. This information they already knew. However, the reporter intimated that it may have been a contract killing. Both Frank and Maudasi watched the report grim faced.

Frank spoke first, 'Why kill them?'

Maudasi was impassive, but philosophical. 'Why is of no consequence. What matters is who. Because, when we know who, we find the diamonds.'

Frank shuddered as he considered what Maudasi's answer would be to the question "What then?"

The brooding look on Frank's face prompted Maudasi to ask. 'Why the long face Frank? Is there something on your mind? Something you would like to say?'

Frank wrestled with his thoughts and words for a few moments before speaking, 'Sadim, forgive me for asking, but why is Dragan harassing my friend?'

Maudasi gave Frank a curious look, 'I wasn't aware that he was?'

Frank wasn't in the mood for more cat and mouse games and just came right out with it.

'My friend Dirk, the one staying in my apartment, informs me that Dragan came to see him yesterday and asked about Jason Sinclair. He wanted to know if he had any more coins to sell.'

Maudasi was unashamedly forthright in his reply. 'Do you have a problem with that? I asked Dragan to find out if your friend had anything that may be of interest that's all. I didn't see any point in letting an opportunity go to waste in your absence.'

Frank hesitated before answering, 'Well, that doesn't explain why Dragan was in the apartment when my friend was out.'

Maudasi looked mildly mystified, 'Why don't we ask Dragan to explain his actions tomorrow?'

Now it was Frank's turn to be mystified, 'Tomorrow?'

'Yes, I don't see any point in remaining in Geneva, do you?'

Chapter 45

Neither Frank nor Maudasi received any more calls for the remainder of the evening, for which Frank was truly thankful. Desperate to get away, he manoeuvred his exit by asking what time he should return in the morning. "Early" was the curt reply. Hong Kong was seven hours ahead and there was much to do. Maudasi finally dismissed him just before midnight.

Frank pulled his Porsche into Natalie's driveway and turned off his adrenalin. He didn't get out. Just sat there listening to the noises of the engine as it settled and began to cool off. It had been a prolonged and arduous day and he needed to do the same. He was desperate for answers.

Natalie's Porsche was parked beside his. The two cars were identical, apart from the steering columns. They were on opposite sides. He glanced at it introspectively and desperately wanted to speak with her. Exhausted, he remained in his car for several minutes before heaving himself out of the low slung driver's seat and into the house.

The panoramic lounge window gave him enough light with which to see, without having to turn on the lights. In the soothing gloom he walked over to the drinks cabinet and fixed himself a generous glass of Armagnac. Took a long drink and topped it up. Turning around, he walked across the great room and up the three short steps to the large window overlooking Lake Geneva. The evening view of the tranquil Lake usually provided solace, but as he looked out and sipped his elixir he could see only the image of an aged and anxious man staring back. He took another drink and felt its fire within trickling down his throat and into his tumultuous stomach. His wretched reflection held his stare for a long moment, until he had to turn away.

He walked back down the three short steps. Kicked off his shoes and went upstairs, drink in hand, to run a bath. On entering the bedroom, he glanced with melancholic longing at the emptiness of the bed, where he'd spent countless memorable moments with Natalie. Continuing on through to the en-suite, he proceeded to fill the sizeable sunken bath with hot water. As the water tumbled out, he added some bath foam and left the water running while he stripped off. Sitting there, on the lid of the toilet seat, waiting for the bath to fill, he regarded his now depleted glass and decided to top that up too. He trotted back downstairs naked and filled it almost to the brim. By the time he got back upstairs, his foaming therapy was ready and waiting. After checking the temperature of the water, Frank stepped in and lay down. His plan was to soak in it until he had fully imbibed his generous anaesthetiser. He also planned to sleep downstairs in the lounge tonight, on top of the supersized L-shaped sofa. The early morning sunlight streaming in through the large window would ensure he didn't oversleep. As he lay in his bath, under the subdued overhead lighting, he closed his eyes and tried to push all negative thoughts out of his head. Nothing had come off the rails yet. Not as far as he was concerned. However, he needed confirmation before he could genuinely feel secure. Suddenly, his security was rocked to its core and his nervous system took another jolt, when the smoky voice standing in the doorway fractured the silence, 'Bonsoir Francois.'

The unexpected presence shattered his fragile peace. Frank banged his head against the rim of the bath and almost dropped his glass into it. 'Jesus Christ, you almost gave me heart failure. When did you get here?'

She came all the way into the bathroom and looked at Frank lying in his bubble bath: a flaccid wet form, pink and hairless. 'You don't have a heart Francois.' she said pointedly.

As she stood there looking down at him, Frank suddenly felt exposed and vulnerable. 'Pass me that towel over there, will you'.

'Please, remain where you are. I'm sure you've had a very distressing day. Relax and enjoy your Armagnac.'

Frank did as he was told and sank back into the water, but regarded her with suspicion. 'Did you kill Chong?'

'Yes, I'm afraid I did.'

'And his wife too?'

She gave him a withering look.

'Why?' demanded Frank.

She shrugged nonchalantly. Killing Chong and his wife had not bothered her in the slightest. They had merely been a means to an end. Her real concern had always been that once Chong and his wife had seen her, they could identify her. She gazed at the large diamond ring on her finger. It was a little tight for her third finger, but fitted her little finger perfectly. She would have it resized when she had the time to do so. 'I saw an opportunity and I took it.' She said, holding up her hand and wiggling her fingers.

'I had a call from the Hong Kong police.' said Frank.

'You did?'

'They want to talk to me again about Chong.'

'They do?'

'There was a report on CNN this evening about it; they're calling it a contract killing.'

'That sounds like good news. No?'

'No, it's bloody well not. We don't need the Hong Kong police involved and that's what you've done by killing Chong and his wife.'

She shrugged again, 'It takes the focus away from anyone else; namely you Francois.'

'Maudasi is outraged. He'll look under every rock and every stone until he's satisfied. If you hadn't killed Chong it would have just been his word that he was robbed…against a ghost's.'

She remained unperturbed. 'I am so glad you mentioned rocks and stones Francois. For a moment I was beginning to think you'd forgotten.'

She knelt down and ran her fingers in his bath water. Frank continued to look at her warily. He swallowed hard and took another drink, then made an attempt to change the subject. 'I always liked that dress. You do it justice.'

'Thank you Francois, it's very gracious of you to say so. However, I am not here for compliments.'

Frank wished his glass was fuller. 'So, why are you here?'

'Well, I decided I couldn't wait, because I believe if I did, I don't think the diamonds would be safe for very much longer.'

'What do you mean?'

She gave Frank a reproachful look. 'You know what I mean Francois. I've checked the diamonds and I know they are fakes. You have some explaining to do.'

Frank was in no position to contradict her. Instead, he attempted to rationalise her discovery. 'I thought that if you knew they were fakes, then you might have handled things differently.'

She was no fool. 'I did handle things differently; I killed Chong…and his wife. But I fail to see any logic in your explanation other than to trick me into thinking I was stealing actual diamonds.'

Frank had his speech all prepared. 'That's exactly what I wanted you to think. Consider this; what if Chong had opened up the cigar box and discovered that there were no diamonds in there at all, just cigars? We would have blown it immediately right? But if he did open one or even two, then he would have seen what he thought were real diamonds. He would never have suspected in a million years that he'd been given fakes. He would never have scrutinised them. Now, these synthetic stones would have been immediately spotted as fakes if he'd attempted to present them at the trade; that's why he had to be relieved him of them. He reports back to Maudasi that they've been stolen, but we've had the real stones safely hidden away the whole time. No one is any the wiser.'

Frank showed balls, sitting there naked in his bath, lying to her face. She was impressed, but her patience was thin. 'Why not just tell me this and I could have just dumped the fakes in Hong Kong Harbour, instead of risking customs by bringing them back. Were you hoping I'd get caught?'

'No, don't be ridiculous. It was…it's just…look, knowing you as I do, even you have to admit, had you known they were fakes, you wouldn't have been as motivated to recover them.' Frank risked a smile before continuing. 'It worked didn't it…and another thing…these fakes, as you put it, are worth a quite a bit of money. I wanted them back.'

She smiled back and continued to run her hands through the bubbles in the bath water. 'So, Francois, where are the real diamonds?'

Frank made a valiant attempt to sound confident and reassuring, 'Don't worry, I have them in a safe place under lock and key.'

'Where?' she asked again.

'Don't you trust me?'

'No Francois. I don't'

Frank couldn't think of an answer to that, but made an attempt to gain control of the situation. 'Let me get out of this bath before I'm cooked and I'll tell you ok?'

'No, it's not ok. Tell me where the diamonds are. Right now.' she demanded, this time with a lot more menace in her voice. Frank protested like a petulant child and started to get up. 'Look, I'm tired and I need to get some sleep. I have to deal with Maudasi really early tomorrow, so enough of this nonsense, I'm getting out.'

She raised her hand and pointed a gun at him. Frank almost flavoured his water at the sight of it. But then he relaxed. The gun she held was an 1892 French military revolver, from his private collection of antiques. 'That's mine. What are you doing with it?' he asked with indignation.

'What do you think I am doing Francois? I am here, with you, discussing diamonds. Now, I want to know where they are and don't lie to me again.'

'What are you going to do, shoot me?' asked Frank, with a touch of bravado.

Still pointing the gun, she said. 'I'm going to give you one last chance to tell me where they are and then I'm going to shoot you.'

'I can't tell you where the diamonds are if you kill me?'

She cocked the hammer. 'If you don't tell me where the diamonds are, I *will* kill you Frank.'

He failed to notice that she had switched from calling him Francois to Frank, as a way of re-categorising him. However, he was fully aware of her stoic determination and knew she wasn't bluffing. 'OK, stop. STOP! They're in Holland, they never left.'

Her pupils dilated and she leaned in closer, 'Where in Holland…your apartment?'

Frank swallowed hard as the gun pressed against his head. 'If I tell you that, there's nothing to stop you killing me is there?'

'Where are they?' She demanded again.

Frank cowered behind his large crystal goblet. 'Ok…I'll tell you…I have them safely locked away…please…be careful with the gun.'

Complying with his request, she lowered the weapon slightly, but kept it pointed at him. She waited for him to talk and talk he did, however he didn't have the good sense to stop lying. 'Look, I'm telling you the truth about why I gave Chong fakes…I only kept it from you as a precaution…'

That was Frank's undoing, she'd had enough. She wasn't going to give him the opportunity to come up with yet another bullshit tale. Pressing the gun against his temple, she demanded harshly, 'Tell me where the diamonds are NOW?'

Panic and fear triggered a jerk reflex and Frank made a grab for the gun. His sudden movement made her grip tighten and the ancient revolver discharged. As the bullet entered his skull, the answer to her question died with him. His glass dropped to the tiled floor and smashed in a glittering array of small sparkling crystals. His body thrashed and splashed about as the bullet bounced around inside his skull, turning his brain to pottage. She waited for the bath water to settle, before dropping the gun in with his juddering corpse. When the crimson water became still, she turned on the hot tap and left it running. Without another moment's pause for thought or remorse, she went to search through Frank's effects before heading for the airport and the next available flight to Amsterdam.

Chapter 46

Friday Morning. 6th May. Geneva.

The steam from the bath water filled the room. Maudasi inhaled deeply and felt his airways expand and his mind begin to clear. A man servant massaged his head and neck while he soaked up the soothing sensations. Soon he would rise and face the demanding day ahead of him. Wheels were already set in motion. Dragan had been given instructions to contact an associate in Amsterdam's Chinatown and inform him of their unfortunate developments. This old friend and erstwhile business partner had vowed to make swift enquiries. However, with every passing hour, Maudasi's patience was growing thinner. He was desperate for information before he left Geneva for the Netherlands and if he didn't receive any soon, he would require more than just a neck massage.

When Frank hadn't shown up by seven, Maudasi checked his watch and frowned. Thirty minutes later, he descended the stairs and discovered that Frank still hadn't arrived. This stretched his patience further. He expected to be obeyed. Maudasi requested breakfast and instructed a servant to call Frank on both his home and cellphone numbers to *"see what the hell was keeping him"*. Neither yielded an answer. By eight, Maudasi was sick of waiting. He barked instructions at his staff to dispatch a driver to go and bring Frank here no matter what the problem was with him.

~

As Maudasi ranted, a maid cleaning service arrived at Natalie's house in Cologny, just as they did every Friday morning. The two female cleaners, Maria and Marcella, always rang the doorbell as a courtesy before entering the house unannounced. Both were in the employ of the security firm responsible for the high tech alarm system and could be granted access remotely, if the house was unoccupied, in order to perform their duties.

At first there was some mild concern from the security technician, who informed them that the alarm had not been reset and that the owners were not answering the telephone. However, it had been disabled by someone using the correct protocol the previous evening. Having no real reason to be unduly concerned, the technician unlocked the door for the two cleaners.

Not wanting to catch anyone in a compromising situation, they entered the house cautiously; although it wouldn't be the first time they had been witness to bizarre scenes involving a client. It was immediately apparent that the downstairs lounge area was unoccupied and there was nothing obvious out of place. Marcella walked into the large kitchen and proceeded to make coffee. The other cleaner, Maria, began to look around for any signs of occupancy. She called upstairs and announced herself, but got no reply. She ventured upstairs and listened at the bedroom door. She could hear the sound of water running and assumed that the Madame or Monsieur was in the bathroom. She knocked once, announcing herself again, but still there was no answer. Deciding not to disturb what might be an intimate or private moment, she retreated and went back downstairs.

Her colleague had made coffee and turned on the radio she always brought with her, so they went about their duties. The owners would surely hear them soon and make an appearance. After what she determined to be an appropriate amount of time to wait before trying again, Maria went upstairs again to ask if they would like some coffee. The Monsieur and Madame were always generous with her and her little cleaning friend and therefore, it was always good to provide a little extra service whenever possible. She could still hear water running and thought it a bit strange, but once again she knocked on the bedroom door and announced herself, 'Bonjour Madame et Monsieur. C'est moi, Maria, comment ça-va?'

Again, there was no answer. Tentatively, Maria pushed open the bedroom door and peered in. She was astonished by just how much steam there was. It almost filled the entire room. Concerned at this, she walked over to the bathroom door. It was slightly ajar. She knocked and announced herself again. Still there was no answer. There was no sound from within, nothing apart from the sound of water running. Nothing was visible. Everything was concealed by a wall of steam. She was beginning to feel afraid and considered going back downstairs to fetch her friend, but the surreal haze generated a hypnotic pull. She nervously entered. The air was thick and wet. She waved her hand in front of her face to fan the steam away, but couldn't see anything in this fog. No one appeared to be in here. However, when she reached the edge of the bath and encountered the grotesque sight of the giant lobster bisque staring up at her through bloodshot, bulging, eyeballs she was sent skittering backwards, until she slipped on the wet tiled floor and fell down on her ample sized butt. Hearing the dull thud from above, her colleague called out for her. 'Maria, what was that? Are you alright?'

Maria replied with an octave that almost shattered the panoramic lounge window.

Chapter 47

Maudasi's driver returned with disturbing news. As instructed, he'd driven over to the Frank's house to bring him here, only to discover a lot of activity outside. He hadn't stopped. There were two police cars, a security firm car and a service industry van of some description parked outside the house. He also said that as he was driving back out of the area, another two police cars and an ambulance were driving in. It was definitely the house where Frank Perrier lived, he was absolutely sure of it. Maudasi immediately called Dragan with this additional good news. Dragan advised him not to wait any longer in Geneva and leave sooner rather than later. Just after midday Maudasi was on his way to the airport and had still heard nothing from his Chinese business associate or had any idea what had happened to Frank. He was now definitely in need of something more than just a neck massage.

~

It was almost three pm when Maudasi touched down at Schiphol airport. He strode across the tarmac towards the waiting Bentley. Dragan could see his master was in a foul mood, but greeted him courteously and opened the car door for him. Dragan got into the front seat and proceeded to relay what his Chinese associate had uncovered regarding Chong's death. There was still no clear identity to Chong's assassin, but the Chinese were sure it was a woman. They had been able to ascertain that the assassin had gained entry dressed as a maid. The hotel also had security video footage of a woman carrying a silver attaché case. She was clearly trying to conceal her face as she was leaving the hotel, minutes after the shootings.

His associate had also expressed the disappointment of his friends in Hong Kong, at not being told of Maudasi's involvement with the gold deal on their territory. Had he been more forthcoming with his generosity in sharing, he would be a wealthier man today. However, if he was still interested, they would be willing to enter into negotiations with him. The Chinese were toying with him. They were telling him they now had possession of the gold and possibly more and that he would have to play nice with them. Maudasi was livid, but at least he was better informed than before. Without waiting to be asked, Dragan told him that Frank had been found dead in his bathtub; an apparent suicide according to a reliable source.

Maudasi didn't say a word. He couldn't, because his jaws were clenched so tight that he almost ground his gold fillings down to the jawbone.

Chapter 48

As soon as he got up, Dirk hid the fifty thousand euros inside Helena's oven. She had left for work early again. After his customary two cups of coffee he showered, got dressed and went downstairs. He checked the paper in the door jamb. It was still in place. Confidently entering the apartment, he went straight into the kitchen and put his clothes from the yesterday into the washing machine. With Frank due to return any day, he wanted to keep on top of things. He threw in some washing powder and turned the machine on then set about cleaning the apartment. There wasn't much to do because he hadn't been there the past two nights, so it took no time at all to tidy things up. He opened the window to air it a bit and made a pot of coffee. That was always a welcome smell to come home to. Finally, with nothing more to do, he sat down on the sofa and turned on the Euro news channel. He smiled as another bright and breezy weather girl was telling the European populous how bad the rain had been and that it was only going to get worse, culminating in a hurricane of dam bursting proportions by the end of the week. She concluded her report by wishing everyone a great weekend. At this cheerful announcement he glanced outside at the darkening skies.

Not feeling much like going out on such an unpredictable day, he poured a mug of coffee and fixed himself a bowl of granola. Wolfing it down, he finished off with a Red Bull. When the washing machine came to the end of its final spin cycle, he went over and transferred his wet clothes to the tumble drier. The lazy morning drifted along, until Helena texted and informed him that she and some of her colleagues were planning on going out for a drink sometime this afternoon and that he was welcome to join them. She said she would call later to let him know where they were going when the time came. He texted her back and said he couldn't wait. She replied with three kisses. By the time his laundry had dried it was only midday. Being still in possession of the ironing board and the iron, he ironed the lot to get it out of the way for the weekend. When he'd finished, he grabbed his Jacket and hat and headed out for some lunch. He'd walked no more than ten metres from the building when the heavens opened and he had to run for it, as the rain hit the ground all around him like a hail of bullets.

On the opposite side of the canal bank, from within the interior of a black BMW, keen eyes watched his progress.

~

Seeking shelter in a nearby internet café, Dirk settled down to wait out the rain. After an hour of surfing the web and a delicious pastrami baguette, he received a call from Helena. She told him where she and her colleagues were going for a drink and that they would probably be leaving work around three. When he hung up, he checked Google maps to see where the bar was. It was only a ten minute walk from his current location. He checked his watch. It was just approaching two. With the weather showing no sign of improvement and an hour to kill, he booked some more internet time. He spent it constructively, searching for information on the Queen Anne coin and even googling the name Maudasi. The latter yielded nothing.

Antwerp diamonds were next on his list. He found a website providing an idiot's guide on *how to buy a diamond ring in Antwerp*. It contained useful information on tourist traps and pitfalls to avoid. There was also an article on where wealthy buyers should obtain their diamonds. The article recommended the larger shops, set up by the government, that are part of the Antwerp Diamond Jewellers Association. It ended with a topic on ethical aspects alluding to the fact that some of these diamonds may, in actual fact, be blood diamonds. This news didn't make him feel any better. He was under no illusions regarding Frank and Maudasi's source. But he was certain of one thing, it would not be government endorsed.

The rain eventually died down to a light drizzle by the time it came for him to head off. He stepped outside the cafe and turned his collar up and pulled his hat down. Standing in the doorway, furtively looking up and down the street, checking for any suspicious characters lurking behind lampposts, he looked reminiscent of a third rate actor in a post-World War II spy movie. Satisfied all seemed as it should, he stepped into the wet street and set off for his rendezvous at an even pace.

He met Helena and her colleagues at ten past three in an Irish themed bar not too far from Leidseplein. The location was ideal, but the choice of venue wasn't. Dirk hated theme bars and pubs. They were usually too loud and full of tourists and ex-pats, all wanting to know which football team he supported; like he gave a shit. Helena saw him come in and greeted him with a great big affectionate hug and a kiss, way too passionate for public consumption and much to the consternation of her male colleagues. Dirk could almost appreciate their annoyance at this foreign usurper encroaching on their top piece of totty, but looking around he couldn't see any serious competition. They were all either too thin or too fat, too bald or too old. Too bad! They were a nice bunch of people and took to him readily enough. Especially the women who were interested to know what he was doing in The Netherlands and if he was staying long. He announced, with a twinkle in his eye, that Helena had asked him to marry her and he had no choice now but to stay. This statement elicited a shriek of delight from Helena's female colleagues and a playful slap from her, followed by a look that said *"Really? Would you like that?"* It shocked him to know what his answer would be. Fortunately someone changed the subject by ordering another round of drinks. Helena stayed close to him for the rest of their stay.

Around five, before the rush hour traffic began to build up, people started drifting off home. Two badly dressed, middle aged, overweight, bald guys displayed no signs of leaving the bar and started making noises about getting something to eat. Helena sniggered into her drink, when she saw the look of horror that crossed Dirk's face at the thought of dining with the righteous brothers. Helena rescued the situation by reminding them that she was working in the morning and bid them both 'goodnight' as she ushered Dirk out the doorway by his elbow.

'Too much of a good thing can be detrimental to your health.' said Dirk.

'Where do you want to marry?' she chirped, playfully.

'What?'

'Where do you want to eat?' she said with a mischievous grin.

'I think lack of food is affecting my hearing, let's find somewhere to eat.' said Dirk, skirting the topic. But when she smiled her Marilyn Monroe smile, he seriously considered getting down on one knee.

Since the apartment wasn't far, they decided to drop off Helena's camera and stuff before heading back up to Leidseplein for the evening. They walked back holding hands, laughing and joking about her colleagues. Dirk teased her about how many of the guys in her office had asked her out on a date. They laughed even more when she said all of them had and she was sure that at least two of the women had shown an interest too.

Turning serious for a moment, he asked 'Do you really have to work in the morning?'

She shrugged, 'Yes, if I want to get ahead with my article. The ICC is quieter on the weekends and I sometimes go in from ten until two. It's enough, you know?'

Dirk looked a little disappointed at this news. She responded to his frown by making a big pout with her bottom lip. He was about to make a suggestion, but as they turned the corner into their street Dirk's question died in his throat. Standing on top of the front steps was the imposing figure of Dragan.

'Shit!' exclaimed Dirk.

'What's wrong?' asked Helena, confused by his strange reaction?

He nodded over to their apartment building. 'That guy standing outside. He's been in the apartment twice this week already; once when I was out.'

They both stopped and watched what he was doing. Dragan hadn't spotted them.

'Who is he, your landlord?' asked Helena.

'No, but he works for the guy who owns the apartment; the same guy Frank works for.'

'OK, let's get some evidence.' said Helena.

'What do you mean?' asked Dirk.

Helena nodded towards the apartment. 'If he opens that door now and enters your apartment illegally, you can sue because you'll have me as a witness and photographic evidence to prove it.'

Dirk made a face. 'Well, technically it's not my apartment, it's my friend's. Or more to the point, my friend's Boss's and this guy works for him. So, I'm not really in a position to sue anyone am I?'

She waived her hand dismissively and proceeded to take out her camera to photograph Dragan who remained standing, stock still, at the top of the front steps. He looked contemplative somehow. Another full minute passed before he walked back down the steps and got into the Bentley. His behaviour puzzled Dirk. It didn't conform to conventional forms of breaking and entering or even illegal entry. What was he up to?

They remained at a distance and watched. Dragan

just sat there, unseen behind the car's tinted glass, apparently in no hurry to go anywhere. Dirk decided to call Frank again and sort this out. He was supposed to be having a holiday for Christ's sake, not having to avoid this big bastard. He called Frank's number. It rang out for a long time then went to voicemail. Dirk left a message: 'Hi Frank, it's me, Dirk, just a quick call to find out when you get back. Give me a call as soon as you can and let me know. Bye.'

As they stood there watching the dark car and its shrouded occupant, Helena could see Dirk was agitated and asked if he wanted to call the police.

'I can't just call the police; he hasn't really done anything has he? To tell you the truth, he could be here for completely innocent reasons. Maybe he just wants to ask me some more irritating questions about coins, which I know nothing about. His other question will probably be about the whereabouts of Jason Sinclair and I can't answer that one either. '

Helena gave him a puzzled look. 'Who's Jason Sinclair?'

Dirk blew a heavy sigh, 'He's a *business associate* of Frank's and not a very nice one I have to say.'

Helena nodded in Dragan's direction again, 'It doesn't look as if he's in a hurry to leave. Let's go ask him what he wants…together.' She squeezed Dirk's arm in encouragement and support.

He responded with a smile. 'I don't want to invite him inside and I definitely don't want to introduce him to you.'

'Scared he might steal me from you?' she said, with a mischievous smile.

'He'd have to kill me first!' He said and gave her a kiss.

Dirk realised Helena was right, they couldn't just stand there and wait for Dragan to leave, he could sit there all night. He told her to wait while he went over to speak with him and see what he wanted. She was having none of it and said she wasn't afraid of any big bad wolf. She also pointed out that it would prevent anything illegal happening while she was there as a witness. Dirk smiled at her determination. 'Alright, but you go straight into the building and drop off your stuff. I'll talk to him on the street. I don't want to give him any more time than I have to. I'll come up when I've finished with him. OK?'

She shrugged and nodded in passive agreement, but took his hand as they strode towards the apartment. When they reached the bottom of the steps, Helena gave him a kiss on the cheek before bouncing up the steps to the front door and into the building. As the door closed behind her, Dirk turned around and looked straight at the Bentley and waited. The car door opened and Dragan got out. As he approached he nodded towards the front door, 'Nice looking girl, you move fast Mister Dirk.'

Dirk wanted to kick him in the balls, 'What can I do for you *Mister* Dragan?'

'Let's go inside and talk.' he said, more in the form of a demand rather than a suggestion.

'No, outside's good enough. What is it you want this time, coins? Jason Sinclair? As I've said before, I don't know where to get hold of either of them.'

Dragan glowered slightly and then surprised him

with his next question. 'When did you last speak with Frank Perrier?'

Dirk frowned, 'Yesterday afternoon, why?'

'And you have had no further contact with him since then?'

'Actually, I tried to call him just a couple of minutes ago, when I saw you standing there, but he didn't answer. I did, however, leave him a message asking him to call me back as soon as he could.'

Dragan looked a little mystified by this statement. 'You called him just now?'

'Yes, I just said so didn't I?' replied Dirk, getting exasperated.

'Why did you call him?'

Dirk decided to take the gloves off. 'That's really none of your business is it?'

Dragan gave him a stern look, but Dirk didn't back down, 'That's another thing, I don't like people giving me dirty looks and I don't like your threatening behaviour. Now, if this is about me being in the apartment when Frank isn't here and your boss wants me to get out then it's done, I'll leave right now. But I thought I was a guest of my friend and I don't think he'd appreciate me being harassed like this.'

Dragan went to speak, but Dirk shouted him down, '…and another thing, Frank wasn't too pleased when I told him that you'd let yourself in the other day.'

Dragan appeared to be even more mystified by this statement, 'But, you let me in.'

Dirk gave him a reprehensible look, 'Come on, you know exactly what I'm talking about, you even left a couple of calling cards for effect.'

Dragan gave him a confused look. 'When was this?'

Dirk was becoming exasperated, but didn't want to argue, 'Tell you what, you wait here for five minutes and I'll get my shit together and move out, then everybody's happy ok? You and your boss can sort all this out with Frank when he gets back, because I can't be bothered with this crap anymore.'

Dirk turned and stormed up the stairs. Dragan called after him, 'I really think it would be best if we talked inside.'

Dirk stopped at the top of the stairs and took out his phone, 'Fuck this. I'm calling Frank again right now, you can talk to him.'

Dragan dropped his bombshell. 'That won't be possible. Frank Perrier is dead!'

Dirk stared at him open mouthed, struggling to take in what he'd just been told. All of his senses had gone numb and he felt as though he was swimming underwater. He swayed slightly, but Dragan suddenly appeared beside him and put a hand on his arm to steady him. Dirk didn't object. He hadn't even been aware of Dragan ascending the stairs. This sudden physical contact brought him out of his fugue state. 'DEAD, what do you mean dead?'

'He was supposed to turn up for an important meeting early this morning, but failed to do so.' said Dragan.

Dirk was still staring, wide eyed, 'That doesn't mean he's dead. Have you tried to contact him? What about your boss, what does he think?'

Dragan answered with some detachment. 'Mister Maudasi is very distressed by the news. We had hoped that you could provide us with some helpful information. Let's go inside and talk.'

Dirk was nodding, but not really taking in any of what was being said to him. He opened the front door and stumbled inside. Dragan followed close behind. When they entered the apartment, the scene that lay before them was one of devastation. It looked like it had been ransacked by someone possibly related to Edward Scissorhands. The sofa and its cushions were slashed beyond repair, drawers had been pulled out and their contents strewn all over the floor. Broken glass was everywhere. Dirk couldn't believe what he was seeing.

Dragan surveyed the mess and remarked. 'Been having some wild friends over Mister Dirk?'

Dirk rounded on him, 'You fucking bastard. You did this, didn't you? You weren't waiting at the front door…you were just fucking leaving when we turned up and caught you.'

Standing close to Dragan, Dirk's anger boiled over and he lunged. Dragan was way ahead of him and pulled out a slim, extendible, steel baton. Gave it a sharp flick and rammed it into Dirk's abdomen. The severity of the blow took the wind out of him. He doubled up and crumpled to the floor in agony. He wanted cry out but couldn't. He had no breath. Dragan casually walked over and closed the apartment door. No witnesses. Dirk tried to stand up, but Dragan came back over and placed his foot firmly on his back, forcing him to lie still.

Looking around at the ruination of the room, Dragan came out with a surprisingly candid question. 'You think I am responsible for all of this?'

Dirk turned his head, 'Of course it was you, we just caught you coming out didn't we?' he snarled.

This earned him another stab in the ribs with the baton. Dirk cursed.

'Who's the girl?' asked Dragan.

'Just a neighbour.' replied Dirk.

'*Just* a neighbour?' asked Dragan, seemingly unconvinced.

Dirk desperately wanted to shove Dragan's night stick or whatever the hell it was where it wouldn't show, but he couldn't move. Dragan was standing behind him and out of reach. Dirk just lay there in his undignified state and did nothing, as advised, for the moment.

'Tell me. Why do you think I would do this?' puzzled Dragan.

'You tell me; envy, frustration, an underprivileged childhood?' Dirk replied, scathingly.

Dragan glared at him and said, with stern finality, 'I'm sorry to disappoint you, but I am not responsible for this. Now, let's move on'

Dirk detected impatience and anger creeping into Dragan's voice and said nothing more to antagonise him.

'May I get up?' requested Dirk, immediately regretting the sarcasm in his voice.

Dragan thought about this and tapped his baton against his leg, 'Yes, you may, but if you try something stupid, I *will* break something with the next strike. Think about what that pretty girl would think of you with a ruined nose or fractured eye socket?'

Dirk had the distinct feeling this guy enjoyed inflicting pain. Sizing up the situation, he realised this was the first time he could think of that he really wanted to kill someone. Sure, people say it all the time and even think about it, but deep down they don't really mean it. But, on this occasion, he genuinely wanted to get up and beat another human being senseless. However, he had the good sense to realise he was no match. Taking on a guy like this could get you killed. Dragan backed away to allow Dirk to sit up, but only as far as the floor. Dirk leaned against the shredded sofa and rubbed his aching stomach and ribs.

'So, you don't have any idea who you think might have done this…apart from me?' asked Dragan facetiously.

Dirk shook his head.

'What do you think they were looking for Mister Dirk?'

Mister Dirk, there it was again, Dirk gritted his teeth and swallowed his anger, along with his pain. 'I thought you wanted to talk about Frank? What happened? How did he die?'

Dragan conveyed his condolences in his inimitable style. 'Suicide! ' he announced bluntly.

'Suicide?' Dirk was incredulous. Frank hadn't sounded suicidal on the phone yesterday, not even in the slightest bit depressed. Pissed off, sure! Upset possibly and maybe even a little bit anxious, because of what had happened on Monday, but suicidal? Not a frigging chance.

'We had a conversation about Monsieur Perrier once before and I asked you if you knew what business he was in, do you remember?' asked Dragan.

'How can I forget?' said Dirk through gritted teeth.

Dragan gave the baton a little twirl, as a reminder who was in charge and asking the questions. Dirk got the message and sat up a little more. 'Banking, I told you, that's how I know him. We both worked for the same bank many years ago. Look, what's this got to do with anything?'

'Bankers do commit suicide, it's not uncommon. What business is your friend Jason Sinclair in?'

Dirk wasn't sure if that was supposed to be an answer or not. He didn't know what was more surreal, the news that Frank was dead or the sudden switch to questions about Jason.

'We've had this conversation before too. He's not my friend and I have no idea what business he's in, apart from selling coins…and I've only seen him do that once. Look, you said you wanted to talk then you tell me my friend is dead and then you beat me up. What the fuck's this all about?' asked Dirk.

'I was merely taking defensive action.' said Dragan flatly.

'And you just happened to have that thing handy?' spat Dirk, referring to Dragan's cosh.

Dragan collapsed the baton and put it away. Held up his empty hands as a moot gesture of truce then began asking questions about Jason again. Dirk had a bad feeling that this conversation could easily end with him in a body cast or a wooden overcoat, if he didn't take care with his answers.

'Dragan, how many times do I have to say it? Jason Sinclair is not my friend and I still don't know where he is. I met him for the first time on Queen's day. I was with Frank when Jason turned up and yes, I saw him in the Sea Palace on Sunday, but again he just turned up unannounced. Frank arranged to meet him on the Monday to buy a coin. But you already know all this, you saw us in Den Haag. Frank bought me lunch. I just went along for the ride.'

'Just for the ride?' scoffed Dragan.

Dirk didn't like this big thug or the accusatory tone in his voice and tried desperately not to let his feelings show. The conversation wasn't going anywhere, except round in a circle. It had to end before Dragan got his stick out again. 'Look, I really don't know what's going on here, but I need to find out about Frank and I'd like to speak with Mister Maudasi. Can you arrange that Dragan?'

'Why?' shrugged Dragan.

'Why? Because you've just told me my best friend is dead and I'm here, in his apartment and you've obviously felt the need to contact me…and beat me up.'

Dirk regretted his words immediately and hoped they wouldn't be his last. To his relief, Dragan's cell phone rang and stopped him from pulling his stick. He watched as Dragan listened intently to the caller for about ten seconds then hung up. 'It would appear you *are* psychic', said Dragan, mocking the remarks Dirk had made on their first encounter, 'Mister Maudasi wants to see you too.'

'When?' asked Dirk.

'Right now, he's outside…in the Bentley.'

Chapter 49

Dirk slowly got to his feet and limped over to the window. He looked down at the ominous black Bentley. It totally reminded him of a hearse. Dragan led the way and Dirk followed him down the steps, like one of the walking dead. Dragan went over to the car and opened the rear door, holding it open as a gesture for Dirk to get in. Dirk shuffled closer and bent down to get a better look at its occupant. Within the gloom of the car's interior, he saw a distinguished looking man, somewhere in his fifties, sitting regally on the back seat. Dirk got in and the gentleman introduced himself with a voice that, like his eyes, conveyed no emotion. 'I am Sadim Maudasi. I have some bad news about your friend, Frank Perrier.'

Dirk felt sick, but managed to nod. Dragan had gotten into the driver's seat and sat with his back to them. Maudasi could see that Dirk was in obvious physical distress by the way he was clutching at his stomach. 'Are you in some kind of pain Mister Dagger?'

Dirk replied without reservation, 'Ask your boy here, he just beat me up.'

Dragan turned his big head around and glared in at Dirk through the Plexiglas that was separating them. He gave his master a succinct account of events. 'The apartment has been ransacked and an accusation was made against me, with significant prejudice. I defended myself.'

Maudasi looked back at Dirk, 'Is this true Mister Dagger?'

'Yes, that cunt hit me with a stick.' Replied Dirk, bitterly.

The caustic remark caused Maudasi to pause for a moment. 'Who is responsible for this?'

Dirk was about to thank Maudasi for his concern for his welfare, but simply said 'Ask him, he seems to have all the answers.'

Puzzled by this remark, Maudasi asked. 'Why do you say that, Mister Dagger?'

'Because, on Wednesday, when I was out, he was in the apartment uninvited; that's why.'

Dragan turned around some more at the accusation and his glare intensified. Maudasi said something to Dragan, in a language Dirk didn't recognise, who answered by shaking his head. Dirk got the gist of their conversation. However, he wasn't letting it go. 'Well, if it wasn't him, then who the hell was it that came in and left a cigar in the ashtray as a calling card?'

Maudasi brought order to the proceedings. 'There is no need to raise your voice Mister Dagger. I believe Dragan. Now, let us discuss this in a civil manner. Why do you think someone was in the apartment on Wednesday? Was anything stolen then?'

'I don't have an inventory to cross reference with. You can always come inside and see for yourself, it is your apartment after all Mister Maudasi; as Dragan here keeps reminding me.'

This earned him another dirty look from Dragan, which he ignored and continued with his break-in theory. 'Whoever it was that came in, left a cigar in an ashtray in the downstairs lounge. They also used the upstairs toilet.'

Maudasi gave him a questioning look and waited for further explanation. Dirk outlined his theory, leaving out the part that he likes to sit down when he pees. 'I know the cigar wasn't mine, because it was a Cohiba and I prefer Montecristos.'

Maudasi didn't ask him to expand on how he knew someone had used his toilet, but questioned the cigar.

'Maybe the cigar was there all along and you just didn't see it?'

'No. Neither Frank nor I have smoked any cigars in the apartment since I arrived. I've often sat at that table and there has never been a cigar in the ashtray. I'm certain of it.'

Maudasi shrugged and waived his hand in the air nonchalantly. 'And what about now, do you think this was done by the same person?' he asked in reference to the devastated apartment.

'Well, if it wasn't him, that would be my guess.' said Dirk, nodding at Dragan and endearing himself further. Maudasi calmly continued with his questions, which notably still contained no mention of Frank. 'If what you say is true, what do you think they were looking for Mister Dirk?'

Dirk flinched. What was it with these arseholes calling him *Mister Dirk*? First off Jason and now these two, although at this moment he would have preferred it to be Jason. Focusing on the question, he thought about suggesting that Frank has a lot of really nice wines, expensive too, but these guys were humourless. He tried to keep it real. 'I don't know? What do people who break into houses normally look for? Anything of value would be my guess.'

'Have you informed the Police of this?' asked Maudasi.

'Not yet. I only just saw the damage when I went in with him. I'll do it now.' replied Dirk.

Maudasi waived his hand again, 'Leave it. I will have someone come round and take care of things.'

'Are you telling me not to call the Police Mister Maudasi?' asked Dirk, with growing concern.

Maudasi sat tall in his seat, like a Cobra getting ready to strike. 'Let us first consider the facts Mister Dagger. Frank Perrier was found dead this morning and his apartment has been broken into on the same day. So until I have more information, I would prefer it if the police were not involved at this time.'

Dirk was still trying to get his head around what Maudasi had meant by '*having someone come round and take care of things*'. He didn't like what this implied or the way it had been spoken. Dirk felt queasy and experienced a twinge of pain in his tender midriff. He grimaced and wanted to throw up, all over Maudasi, but swallowed it down and tried to appear normal.

'Is it true about Frank? Is he really dead?' asked Dirk.

Maudasi nodded, 'Regretfully, yes.'

Dirk was anxious for answers about his friend. 'When did it happen? When did you find out?'

Maudasi looked at Dragan before answering. 'I don't know exactly when. I only found out myself this afternoon.'

'Are you sure it was suicide?' asked Dirk.

'I'm not sure of anything yet.' replied Maudasi.

Dirk shook his head 'It doesn't make any sense. He was due to come back this weekend. He was looking forward to it. Frank wouldn't just...' his words trailed off in disbelief.

Maudasi was surprisingly philosophical in his answer, 'There is nothing more complex than the human mind. When did you last speak with him?'

Dirk felt as though he was swimming under water again. He suddenly couldn't remember when he last spoke with him and he desperately wanted to go back upstairs to Helena. Maudasi continued to probe. 'Can you tell us anything that could help us better understand these *tragic* events?'

'Uh, no...I...I'm...it's so...this is unreal...' Dirk stammered.

Maudasi continued with the same detached and unconvincing philosophical discourse, 'Yes, we are all puzzled and saddened by this, but I am sure someone, somewhere, will provide an explanation. However, these events have caused me a problem.'

'A problem..?' asked Dirk, his voice sounding far away in his own head.

'Yes. As you are no doubt aware, Frank Perrier was my banker. He was pivotal in a forthcoming acquisition and this...*tragedy* has thrown things into chaos somewhat. I'm sure you can appreciate the ramifications of this Mister Dagger.'

The change of tact by Maudasi from concerned employer to hardnosed businessman was subtle but swift. His voice no longer sounded philosophical. It was just harsh and it was coming in loud and clear. Dirk picked up on the fact that Maudasi had dismissively and casually referred to Frank in the past tense. The hair on his neck was bristling and he felt he was swimming in shark infested waters. Swallowing hard, he found his voice. 'Uh, yes, he mentioned he was working on something important…for you in fact, but he didn't say what. I only know that he was excited about it.'

'Was he indeed?' said Maudasi, raising an eyebrow and glancing at Dragan, who glanced back in the rear-view mirror. 'Now then Mister Dagger, perhaps you can tell me, was Frank involved with anything or anyone else regarding business dealings of any kind?'

The tone of the conversation made Dirk's already painful gut tighten some more. 'To tell you the truth Mister Maudasi, I hadn't seen Frank for some time; not until he came to visit me in England two weeks ago and invited me to come over here for Queens day. So the answer is no, I don't know what he's been working on or with whom, but he did buy a very valuable coin from someone called Jason Sinclair on Monday.'

Maudasi paused to consider this. Dirk could see he was deliberating the forthright way in which he had answered the question by bringing Jason into it. Another glance was exchanged in the mirror.

'Dragan tells me that you and Frank met with this Jason person several times before Frank went to Geneva. Is that correct?'

Dirk answered with a question of his own. 'Mister Maudasi, I'm confused. What has any of this got to do with Frank's death?' His own words rang in his ears, as he heard himself speak his friend's name and death in the same sentence.

Maudasi raised his hand, 'Indulge me.'

Dirk was growing increasingly uncomfortable. He could feel a chill sweat on his back and neck. 'Yes, we met him on a couple of occasions. Jason hounded Frank quite a bit with this coin he sold him.'

'Why do you say hounded?'

'Well, Frank hadn't invited him and I got the impression that he was angry at the possibility Jason had followed him here...to Amsterdam...to sell him another coin.'

Maudasi feigned ignorance, 'Another coin?'

'Frank mentioned that he'd bought some coins from him before. He also told me you were a coin collector too, Mister Maudasi.'

Touché thought Maudasi. 'Do you know what he paid for these coins Mister Dagger?'

Dirk knew the answer Maudasi was looking for and played it low key, 'No, I don't, although he did say he thought he'd paid too much for them.'

'So you didn't see any money or anything change hands between Frank and Jason Sinclair at any time?'

'No.' Dirk lied again.

Maudasi looked thoughtful for a moment. 'Could you find out from Mister Sinclair, what Frank paid him for these coins?'

These guys never gave up. 'Mister Maudasi, as I've told your...assistant here, I don't know Jason Sinclair and I have no idea where he is.'

'When did you last see Mister Sinclair?' asked Maudasi, with an air of conceit that made Dirk suspect he already knew the answer.

'I saw him yesterday afternoon, in a little café across that bridge over there.' Dirk pointed out the car window.

Maudasi's next question was more direct. 'You say

you don't know him and yet, you met him yesterday. Why? Did he have a business proposition for you?'

Dirk didn't like the way the conversation was going, he was now feeling very uncomfortable and very vulnerable. He was wet around the gills with sweat, which surely must now be apparent to these bastards. He had to act quickly and get out of this hearse. Going for a direct approach, he asked straight out, 'Mister Maudasi, what's all this about? Do you think Jason had something to do with Frank's death?'

'No, but I would like to find out why Frank took his own life and who broke into his apartment, as I am sure you would too.' said Maudasi, condescendingly.

Dirk desperately wanted answers about his friend's death, but right at this moment he wanted out of this car more than anything else. He knew his best option was to play along.

'I met Jason Sinclair yesterday at lunchtime, but not for lunch and not for a business meeting. I received a note from him on Thursday morning, asking me to meet him in Café Heuvel at noon. The note was unsigned and at first I assumed it was from him.' said Dirk, jerking his thumb towards Dragan.

Maudasi spoke again to Dragan in the same strange language and they both laughed. Maudasi was still laughing when he turned back to Dirk. 'Why would you believe Dragan to be sending you little notes?'

'Because I suspected him of being in the apartment, that's why. I thought this was another form of harassment.'

Dragan looked at Dirk like he was about to come crashing into the back seat and tear him apart. Maudasi shook his head. 'Dragan says he wasn't, so let's leave it at that. What did Mister Sinclair want?'

Dirk had no intention of talking about diamonds or any of the fantasies Jason had proposed during their last meeting, so instead he recounted an earlier encounter he'd had with him. 'At first he said he just wanted to start over and be friends, because he felt we'd got off on the wrong foot, but then he started talking about the coin he'd sold to Frank and asked if he was happy with it.'

'Was he?'

'Was Frank happy? No, I don't think it gave him any pleasure at all, do you?'

Maudasi didn't respond to Dirk's subtle rebuke. 'Did Mister Sinclair offer to sell you some coins?'

Dirk was tired of all these damned questions. He was angry and upset at his friend's death. He wanted to tell Maudasi where to stick his coins and his money and his big fucking car. He also didn't want another beating. 'No, but he did ask if I would ask Frank to reconsider.'

'Reconsider what?'

'When Frank bought the coin from him in Den Haag, he told Jason that he was finished doing business with him. Jason thought I might be able to put a good word in for him with Frank and get him to change his mind.'

'Did you...*put a good word in* Mister Dagger?'

'No. I told him it was none of my business.'

'How did Mister Sinclair take this rejection?'

Dirk shrugged, 'I think he'll find a way to get over it.'

Maudasi leaned back in his seat, pondering what Dirk had just said. 'Are you implying that it was your friend Jason who entered your apartment to look for the coins he sold to Frank, in order to steal them back?' asked Maudasi.

'I'm not implying anything and Jason is not my friend and it's not my apartment...as I keep being reminded.'

Dragan was glaring in at him with murderous intent.

'Do you think it could have been this Jason fellow who was in the apartment?' asked Maudasi.

'It depends on how badly he wanted his coins back, but you still haven't convinced me it wasn't him either.' Dirk jerked his head towards Dragan, who was now bearing his teeth.

'You seem extremely focused on provoking Dragan, Mister Dagger. He is not someone you would wish to make angry, let me assure you.'

Suddenly it felt like Nazi Germany inside the car. Dirk switched back to diplomacy.

'Mister Maudasi, with all due respect, the news about Frank's death has deeply upset me and this line of questioning isn't helping either. I'd really like to help, if I can, it's the least I can do. So, please, tell me what it is that you want from me and how we can help each other.'

Dirk could see that Maudasi hadn't anticipated such a profound and emotional response from him. Maudasi and Dragan exchanged a silent, but definitive communication and the air in the car felt no less oppressive. Dirk didn't like the feeling that had descended and desperately sought for a way to get out of the car PDQ. Fortunately, if that was the correct way to perceive what happened next, Dragan had inadvertently provided him with a solution. Dirk's sensitive stomach, together with the claustrophobic heat of the car, was making him nauseous and he began breathing heavier. He clamped a hand over his mouth and started heaving. Maudasi was aghast when he realised what was about to take place and screamed at Dragan for assistance. Dragan was faster than shit off a shovel at his master's command and sprung out of the driver's seat, yanked open the passenger door and manhandled Dirk onto the street. Dirk staggered around to the back of the car and continued to heave and retch, bringing up his last beer in a foaming fountain of bile, all over the lovely car's rear bumper, much to Dragan's disgust. Dirk could hear Maudasi talking from inside the car and hoped he was giving Dragan a stern admonishment. The sound of Dirk clearing his throat and nostrils sounded like a malfunctioning Cappuccino machine and ended their conversation. Dragan enquired if he had finished, but conspicuously not how he was feeling. Dirk stood up and slouched into a position, against the car, where Maudasi could see him out of the rear door. 'You can thank him for that Mister Maudasi' said Dirk, aiming his wet chin in Dragan's direction. Maudasi was studying him from the gloom of the car's interior, his grey blue eyes piercing through it like laser beams. Dragan was standing at Dirk's back, in what could be perceived as a position to manhandle him again. Dirk suspected the interrogation wasn't over yet, but there was no way he was getting back into that car under any circumstances. However, Maudasi relieved him of making any drastic decisions. He said something in his Slavic tongue, or whatever it was, prompting Dragan to get back into the driving seat of the Bentley. Dirk walked back around to the open passenger door and into full view. Maudasi surveyed the splash marks on Dirk's T-shirt from his sudden evacuation. 'You need cleaning up Mister Dagger.'

Dirk wanted to kick the bastard in the teeth, but thought better of it. How many people get to do that with a guy like this and live to brag about it? He spat on the road in front of the open car door. Maudasi didn't miss the significance. Without another word he slammed the door shut. A moment later, the car silently moved off, leaving Dirk standing there wondering what the hell alternative universe he'd been transported to.

As soon as the car turned out of sight, Dirk was up the front steps and into the building. He was desperate to see Helena, but he'd just thrown up. He dived back into the ruined apartment and grabbed a Red Bull from the fridge, downing it in a single gulp. No sooner than he'd drained the last of it when Helena, who had been watching events unfold from her upstairs window, charged into the devastated apartment. Taking in the mess, she came to a dead stop. 'My God, Dirk, where are you? DIRK?'

'I'm back here Helena.' he called out.

She came all the way in, outraged at what she was seeing. 'Bastards! I'm calling the police.'

Dirk put a hand on her. 'Not so fast, let's look around first.'

She was bewildered by his reaction. 'What did those bastards do to you?'

'Nothing, I'm ok, really. Did you get lots of nice pictures of me making a pavement pizza?' he asked, attempting to be light-hearted, in a vain attempt to convince her everything was cool.

She wasn't, but answered his question. 'Yes, several, all in high resolution.'

Dirk nodded his approval and announced that he needed a drink to calm his nerves. He went into the kitchen to get two beers from the fridge. There was broken glass all over the kitchen floor and he had to step carefully to avoid it. He returned and handed her a beer, then started talking about everything and nothing with a frenetic urgency that scared her. She could see something was very wrong and put her hand on his face. Her calming touch halted his rant. His shoulders sagged and his eyes filled with tears. She put her arms around him and he told her the grim news about Frank. Now she understood his bizarre behaviour and was saddened to see him in such turmoil. As he went through the details of what he'd just learned, she grew concerned when he described the line of questioning Dragan had taken and what followed inside the Bentley. He left out the bit about Dragan getting the better of him, but told her most of what had happened since he'd arrived in The Netherlands. When he had finished, she acknowledged that his friend Frank had gotten himself involved with some dangerous people.

Helena was intrigued to know more about the coin Frank had bought for so much money, but Dirk thought it wise to play it down. He began to wish he hadn't told her anything, because the more he thought about the whole thing, the more it worried him. She urged him again to call the police and tell them everything that had happened. He shook his head. 'What could I tell them?

My apartment's been broken into, but wait it's not really my apartment it's my friend's. No, wait he's dead and anyway it's not really his, it's his boss's, but don't worry about it, he knows and doesn't want me to report it because he said he'll *take care of it*.' Dirk animatedly raised a thumb and forefinger to his head as he raved on. Helena endeavoured to be the voice of reason. 'You can tell the police what they said to you. You must Dirk.'

'It would be my word against theirs. All I could really tell them is that they came to inform me my friend was dead. That's all.'

'That's not all, it was the way they came to you and the questions they asked. You can tell the police that one of them was in the apartment illegally too.'

'I've no proof of that either have I?'

Helena was adamant. 'You have to call the police and tell them about the break-in, you must at least do that. Look at the damage that's been done. Look at the sofa, it's...' She seemed to pause as she considered the type of weapon that the perpetrator had used. 'No, Dirk, you must call the Police. It's wrong that they told you not to.'

Dirk thought about everything she said and then some more about his experience with Maudasi and Dragan. Helena was right. He should report it, to hell with Maudasi. 'Ok, but you'll have to do it.'

Helena called the local police and explained that there had been a break-in to the apartment below hers and that she was here now with the resident, who was not Dutch but wanted to report it and make a statement. She gave the police controller her name, the building address and a contact number then passed the phone over to Dirk. He made a statement of his name, passport number, cellphone number and the address he was staying in Holland, which seemed pointless as Helena had just given her address as the flat above where he was staying; bureaucracy in progress. When he was done, he put Helena back on and she confirmed Dirk's details in Dutch. She requested a time when they could expect someone to turn up and process the crime scene, but was told as it was a Friday evening and the start of the weekend it would probably be tomorrow before someone would be available. The controller requested they touch as little as possible, until someone turned up, as it could hinder the investigation process. Helena thanked the operator and hung up.

Dirk dreaded going up to his own living quarters to see the damage, but they didn't put it off and went to look together. It was more of the same. *Scissorhands* had cut up all his remaining clothes, including his Hugo Boss suit. His small settee had undergone the same treatment and was beyond repair. Dirk didn't have a kitchen so there was no broken glass like downstairs. However, the one notable difference he could make out from the mess in Frank's place was the fact that all of his cigars had been taken out of his humidor, broken into pieces and strewn everywhere he looked. Some people really hated a smoker. Dirk suggested Helena take photographs of the damage, in case Maudasi sent someone round and removed all evidence of a break-in. She clicked away with her camera, recording the destruction, while he sifted through his tattered and ruined belongings. Somehow he didn't feel the need to ask if it was alright if he moved in permanently with her, she seemed to accept this as a given. When they could do no more, they salvaged two of the remaining bottles of Frank's wine and left. It was almost seven pm, but the day was far from over.

Chapter 50

The Bentley pulled in behind a Porsche Cayenne four wheel drive that looked like it had just been driven out of the showroom. In front of that was a Mercedes and in front of that a BMW. All of them black and lined up like a rock star's funeral. Although no signs were visible indicating exclusive parking rights, no other cars were present. The main drag, at the far end of this quiet side street, led into busier streets, where numerous bars and restaurants vied for tourist business amongst the dwindling number of sex clubs and scantily clad girls touting in windows. Dragan switched off the engine and waited. Maudasi got out of the car. Glanced to his left and then to his right before opening the front passenger door and getting back in. A moment of heavy silence passed before a word was spoken.

'Do you think he's involved?' asked Maudasi.

'I'm not sure, but he knows more than he's telling us. I don't believe him to be just a friend here on vacation.'

'I agree. Do you think we came on too strong?'

Dragan shrugged, 'If he is involved it will have shaken him up, if not then no matter.'

'We'll know soon enough. What about the apartment, do you think he could have caused the damage himself?'

'It's unlikely. I think he was genuinely shocked and angered when he saw it. If you consider it, he didn't have to take me inside.'

'Do you think it could have been the other one...Sinclair?'

'It's possible, if he was looking for coins...or diamonds. Maybe he just wanted to rob Perrier because he knew he wasn't there but...'

'But..?'

'...but what if it wasn't either of them?'

Maudasi thought about this for a long moment. 'Let's go through what we know. Wednesday morning Chong and his wife are killed in Hong Kong. This morning Perrier is found dead in Geneva. It doesn't take a genius to figure out there's a connection. Then, this afternoon, Perrier's apartment, here in Amsterdam, is turned over; coincidence?'

'No. It has to be connected.' said Dragan.

They both sat in silence contemplating these facts. 'When exactly was Chong killed?' asked Maudasi.

'Wednesday morning around ten a.m. Hong Kong time, which would make it three a.m. European time.' recounted Dragan.

'Where were Perrier's two friends?'

'I spoke with Dagger on Wednesday, he was here in Amsterdam and he just said he saw Sinclair on Thursday at midday.'

'Perrier left my house late last night and was dead by this morning, possibly soon after he arrived home.'

Without it having to be spoken, the suggestion of Frank having committed suicide had been swiftly dismissed out of hand.

'Two different continents two different killings...' said Dragan.

Maudasi finished the sentence '...but sufficient time between the two.'

'It's not impossible, if you consider the timeline.' Dragan speculated. 'It does shed new light on the situation.'

'Someone else knew Chong was in possession of the diamonds and killed him for them. But why kill Perrier?'

As if he knew what Maudasi wanted to hear, Dragan speculated again, 'It would suggest that Perrier was involved and his partner, or partners, decided not to share. But, as you say, why kill him? Why not just disappear? It isn't as if he could complain to anyone that he'd been double crossed.'

'A silent partner is better than a bitter partner.' declared Maudasi. 'Let's begin with Frank's two friends, Dagger and Sinclair. It isn't feasible for either of them to have killed Chong...or Frank, but what about the girl who was with Dagger just now? Do you think she's involved too?'

'We can't rule anyone out. The one called Sinclair had a Chinese girl with him when he met Perrier and Dagger last weekend.'

Maudasi nodded. 'So, we have a potential clique of four: Dagger and Sinclair, the girl with Dagger just now and the Chinese girl with Sinclair.'

'Our associate reported that whoever killed Chong was a woman and we now have two women in the frame, both unaccounted for at the time of the deaths. I think we need to talk to them all as soon as possible.'

'I agree. Go back to the apartment and confront Dagger again...and the woman too. I think he will be more inclined to tell us what he knows if he thinks she's being threatened.'

Dragan nodded then added. 'What about the other one...Sinclair?'

'We'll get to him later. He wants to sell coins and he probably still has the diamonds Perrier gave him. We can relive him of both when the time comes.'

Chapter 51

Jason Sinclair had watched the news report of Frank's demise with a mixture of glee and regret. His golden goose was gone, but it presented a new opportunity. His brief foray into the apartment earlier in the week had been somewhat fruitless. He had only wanted to get a better look and feel for things and hadn't wanted to disturb anything. Getting in had been easy, he was adept at getting past locks. He'd done it often enough at his parent's home, after they'd taken away his keys. Now he was back to conduct a more thorough search, except this time someone had beaten him to it and judging by the extent of the damage, that someone had been unsuccessful in their search.

As he walked around in the wreckage, pondering who could have been responsible for such wanton destruction, he froze. Someone was inserting a key into the door of the apartment.

~

Dirk and Helena had gone upstairs to her apartment in silence. On entering, a wave of nausea came over him and he felt like throwing up again. He headed straight for the bathroom, locked the door and sat down on the toilet seat with his head in his hands. This had to be a nightmare that he was about to wake up from and swear never to drink ever again. Then Helena drifted into his thoughts. She could never be part of anyone's nightmare. He remained like this for about ten minutes, reliving conversations and events, trying to make sense of it all. A gentle knock on the bathroom door, followed by Helena's voice, brought him back to reality. 'I think there's something on TV about your friend.' she said softly.

Dirk was up and out like a shot. The TV was on in the lounge and there it was, running along the bottom of the screen on the BBC24 news channel.

'Swiss Banker, Francois Perrier was found dead at his home this morning in the wealthy Geneva suburb of Cologny. It is believed he took his own life. His family in France and England have been notified of his death.'

There was a picture of Frank accompanying the article. It had been taken a couple of years ago and it showed him smiling, with the Swiss Alps as a backdrop. This hit Dirk hard and his eyes welled up. Helena came over and hugged him and he held on to her tightly.

'I'm so sorry Dirk.' she whispered.

The article ended and Dirk switched off the TV. He was stunned. Up until this moment he still hadn't believed it, but this really brought it home and now it was official. He thought of Frank, but couldn't see his face even though it had just been on TV. He'd heard of weird stuff like this about the dead. He could clearly visualise Maudasi's face and Dragan's and even Jason's and that made his blood boil. His head was suddenly filled with images of the break-in and he turned to Helena. 'I have to go back downstairs.'

Helena followed him down to the ruination of dead

Frank's apartment without question. She assumed this was a knee jerk reaction to the bad news and the need to experience some kind of closeness with his departed friend. But when they entered the apartment and he began pacing around the room around with a deranged determination, she realised it was something else entirely.

'What is it Dirk?' Helena asked.

Now wary and aware, he took a long moment before answering. 'I'm not quite sure. Look at all the stuff they could have taken: Frank's computer, his big TV, his stereo. In fact, look there, his iPod's still sitting in the Bose speaker system. All classic items a burglar would take, but... '

As he spoke the words, he realised they'd stumbled upon something more sinister. '...something's not right. Why would someone break in and not take any of this stuff?'

Helena's eyes followed him around the room as he continued with his observations. 'It's a hell of a coincidence that Frank turns up dead and his apartment is broken into on the same day, don't you think? Even Maudasi said as much.'

Helena nodded, 'I think you should call the police back and tell them about Frank too?'

Dirk shook his head, 'It's something else, come on think.'

'I'm trying.' protested Helena.

'I'm sorry Helena, I didn't mean you. I was thinking out loud. Maybe Jason *did* break in to look for the coin he sold to Frank...and steal it back. But maybe it was something else too...' He stopped himself from saying too much and paused for thought, 'Ok, let's try and figure out what's going on before we make wild accusations.'

They sat at the table by the window, looking at the overall scene of devastation and tried to make sense of it all. Dirk began. 'Ok, I left the apartment today just before one and everything was fine. We got back here at what...five...five thirty? Maudasi and his bully boy were already outside. They tell me Frank's dead and then ask when I last spoke with him, which is odd in itself. Anyway, the apartment's been done by this time and we can be sure it was sometime within that four hour window. That's plenty of time to create this amount of damage. Maybe they watched me leave?'

Helena simply looked on, neither agreeing nor disagreeing with his supposition.

'But then...and this is the puzzling part...they grill me about Frank's business dealings with Jason and I'm supposed to believe Frank's death was a suicide. Bullshit.'

Dirk stood up and started pacing around the room like a caged lion. 'I think they did it, you know that.'

Helena was alarmed by this statement. 'Did what? Killed your friend?'

'No, the apartment, all this crap...' said Dirk sweeping his hand in an arc over the mess.

Helena shook her head, 'But why smash up their own place, when they can just ask you to leave and then take all the time they need to look around for what it is they are looking for?'

Dirk sighed. He knew she was making more sense than he was. 'I don't know, but who breaks in and leaves all this stuff behind?'

Helena put a hand to her mouth as if she'd just realised something. Dirk looked at her 'What?'

'Maybe Frank has a woman? Yes, a woman he has done something bad to. This seems like the kind of thing an angry or jealous woman would do, no?'

Dirk had to smile at her deduction, 'No, Frank just isn't the type for affairs. If you saw his girlfriend, Natalie and where they live, you'd know he wouldn't risk all of that just for a fling.' His smile faded. 'But there's no sign of a break-in and the locks are undamaged, so it must have been someone with access and that points to Maudasi and his goon. They were here when we got here.'

Helena wasn't buying it. 'I have to say it again, why would they do so much damage when they have access and ownership?'

Dirk was scratching his head. 'You're right, that doesn't really make any sense does it? Maybe it *was* Jason and he was just pissed off and wanted to get back at me and Frank. But how did he get in?'

'Maybe it wasn't him, maybe it was someone else?' suggested Helena.

Dirk stopped pacing and looked at the mess all around them, 'But what were they looking for, if all of this valuable stuff they left behind didn't interest them?'

'My guess is money. You said your friend was a Banker, so that means cash right?' Helena said.

'No, that's not it. Nobody, not even a Banker, keeps huge sums of money lying around.' As Dirk said it, he remembered the fifty thousand euros Frank had given him to look after. But that was between the two of them. No one else knew about it, apart from Maudasi and he wasn't likely to do this for a mere fifty grand. No, it wasn't money they were after. Dirk cursed in his frustration. 'It must be those damned coins that Frank collects, they're worth a hell of a lot of money and Jason knows exactly how much they're worth.'

He was guarded in what he said around Helena and careful not to mention diamonds. He paused for thought again. 'Nothing's been stolen that I can see, even Jason would have taken the iPod, so that means the thief was looking for something specific and not just stereos or something like that to steal, right? But if it wasn't Jason and it wasn't Maudasi, then it must be someone else like you said…but who?'

They sifted through the broken objects and contents of the emptied drawers and closets, trying to figure out why the mattress, the sofa and all of Frank's clothes had been slashed. Maybe Helena was right. This did seem like the work of a scorned woman. When they stood in the kitchen something odd struck them both. It was the broken glass all over the tiled floor. Dirk picked some pieces up and studied them. They appeared to be the remains of what looked like glass jars of food, taken from the kitchen cupboards. Their contents were spread everywhere.

'Why would they smash these up?' he said out loud.

'Maybe they were looking for something inside them. I used to keep coins in a jar when I was a child, didn't you?' Said Helena.

'Well, yes, an empty jar to keep all your loose change in, but never a full one.' replied Dirk.

'But if you wanted to conceal something small and valuable, like the coins you mentioned, then a jar of pesto or whatever would conceal them and they could easily be cleaned.'

Dirk shook his head, 'No, the coins Frank buys are worth a lot of money, he would never put them inside a jar of pesto or any other kind of sauce that could damage and devalue them. You've seen what tomato ketchup can do to old coins.'

'But it does look as if they were looking for something small and easy to conceal, yes?' suggested Helena.

Dirk was aware of the other small sparkling commodity that Frank would stash securely, but knew he hadn't kept those here either. As he scanned around the wreckage, something Helena had said resonated within him and it struck him like a thunderbolt. He leapt over the broken glass and landed in front of the wine rack, startling Helena with the suddenness of his actions. He pulled out the bottom bottle on the far side and slid his hand inside. The little gold key he had found days earlier was still there, concealed in the shadows at the back of the wine silo, undiscovered. He held it up and regarded it pensively. Something clicked and he looked over at Helena as if he'd just been given next week's winning lottery numbers.

'What? Tell me. What is it?' she asked.

Dirk slipped the key into the small pocket on his Levis, the one originally designed for a fob watch but now useful for secreting lighters, cigar cutters, condoms and little gold keys. He patted it down and turned to Helena.

'Come on, we're not staying here tonight. Grab some clothes for the weekend.' said Dirk.

Helena was still puzzled and shaking her head. 'Where are we going? I have to work at the ICC tomorrow, remember?'

'Then that's perfect, because that's where we're going right now. Den Haag.'

~

When the apartment door closed behind them, Jason came out from his hiding place behind Frank's bedroom door and smiled to himself. It *had* been worth coming back here after all.

Chapter 52

In less than fifteen minutes they were packed and ready to go. Dirk grabbed his laptop and the money Frank had given him. He felt guilty for considering it now belonged to him, since Frank was dead, but knew it was going to provide the means to move them out of harm's way. He made no mention of it to Helena.

The decision to leave was his, but he was glad she agreed with him. She no longer felt comfortable staying there either and actually seemed quite excited about it. She was a journalist after all and this had all the ingredients of a good story. Dirk couldn't think of anyone better to have along under the circumstances. He *Googled* Hotel des Indes on his smart phone and found their website. It was fully booked apart from one executive suite at a really expensive price. He didn't hesitate when he saw the rate and booked it straight off. If they had to run and hide, they'd do it in style.

Before leaving the apartment, they agreed upon a plan of action regarding the direction they would take when they left the building; just in case they were being watched. This time she made no jokes about his paranoia when he risked a look out of the window at the quietened street below. It looked as normal as he dared consider it to be. Without a word, he turned around and walked towards Helena standing by the door. He thought she looked anxious, but didn't say anything. His throat was too dry. He nodded and she responded by opening the door. She closed it behind them and locked it, the small click making them both cringe.

Moving silently, they descended the stairs. At the bottom they tiptoed past Frank's apartment door, although they didn't know why. It just seemed like the instinctive thing to do. Dirk put his hand on the outside door handle and glanced back at Helena in the dark hallway. She appeared to be holding her breath. He was doing the same. Dirk was carrying his travel case. It wasn't so large that it gave them the look of two people running away. It contained their laptops and a change of clothes for them both. Although for Dirk, this meant the one intact T-shirt he had remaining. Helena carried her camera over her shoulder. He gave her a faint smile then, slowly and very carefully, opened the front door and stepped outside. She quickly followed and they walked smartly, but not hurriedly, down the front steps and turned right.

They turned left at the end of the street and crossed over a bridge then turned down a one way street, so anyone following in a vehicle would have to go the long way round. Encountering a bar that had an entrance on both sides, they walked in and straight out the other side; doubling back on themselves. About ten metres into another one way street, they stepped into a darkened doorway and listened for footsteps or a vehicle slowing down. They remained like this for several minutes and waited, huddled close to another. To a passer-by they would have looked like any other young couple sneaking a secret tryst. Dirk felt her breath on his mouth and bent his head slightly forward until his lips brushed hers and he kissed her softly. She responded and kissed him back. The kiss was tender at first, not passionate, but as they held each other and she began to squeeze tighter, their passion ignited.

For several more minutes they lingered like this, almost forgetting where they were and why, until Dirk broke off and said they had to go. After a quick glance in both directions of the street they continued with a similar zigzag pattern, until they were sure no one was following and hailed a taxi without any trouble. Dirk asked the Indian cab driver to take them to Den Haag. The cabby's eyes lit up at the prospect of such a lucrative fare and he was about to start the haggling process for the cost of the journey, but Dirk told him that if he could get them there safely and promptly, he would give him two hundred euros. The cabby beamed and shook his head from side to side and turned up his radio in apparent celebration at his good fortune. The loud and lively music made it possible for them to converse without the driver eavesdropping, thus allowing Dirk to outline briefly what he intended to do when they got there. He held Helena's hand as Amsterdam faded into the distance behind them.

~

The cab driver dropped them off at their hotel exactly forty minutes later. Dirk handed him two, one hundred euro notes. The cabby kissed the money and made a gesture that looked like he'd given them a Hindi blessing or something. They both smiled as their happy chauffeur sped off, his Bhangra music blasting out.

It was nine pm by the time they were checked in. Their room was huge and it overlooked the park outside the front entrance. Helena went into the en-suite to freshen up. Dirk drew the curtains and located the hotel room safe. He took the remainder of the fifty thousand out of his jacket and removed two hundred, to replace the two he'd used to pay for the taxi, before locking the rest away.

When Helena came out of the bathroom, Dirk asked if she was ready to go downstairs. She said yes, but asked him first to tell her again what he'd told her in the taxi. He explained that he'd met Frank, here at the hotel, for lunch on Monday and had then gone on to meet with Jason Sinclair. She was astounded when he told her Frank had simply handed over Jason's asking price of forty thousand pounds for a coin. Dirk didn't mention the payment was in diamonds. He went on to explain his theory about where Frank may have stashed his valuables and that was where the little gold key came into the picture. She concurred that his logic was sound, but shouldn't he be telling all this to the police. He explained that it was just a theory and could have no bearing whatsoever regarding the break-in. She made a face, saying that her journalistic intuition told her it wasn't likely. He admitted that he had considered someone else may have come to the same conclusion and that was why he wanted to check it out. Helena could see he was hesitant and uncertain, so she stood up. Walked over to the door, turned and looked straight at him. 'Well, what are we waiting for? Let's go check it out!'

Dirk was thrilled she was with him on this and didn't consider him to be nuts for doing what he was doing. They walked downstairs and went directly into the cigar lounge. The room was brightly lit, but more importantly it was empty. A member of the hotel staff came in to take their drinks order and recommended the Malbec-Merlot "Trumpeter" from the Mendoza Valley in Argentina at €33.50 a bottle. Dirk played the part of the uninformed tourist and accepted the recommendation. Five minutes later the waitress delivered their wine and some Indonesian spiced nibbles. When she had poured them each a glass and departed, they looked at each other with excitement and trepidation before turning their focus towards what they had come to investigate.

Just inside the entrance to the lounge, lined up against the back wall, was an array of cigar safes. There were about forty in total and Dirk would try all of them if necessary. He took out the little gold key and they both regarded the cigar safes with caution. There appeared to be an alarm system in place that matched each safe with its own specific key. Dirk looked crestfallen. This meant they couldn't just try them all in turn. They would have to be spot on in their selection to avoid setting off an alarm. Most of the safes higher up didn't have nameplates on them, so they disregarded those for now. This left about maybe a dozen with nameplates that were in use. Dirk began at the lower left hand side and Helena at the right, trying to figure out which one belonged to Frank. There were actual names on some and symbols on others. Many of the names were arcane and belonged to cigar clubs while others had the name of the individual; genuine or otherwise. Dirk tried to imagine what kind of name Frank would choose and carefully perused the remaining safes. One caught his eye. He took out his smart phone and entered it on Google. Within a couple of seconds several translation sites popped up and Dirk announced, 'I think we have a winner.'

Helena looked up. On the third row from the bottom, second door in, he pointed to a nameplate that bore the words '*Ignis Internum*'.

'What does it mean?' asked Helena.

Dirk explained, 'It's Latin and it translates to '*Fire Within*'. Speaking the words aloud elicited a big grin from him. Helena was still confused, but it all made sense to him. On Monday, in the cigar cellar, when Frank handed out cigars, he'd said something odd at the time to Jason; something Dirk hadn't quite understood. It was a reference he'd made about the cigar tube having its own fire within. Frank had been punning, referring to the diamonds that he'd just handed to Jason. He'd been alluding to their lustre, like a fire within the stones. However, cigars have their own fire within too; thus making it a flawlessly inspired name to have written on a cigar safe. It was the perfect smoke screen and typical of Frank's humour. Genius: *Ignis Internum: Fire Within*. Dirk suddenly realised this presented another dilemma. What would he tell Helena if he opened it and discovered a fortune in diamonds?

'Are you sure this is the correct one?' Helena asked again.

'I'm pretty sure. It's exactly the kind of wording Frank would put on something like this and it's a good place to hide other stuff too, like coins right? It is a safe after all.'

Helena smiled and squeezed his hand. He gave her the same hopeful look and inserted the key carefully into the lock. The key turned and the lock clicked.

Bingo. He opened the door and they both leaned forward to look inside, with the anticipation of children on Christmas morning. Lying within the darkness of the small safe was a simple wooden box. Dirk lifted it out and immediately recognised it to be a box of twenty five Montecristo No 2 cigars. Exactly like the one Frank had given him in Bristol. They both looked back into the safe, but could see nothing else. Helena ran her hand around inside to make sure and found nothing more. They sat back down and stared at the box. Dirk seemed afraid to open it, but not her, 'Go on, what are you waiting for? Open it.' she urged.

Dirk used his thumbnail to prise the little nail that fixed the box shut and pulled it out. Inside the box was a layer of about a dozen cigars. Puzzled, he glanced at Helena then lifted up the top layer and looked at the layer underneath. It revealed more of the same, nothing else, just cigars. Dirk shook his head in disbelief, 'This can't be it, surely? I mean, we figured it all out. We found the key, beat the bad guys to it and I've even got the girl, but where's the treasure? Who wrote the script for this?'

Helena smiled at his analogy of himself as the Hollywood hero and touched his face. Although disappointed, he smiled too. 'Let's have a toast to my wonderful friend Frank.'

She raised her glass to his, 'To Frank.'

They remained in the cigar lounge only for a short time, while Dirk pondered their frustrating discovery. Finally, he managed to shake off his melancholy. 'Come on, there's nothing more to see here. I'm sorry for the big let-down.'

Helena regarded him with puzzlement. 'Why are you sorry? I think your theory was correct, but I think your friend removed whatever else might have been in there. Finding cigars in a cigar safe is not really such a big surprise, is it?'

Dirk smiled again at her observation and said, 'No, I suppose not.'

'Are you going to take them with you or leave them here?'

Dirk thought about it and said, 'I might as well leave them here, where they're kept cool in the humidifier. I can come back for them any time. I know Frank would want me to see they found a good home.' He tried to sound jocular, but there was a lot of pathos in his voice. Helena felt his pain and stroked his hair. Dirk placed the box back into the cigar safe and the little gold key into his Levi jeans fob pocket.

Chapter 53

On the canal bank on the opposite side from the apartment building, screened behind the dark tinted windows of her rented black BMW, she had watched events unfold through a zoom camera lens. Her rage had subsided considerably since her frenzied search of the apartment yielded nothing. She'd spent over two hours turning it inside out looking for the diamonds, but unless they were under the floorboards they clearly weren't there. She cursed Frank for getting himself shot in the head like that. She was sure he would have capitulated in the end and told her everything, but the stupid bastard was dead and there was nothing she could do about it now. She considered the possibility that Dirk was his real partner and maybe Frank had told him where the real diamonds were hidden. However, as she'd waited for his return, her plans were dramatically altered by the sequence of events that followed:

First the Bentley turned up and Dragan got out. Walked up the front steps and rang the doorbell of the apartment. She watched while he waited patiently for an answer she knew would not come. She didn't know who he was, but knew the car belonged to Maudasi from her conversations with Frank. A thrill ran through her when Dirk and Helena appeared. Then, her smile broadened when she recognised from Dirk's body language that Dragan had conveyed the news of Frank's death. When he and Dragan disappeared inside the apartment for a short time, she grew impatient then curious when they re-emerged. There was a visible change in Dirk's demeanour, he looked smaller somehow and more subdued. She almost started her car to follow when he got into the Bentley, but the vehicle didn't move away and she continued to watch. The reason for this soon became apparent when Dirk got back out of the vehicle and proceeded to throw up. She could see Dragan was in conversation with someone in the back of the car and knew that it had to be Maudasi, recently returned from Geneva and pissed off. The thought of that made her smile. When the Bentley eventually drove off, leaving Dirk standing in the street, she remained in her car and watched him re-enter the apartment. Less than a minute after Dirk had gone in, the girl he'd arrived with came into the apartment. This presented a problem. It wasn't that she couldn't handle them both together; she was well practised on that score. The problem the girl presented was that of a potential witness or potential corpse that would incur police involvement, blowing away any chance of locating and retrieving the diamonds.

Secondly, as she sat in comfort and gloom considering how to handle the situation, another young man turned up and furtively looked around before skipping up the stairs to fiddle with the front door lock. Zooming in with her telescopic lens, she could see his shadowy form rummaging around inside the apartment. He appeared to be searching for something. The sudden realisation of what that something was almost stopped her heart. She had competition. When he disappeared further into the shadows she lost sight of him. Suddenly the lights in the apartment came on and Dirk and Helena reappeared. The young man could no longer be seen and didn't make his presence known to them.

Thirty Minutes later Dirk and Helena re-emerged from the building and looked like they were going somewhere in a hurry. What did it mean? Had they discovered the intruder? Had they killed him? What was she to do? She was about to get out of the car and go over to the apartment and find out for herself when the Bentley returned and Dragan got out.

Moments later, the front door opened and the young male contender was confronted by the large man at the base of the steps. Both men just stood and spoke to one another from their respective positions, until Dragan put a foot on the bottom step and made a gesture with his hand towards the Bentley. The young man smiled and came down the steps, shook Dragan's hand like an old friend and got into the Bentley with him. As they moved off she started her engine.

Chapter 54

Back in the secure comfort of their hotel room, Dirk brooded over their find. A box of cigars, surely that wasn't all there was to it? But maybe it was and whatever Frank had hidden in the safe was now long gone. Who knew? Frank certainly couldn't say. They'd brought the remainder of their wine from the cigar lounge and Helena poured them a glass each. Dirk emptied his coat pockets of all his bits and pieces and put them away in the desk drawer: cellphone, keys and wallet. He shrugged off his coat and tossed it over a chair. Last, but not least, he took the little gold key out of his pocket and stared at it, turning it over in his hand. He was still shaking his head in disappointment as he dropped it into the drawer beside his other stuff.

Turning to Helena, he asked if she would like to have a nice relaxing bath. She liked the idea, but suggested they eat something too. Dirk went into the en-suite to start running their bath, while Helena set about organising her own things. She took out her laptop and proceeded to upload her camera. While the images were uploading, she called room service and ordered a couple of club sandwiches and a mixed selection of Bittergarnituur and Bitteballen. Next, she switched on the TV and flicked through the news channels. There was nothing more on Frank, but there was something about a double murder in a Hong Kong hotel room. She made a mental note to lock the hotel room door after their food had been delivered. Dirk was singing in the bathroom, he had a strong voice and it brought a smile to her face. When the upload completed, she called out to him, 'Hey cowboy, want to see your pavement pizza?'

Dirk came out of the bathroom. 'Sure, I could use a laugh.'

Helena didn't respond. She was fixated on something on her computer screen that had dramatically altered her demeanour. Dirk said, 'What's up? You look like you've just seen a ghost.'

Helena turned to look at him and her expression startled him. 'Maybe I have.' She said.

The image on the screen was that of Dragan, standing atop the apartment building stairs. It was a good clear shot and it looked like he was actually staring directly into the camera, although he hadn't seen them watching at the time. Dirk waited for Helena to enlighten him further, but she said nothing.

'What is it? What am I missing?' Again she was silent. 'Helena?'

Helena's response was flat but definitive, 'I've seen this man before.'

Where? When? At the apartment?'

Helena shook her head, 'He's supposed to be dead. Like all the others.'

'What others? Who do you think he is?' asked Dirk, but she didn't respond. She was staring intently at the image of Dragan staring back at her from the laptop screen.

Dirk studied the shot of Dragan again. His bull neck was turned towards the camera and his head was tilted slightly back. His lips were parted as if he was drawing breath in the chilly evening air, giving his countenance a kind of grimace. Like a snarl.

'Helena, what is it? Who do you think he is?'

'He looks like someone I thought I knew to have been killed, but...' Dirk waited for her to continue.

She reminded him of her assignment and of the large folder she had shown him, containing news articles, letters, documents and photographs from the former Yugoslavia during its bloody civil war. He recalled the active and inactive files on war criminals and how shocked and disgusted he'd been to see that the soldiers responsible, for the perpetration of heinous crimes against humanity, were all very young.

She briefly recounted her research on the groups of militia who roamed over the countryside, rounding up and killing civilians in their crusade of *ethnic cleansing.* Dirk nodded as he recollected the news coverage of the time. Helena went on to say that of all these groups, none were so prolific and committed as a particularly nasty group of young Serbs who called themselves "*The Wolfmen*". She paused for a moment to consider her next sentence. Of all the men in the horrific documented photographs she had poured over in her research, one stood out in her mind more than the others. It was his smile. It conveyed an arrogant supremacy and was somehow disturbing to behold, even in a photograph. It was an evil smile, pure evil. It was him.

When she had finished, Dirk tried not to sound unconvinced. 'Do you really think it could be him? I mean, it was twenty years ago. People can change a lot in that time and besides we don't even know what nationality he is. Granted, he's a big scary thug, but guys like that are all the same. It could just be the way he

360

looks in that picture that triggered something in you.'

She was still staring at the image on screen, trying to convince herself, the journalist in her wanting to believe it. 'I'm almost certain. The likeness *is* there and I have really a strong feeling, but…to be absolutely certain, I would have to see him again…up close …and see that smile.'

'That might be difficult, I was hoping never to bump into Dragan again.' said Dirk.

She paused and looked up at him with disbelief. 'Dragan…his name is Dragan?'

'Yes, that's what he calls himself, why?'

'Dragan is a Serbian name.'

Chapter 55

Jason was caught and the guy even knew his name, what the hell? The large man's opening question had been about Frank and if he'd spoken with him recently, which he found vaguely unnerving because he'd just seen the news of Frank's death on television. Jason didn't allude to having this knowledge and merely said he hadn't spoken with him for quite some time. He was quick to point out that he had just come here in the off chance of seeing him, but it appeared he wasn't home. Jason then inquired, with all the insouciance he could muster in the awkward circumstances, if the gentleman was a friend of Frank's. The gentleman didn't confirm or deny that he was, but simply asked if he was here to sell more coins. This unexpected question caught Jason completely off guard. He was taken aback, but simultaneously relieved that the big guy didn't ask him how he'd gotten into the building. Jason didn't offer an explanation.

As he stood there trying to size up the situation, he added two and two together and came up short. It suddenly dawned on him that this must be Frank's source for the diamonds, or at least someone who could get him access to them.

Jason turned on his charm and announced that he had come round to discuss that very thing. Dragan, who still hadn't introduced himself, claimed that he too had been unable to contact Frank and informed Jason that he represented a person of interest, who would be willing to purchase anything of singular collectability and value. He enquired if Jason would like to meet with his client to discuss these matters. Would he indeed? Jason jumped at the opportunity and eagerly offered his services. Without having to be asked twice, he gladly got into the Bentley and was taken to meet his new benefactor.

Throughout the short journey, Jason repeatedly tried to get Dragan to introduce himself. Dragan, however, simply parried these questions with some of his own, conspicuously involving coins and their value. He skilfully implanted words like *gold, money* and *substantial* liberally in his conversation and smiled as Jason bit the *carat* each time.

~

The Chinese restaurant was busy, but as they walked in a waiter came over immediately and beckoned them forward. Jason didn't consider it odd when they were led straight through the restaurant and into the kitchen at the back. At first he assumed there was another dining area on the far side, but he began to experience a quiver of nerves when the waiter led them up a steep and narrow, dimly lit, staircase with Dragan at his back.

At the top of the stairs was a long dark corridor, down which they continued walking until the waiter came to a stop at an ornately carved black and red door. He knocked once and an oriental voice barked a short sharp reply. The waiter opened the door and stepped aside to allow Jason and Dragan to enter. Jason nervously stepped across the threshold and saw two men sitting at a large carved rosewood table with a glass top. One of the men was a distinguished looking European gentleman in a dark suit and tie. The other, equally distinguished, gentleman was Chinese; dressed in a Hanfu silk jacket. The waiter closed the door behind them and Jason suddenly felt entrapped.

The room was about twenty five meters squared and the lighting subdued. Apart from the large table in the centre of the room, there was no other furniture. Jason couldn't make out what the room was used for. Was it a dining room, an office or simply a meeting room for business? Notably, there were no windows. No introductions were made. Dragan curtly ordered Jason to sit down on the solitary chair that had been strategically placed in front of the table and announced. 'I caught him leaving Perrier's apartment.'

The Chinese man sat there impassively with both his hands splayed flat on the table top. An odd posture thought Jason, but when he looked at the man's hands he observed that he didn't have any fingernails. Jason tried to swallow. His throat had gone bone dry. He looked around at Dragan who was looking directly at the man in the suit, evidently awaiting instructions. Jason desperately wanted to pee.

No one said a word for about a minute, but to Jason it seemed infinitely longer. Eventually he found the courage to speak. Maudasi beat him to the draw.

'Did you find what you were looking for this time Mister Sinclair?'

Jason was dumbfounded. Here was another stranger who knew his name and what he'd been doing. Who were these people? The big guy who'd just driven him over here hadn't telephoned ahead. Jason looked at

Dragan again, as if he was going to offer an explanation. The Chinese gentleman remained as impassive as a stone statue, with *those* hands fully on display. Jason didn't want to think about *his* role in all of this.

'I...I...was looking for Frank Perrier...I didn't...' Jason managed to stammer before his words trailed off and his throat got even drier. He was in neck deep and he knew it. He could feel his bladder starting to let go and grabbed at his crotch. Maudasi was regarding him with complete detachment. 'I take it Frank wasn't there. Did you let yourself in again Mister Sinclair?'

Jason was stricken, how could they possibly know he'd been there before? Was he being watched? Was there a hidden camera in the apartment? Before Jason could even consider all the possibilities Maudasi spoke again, 'It must be something very important for you to keep going back.'

Jason was still grabbing at his dribbling appendage and he saw the Chinese man's face crack into a smile, his eyes disappearing almost completely into his laughter lines. Before Jason could relinquish any more control, Maudasi took it. 'Do you wish a moment to consider your answer Mister Sinclair?' Jason nodded profusely. Dragan put a firm hand under Jason's armpit and heaved him to his feet like he was a broken marionette. He was frog marched outside and taken to an unlit toilet further along the dark corridor. Dragan ordered him to leave the door open. Jason's relief was brief and he washed his face and hands with cold water. Dragan gave him just ten seconds to dry off before he snapped his fingers at him to get a move on. When they got back to the room, Jason was further relieved to find that only the man in the suit remained. The man with no nails had gone. Dragan closed the door and pushed Jason towards the chair, placing a heavy hand on his shoulder as a command he should sit back down. Maudasi didn't waste any time in resuming his inquisition. 'Let's begin again shall we? Have you found what you were looking for?' He asked in a flat tone.

Jason had the good sense not to hesitate in answering, but none when it came to telling the truth. 'I was looking for Frank Perrier.'

There was movement behind him and an instant later Jason thought he'd been shot, such was the scorching pain in his side. Dragan had produced his extendible baton and rammed it into Jason's ribcage, spilling him out of the chair and onto the floor. The pain was so intense it cut his airways. He couldn't even cry out in pain, his breath was gone and he thought he was going to pass out. Dragan picked him up like he was nothing and dropped him back into the chair. As Jason fought for breath, Maudasi asked him a loaded and very mortal question, 'Who knows you are here Mister Sinclair?'

Jason looked beseechingly at him. He was frantic with fear, but had no voice with which to plead. Maudasi leaned on the desk. 'Exactly, no one does. Now, I will ask you again, have you found what you were looking for?'

Jason was hoarse and he desperately wanted some water, but knew it would be pointless to request some. He swallowed hard and found his voice, 'I...I saw the news this evening...it said that Frank Perrier was dead and I...I went round to his apartment with the idea that

I might…get back the coin I sold him.'

'You mean this coin?' Maudasi held up the Queen Anne and slapped it down hard on the glass table top. Jason recognised it immediately and noted that it had no protective plastic casing around it. He tried as best he could to look remorseful, 'I feel really bad about what I've done…'

His act didn't cut it. Dragan delivered another gut bursting blow to discourage any further attempts at lying and Jason went down again. He lay there in agony and watched Maudasi's foot, under the table, tapping on the floor. Maudasi spoke again. 'Is that all you were looking for?'

Jason was doubled up and face down, clutching his aching ribcage. The floor was cool against his cheek. It smelled of bleach; a disturbing indication that it had been scrupulously washed recently. 'Y…yes, I swear…'obvious

Dragan hauled Jason to his feet and rammed a big fist into his battered ribs, causing him to buckle and collapse to the floor yet again. As Jason writhed around, the door opened and the waiter returned with a tray containing a pot of Jasmine tea and some cups. He stepped around Jason's twisted form and placed the tray on the table in front of Maudasi and departed, as if nothing was out of the ordinary with the happenings inside the room. Maybe he cleaned the floor on a regular basis? Maudasi poured himself some tea and gave Jason an ultimatum. 'I wish to be gone from here soon Mister Sinclair, therefore I suggest you tell me the truth or you too will soon be gone and you will not be coming back. So tell me, what were you really looking for?'

Jason didn't answer quickly enough. Dragan picked him up and dumped him into the chair again. This was the first time Jason noticed that Dragan had donned black leather gloves. That didn't bode well. Jason reeled and his vision faded in and out. As Dragan lined him up to deliver a devastating blow to his face, Jason miraculously found his voice before he completely lost his countenance and managed to blurt out, 'Diamonds…I was looking for diamonds.'

Chapter 56

After his true confession, Jason sang like a canary on acid and told them everything. He even owned up to receiving diamonds from Frank in London without being asked. When he began talking about additional business deals Frank had brokered for him, Maudasi stopped him. He was only interested in two things: when Frank had given him diamonds and how many.

'What led you to believe he would keep something so valuable in his apartment?' asked Maudasi.

'I…I just hoped I might find something, if not diamonds then maybe the coins I sold him. I assumed he must keep them somewhere, why not his apartment?'

Maudasi interrupted him, 'You've made quite a mess in your search Mister Sinclair. How do you propose we settle this?'

Jason looked at Dragan before answering. 'I…I didn't do that…I didn't touch anything.' He held up his hand, more for a stay of execution rather than a feeble attempt to protect himself from a further beating. 'Y…yes, I was in the apartment tonight, but that's exactly how I found it…I swear.'

'But why did you return to the apartment at all? Were you unsuccessful on your previous incursion?' asked Maudasi.

'What…I was…no…I…?' Jason struggled to find the words.

Maudasi glanced at Dragan. That was enough to get Jason squawking.

'Ok. I admit I was there on Wednesday, but just to look around. I didn't touch anything, I swear.'

Maudasi smiled and informed him of his incompetence, 'But you did leave some smoking evidence behind.'

At first Jason was bemused by this statement, but then it dawned on him just how they knew he'd been there before. It was the damned cigar. He cursed his own stupidity and carelessness.

Jason was suppliant. 'Ok, I've let myself in twice, that's all. I swear it. When I went in to the apartment tonight, the damage was already done. It wasn't me; I swear it wasn't me.'

'Then who else could it have been? Would you care to propose any theories of your own Mister Sinclair?' asked Maudasi.

'I…I don't know, maybe Dagger did it himself for all I know. He saw Frank's diamonds in the cellar…and the coin. He knows how much it's worth.'

Maudasi considered what Jason had just said and exchanged a glance with Dragan. 'Tell me about Mister Dagger, you and he are friends and business associates of Frank Perrier; yes?'

Jason adamantly shook his head. 'No, we're not friends. I only just met him last week. On Queen's night I think it was. He was with Frank. I met him again the following day, in the Sea Palace floating restaurant. Again, he was with Frank. The next time I saw him was when Frank and I met on Monday to trade the coin. Dagger accompanied him.'

His answer corroborated all that Dirk had told them earlier. Maudasi probed further.

'Would you say Perrier and Dagger are business partners?' asked Maudasi.

Jason intuitively grasped that Maudasi was looking for something else entirely, but now was not the time to ask, so he played along. If Maudasi wanted a scapegoat then he would provide him with one. 'It certainly looked that way. When I asked them if they were working together, they both got very cagey and were quick to dismiss the subject. Dagger took a leading part during the purchase of the coin.'

Dragan asked the next question. 'Do you know where Dagger is now?'

Jason suspected that if he said he didn't, he would receive another beating. 'I think he might have gone to Den Haag.'

Maudasi's eyes grew keener, 'Why do you think that?'

Jason told as little of the truth as he dared. 'Because, when I was in his apartment just now, Dagger came back with a woman and I hid in the bedroom. They didn't find me, but I heard part of their conversation.'

'Go on.' instructed Maudasi.

'They started discussing the nature of the break in and the fact that nothing seemed to have been stolen; things like Frank's laptop and his iPod, you know. But then Dagger seemed to have a revelation about something, because soon after that he announced they were going to Den Haag and rushed out of the apartment. Shortly after that, I encountered this gentleman.' said Jason, indicating Dragan.

'Where in Den Haag do you think he would go Mister Sinclair?' asked Maudasi.

'I don't know, but my guess would be somewhere he'd been before…with Frank.' said Jason.

Maudasi exchanged a glance with Dragan as he considered this. Dragan conveyed his opinion with a nod, signifying that this was a fair assumption and that Jason wasn't lying any more.

'That's another thing, why did you go back to the hotel des Indes after you followed Perrier and Dagger on Monday?' asked Maudasi.

"Jesus Christ", gasped Jason, *"isn't there anything these guys don't know?"* He swallowed hard and hoped his answer would sound feasible. 'I just wanted to get a feel for things in their shoes. It seemed like a good place to think, that's all.'

'Where was the last place you saw Frank Perrier?' asked Maudasi.

'In the Sea palace Chinese restaurant on Tuesday, he was having lunch with Dagger…I followed him there.'

Maudasi and Dragan exchanged another glance. Jason recognised by their expressions that this was something they didn't know, but it meant something to them.

Maudasi stood up and poured some tea into another cup, walked around the table and handed it to Jason and smiled.

'I think I might have some use for you Mister Sinclair.'

~

Maudasi had one final question for Jason before he dismissed him. He wanted to know who the little

Chinese girl was that had accompanied him to the Sea palace on Sunday. Jason almost soiled himself again when he realised they had known about him for at least a week. Without hesitation he told them, unreservedly, who she was and where he'd met her. Including how much he'd paid for her services. Dragan, without being prompted, walked over to another door. One that Jason had failed to notice until now and knocked on it softly. He didn't dare look up to see who opened it, but shuddered at the prospect of who might be behind it. Dragan disappeared into the room beyond and reappeared one minute later, accompanied by the man with no fingernails. Jason visibly shrank at the sight of the two men approaching. Maudasi ordered Jason to repeat the name of the girl and the name of the place he'd procured her from. The man with no nails listened intently to what he had to say and then went back through the door to his inner sanctum, or whatever the hell it was, to make a call. Ten minutes later he returned and confirmed that there was indeed a prostitute called Mei Lei working in the establishment Jason had given them. She had been working there all week and confirmed that she was with a client last Sunday at the Sea Palace. Maudasi was satisfied. Another person of interest had been crossed off the list.

They took details of Jason's hotel and room number. Dragan entered a number into Jason's cellphone and told him to contact it, should he see or hear anything of Dagger and the woman. Jason still had no idea who these people were, no introductions had been given, but he obsequiously agreed to do everything they asked. When Maudasi dismissed him, he was offered neither a lift nor an apology. Not that he expected the latter. But to his utter dismay, he was offered no deals regarding coins or diamonds. The only thing on offer had been his life and Jason knew that came with no guarantees. His one consolation was that they hadn't demanded he hand over the diamonds Frank had given him. Not yet anyway. When he was finally ejected into the street, Jason had gone into the first coffee shop he found and emptied his bowels. The amount of blood in the water made him wince. Before he left, he purchased two spliffs. Then, on the walk back to his hotel, he scored some Charlie white powder and a few other goodies from a cheerful African dealer; just in case the pain in his gut and sides didn't abate. Once back in the relative safety of his hotel room he took a large swig of neat vodka, before lighting up his weed and collapsing onto the bed. The experience of his ordeal eventually overwhelmed him and he passed out, fully clothed and totally wasted.

Chapter 57

Dirk and Helena forgot all about sharing a bath and let it go cold. Their food arrived, but their appetites had deserted them. Relaxation was impossible after her shock revelation and the potential unearthing of a dangerous war criminal. As Helena outlined her facts and theories, Dirk struggled to comprehend it all. He was still trying to come to terms with the death of his friend, now he had to consider the very real possibility that one of Frank's business partners might be a mass murderer. He shuddered at the memory of Dragan standing over him with his baton and concluded that Helena might not be far from the truth. Helena intensely searched the web for more information, while Dirk searched through the news websites for updates on Frank's death. Nothing; dead bankers didn't merit a second mention it seemed.

It was getting late. Helena resolved to review the archive documents in the International Criminal Court in the morning with a fresh head. They discussed Dragan some more and Dirk concurred with her about the cruel smile. Dragan had most definitely graduated from the school of sociopathic maniacs. However, they needed more conclusive proof than just conjecture. They agreed that they should inform someone about their findings and forward the photographs she had taken of Dragan to her magazine. Helena emailed them to one of her journalist colleagues and asked for his help in researching her theory further. The guy she mailed was one of the geeks from the Irish bar. He responded almost at once with enthusiasm and arranged to meet her inside the ICC, at ten the following morning. What journalist would pass up on an opportunity to bring down a war criminal? Dirk, however, suspected that Helena's colleague was more enthused by the prospect of spending the day alone with her. Dirk offered to accompany her, but she told him her pass didn't have the necessary privileges that would allow her to sign anyone into the building. Disappointed, he let it go.

Fatigue caught up with them both and they went to bed, but neither of them could sleep. They just lay there, staring at the ceiling, unable to expunge their private fears and feelings. Helena turned over and put her arms around him. The weight of their troubled thoughts sparked the need for closeness and the comfort of another. Soon they were making love. It wasn't overtly passionate, but slow and caring as if the experience of being one, in such an intimate way, unified them and strengthened their resolve. After their cathartic fusion they slipped into a restless kind of half sleep. However, Dirk fully awoke in the early hours and felt slightly guilty at having done so. Helena, in her drowsy state, could feel his hardness and squirmed against him in approval of its exigencies. As he spooned her, he slipped easily inside and they moved to the rhythm of their heartbeats, until their passion peaked and waned and they both fell back into a deep and restful slumber.

Helena awoke just before nine, sprang out of bed and into the shower. She was dressed in minutes. With her hair still wet, she kissed Dirk goodbye as he lay, half awake, in bed. As soon as she'd gone, he got up and made himself a coffee. Drained the cold bath and ran another. He spent an hour lying in the warm soapy water, turning over the events of his surreal time in Holland. He thought back exactly a week ago, to Queen's day and closed his eyes when he thought of Frank and the laughter and fun they'd shared. Had his world changed so much in just a week? It was hard to believe, but believe it he did. He got out of the bath, quickly dried, got dressed, then telephoned room service and ordered a club sandwich and a pot of strong coffee. After his light brunch, he spent the rest of the morning surfing the web for any information on "*The Wolfmen*" and other war crimes of the conflict. He didn't find anything insightful that could tie Dragan to it. There were still no news updates about Frank either. He emailed Helena and told her he was still in the hotel, but would be going out at some point soon. He also said he would book a restaurant for around eight pm for dinner. She mailed him back to say that she was still at the ICC with her colleague and that she would probably be finished around five.

Dirk gazed out of the window. It was an abysmally wet day. No sunshine whatsoever; just threatening black clouds and the distant rumble of thunder.

Chapter 58

Jason's sleep encrusted eyes blinked open and he lay for several minutes staring up at the ceiling. Both sides of his ribs ached. His back and stomach too. Rolling himself off the bed and into an upright position, he looked at his image in the mirror on the dresser. He was a mess. His clothes were crumpled and his face was puffy. He cursed the bastards who'd done this to him. On the nightstand was a packet of painkillers. A bottle of Vodka was also close to hand and he washed two down neat. When he could stand, he went into the bathroom and stood under a hot shower until he could feel the blood beginning to pump again.

Vertical and dressed in a crisp white cotton shirt, a clean pair of jeans and a blue blazer, he looked marginally better but still felt washed out. Pain and stress were etched on his face and he was hurting all over. He went into the bathroom again, where he drew two white lines on top of the toilet cistern and assuaged his discomfort through the conduit of a rolled up fifty euro note.

It was midday when he descended the stairs and entered the hotel bar. He ordered a double espresso and lit up a cigarette. The hotel was old and low budget and no one objected. The weather was appalling outside and he didn't relish the idea of venturing out in it, but he had an agenda. He hadn't received any calls from his new associates and had no intention of calling them. Moreover, he had no intention of just sitting still and waiting for things to happen. He'd decided to go and see

Dagger again and make him a proposition. Jason knew Dirk had discovered something in Frank's apartment and he was pretty sure he knew what it was. He'd retraced their steps on Monday, over and over again and had come to a conclusion; one that seemed too good not to be true. He was sure Dirk had figured it out and that was why he had dashed off so smartly to Den Haag. But maybe Dirk was back in Amsterdam now and a richer man for the experience. If he was, then he was about to hand over half of what he'd found. If not, then Jason would threaten to spill it about his theory and let others handle it from there. He also knew he would have to be cautious, because he didn't want to catch another beating on top of the two he'd received. Dagger looked like he could take care of himself. After he'd finished his second double espresso, he *borrowed* an umbrella from one of the patrons drinking at the bar and headed out into the gathering storm.

Chapter 59

Alarm bells went off when the Hong Kong police, following up on their enquiries, had tried contacting Frank on his cellphone, only to have it answered by the Geneva police. They, in turn, had immediately contacted Interpol who confirmed they had also spoken with the Hong Kong police, regarding the murders of a husband and wife in a hotel there. The husband had been identified as a suspected smuggler, but they had no idea what had brought him to Hong Kong. The Geneva police had been attempting to build up a profile of events leading up to Frank's death, by establishing the identities of all those with whom he'd been in contact. Although this new information didn't immediately indicate a definite link between the deaths, Frank's suicide very soon became a murder enquiry. All numbers received and dialled on both Frank and Chong's cell phones were entered into Interpol's database. Dirk's number was at the forefront, because he had been the last person to call Frank only a few hours before his death. Soon the police had a name to the number. Dirk's passport details were brought up, showing that he'd recently entered The Netherlands and was apparently still there. Interpol contacted the Dutch police and the information was relayed through.

Inspector Arjan Lander, of the Amsterdam police, sat at his desk going through the previous night's reports when the call came in. His superior officer called his attention to it and handed him the details he'd been given by Interpol, saying that they wanted to speak with a British tourist named Kirk Dagger thought to be residing at an address here in Amsterdam. The request was marked urgent. Lander said he would get right on it. However, when he looked at the name on the sheet of paper he'd been given, something clicked inside his head. His Commanding officer picked up on the subtle change in his expression immediately. 'What?' he asked.

'This is the person they want to interview?' asked Lander.

'Yes, they e-mailed his details a minute ago. I just printed it off, why?'

'Wait just one moment Sir.' said Lander, going back to his desk to look through his in-tray. 'Shit', he said when he saw the report sheet again. He dashed back to his boss's office, 'You won't believe this, but this man they want to interview…Kirk Dagger? He reported a break-in at his apartment last night.'

Lander immediately called Dirk's number. It went straight through to voicemail. He also tried Helena's, as she'd given her details to the police operator, but hers went straight to voicemail too. Due to the urgency of Interpol's request, he decided to investigate in person and requested a car to take him round to the address. When he arrived at the apartment and looked through the window at the extent of the destruction within, he immediately called it in.

~

Concealed behind the tinted glass of her hired car, she had watched the police car turn up and cursed her bad luck. She realised what this meant, events were catching up and her prize was slipping further away. But suddenly, standing right in front of her car was a young man. It was the one from the previous evening, the one who'd let himself into the apartment; the same one who'd gone off in Maudasi's Bentley with Dragan. She regarded him closely and could see by his pinched expression that he hadn't fully recovered from whatever had taken place inside the Chinese restaurant. Last night, she had watched him limp out of the restaurant and scurry away. She'd tried to follow him, but by the time she got out of her car he had turned the corner and disappeared into the crowded streets of Chinatown. Now he was standing no more than five metres away, staring anxiously at the scene outside the apartment building. She surmised from recent events that neither he nor Maudasi had found the diamonds, but maybe he would lead her to them. When he walked on, she got out of the car.

Chapter 60

Sadim Maudasi was having breakfast in his conservatory. Dragan sat opposite. The previous evening they'd had an intense discussion, deliberating everything Jason had divulged. Not that they'd given him any other choice. Jason had left nothing out when he'd recounted all the places he'd met with Frank and Dirk since the weekend: the bar, the restaurant, the apartment and the cigar cellar where the transaction took place on Monday afternoon. It was of particular interest to Maudasi to discover Frank had taken such an enormous risk to leave the airport and return to Amsterdam to meet with Dagger. Especially since he knew he was being watched. Maudasi and Dragan had carefully considered the roles of all parties and drawn their own conclusions. When Maudasi asked Jason why he'd returned to the hotel des Indes, Jason had said that he wanted to *"get a feel for things in Frank's shoes"*. Now, having slept on it, Maudasi was still pondering over this statement and appraising everything else Jason had told them; coupled with the facts he already knew.

'Dagger lied to us. He knew exactly what Frank paid Sinclair for the coin. He was witness to it.' Said Maudasi, grim faced.

Dragan concurred with his master. 'It would appear so and for the same reason Sinclair lied. He wants to help himself to whatever Perrier has hidden away; now that he's dead.'

'What was it Sinclair said about Dagger? Something about him suddenly wanting to rush back to Den Haag after having a revelation of some kind? What kind of a revelation would make someone do that, considering he'd just learned about his friend's death?'

'Sinclair did suggest he would probably go somewhere he'd been with Perrier. Maybe he too wants to get a feel for things in his shoes.' said Dragan.

Maudasi had his own theory. 'Sinclair did admit he was looking for diamonds. Maybe Dagger is too and has figured out where Frank keeps them?' He paused for a moment. 'Both Dagger and Sinclair deny ransacking the apartment. Do you believe them?'

'I won't rule anything out. But, yes, it is possible they are both telling the truth on that score.' said Dragan.

'When did this alleged break-in take place?' asked Maudasi.

'It took place yesterday afternoon, if Dagger is to be believed.'

Maudasi was still considering the facts. 'Frank was found dead early yesterday morning.'

Dragan nodded.

'Now if Dagger and Sinclair are to be believed and it *was* a third party, another partner perhaps, then it brings a lot into question…and into focus.' Maudasi continued to theorise. 'If the apartment was ransacked before Frank was killed, then I would agree that it might be a partner not wanting to share. But to do it after he was killed implies they haven't yet found what they're looking for.'

Dragan said nothing. He knew his boss didn't want his opinion, not immediately. Maudasi was turning all the facts over in his head and coming to a conclusion. 'I believe they *are* telling the truth, that it was indeed a third party and this third party is looking for the same thing Sinclair was: diamonds, but…an entirely different set of diamonds.'

That was Dragan's cue. 'Are you suggesting Perrier never gave Chong the diamonds on Monday?'

'Is such a concept so hard to imagine?'

'But Chong confirmed he had them, did he not?'

'Chong confirmed he had something, but he can't confirm anything now, can he?' declared Maudasi.

Chapter 61

Dead, he couldn't believe it and there was nothing he could do about it. In all the excitement and rushing around, Dirk hadn't remembered to pack the charger for his cellphone. He'd only just discovered it was dead when he'd tried to check for messages. He emailed Helena to let her know he was *off the grid* and outlined where he was going and what he was planning to do. He told her that if he wasn't in their hotel room when she got back, then he would probably be in either Momfer de Mol or La Grenouille. He also said he would book a table in the steakhouse on the same street for dinner at eight. He signed off with three kisses and waited for a response before leaving. She replied almost immediately. *'Cool, I'll find you.'* She signed off with four kisses. That made him smile. Dirk was in a melancholy mood and still undecided as to when the best time would be to contact Natalie. He wasn't looking forward to that. As he thought of his friend he realised that Frank should be here with him at this moment, enjoying and drink and a cigar; enjoying life. Thoughts of cigars made him reflect upon their disappointing discovery. He decided to go back down to the cigar lounge and smoke one of Frank's cigars in remembrance of good times past. Shrugging on his coat he walked over to the desk and removed three hundred euros from his wallet, then put it back in the desk drawer along with all his other junk. He picked up the little gold key. It still bothered him that he'd been wrong about it. He stared at it for a long moment before placing it securely back into the fob pocket of his jeans. As he was leaving the room he stole a final glance at his image in the mirror, pulled on his hat and headed down to the cigar lounge.

Outside, the storm was building up. The rain was pelting down and the wind tore at the trees. He shivered as he looked out of the window and requested an Irish coffee. When the waitress had gone, he turned to the cigar safe and ran his finger over the Latin phrase written on the brass nameplate. He smiled. *Ignis Internum*. Only Frank could come up with something like that. He took out the little gold key and opened up the safe and stared in at its contents. Just a box of cigars, no receipts or notes of paper or anything to give him a clue; nothing, zip, nada, fuck. He removed one of the cigars and relocked the safe. Put the key in his top coat pocket and placed the unlit cigar in the ashtray. The waitress returned with his coffee and he put it on his room tab. When she left, he glanced around the room and reconsidered where Frank could have gotten his diamonds on Monday.

Sometime later the waitress reappeared and asked if he would like anything else. He declined, but enquired how he would go about obtaining access to, or leasing, a cigar safe. She suggested that someone could come in and provide him with all the information and even get it set up today, if he desired. When he conveyed a genuine interest in finding out more about it, another smiling female member of the hotel staff was quickly dispatched to take him through all the complexities of the safes. This included the humidifying process, the security and most importantly, the fees. She also informed him that he could lease one for a minimum of three months or, if he was a guest in the hotel, have the use of one, free of charge, for the entirety of his stay. He asked if the hotel supplied cigars by the box and the girl happily informed him that they could cater for all of his needs.

~

As Dirk stood in front of the cigar safes, absorbing this information, another interested party watched his every move from across the street.

Chapter 62

When he had finished his coffee, Dirk left the cigar lounge and the remains of his discarded cigar in the ashtray. Feeling quite flush, he returned to the room and splashed his face with cold water. He still had to make dinner reservations for this evening, but was reluctant to leave the hotel. Following several minutes' deliberation, he decided a brisk walk and maybe even a beer would do him some good. The driving rain hastened him on and he covered the short distance to the restaurant in just over five minutes. After making their booking, he came out of the restaurant with his head down against the rain and walked blindly into another pedestrian. Raising his head to apologise, he groaned when he recognised who he'd collided with. Standing before him, under a large umbrella, was Jason Sinclair. Dirk could feel his anger rising, but he reined it back in. Jason surprised him by offering his hand, in what appeared to be sincere regret at hearing the tragic news of Frank's death. Dirk wasn't buying it and asked if he'd come all the way to Den Haag just to convey his condolences. Jason claimed he had no idea Dirk would be here and that it was Frank's death that had prompted him to embark on his own *pilgrimage.*

'Why don't we drink a toast to Frank and have a cigar in the downstairs cellar again? For old times' sake.'

Dirk's first thoughts and answer would have been wholly inappropriate for public consumption, but he checked his sentiments and simply said, 'Why the hell not?'

They walked the few yards to the cigar shop in silence. Jason selected two cigars and four small, twenty five centilitre, bottles of wine and insisted on paying for it all. Dirk was too weary to object. One of the ladies in the cigar shop came down to the cellar with them and turned on the lights. Dirk was glad she had accompanied them, because her presence prohibited him from kicking Jason all the way down the steep staircase. Jason remained reverently silent and went over to the little bar area to open two of the small bottles of wine. Dirk declined the cigar Jason offered him, but accepted the glass of wine. Jason raised his glass. 'Here's to Frank. I was truly sorry to learn of his death. He was a decent sort, really he was.'

Dirk responded by giving a small toast, 'To my friend Frank, I'll miss him.' They sat in silence for a couple of minutes. Then, with respects appropriately observed, Dirk looked straight at Jason and asked bluntly, 'Why did you break into Frank's apartment?'

Jason adopted the look of schoolboy innocence, 'Someone broke into Frank's apartment? When? Did they steal anything valuable?' he asked coyly.

'You know when, yesterday afternoon while I was out. You found out Frank was dead and then you broke in looking for coins...and diamonds; didn't you, you miserable fucking shit?' Dirk spat the words at him, but Jason was unfazed by his aggressive tone. He lit up his cigar and changed the subject. 'I had a chat with Frank's business partners yesterday.'

Dirk looked at him like he'd just picked his nose. Jason put up his hands, 'Oh no, it's not what you think. I was just minding my own business, having a drink in that little café you and Frank like to frequent.' He stopped himself as he mentioned Frank's name in the present tense, 'Sorry.'

Dirk glared at him. 'What did Maudasi want with you?'

Jason was elated. Dirk knew exactly who he was referring to. Now he had a name.

'Actually, it was you they wanted to speak with but they knew who I was, which quite took me by surprise. They asked me if I'd spoken with Frank and did I know how to get hold of you.'

'What time was this?' asked Dirk.

'Oh, around about tea time, five o'clock I suppose.' Jason lied. 'They asked if I had some more coins to sell. They even showed me the Queen Anne I'd sold to Frank, which surprised me. I had no idea he'd sold it on so soon, did you?'

'Frank did say he got you a deal didn't he? That was the one he made for you...with those guys. Did they scare you Jason?'

'Not at all, I found them most accommodating.' Jason lied again.

Dirk was seriously considering jumping on the bastard and shoving his cigar down his throat, but rationalised the consequences of such a barbaric act on foreign soil and deemed it not worth it. Not just yet anyway. He wanted to find out more about Jason's chance meeting with Maudasi. As Dirk was considering accidently spilling his red wine all over Jason's natty outfit, he surprised him again with his next statement.

'Look Dirk, I've been thinking. I realise I offended

both you and Frank the last time we were all here and I want to apologise.'

'It's a bit late for that Jason. Frank's dead, remember?'

Jason didn't skip a beat as he moved on to his main agenda. 'That's something I want to discuss with you. Don't you find it somewhat odd that he's only just dead and these people are going around asking all sorts of questions about him?'

'Maybe they knew he was dead when they asked you about him. You said you spoke to them around tea time right? Well, they spoke to me round about the same time; strange coincidence huh?'

Dirk was on the ball, but Jason let it wash over him and continued with his circumlocutory pitch. 'Do you remember I put it to you that I suspected Frank has a stash of diamonds hidden somewhere he could easily access? Well I think these friends of his know it too and they're looking for it.'

Dirk didn't like the turn the conversation was taking.

'Well good luck to them. I don't want to get involved with those people.'

'What if we don't get involved with *those people*?' said Jason.

'What do you mean *we*?' growled Dirk.

Jason smiled his treacherous smile, 'I think I know where Frank's secret stash is and I know you've been thinking about it too. In fact, I'll go one better. I think you know exactly where it is and I think you've already been and taken a peek inside.'

'What makes you think I know anything Jason?'

Dirk tried to be poker faced but, amidst his anger,

his emotions failed him. Jason was quick to spot *the tell*.

'Because, like me, you've no real reason to come here the day after Frank's death; do you?'

Dirk had had enough and started to get up to leave, but Jason played his ace. 'Wait! I wouldn't be so keen to rush off if I were you *Mister* Dirk. Not if Frank's partners were to find out that you had the key that unlocked all his secrets.'

Dirk stopped rising from his chair and scowled at Jason who was looking back at him with an infuriatingly smug expression. 'So, what does Frank keep in that little cigar safe of his Mister Dirk? More diamonds, coins, cash? All of the above?'

Dirk couldn't believe Jason had followed him again so successfully and without him even suspecting it. He knew there would be no point in trying to bluff it out. However, he tried his best not to look too surprised and shrugged, 'Cigars.'

Jason smiled victorious, 'Why don't we go there now and take a peek together. We can split the contents between us, without telling Frank's partners anything?'

'If it's cigars you want Jason, you can buy them upstairs.'

Jason ignored Dirk's inane quip, 'I bet you have the key on you right now.'

Dirk's anger turned to apprehension. He realised that if Jason had figured all this out by himself, then so too would Maudasi and Dragan. So what was the problem? He wasn't lying, there really was nothing but a box of cigars in Frank's cigar safe, but what was he to do? Jason wouldn't accept it if he just told him to get lost. He'd run straight to Maudasi and Dragan and if they found out that there were only cigars in the safe, Dirk knew they wouldn't believe him either. He considered just giving Jason the key to Frank's safe, but then immediately thought better of it. Jason would never believe the contents of the safe was all there was. When Dirk didn't come back with an answer Jason smiled triumphantly, 'Let's finish our drinks and take a stroll round together…partner.'

Jason got up and went over to the bar where he'd left the other two bottles of wine and poured them both a second drink. Dirk sat there desperately trying to come up with a way out of the situation without bashing Jason's brains in. He was horrified when he considered the possibility that his life might depend upon it if he didn't.

Chapter 63

Hidden amongst the patrons seeking shelter in a convenient café on the opposite side of the street, she waited for them to reappear. After Jason presented himself in front of her car in Amsterdam, she knew she couldn't afford to lose him again and shadowed him all the way here. Her main problem had been getting too close and giving herself away. However, she needn't have worried. He'd been so intent on fleeing the scene outside Frank's apartment that it inhibited his awareness and he failed to notice he was being followed. Jason had been so preoccupied that he'd walked the entire distance back to Amsterdam Centraal Station, where she watched him board the train for Den Haag. She had taken the next carriage and remained vigilant.

When they arrived in Den Haag, she observed him weave through the crowd on the platform and get onto a number 17 tram outside the station. She managed to catch up and get on just as the doors were closing. At that moment he turned around and she thought she was caught, when he looked straight at her. However, a group of teenage girls got on and diverted his attention. When he got off, two stops later, she had gotten off with him using a different door to exit the tram. She'd kept her distance, following him through a dark and rain swept, tree lined, park towards an elegant hotel at the end. He walked purposely and she was hopeful of something positive when they reached the final destination. However, when he came within striking distance of the hotel, he suddenly stopped and hid behind a tree. She moved out of sight, behind a parked van. He remained behind the tree for several minutes and appeared to be directing his gaze at something or someone inside the hotel. She couldn't make anything out from where she stood. Risking exposure, she moved closer and aimed her telescopic camera lens at the hotel to get a closer look at the reason for his odd behaviour. The person he so badly wanted to avoid was visible through the ground floor window. His back was turned and he appeared to be in conversation with someone else in the room. However, she recognised him by his hat. Dirk was standing at the back wall with his hand outstretched, touching something.

For almost an hour she had patiently watched Jason, who not so patiently watched the hotel. Dirk eventually came out and walked away from the hotel, through the park, perpendicular to the way they had come in. Jason remained out of sight behind his tree for another minute or so. Then, staying behind the tree line, he fell in behind Dirk and followed him. Keeping them both in her sights, she ventured closer to the hotel and looked in through the window where she'd seen Dirk standing. As soon as she saw the cigar lounge and all the little safes lined up against the back wall, she knew. She knew because it was as brilliant as it was simple. Satisfied, she turned away from the hotel and fell in behind them both until they disappeared underground.

Chapter 64

Maudasi had come to a decision. He would do exactly what Jason Sinclair had done: retrace the steps Frank had taken on Monday and *get a feel for things in Frank's shoes.* Now, as he sat in the cigar lounge of the Hotel des Indes and sipped an eighteen year old Macallan Scotch whisky, his eyes tracked around the room like Schwarzenegger's terminator, 'Are you getting a feel for anything yet Dragan?' he asked.

Dragan glanced around. 'Perrier was last seen with the package in this room. He came straight from your home and was dropped off here, at the hotel, on Monday morning. Ulyana reported seeing him in here, drinking coffee and watching TV, prior to meeting up with Chong...'

Maudasi was sitting back in his chair; malt whisky in one hand, cigar in the other. He closed his eyes and considered Dragan's every word.

'...After Chong left, Perrier returned to the cigar lounge and remained there until he went to meet his friend Dagger. He returned with him just after one pm. Ulyana and I observed them having lunch in the restaurant. At no time during this period, did Perrier or Dagger have a bag or anything that could have contained something the size of a box of cigars. The rest we know, both from Sinclair's account and what I myself observed. After they traded with Sinclair they came back here again, late in the afternoon, smoked cigars and drank some wine before returning to Amsterdam.'

Maudasi was deep in thought. 'That makes it three times Perrier was here on the same day; coincidence or convenience? Let me put something to you. Supposing you were going to steal something from someone…someone close. In fact you were going to steal it right from under their nose. How would you do it?'

'Very quickly.' replied Dragan.

'And the same could apply to a switch couldn't it?'

'Even simpler, because nothing would seem amiss.'

'And where would you hide it?'

'Somewhere close by; somewhere convenient and easily accessible.'

'Somewhere in plain sight perhaps; somewhere so obvious that no one would even think to look?'

Dragan knew exactly what Maudasi was alluding to, but he would not steal his master's thunder. 'Do you think it's in this hotel?'

Maudasi opened his eyes. 'I think it's in this room.' he replied, exultantly.

Chapter 65

Thirty minutes had gone past and she was considering going down to confront them, but scratched that thought. Cellars are man-made traps and she didn't know the layout or how many people might be down there. Worst case scenario: she could be forced into killing them. That was out of the question. Not without the diamonds.

Her best option was to wait it out and follow the hat, because there was now no doubt he was the key player in the game. He was the one Maudasi had sought after Frank's demise and he was the one being sought, at this moment, by the other player in the game. The minutes ticked slowly by. Then, without warning, as if in announcement of an impending event, came a flash of lightning that illuminated the darkened street followed by an almighty crash of thunder that shook the windows of the cafe. Everyone in the café whooped and jumped with a mixture of fright and delight; all except one. As rain poured off the canopy of the cigar shop, a lone figure emerged from the cellar. It was show time. She watched as he turned his collar up and pulled his hat down against the rain before walking off. Standing up, she placed twenty euros on the table and stepped out into the downpour, carefully concealed under her umbrella. She followed him back in the same direction they had come from the hotel earlier, through the tree lined park. She appreciated the display of sculptures and grand buildings, although not for their design or their beauty. It was more for the convenience they provided.

If he was to suddenly turn around and look back, she could stop and pretend to admire something. However, the abysmal weather forced his pace and he continued to walk purposefully on without stopping or looking back. When they had almost reached the hotel, he behaved in a manner she hadn't anticipated. He sidestepped off the path and hid behind the last in the line of trees. She ducked out of sight, underneath the giant sculpture of the kneeling bronze giant. His behaviour was puzzling. Why was he being so cautious? A quick glance in the direction of the hotel told her why. Maudasi's Bentley was parked right outside the front entrance.

She moved to a better position and zoomed in on the hotel windows with her long camera lens. Maudasi and Dragan were standing in the cigar lounge. A waitress entered carrying drinks, making it apparent they weren't leaving any time soon. She was philosophical about the timing of their arrival. Albeit somewhat inopportune, she considered it to be a fortunate occurrence. It would have proven awkward had she been in there when they'd turned up. Now, at least, she had them in her sights. She smiled at how agitated it made her friend behind the tree behave, knowing he had to wait for them to leave before he could enter. However, she saw no reason for her to stand in the rain waiting for Maudasi and his formidable driver to leave. Putting her camera away, she slung her bag over her shoulder and glanced around the surrounding area. There were no other people in the park. The weather had driven them all indoors. She looked up at the sky. It was as dark as night and a lot more rain was threatening to come down. He obviously thought so too, pulling his coat collar up higher and readjusting his hat in preparation for a long wait. She approached with stealth and pressed the barrel of the gun hard into the back of his neck. 'Don't turn around.' She ordered flatly.

Such was his surprise he almost did the exact opposite, but she held the gun firmly in place and informed him he would receive the same send off as Frank Perrier if he tried it again. This seemed to convince him of her convictions.

'Who are you? What do you want?' he asked.

'You know what I want. I know all about that room over there and what it contains.'

'I don't know what you're talking about? What room?'

She pressed the gun harder against his neck. 'I'm not here to play games, so don't lie to me again. I know why you're here. I watched you earlier. Now, are you going to give me what I want or do I take it off your corpse?'

'You're not going to shoot me in broad daylight.' He replied, with surprising self-assurance.

She looked up at the ever darkening sky, 'What daylight? Now, either you give me what I want, right now, or I'll kill you and go through your pockets to find it. I'll count to three: one, two, thr...'

'Wait, don't shoot...it's in my coat pocket...I'll get it. Just don't shoot me ok?'

Holding the gun firmly in place, she asked. 'What's the name on the safe?'

'I don't know.'

She pressed harder with the gun.

'I honestly don't know. I haven't figured that out yet.' He said.

She glanced at the hotel. 'Do they know the diamonds are in there?' she asked, gesturing to Maudasi and Dragan.

'It looks that way doesn't it?'

'Then we'll just have to convince them to leave, won't we?' she announced.

Lightning flashed and a cloud burst overhead with a deafening boom. His face butted off the tree as she fired point blank at the back of his head. He rebounded violently with the recoil onto the wet gravel pathway, landing flat on his back in a dead heap. She casually glanced around again and saw not another living soul.

Quickly going through his pockets, she found his passport and wallet. There was three hundred and twenty euros in it. She removed the money and continued her search. In the top right hand breast pocket of his coat, she found what she was looking for. It was surprisingly more solid and heavier than she'd imagined it would be, but then again it came with a heavy price. Wasting no time in celebration she quickly checked all his remaining pockets, but found nothing more of interest or value. Satisfied she hadn't missed anything she dropped the contents of his pockets onto the ground, beside his twitching form and walked unhurriedly away from the macabre display she'd just created. She didn't look back and continued her steady march past the gothic and sometimes grotesque sculptures, admiring each one in turn. They appealed to her cultural sensibilities. When she reached the kneeling bronze giant, at the far end of the park, a siren wailed in the distance. She didn't panic or break into a sprint. The sound was coming not from behind her, but in the direction she was headed. Her pulse quickened slightly, but not her pace. It was way too soon for anyone to have discovered the body she had only moments ago left lying in a dark puddle. Maintaining her resolve, she crossed over the tram lines and disappeared amongst the diminishing crowd of straggling shoppers. By the time she planned to return to claim her prize, the police would have scared off all the competition.

Chapter 66

Helena finished her research in the ICC around six o'clock in the evening; later than she'd anticipated. Her colleague couldn't see a resemblance to any of the few grainy photographs she'd managed to dig out of the archives, with the recent ones she'd taken of Dragan. There were descriptions that could relate to a man like him, if you turned the clock back twenty years, but only in approximate height and build. However, she was resolute in her belief. Her colleague sympathised, saying that he understood her ambition, but told her they had little or no evidence with which they could proceed. She didn't see any point in telling him about what had happened to Dirk's apartment and felt he was being a little too patronising. She capitulated for the time being and thanked him for his help. As a courtesy, she invited him to join her and Dirk for a drink and experienced a slight pang of guilt at feeling relieved when he declined her offer. She'd much rather be alone with Dirk.

When she got back to the hotel, she was surprised by the large crowd gathered outside the entrance. There were at least six police vehicles, all with their lights flashing. Paramedics were there too, but they appeared not to be in a heightened state of emergency. The roads either side of the hotel had been blocked off to traffic and pedestrians alike. Helena was only allowed through when she told the police she was a guest in the hotel. Once inside the cordon she asked one of the police officers what the problem was. He was unforthcoming. She flashed her journalist ID at him. This elicited an even more negative response and she was curtly told that there would be no comment at this stage.

Inside the hotel she found out from one of the hotel staff that a body had been found in the park. A dreadful fear gripped her and she ran up to the room. Dirk wasn't there. She was about to call him, but remembered switching off her cellphone in the ICC building and hadn't switched it back on. Her heart sank when she dialled his number and it went straight to voicemail. It sank further when she saw his phone lying on top of the desk...dead. But then she remembered the email he'd sent telling her about it. She listened to her voice messages in the vain hope that somehow he'd left one for her. There were several and she listened to them all. None of them were from Dirk. One was from the Amsterdam police regarding the break-in to his apartment. The officer had left his number and requested she call him as soon as possible. Going back downstairs to the hotel reception, she enquired if there had been any messages left for her. There were none and her dread worsened. She looked in the cigar lounge in case Dirk was watching the scene from in there, but there was no sign of him. Stepping back outside, she tried desperately to find out more about the dead person in the park and was again sternly rebuffed by the police. She thought it best to let it go for now. It would do no good if she got herself arrested for interfering with police procedure. Her mind raced and she remembered Dirk saying that if he wasn't in the hotel room, he would be in one of the bars near the restaurant where they were supposed to be having dinner.

With a flickering flame of optimism, she headed for

the bar with the great Stoofvlees first. He wasn't there. She looked in the bar across the street. No luck there either. With increasing despair, she walked around the corner and went in to La Grenouille. Again, she was out of luck. There was no sign of him anywhere. Helena described him to the barmaid who told her that there had been no one in who matched his description, but asked her to send him round immediately when she found someone who did. Helena laughed meekly. She returned to the first bar, thinking they might have missed each other, ordered a drink and sat down to wait and hope.

Forty five minutes later he still hadn't turned up. Tired and despondent, Helena went to the restaurant for their eight o'clock booking still hopeful and praying he'd show up. She sat there on her own for thirty minutes, then left without ordering anything and returned to the hotel. The area was still cordoned off and a substantial police presence remained. Now fearful of any information the police might provide, she went back into the hotel and asked reception if there had been any messages. She was disappointed again. Back up in their room, everything looked normal. Nothing was out of place, no signs of a break-in or a struggle. She sat there worrying and wondering what to do and if she should go back out and talk to the police again. She glanced over at Dirk's dead cellphone. It was now nine thirty and he was missing. She listened to her voice messages again and made a single call. It was answered on the first ring. 'Inspector Lander.' announced the keen voice.

Chapter 67

As Helena made the call, Dirk's passport details were being entered into the Den Haag computer system. Almost instantly this flagged an Interpol alert and communications flashed between police departments and international borders. Twenty minutes later, she opened the hotel room door to a uniformed officer accompanied by a man in plain clothes. He introduced himself as Inspector Jan Alphenaar of the Den Haag police force and seemed almost as relieved to see her as she was of him. The urgency in Lander's voice had panicked her when he'd instructed her not to leave the hotel room until he could send someone. He refused to elaborate or tell her anything. She was worried sick and wanted to know what was going on. Most important of all, she wanted to know what had happened to Dirk.

Alphenaar stepped over the threshold, shook her hand and requested they sit down. His tone of voice and sorrowful demeanour didn't fill her with confidence. She sat down in an armchair that almost swallowed her up. He took a seat at the desk. The other officer remained standing.

'I'm guessing this isn't about the break-in Inspector.' she said, with a large dose of irony.

'That *is* part of it,' was all he said.

She looked at him imploringly and seemed to shrink deeper into the low chair.

'What's happening outside Inspector? Please tell me? Is it Dirk?'

Alphenaar drew breath and glanced at the officer

standing by the door and then back at her. 'A man was killed in the park just opposite the hotel. The passport we found beside the body belongs to a Mister Kirk Dagger.'

Helena put her head in her hands and wept.

~

Helena wanted to see Dirk's body, but it was suggested she wait until he was made more presentable for viewing. She appreciated the delicate way it was put. She still didn't know how Dirk had died and asked if the police thought his death was related to the break-in at the apartment. Alphenaar said he couldn't really say anything more at this time.

They remained in the hotel room while the uniformed officer wrote down her statement. Helena recounted all that had happened since they'd turned up at the apartment last night and found a man waiting on top of the front steps. She described Dirk's disposition when he'd gotten into the big black car and his condition when he got out again in some distress. She illustrated the bizarre characteristics of the burglary and their hypothesis for the reasons behind it, mentioning the gold coin and how much Dirk's dead friend Frank had paid for it and that Dirk suspected the coin was the main reason for the break-in. Alphenaar nodded grimly as he listened to her tearful account of events and asked her for the names of these men. She gave up Dragan, but couldn't remember the name of the man in the car or the one who'd sold the coin. Appreciative to the fact she was stressed and upset, Alphenaar gently cajoled her into trying to recall some of the things Dirk had told her. She remembered that the two men in the black car seemed very interested in obtaining more coins and that Dirk suspected the one called Dragan had been in the apartment before the break-in. Alphenaar asked if she could provide descriptions. She said she couldn't describe the one who remained inside the car, but thought he might be the landlord and mentioned the disturbing fact that he had threatened Dirk about contacting the police regarding the break-in. Alphenaar immediately instructed the uniformed officer to track down the owner of the apartment. When he prompted her to continue with her description of the man at the top of the stairs, he noted the dramatic change in her demeanour.

She told him about the pictures she's taken of Dragan and took out her laptop to let him see. As Alphenaar perused the photographs, Helena dropped her bombshell. She told him what she had been researching at the ICC today and why. He had to do a double take on what she said. When she had finished repeating what she had just told him, he looked like he was going to pop. He immediately got on the phone with his superiors and relayed this startling information about the possibility of a war criminal being involved. They, in turn, informed Interpol and the investigation went into top gear. Helena provided them with copies of the photographs she had taken of Dragan and gave them reference numbers to the files containing grainy pictures of suspected war criminals. When Alphenaar finished talking with his superiors, he attempted to resume the interview. Helena had regained some of her composure, but only wanted to talk about one thing and cut him off with a single question. 'How was he killed Inspector?'

Alphenaar hesitated momentarily before answering. 'He was shot.'

She closed her eyes and he knew the interview was over.

~

Helena was driven back to police headquarters by Alphenaar, who was keen to keep a tight lid on the investigation. On arrival, he received another call from Inspector Lander of the Amsterdam police. Lander had been the one who'd contacted him and informed him of Helena's phone call and whereabouts. He said he was calling to enquire about the welfare of the girl, but he also stipulated that Dagger and Helena had first contacted his department about the break-in. Alphenaar knew what Lander was angling for. However, murder superseded burglary. It was his case now and it was becoming a complex one: murder and war criminals. All in a day's work he thought ruefully.

Helena remained under police protection for the entire night at the police station. Alphenaar asked if she would like to call anyone for support. Her editor fleetingly crossed her mind, but she'd been too upset to answer any more questions and had silently shaken her head. In the morning she was asked if she felt up to identifying the body. She nodded her head slowly. Alphenaar contacted the hospital in Den Haag and spoke with the morgue supervisor, who said they could come down anytime they were ready. He asked Helena if she wanted a coffee and something to eat first. She requested only a coffee. Thinking the girl had been through enough to be subjected to further distress by the coffee they served in the police station, Alphenaar went out to get her something decent. While he waited for his order of coffee and croissants his cellphone rang.

'Alphenaar' he answered in his inimitable gruff voice.

Chapter 68

He was still out of it. The authoritative and capable young female doctor insisted they let him rest. Alphenaar was perusing the medical report. The Doctor said that it was uncommon for this type of drug to be found in men and that the dosage was a little high, but that happens with the misuse of unregulated drugs. What she couldn't understand was why he had taken Rohypnol, which is more commonly known as "the date rape" drug and why he had taken it in the location where he was found. It was a puzzle that would have to wait until he had slept it off and came around.

Alphenaar asked to see the patient's personal effects. He'd been brought in wearing a pair of Levi jeans, in good condition, an expensive pair of boots and a fine quality cotton shirt. No jacket. No identification or cash had been found on him either. At first it was suspected someone had drugged and robbed him, but he was still wearing his watch. It was an expensive Tag Heuer. Alphenaar didn't think anyone would have gone to the elaborate trouble of drugging and stripping someone of their valuables, only to leave behind a three grand watch. But if it wasn't robbery then maybe he'd just tried to get stoned and bought the wrong drug. It happens with tourists. Alphenaar wasn't buying it. He got out his cellphone and dialled a number. It was answered after just two rings. He spoke quietly with the person on the other end of the phone and nodded, all the while looking at the sleeping patient. He ended the call by inviting the person he'd dialled to join him in the ward. He hung up and said to the young Doctor, 'Maybe we can clear this up right now?'

The ward doors opened and the Doctor looked up to see a pale faced, terrified, young woman enter with trepidation. Alphenaar walked over to meet her and led her over to the bed. 'Don't worry, this isn't the morgue. I just want to know if you recognise him.' He said, indicating the patient lying on the bed.

'Dirk!' screamed Helena, prompting the Doctor to immediately order her to be quiet. But there was no stopping her now as she pushed past and rushed round to Dirk's bedside. She stroked his hair and covered his face with kisses and rivulets of tears; such was her elation and relief at seeing him alive again. Her joy suddenly stalled and she looked anxiously between the Doctor and Alphenaar. 'Is he...?'

'He's fine, by all accounts. He's just had a disagreeable dating experience, that's all.' said Alphenaar.

Helena was confused by his statement, but he came over to her and suggested they leave the hospital staff to get on with their jobs. He gently led her out of the ward and told her what the Doctor had told him: Dirk was expected to wake up and fully recover in a few hours. He explained what had happened to him and where, but couldn't say why. He quickly moved on to the subject that had originally brought them here; the body in the morgue. Helena recoiled at this and said she didn't want to go there now, since it wasn't Dirk and that looking at an unknown dead person would do her beauty sleep no good at all. Alphenaar accepted her point. Then, as an afterthought, he asked her if she knew someone called

Jason Sinclair. Expecting a negative answer, he almost had a seizure when she said she remembered Dirk mentioning that name to her before. He was the one who had sold Frank the gold coin.

Chapter 69

Dirk awoke from his latest nightmare demanding to know what time it was, where he was and why he was handcuffed to the bed. A policewoman was summoned and it was explained to him that he was a person of interest in a murder inquiry. Dirk rattled his shackles like Marley's ghost and demanded to be released, but settled for the cup of tea he was offered by the hospital staff. Ten minutes later Helena came running in to the ward and jumped onto his bed. She was horrified when she saw the handcuffs. Fortunately, Alphenaar had accompanied her and the restraints were removed.

'You look good for a dead man Mister Dagger.' remarked Alphenaar.

'I'll take your word for it, I haven't seen what I look like yet.' replied Dirk, with no idea to whom he was speaking.

Alphenaar introduced himself and shook Dirk by the hand, indicating that he was in no way a suspect. Not yet anyway. Then, without any further pleasantries, he requested the nurse draw the curtains around the bed for privacy and began asking questions. 'Do you know someone called Jason Sinclair, Mister Dagger?'

'I'll say I do. He's the bastard that put me here.'

Alphenaar frowned slightly at Dirk's colourful rhetoric. 'Do you remember what happened to you?'

'Yes, I went out for a walk and bumped into Jason Sinclair.'

'Bumped into?' queried Alphenaar.

'Accidently met him by chance.' clarified Dirk.

'Why do you say he was responsible for your current condition?'

'Because I was alright before I met him.'

'Do you know what he gave you?'

'He slipped me a mickey?'

'He did what?'

'Slipped me a mickey…a Mickey Finn; it means he put something in my drink.' explained Dirk.

'Did you see him do this?'

Dirk looked at Alphenaar as if he was an idiot.

'I have to ask, you may have requested it. It's for the record, alright?' said Alphenaar, unashamedly.

Dirk sighed, 'Jason poured the wine, so I couldn't really see if he put anything in it apart from wine. I never expected it you know?'

Alphenaar nodded, 'Why did you go downstairs with him?'

'It's a smoking cellar for people who've bought a cigar from the shop upstairs. They sell the wine too. It's normally a nice, safe place to go.'

'So, you've been there before?' asked Alphenaar.

'Yes…once before.' Dirk hesitated and Alphenaar picked up on it, 'Recently?'

'Yes, on Monday as a matter of fact.'

'Were you on your own or did someone accompany you?'

Dirk appreciated that this wasn't a formal police interview, but he didn't want to appear cagey or worse, guilty of something. 'I was with my friend Frank Perrier and…Jason Sinclair.'

Alphenaar put his hands on the bottom of the bedstead and looked straight at Dirk. 'Did you go there to conduct some private business with them Mister Dagger?'

'No, I'm here on holiday.'

Alphenaar smiled at this. 'Are you having a good time?'

Dirk immediately grasped what his smile was about. Helena must have told him about the coin and Frank and possibly more. 'I've had better. Can I get dressed and get out of here Inspector? Do you have Jason in custody?'

'Yes…and no.'

Dirk looked at Helena then back at Alphenaar. 'I can identify him…and I'll press charges for what he did to me.'

'I'm pleased to hear it Mister Dagger, because I do have someone that requires identification. He's lying in the morgue.

~

Helena didn't have any objections when she was asked to wait until they got back. Alphenaar escorted Dirk down to the morgue, where he was shown some clothing and other personal effects taken from the body. He identified his own hat and coat and obviously his passport. He noted there was no little gold key amongst them. The Police had gotten Jason's name from a casino membership card found in his wallet and a maxed out credit card bearing the same name, but nothing with photographic identification. Not that it would have helped. Jason was a bloody mess. The bullet had exited at the bridge of his nose, blowing most of it off and taking out his right eye socket. The swelling to his lips made him look like he was puckering up for a big wet one and might have seemed comical, if that was all the damage done to his devastated features and he wasn't dead. Dirk was surprised by how much sympathy he felt. FUBAR as Jason was, he could still tell it was him.

Dirk officially identified him and signed a form attesting to his positive identification. On the way back upstairs, he asked about his passport and when he could have it back. He was informed that all his effects would have to be retained as evidence for the time being, including his passport. He wasn't worried about getting his hat and coat back; they were a bloody mess too.

Alphenaar drove Dirk and Helena back to police HQ in Den Haag, where he began the formal process of interviewing them. He began by asking them how they knew each other. They held hands as they told him how and when they met. That brought a smile to Alphenaar's face and he said something in Dutch to Helena, who squeezed Dirk's hand but didn't translate. Dirk explained about the break-ins and who he thought was responsible; he professed that it could have been either Jason or Dragan or both, on separate occasions, but expressed misgivings about his theories due to recent events. Alphenaar didn't offer an opinion.

The police quickly established that Helena's involvement was purely circumstantial and Dirk was really the one they needed to be talking to, not least because of the request from Interpol. He was taken into another room to provide confidentially and privacy, so he was told, accompanied by Alphenaar and two other police officers. They began, very cordially, by asking how he was feeling after his trip with Rohypnol and if he would like another cup of coffee. It was all seemingly very relaxed, but he knew it was only a matter of time before they would get to the point. Being astute enough not to volunteer anything to men with an agenda, he let them ask their questions. They asked him again how he knew the deceased and he gave the same stock answers he'd been handing out all week: that he didn't really know Jason, but had met him through his friend Frank Perrier. He was asked to expand on this and the relationship between Jason and Frank. He answered truthfully; telling them Jason was a client of Frank's and had come here to sell him a gold coin. When they asked him to tell them more about the gold coin, he wrote down the details he remembered of it. One of the officers Googled it on his smart phone and it spoke for itself.

'That's a very valuable coin to be carrying around and you say Mister Sinclair came all the way over here from England, just to sell it to Monsieur Perrier?' Asked Alphenaar.

Dirk suspected the police already knew the answers from Helena. She had probably told them everything, thinking he was dead. Alphenaar further confirmed Dirk's suspicions when he enquired if the trade had taken place in the cigar cellar, where he'd been drugged. However, before Dirk could answer and much to Alphenaar's consternation, one of the other officers unexpectedly jumped the gun. 'How much did he pay for it?'

Dirk answered unwaveringly. 'Forty thousand pounds!'

The officer did a quick mental calculation. 'That's almost fifty thousand euros and he handed it over just like that, in a public place? That's more than I earn in a year.'

Alphenaar shot the officer a look that told him he'd be staying on the same pay scale for some time to come, then took the lead again. 'Did you witness this transaction Mister Dagger?'

Dirk looked him straight in the eye. 'Yes, I did.'

'And was it exactly forty thousand pounds? Did Mister Sinclair count it?' Asked Alphenaar.

'No, he didn't. I guess he trusted Frank. I believe it wasn't the first time they'd done business of this sort together.'

The interview then followed on with questions about his relationship with Frank and why he'd come to Amsterdam. Dirk recounted their long friendship and that he'd come here to visit his friend for Queen's day. It became more like an interrogation as time went on. They asked him to explain his relationship with Jason and then Frank again, switching between the two in an attempt to trip him up. He wearily gave the same answers to almost exactly the same questions asked by Dragan and Maudasi on Friday. Alphenaar asked him about the break-in again and why he thought it might have been Jason and Dirk recounted it all again. When Dragan's name came up he was asked to explain his relationship with him and did he also think that he was a war criminal. Dirk said he couldn't attest to him being anything other than the bastard who beat him up, but had confidence in Helena's judgement. He made it clear that there was no relationship and outlined that he had only met Dragan on three separate occasions, but not sociably. Friday's encounter had definitely not been sociable. He gave them a detailed account of the aggressive line of questioning Dragan had taken with him, followed by the beating he'd received at his hands and the weapon of choice he had used. Finally, this seemed to cause the police some concern.

Following on from this were questions regarding the mysterious Maudasi. Dirk recounted his conversation with him in the Bentley and told all he knew about him from what Frank had told him; that he was super rich and loved gold. They asked what business Frank had been involved in with these people and Dirk simply said that apart from buying the gold coin from Jason, on behalf of Maudasi, Frank provided private and personal banking services. Dirk stringently emphasised that up until this week he had never met any of these people, but they all seemed to want cause him harm. One of the other officers suddenly changed tack and asked why he and Helena had come to Den Haag. Dirk reminded them of what they had just been talking about and they seemed to accept his reasons for not wanting to stay in the apartment. Well, who would after a break-in, the death of his friend and a beating; all three connected with the same place.

When the questions had seemingly ended, two officers arrived from Interpol and the questioning began all over. Dirk went through it all again with monotonous repetition. However, like the Dutch police, Interpol seemed to be more interested in Dragan and were keen to interview Helena. Careers could soar on a collar like that. At no time during any of the interviews did the subject of diamonds or little gold keys enter into the conversation.

Chapter 70

Sunday 8th May, Den Haag.

There was still a lot of police and press activity in the park the day after the fatal shooting, but the roads and sidewalks accessing the hotel were no longer blocked off. The hotel staff and guests alike were so agog about the murder on their doorstep that she walked casually into the hotel. Unimpeded and unobserved. However, when she entered the cigar lounge she cursed her bad luck again. There were several people smoking and drinking and ogling the scene outside, obstructing her access to the prize inside. She could do nothing for the moment except pretend to be intrigued by the ongoing activity. A dapper old gent enjoying a sherry was only too happy to enlighten her. While he talked she furtively scanned the cigar safes, counting forty in total and observing that less than half had a name or symbol of ownership inscribed on them. None gave a clue to which one was Frank's. She knew she couldn't just try them all with so many people around. Even more disconcerting, there appeared to be an alarm system in place. She suspected the key contained a security chip of some description that was matched with its parent safe. If that was a possibility and she didn't insert the key into the right safe, it could set off the alarm. Damn Frank!

Knowing she couldn't afford to get it wrong or take any more unnecessary risks, she tried to recall what she had observed through the window last night with her camera lens. Dirk had been bending over slightly, touching one of the safes; possibly *the safe*. Positioning herself in front of the wall of safes, she tried to imagine which one he was touching. It was somewhere around about…Damn. The old gent had nudged her and asked if she would like to join him for a drink. Realising she would have to bide her time and wait for a better opportunity, she politely declined and made her escape.

Once outside, her thoughts became clear again. She rationalised that she'd been looking for the wrong thing in Frank's apartment and her temper had gotten the better of her. Silly really, Frank had a lot of nice stuff too. She'd been searching for the diamonds when she had overlooked the fact that Frank had cleverly secreted them someplace else. Well, now she knew exactly where they were hidden and with both Frank and Dirk out of the way, there was nothing to stop her going back to Amsterdam and searching the apartment again for a clue to the name on the safe. She might even pick up a few keepsakes this time.

Chapter 71

The death of Jason Sinclair puzzled Maudasi, what did it mean? Had he stumbled across the diamonds or had he come to collect? Had his partnership been terminated like Frank's or had he just been in the wrong place at the wrong time? No matter what the reason, it made Maudasi very uncomfortable to consider that he'd been killed right outside the hotel at the exact same time he'd been in there.

~

Last night, as Jason lay drinking a cocktail of his own blood and rain water, Maudasi had been drinking quality malt whisky in the cigar lounge. He and Dragan had been discussing their current predicament and drawing their conclusions, when a piercing wail of sirens interrupted their deliberations. Outside the hotel, the arrival of several police vehicles and an ambulance alerted them that something was very wrong. They had watched the frenetic activity of the emergency services unfold and erect a cordon around the area, making it impossible to see anything. Dragan had gone to find out what was going on and the concierge informed him that a body had been discovered in the park just across from the hotel. No more than ten or fifteen metres away. This information had given Dragan a very bad feeling and he'd instinctively dialled Jason's cellphone. It rang out for a long time before going to voicemail. On his return to the cigar lounge, he passed on the disturbing news.

Maudasi continued to view the dramatic scenes in the dark and sodden park and instructed Dragan to keep trying to get hold of Sinclair. However, the second time Dragan rang Jason's number it was answered by a policeman. Dragan instantly hung up, removed the SIM card from the cellphone and broke it in two with his thumb and forefinger. Wasting no more time he turned to Maudasi and issued a grim directive. 'We need to leave this place *now*!'

~

Maudasi had come to a decision. The hotel was where the diamonds had begun their journey at the start of the week and that was where they were now. Jason's death confirmed his theory. Perrier had made the switch and hidden the diamonds in a cigar safe, but which one?

The hotel and surrounding park area were still swarming with Police. Maudasi didn't dare go near. If the diamonds were still in the cigar lounge then the police presence guaranteed their security, for now. Only a fool or a madman would risk coming back for them with all this going on. The smartest place to be would be far away. He also concluded that Jason hadn't just been killed, he'd been executed; but by whom? It drew down focus on the one remaining known associate of Frank Perrier's: Mister Dirk Dagger.

Chapter 72

They said very little to each other in the car. Helena leaned against him and he closed his eyes for the entire journey. Both were drained by their recent experiences. Dirk was still feeling slightly woozy, owing to his Jason induced slumber and he was also still very much in shock over his near death encounter. The police had intimated that Jason's murder may well have been a case of mistaken identity, simply down to him wearing Dirk's hat and coat. Dirk shuddered as he recalled the memory of Jason's ruined face in the morgue.

The Dutch police and Interpol were desperate to haul Maudasi and Dragan in for questioning, but with scanty details on both, the authorities were stymied. Maudasi didn't seem to exist on file anywhere. Even the Bentley couldn't be nailed down without a registration number.

Dirk and Helena had made the decision to stay in Hotel des Indes again that night, rather than return to Amsterdam. However, Helena had requested she be allowed to go back to her apartment and pick up some clean clothes and a few essentials. Dirk had offered to buy her what she needed, but understood when she said she would rather have her own stuff. A police officer had been assigned to drive them to Amsterdam and then escort them back to the relative comfort and security of their hotel in Den Haag, under the protection of the police.

The officer parked in an empty spot near the entrance to the street and remained in the police car, allowing them some privacy. When they entered the building, they walked straight past Frank's apartment and up to Helena's to get what they needed. Neither of them said a word when they entered. The shock and strain of the last twenty four hours had taken its toll. As they stumbled around the apartment, gathering what they thought they might need, they bumped into each other at one point. Dirk looked into her eyes and saw that they had filled up with tears. They both dropped what they were holding and embraced each other. Dirk could feel her body shaking or was it him, he couldn't tell. She began to cry and he felt his own tears well up and a lump form in his throat. He lifted her chin and kissed her wet eyes and cheeks and gave her a reassuring smile. 'Come on, that cop downstairs will be banging on the door any minute.'

She gave a weak laugh and wiped away her tears. He kissed her again and said, 'We'll have that bath tonight and some wine ok? Then we'll get an early night.'

'I can't wait'. She replied, sucking air between her teeth.

When they'd finished collecting what they needed, they went back downstairs. Dirk announced that he wanted to go in to Frank's apartment to look for a jacket or a pullover; just something intact enough to replace his blood soaked Barbour, until the stores opened in the morning for him to buy a new one. Helena looked hesitant, but he assured her he would be in and out and opened the door. Helena reservedly stepped in after him. Dirk went into Frank's bedroom and rummaged around in the trashed clothing for something wearable against the night air. He managed to find an intact fleece and shouted back to Helena that he'd found something. When she didn't answer he called her name again. A primal fear clutched his heart when his second call got no reply and he shivered, even though he'd just pulled on the fleece. He walked back into the lounge with mounting trepidation and was confronted by the brain numbing sight of a wide eyed Helena and a grinning Dragan. His big arm wrapped around her neck. 'Find what you are looking for this time Mister Dirk?'

Helena struggled against Dragan's iron grip. Dirk struggled to remain calm. 'I could ask you the same thing *Mister* Dragan.'

'So, you finally killed Sinclair?' asked Dragan, with a subtle note of admiration in his voice.

'Again, I could ask you the same thing.' replied Dirk.

Dragan donned his inimitable smile. 'Do you have them?'

Dirk slowly shook his head. 'You guys never give up do you? I don't know what the fuck you're talking about. Jason obviously did and it got him killed. So, please, just tell me. What the fuck are you looking for?'

Dragan tightened his grip on Helena and she began to choke.

'Ok, Dragan. Let her go. Tell me exactly what it is you want and I'll try to help ok?'

Dragan looked like he was about to snap Helena's neck just for the fun of it, so Dirk stalled.

'Maybe we can figure out a way for everyone to come out a winner here? How about it Dragan? Please?'

Dragan's smile got wider when Dirk said please. He saw it as a sign of weakness. 'Very well, if you insist on claiming you know nothing, I will tell you. Your friend, Frank Perrier, was responsible for a very valuable package on Monday. It contained twenty million dollars in diamonds, hidden inside a box of cigars. He was supposed to deliver this package to someone in the Hotel des Indes; the very place you had lunch with him on Monday. Less than forty eight hours later, the person to whom he delivered it was killed. Less than forty eight hours after that, Perrier himself was killed and…less than forty eight hours after that Frank's other business associate, Jason Sinclair, turns up dead outside the same hotel in Den Haag. All three of them shot in the head. Coincidence Mister Dirk?'

'And you think I had something to do with it? You must know that's not possible. I don't know who shot them.' said Dirk.

Dragan was losing patience and Helena was losing consciousness. 'Speaking of coincidence, I believe you were in Den Haag yesterday. So don't tell me you know nothing or I will break your girlfriend's neck.'

Dirk looked at Helena as she fought for breath against Dragan's stranglehold.

'Let her go first and I'll tell you everything I know.'

'Tell me first.' barked Dragan, tightening his grip. Helena's feet lifted into the air and she began to dance grotesquely. Dirk couldn't see any other choice and blurted it out:

'The package is in the Hotel. It never left.'

Chapter 73

Helena had lost consciousness, but Dragan continued to squeeze the life out of her. She became a dead weight in his arms and began to slump, forcing him to adjust his grip. That was all the opportunity Dirk needed. He launched himself forward and crashed into them both. Dragan had no choice but to let her go and she flopped unconscious to the floor. Dragan and Dirk grappled with each other. Dirk had the momentum and tried to throw a right hook, but Dragan's reaction was swift and he dodged it; taking it on the shoulder. Dirk realised he was standing on top of Helena and tried to shift his weight off her. Dragan capitalised on his distraction and spun him round, slamming him into the door frame in a bone juddering crunch. In a flash Dragan had produced his extendible baton and swung it in a low arc. Dirk pushed himself off the door frame, but the baton caught him on the hip. Clenching his teeth, he pushed himself forward. His renewed momentum propelled them onto the ruined sofa, toppling it over and spilling them onto the hardwood floor. Almost immediately, they were both back on their feet. Dragan still had hold of his baton and backed away to get more room to swing it. In the second or two it took him to size up the situation, Dirk fumbled for his belt and quickly hauled it off his waistband. Now, he too had a weapon. Dragan thrust out with the baton and Dirk swung with his belt. The brass buckle caught Dragan on the side of his head, but the baton grazed Dirk just below his left eye. Dirk swung the belt again. This time

Dragan caught it in his free hand and pulled. Dirk lost his balance, but managed to push in the direction he was falling and landed hard against Dragan. They crashed on top of a small table, disintegrating it on impact. Dirk could hear glass breaking, but dismissed all thoughts of sustaining serious lacerations and connected his forehead, full force, against Dragan's nose just as Dragan's knee came up to meet with his groin. The electric shock emanating from Dirk's nether regions made him buckle, but he had enough strength and instinct to push himself away from his quarry. Dragan swung blindly with his baton. It connected squarely with Dirk's collar bone and he went down.

Helena was recovering slowly from her undignified and prostrate position on the floor. As her senses kicked in she began to focus on the noise in the room. It sounded like the building was collapsing. Managing to push herself up onto her elbows, she saw Dirk lying on the floor on his side. He was conscious, but appeared to be having difficulty moving. Suddenly another figure came sharply into focus. Dragan was standing above Dirk with a weapon of some sort in his hand, raised in what looked like a killer blow. He was smiling. No, not smiling. Grinning? No, that wasn't it either. It was a strangely animated look. It was the look of a madman. Her breath caught in her throat and then it released in an ear shattering scream. '*WOLFMAN!*'

Time seemed to go into reverse for Dragan as his brain struggled to process what she had shouted at him. He stared at the crazy woman on the floor with bewilderment and confusion. She was staring back at him with wild eyes, saying something to him, using a name he hadn't heard in a very long time. Still doing the breaststroke on the floor, Dirk had been bracing himself for some more of Dragan's majorette skills when his hand touched something sharp. Dragan was standing over him, but his attention was now focused directly on Helena. Dirk picked up the shard of broken glass and with all his remaining strength, rammed it into Dragan's leg just above his Achilles tendon. Dragan howled like a condemned soul as the pain registered and he brought his baton down to reconnect with Dirk's already aching collarbone, sending him back to the floor. Helena scrambled to her feet and looked around the room for a weapon of any kind. Dragan was regrouping fast and Dirk was in no condition to defend himself. Helena lunged for the table by the window and grabbed hold of a large chunky ashtray. Dragan mocked her choice of weapon then, moments later, undoubtedly conceded that it was in fact an excellent choice, when she threw it at the large front window; shattering it and alerting all and sundry to the fact that something was wrong.

Dragan took a step towards Helena and stopped when he glanced out of the broken window. Running at full pace along the street, was a policewoman pulling her standard issue Sig Sauer P250 out of its holster. Dragan looked between the two: Helena with a look of sheer hatred and an oncoming police officer with deadly force. He made a decision. Stepping around the sofa, he gave Dirk a swift kick. This provoked the reaction he had anticipated from Helena. She attacked him with all the ferocity of a lioness protecting her cub. Dragan thrust his arm out sharply and his baton caught her full on the solar plexus, cutting her breath and knocking the fight out of her. Suddenly there was a loud crash as the policewoman forced the front door lock with an explosive brass jacketed key. Dragan had to think fast. Picking Helena up like a rag doll, he threw her arm around his neck and stepped out into the hallway. The police officer was standing just outside the apartment door with her gun raised. Dragan adopted an expression of anguish and distress. 'Please, help us…help us?' he pleaded as he limped out with an unconscious Helena. The momentary confusion of the police officer, at the sight of the woman she was supposed to be protecting being rescued by a stranger, was all Dragan needed. As she checked her weapon into its holster, he delivered a vicious blow with his baton and all of her promotion prospects diminished.

Helena had fallen to the floor again. Dragan decided not to waste any more time on her or Dagger. He'd settle this another time. Now was the time to get away. Once outside the building, he looked left and right. The Bentley was four cars away. It wasn't an option. Too many people had congregated on the other side of the canal to stare at the commotion. He would have to evade and escape on his own. He limped down the stairs and walked away from the scene as quickly as his bleeding leg would carry him, painfully aware of the approaching sirens.

Dirk's eyes came into focus and he glanced around the room. There was no sign of Dragan or of Helena. He hauled himself upright and staggered over to the open doorway. He felt both relief and anguish to see her lying face down in the hallway. She was breathing and moaning, thank God. He propped her up against the wall and then went over to examine the policewoman. She was unconscious, but breathing. Her face had blown up like an orange balloon on Queen's day. He rolled her into the recovery position and made sure she wasn't in any obvious distress. The front door was open and there was a trail of blood leading outside. Dirk followed the trail to the top of the steps and saw that it went all the way down. Dragan must be hurt bad; good! People standing on the opposite side of the canal bank were shouting and pointing at something or someone. Dirk tracked his eyes to where their attention was directed and saw Dragan, almost at the end of the street, half limping, half running and he saw red; a whole trail of it. He started down the front steps, but in his haste lost his footing and tumbled all the way down to the unforgiving pavement below. Cursing, he got back to his feet on jellified legs and gave chase. His pursuit was slow at first and his bladder felt like it was going to burst. His neck, shoulder and balls hurt like a son of a bitch, but this had to end now because the next time Dragan wouldn't announce himself. He'd just kill them.

Dirk turned the corner where the blood led and staggered to another corner, where it led him up a side street behind the apartment building. There was no sign of Dragan. Dirk proceeded warily. Halfway up, the trail took a left turn and he followed it until it turned right onto a wider street. About seventy metres away, still limping, but keeping a steady pace, was Dragan. This led into a busier street where he knew Dragan could disappear amongst the crowds. Spurred on by the thought of losing him, Dirk hurried along at his agonised pace and emerged in time to see Dragan cross the main road. He yelled his name at the top of his lungs. People turned around in shock, to stare at this beaten up banshee making all the noise. Dragan was forced to pick up the pace, much to the detriment of his bleeding wound. Dirk ran across the street, dodging trams and cars, in time to see Dragan turn another corner. Dirk approached cautiously. By now he was familiar with Dragan's dirty tricks and anticipated a counter attack. He came to a stop and listened, then walked slowly around the corner at a wide berth. A couple of meters down the side street was Dragan, hiding in a doorway, sweating and bleeding, waiting with his baton.

With his element of surprise gone and knowing there would be no escape while this amateur was chasing him, Dragan stepped out to face and finish his nemesis. Dirk looked around for something…anything he could use for a weapon. But there was nothing of practical use and he stood there with empty hands. Dragan waited for him to make his move. Dirk didn't budge. The police couldn't be far behind. Dragan knew Dirk was playing for time. However, he also knew that his best defence was attack and he launched it swiftly and brutally, lashing out with the baton. Dirk dodged the first of the blows, but he was weakening. It was only a matter of time before he ran out of steam and then luck.

Dirk caught hold of Dragan's baton and tried to wrestle it from his grasp. Dragan stuck his left thumb into Dirk's eye and started to push hard. Dirk pushed back with his other hand against Dragan's face and heard him grunt, as it connected with his sensitive broken nose. Dirk shook his head and managed to get his eye away from the big thumb and held in close, like a boxer on the ropes. He punched at anything he could connect with, but his blows just bounced off the big tough bastard. Dragan seemed to be doing nothing in return, conserving his energy, letting Dirk expend his. Dirk pushed with all his might against the big man, but his strength was failing. The drugs that were still in his system were closing him down. He was slumping downwards and his legs were starting to give way. His nose was at Dragan's chest and it hurt as it dragged down his coat, tugging at it and pulling it up grotesquely. A rage of fury and injustice surged, fuelling the fire within. He pushed his feet off the ground and rammed his head into Dragan's face, crushing his already shattered nose. The pain must have been excruciating. Dragan roared and brought his big fist down on the back of Dirk's neck, relinquishing him dazed and sprawled on the pavement.

The sound of police sirens alerted Dragan that he had to move. Almost blind from pain and blood, he cut between two parked cars and ran through the growing crowd of terrified onlookers. He couldn't see properly because of his watering eyes and struggled to negotiate a straight path. People darted and jumped out of his way. He pushed on. His heart was beating like a bongo drum and he wondered how much blood he'd lost. Although not arterial, the nature and severity of his wound produced a steady flow and caused him distress. Suddenly a cyclist came out of nowhere, startling him. Stumbling backwards, Dragan stepped off the pavement and straight into the path of an oncoming tram.

As he lay on the road he wondered if the scream he heard was his own. No one was screaming now. In fact he could hear no sounds at all, not even sirens. Maybe he'd gotten away. Then a strange buzzing sound started, it sounded as if a swarm of bees had descended. He was aware of people, lots of people. They were talking and drinking and laughing. It looked like a market square. It looked like fun and he wanted to join in, but when he approached they all stopped and looked at him sternly. An old man among the crowd pointed to a bridge. Dragan felt compelled to go to it. As he got nearer the bridge, the sky grew darker and it looked like a storm was approaching. He turned to look back at all the people, but they had disappeared and he was alone on the bridge. He tried to look over, but it was too high. He tried to climb on top of it and saw that he had no legs. Where were they? He looked around and saw the ends of the bridge were closed off, shrouded in fog. Strange, but where were his legs? He heard splashing over the side of the bridge and hauled himself up onto it and saw that the water was roiling; it was roiling and it was blood red. A bony hand appeared from the water and a faraway voice spoke to him. 'Wolfman.'

He felt cold, as if the bony hand had clutched his heart and he experienced an unprecedented sensation of fear. He tried to get down from the bridge, but found he was sitting on the edge without legs, leaning over and staring into the water. 'Wolfman.' The voice called ominously again. Dragan's heart was racing and it pumped rhythmically in his eardrums. 'Who are you? Where are my legs?' Dragan demanded, but there was no challenge in his voice. Suddenly, there was a blinding flash and Dragan found himself looking into a dark and rain filled sky. He couldn't remember where he was until a face came into view. It was Dagger. Now he remembered everything. As the darkness closed in around him he heard the faraway voice calling one last time. 'Wolfman.'

Chapter 74

Maudasi had watched with morbid fascination when Dagger and the woman turned up and entered the apartment building. Dragan would surely hear them come in and confront them. Now he would have some answers. His optimism turned to absolute horror when a projectile smashed through the front window and disintegrated with an alarming crash onto the street. This was swiftly followed by a policewoman running towards the scene with a gun in her hand. He couldn't have foreseen a development like this. The Bentley had been parked too far away and he hadn't seen them arrive in a police car. He felt his mouth go dry. What should he do? It was too late to warn Dragan. He could do nothing but sit and watch it all play out, concealed within the confines of the car's tinted glass interior. His horror intensified when Dragan stumbled out of the building with blood all over his face, hands and suit. Paused momentarily and stared directly at the Bentley. Maudasi saw something in his eyes that he'd never seen before, something that almost arrested his heart. It was shear panic. He stared in disbelief as Dragan hobbled off down the street and then gasped when Dagger appeared at the top of the steps and promptly fell down them. His blood pressure took an exponential upward surge when Dagger got back up and started running after Dragan, shouting every obscenity in the English language. Moments later, they both disappeared around the corner at the end of the street and were gone. Maudasi continued to stare at the empty corner from the back of his now not so comfortably safe position, stupefied by indecision. The sound of police sirens getting closer jolted him out of his stupor, but in the wasted seconds he'd spent trying to make up his mind whether to get away on foot or drive, his car door was abruptly opened by a woman wearing sunglasses and a large saw tooth cap. She slid in beside him and slammed the door shut.

Maudasi's already grated nerves made him jump. 'Who the hell are you?'

In a flat tone, she coolly announced, '*That* is unimportant, but I think your problems just got bigger.'

'What do you want?'

'The same thing as you Mister Maudasi...diamonds.'

Maudasi was surprised she knew who he was and regarded her contemptuously, 'And what diamonds would those be?'

'Come now Mister Maudasi, the diamonds Frank Perrier stole from you on Monday.'

While he considered what she said, the sound of the sirens grew louder. He didn't want to hang around, but at the same time didn't want to pass up on an opportunity to recover his stolen goods.

'What do you know about that?'

'I know you don't have them and neither does your running friend.'

Maudasi regarded her contemptuously, 'Are you saying you know who does?'

'I'm saying I know where they are Mister Maudasi.'

Maudasi had the gall to chuckle. 'So what do you want, a finder's fee?'

'No, Mister Maudasi, I want the diamonds.'

As Maudasi opened his mouth to convey his feelings,

440

his thick silver mane turned bright red as the top of his head blew off, decorating the rear window of the car with his brains. As his final moments twitched away on the back seat, she checked her image in the car's vanity mirror and made a slight adjustment to the angle of her cap.

Chapter 75

The paramedics made no attempt to resuscitate the legless corpse that was Dragan, pooled in his own blood with a tram on top. They placed a large plastic sheet over him, denying the twittering, blogging, onlookers a social media scoop. Battered and bleeding, his energy entirely sapped, Dirk sat down on the pavement and watched it all with an almost dispassionate sense of gratification and relief. The paramedic crew wanted to take him to the hospital for treatment and the police wanted to question him, but he insisted on returning to the apartment and made a bit of a scene. Inspector Lander got wind of what had happened and Dirk was promptly whisked away in a police car. When he arrived back at the apartment, Lander was at there to meet him. Another paramedic crew had turned up and were treating Helena and the downed officer. The injured police woman had a skull fracture and had to be stretchered out. Helena had bruising to her throat and chest, but was otherwise unharmed. As Dirk came through the front door, he almost had to be stretchered back out, when Helena launched herself at him and threw her arms around his neck. The pain in his collarbone was excruciating.

Lander spoke gently to them, but it was clear he wanted a statement as soon it was feasibly possible. His concern was that other police departments would soon turn up, assert their authority and claim all the glory for themselves. Helena sat on the ruined sofa and gave her statement. Dirk was too wired and remained standing.

The other reason was that his balls hurt too much to sit down. He refused medical treatment and insisted on opening a bottle of wine. He then informed everyone how much it cost and proceeded to offer the cops and paramedics a drink. They all politely declined, saying they were on duty. Dirk persisted, insisting they help themselves and even take a few bottles away with them. It was obvious he was in shock and the paramedics tried in vain to subdue him. However, it didn't even take one glass before he was spent. His adrenaline had all but burned out and he slumped to the floor. Two paramedics kept watch over him as did Helena.

It was suggested they spend the night in hospital for observation in case of delayed concussion. They both said that, if possible, they would like to return to the comfort and safety of the Hotel des Indes. Helena also pointed out that she would need to be in Den Haag tomorrow, to provide a deposition at the ICC of her positive identification of Dragan as a war criminal.

Leaving Dirk and Helena to have a moment alone, Lander spoke with his fellow officers and requested an update on the progress of locating Maudasi and his Bentley. He was knocked over by the efficiency of the officer, to whom he'd given this directive, when he returned five minutes later and informed him that they had located both. Dirk went outside with Lander to look inside the big car and immediately identified the brightly crowned corpse in the back seat as Maudasi. He and Helena felt a tremendous wave of relief, as they realised that the people trying to cause them harm were now dead. However, it raised another serious question. Who killed Maudasi? Had it been Dragan? It was unlikely, but not impossible. He could have killed him before he entered the apartment. When they went back inside, Lander cleared the room of technicians and medics then began asking more questions. However, neither Dirk nor Helena remained in a fit state to do anything apart from collapse. Lander relented and allowed Helena to take Dirk upstairs.

A little over an hour later, they were awakened by the buzz of activity downstairs. Interpol had arrived and so too had Inspector Jan Alphenaar. Helena opened the door to him when he knocked on her apartment door. He showed genuine concern for them both. Dirk managed to get himself up and with a little help from Helena, showered and washed off the last traces of dried blood; some of which was Dragan's. His body ached all over but he didn't think anything was broken, including his collarbone. They were interviewed again by Interpol, who couldn't stress enough the importance of apprehending the killer. Both Interpol and the police had emphatically dismissed any notion that Dragan had killed Maudasi.

Dirk recounted the things Dragan had said to him before they'd fought. He outlined as plainly as he could that, according to Dragan, Frank had been given the task of delivering a package to someone in Hotel des Indes on Monday morning. This person was now dead, according to Dragan. He omitted to mention what the package contained.

'Have you heard of a man called Chong Yuan, Mister Dagger?' asked the Interpol officer.

Dirk shook his head.

The officer continued. 'He's a smuggler or, should I

say, was. Interpol have had their eye on him for years. We believe he was the man Frank Perrier gave this mysterious package to. He was shot in Hong Kong a couple of days ago, along with his wife. It was on the news. Perhaps you've seen it?'

Dirk went white as he recollected seeing the story on CNN earlier in the week. The officer also pointed out that Chong and his wife, Frank Perrier and Jason Sinclair had all been shot in the head at point blank range. They had all been professionally taken out. Dirk already knew these grizzly facts from what Dragan had told him earlier. Maudasi too, still sitting outside in the backseat of his Bentley while the crime scene technicians gathered forensic evidence, had been dispatched with a single head shot. Dirk shuddered as the imagery entered his consciousness.

'It would appear that your friend Frank and his business associates were involved in smuggling something of great value; something that can be concealed in a small package. What do you think that could be Mister Dagger?' asked the officer, the rhetoric in his voice thinly concealing the loaded question.

Dirk shrugged and chose not to offer an opinion. The officer put it to him in another way.

'This killer is very determined. They will not give up until they have what they are looking for. Who do you think will be the next target Mister Dagger?' asked the Interpol officer, letting the question hang.

Acutely aware that anything he said now would undoubtedly raise more questions, Dirk carefully considered what to tell them. But a lot of people were dead and he had to consider Helena. He took a breath and looked at her and then Alphenaar before he spoke. 'Frank bought the coin from Jason on Monday with diamonds…forty thousand pounds worth of diamonds.'

After that you could have heard a pin drop.

Chapter 76

Monday 9th May, Den Haag.

The cigar lounge was empty, but the TV was on. An effervescent weather girl cheerfully outlined the bleak forecast for the week ahead. Outside the rain lashed and the wind howled. Battered and blown out umbrellas were discarded everywhere. The waste bins were full of them. One blew through the park like tumbleweed in an old western movie and came to rest against a tree. Ironically, it was the same tree where Jason Sinclair had come to rest forty eight hours previously.

Dirk looked out of the window and reflected on the past week. Had it only been seven days since Frank had kicked off a chain of events, here in this very room, with such devastating and far reaching consequences? He removed a cigar from his pocket and snipped off the closed end. Struck a match and held it to the business end, gently blowing on its glowing fire to help it along. When it burned bright he drew upon it, taking the cool smoke into his mouth and exhaling a large plume skywards.

A waitress entered carrying a drinks tray. Dirk requested coffee, without sugar or cream and a small glass of port to accompany it. She smiled and he acknowledged her with a slight nod of thanks. When she departed, he sat down in an armchair and appreciated the moment of solitude. Helena crossed his mind and he considered all that they'd been through in the past few days. She'd stood by him throughout. He smiled when he thought of her sitting somewhere within the safety of the International Criminal Court building, nailing Dragan's coffin shut. It was almost over.

His thoughts were dispelled by the striking image of another woman, when the velvet curtains of the cigar lounge parted and in she walked. Dirk recognised her immediately, even under the hat and Jackie O sunglasses. She sat down on the chair opposite, keeping the table between them. She said nothing, but he could see her dark eyes scanning him from behind the tinted lenses.

'Hello Natalie.' said Dirk.

She continued to regard him silently with her inscrutable gaze, her lips curling faintly into a smile. Dirk drew on his cigar once more and blew the smoke away from her. 'I always knew it was too good to be true; I mean someone as beautiful as you hooking up with someone like Frank.'

She almost purred at the mention of her beauty and her lips curled even more. She loved it when men commented on it, her power was their desire. Still she said nothing.

'How long have you been here?' he asked.

Finally, she broke her silence, 'Do you mean since Frank's unfortunate suicide?'

Dirk was casually dismissive and shrugged, as if nothing really mattered; except that she was here now. He asked if she would like something to drink and pointed to the port. She declined. He held up his cigar. 'So, you've come to collect. What do you propose? A fifty-fifty split?' said Dirk, smiling. He had a nice smile and she almost smiled back, but no this was business. The time for smiles and more would come later.

'I think you are overlooking something; I have the key and you don't.' She declared.

Dirk was unimpressed. 'No, I think you are overlooking something; I know which one it opens and you don't.'

She was equally unimpressed and held up a gun. It was fixed with a silencer and it was pointed straight at him. 'Well here's something you can't overlook. Now show me.'

Dirk shrugged again. 'It's the one with fire within.'

Her eyes flashed. She was in no mood for games. Dirk could read it clearly in her expression. Still holding his cigar, he opened his arms and held out his hands in clarification. 'That's the name written on the cigar safe. You know, I'm surprised you didn't figure that out for yourself, Frank always liked a touch of irony.'

She produced the little gold key she'd taken from Jason and placed it on the table. 'Open it.'

'So we're agreed, fifty-fifty?' said Dirk again, with exaggerated optimism.

She continued to hold him in those impenetrable dark eyes and issued her ultimatum. 'Open it or I'll split you fifty-fifty.'

She stood up and motioned with the gun, indicating he should get up too. Dirk picked up the key and solemnly stood. She kept her eyes and the gun firmly focused. He stepped forward, holding the key out in front of him. When he reached the cigar safes she made her intentions clear. 'Don't do anything stupid. I won't give you a second chance.'

Dirk inserted the key into the lock. There was a click and he swung the small door outwards. She ordered him to step away and sit down on the sofa with his hands in his pockets. Keeping the gun trained on him, she looked into the safe and saw the box of cigars. She reached in and lifted it out. Placed it on the table and plucked at the little securing pin that held the box shut, casting it aside. Her moment had finally come. Opening the lid, she picked out a single cigar and allowed herself a smile.

'Don't I get one?' Dirk asked.

'You get to live.' She replied, putting the cigar back and closing the box.

'Well, I suppose that's a better deal than Frank got.' remarked Dirk.

She smiled at his philosophical outlook and dropped the cigar box into her bag. 'I'm so glad you agree. It's the small things in life that are important. So, I guess this is goodbye. It was fun this week wasn't it?'

Still holding the gun on him, she backed towards the exit. Stopped and looked out of the window at the deserted rain spattered street. Her eyes tracked back to Dirk and she smiled again. The force of the gunshot hit him square in the chest, blasting him backwards against the sofa. The recoil of his body propelled him forward and he hit the coffee table face down, cracking his forehead on impact and engulfing him in blackness. As he dropped to the floor, she dropped the gun into her bag and slipped between the velvet curtains.

Chapter 77

Outside, she headed across the park and passed the tree where she had dispatched Jason. Her car was parked at the far end of the line of trees, facing the opposite direction for a quick exit. As she drew closer, she became acutely aware that two people, a man and a woman, were lingering very close to it. They appeared to be having a conversation. Nothing odd about that, generally speaking, but the weather was abysmal and they didn't have umbrellas. They also looked unnaturally casual. Passing a parked car, she glanced into the wing mirror and saw two men walking behind her. There was nothing casual about them. Her adrenalin kicked in and her heart began beating faster. Slipping her hand into her bag, she curled it around her gun.

As her trigger finger tightened, an opportunity presented itself in the form of an elderly male driver struggling to park his small Fiat car while his rear window misted up. When she drew level with him she turned and fired two shots at the men walking behind her, felling one and making the other dive to the wet ground. In a blur of desperate motion, she skipped sideways and dragged the old man unceremoniously from his car. Jumped in behind the wheel and crunched the gears. The car shot forward and she felt a jolt as the tyres ran over the old man's legs. His tortured cries of anguish could be heard above the noise of the screeching engine. She turned the car towards the two men she had fired upon. This offered better odds, because she knew at least one of them was out of action. Glancing in the wing mirror, she saw the man and the woman, who'd been in conversation near her own car, break into a run. They had guns out too. She felt the thud of bullets hitting the car's body, but none had an effect on her or the car's performance. The gears screeched in protest as she grinded them and pushed the little car for all it was worth.

Another car appeared in her left peripheral vision and sped towards her. She veered the Fiat away from its approach, down the street to the right of the hotel. The Fiat's rear window shattered, showering her with glass. A searing hot pain flared in her back as the bullet tore through her flesh. It exited just below her collarbone and smashed into the car's console in front of her. She wasn't wearing a seatbelt and cursed as the jolt propelled her forward. She continued to drive at a dangerous speed. At the junction at the end of the street, she gunned the engine and tried to shoot across the main road. She never made it to the other side. A large utilities van slammed into her rear end and put the small car into an uncontrollable spin. The Fiat bumped up and over the opposite pavement, hit a small embankment and rolled over twice before sliding into one of the few canals in Den Haag.

The cold water revived her senses and prevented her from passing out. Disoriented by the chaos, she groped and fumbled for her bag in a desperate attempt to locate the box of cigars. She managed to get hold of it, but as she pulled the box out of the bag it slipped from her wet hand and opened up. She hadn't replaced the securing pin. She watched in horror as the cigars began spilling out. They were instantly caught in the whirlpool of water gushing in through the open window of the fast sinking vehicle. She frantically grasped at them as they bobbed, sank and resurfaced as if to taunt her. Her hand caught hold of the box again and to her relief, it still contained several cigars. She held on to it for grim death, but the rising level of water necessitated a different course of action.

She tried to pull herself through the open window, but found it difficult with one hand and a bullet through her shoulder. Struggling to get free, she felt panic starting to set in. The car was almost full of water and she knew she had to make a choice. Reluctantly, she relinquished the cigar box and began kicking and pushing, but the force of her struggle turned the small car onto its side and it started to sink down. As the car settled on the shallow bed of the canal, it pinned her from the waist down. She pushed with her one good arm, but the car would not budge. Her lungs were at bursting point. Tantalizingly, the cigar box floated past within reach. She grasped for it and caught it, but in the churning gloom, even with her blurred vision, she could see that it was empty. All of its contents had tumbled out and were already turning to mush, soon to break up and disintegrate.

The lights still burned on the little car and she could make out weeds and other strange dark shapes morphing in the shadows of the murky depths. Something caught the light and her eyes turned towards its sparkle. It was the large diamond ring she had taken from Chong's wife's dead hand. She held her hand up in front of her face. The diamond sparkled and blinked at her and seemed to grow even brighter as she gazed at it. The light reflecting from it was intense, but it only lasted for a moment before it began to fade and was gone. Then everything went dark.

Chapter 78

The hospital staff seemed to be in awe of him. His epic chase through the streets of Amsterdam had already achieved legendary status on You Tube. He was also building quite a reputation with the emergency services; this was the third time he'd received medical treatment in forty eight hours. Receiving a gunshot to the chest wasn't something he'd imagined he would experience on vacation or would ever wish to again. The Kevlar vest supplied by the police had absorbed the force of the bullet, leaving a dark bruise on his chest at the point of impact. His head hurt more and he was receiving the last of ten stitches to it.

'I could have been killed Inspector.' Dirk pointed out aggrievedly to Alphenaar. 'You guys were supposed to be listening. You should've come charging in like gang busters as soon as you were aware I was being compromised. The moment I spoke to her and said her name should have been enough for you to act.'

'The TV interfered with our reception, sorry', was all Alphenaar offered by way of an apology.

'Sorry doesn't really cover it, does it?' said Dirk.

'Well, we couldn't really just charge in without knowing something definite could we? We had to wait until a threat had been made or she said something that indicated we had the right person. For all we knew she could have simply been a hotel guest or just another cigar smoker. We had to wait until she had left the hotel, in case she fired her weapon.' said Alphenaar, in an attempt to rationalise the shortcomings of his department.

'She did fire her weapon…at me.' Spat Dirk.

Alphenaar shrugged, 'At least you survived, which is more than I can say for her.'

Dirk raised his non-bruised eyebrow. 'She's...?'

'Unless she can hold her breath for a very long time; she's still at the bottom of a canal not far from the hotel. We have divers in trying to recover the body.' said Alphenaar.

Dirk nodded grimly. 'I'd like to see Helena and tell her it's over.'

'I think I can arrange that.'

Twenty minutes later a tearful Helena came bounding into the ward and jumped onto Dirk's bed, much to the consternation of the same young female Doctor on duty from his previous visit. On seeing the stitches above his eye and the bruise on his chest, she shot Alphenaar a pejorative look. He favoured her with a sheepish and apologetic one in return then gave them a moment alone. He knew exactly how she felt.

~

When he'd spoken with her on the phone and told her where he was and what had happened, Helena had gone ballistic; screaming a torrent of abuse down the line at him. He'd met her on arrival at the rear entrance to the hospital, where he had attempted to placate her by offering a brief explanation of the events that took place earlier in the day. When he'd finished his summary, Helena called him and his fellow officers, Interpol too, a bunch of reckless incompetent assholes.

~

She gave Dirk and earful too, for not telling her and putting himself in harm's way. Dirk explained that he had purposely kept her out of the loop, because he knew what her reaction would have been. She was angry with him, but didn't stay mad for very long. Helena's journalist colleagues made sure the police didn't harangue them too much and after a brief statement from Dirk, they were whisked back to the comfort of the hotel in a limousine. Helena's magazine had also arranged for Champagne to be delivered to their room. Within the seclusion of their luxurious bathroom suite, lying together in their foam filled bath, Dirk popped the cork and told her everything.

~

When the Dutch police and Interpol had learned that Frank had given Jason diamonds for his coin, they wanted to know everything Dirk knew. Dirk again recounted the events that took place in the days following the trade. Finally, he told them of the key he had found in the apartment after the break-in and what he suspected it opened. That and the things Frank had said at various times in his company had inspired him to go to Den Haag and act upon his hunch with the cigar safe.

The police had been keen to know about the contents. Dirk divulged that, together with Helena, they had opened the cigar safe when they'd arrived at the Hotel and discovered a box of cigars. Interpol were sceptical. Helena corroborated everything he said, including the fact that they hadn't removed any of the cigars from the box. Dirk confirmed that Frank's safe still contained a full box of cigars.

Both the police and Interpol hadn't been amused that he'd failed to tell them any of this before and accused him of withholding information. He'd dismissed it by telling them he hadn't thought it important, because it appeared to be exactly what it was: a cigar safe containing cigars. He also reminded them that Frank had taken him there for lunch at the beginning of the week and had given him a cigar, which had presumably come from his private stash there.

The consensus of opinion was, that the safe must contain the elusive package everyone seemed so desperate to get their hands on and that Dirk and Helena had just missed its true value when they first discovered it. Interpol demanded Dirk hand over the key and were horrified to learn that he'd had it on him when Jason had drugged and robbed him. The police were quick to point out that they hadn't found a key among Jason's effects and had to acknowledge that whoever killed him must have stolen it. The implications of this prompted immediate action. A quick phone call was made and surveillance was put on the cigar lounge, in case the killer was headed back there. Dirk had been quick to interject and offer an opinion. He said that he didn't think the killer would attempt to access the cigar safe yet because they, in all probability, didn't know which one it was. He hypothesised that because of Maudasi's murder, the killer had probably come back to the apartment for the same reason Maudasi and Dragan had: to look for a clue that would point to the name on the cigar safe or confront him and Helena and extract that information.

Interpol wanted to open the cigar safe without further delay and insisted Dirk give up the name written on it. Dirk's main concern with this idea was that any tampering with it would just make the killer disappear, only to have them resurface at a later date with deadly intentions. Whoever it was had already tried to kill him once before, but Jason had got in the way. He pointed out that they would most likely try again and would probably succeed a second time and possibly kill Helena too, out of revenge, if he gave up the contents of the safe to the authorities. Interpol said that if he wouldn't give up the name then they would just open them all and check all of their contents. This suggestion enraged the Dutch police and an argument ensued over legality and statutory rights.

As the arguments raged, Helena excused herself and went back up to her apartment. With her out of the room, Dirk had come up with the suggestion of using himself as live bait.

Chapter 79

The day after the shooting, Alphenaar came back to the hotel to collect Dirk and escort him down to the morgue again; this time to identify Natalie's body. When they arrived at the morgue, he asked an odd question. 'Are you quite sure you can identify her?'

Dirk was somewhat taken aback by this. 'Yes, quite sure, she's not someone you'd easily forget. I recognised her the moment she turned up.'

Her body was lying on a gurney covered by a simple white cotton sheet. As they approached, the morgue attendant pulled back the sheet, revealing her face, neck and shoulders. Her hair had been swept back and the exit wound on her shoulder, made by the police shooting, was clearly visible. Dirk steeled himself to look at her.

'Yes, no mistake, that's Natalie; Frank Perrier's girlfriend.' He said in a sombre voice.

Alphenaar was looking at him curiously. 'What, don't you believe me?' Dirk asked.

'I spoke with the Interpol this morning and they claim to have spoken with someone called Natalie, fitting her description and living at her address in Geneva. She returned from Zurich two days ago, when the police contacted her about Frank Perrier's death. She came back to identify him and is there now.' announced Alphenaar, gravely.

Dirk was utterly perplexed by this alarming revelation. He stared at Alphenaar and then at the corpse again. 'But that *is* her. No doubt about it.'

'That's another thing.' said Alphenaar, gesturing to the attendant who tore off the sheet covering her modesty and revealing her naked form. Dirk was horrified at this total lack of respect for the dignity of the dead, but his eyes were drawn to her. At first he couldn't comprehend what he was seeing until Alphenaar posed the question.' Are you quite sure that is *she*?'

The testicles and penis, although small, were unmistakable. *She* was a *he*.

'Is there anything else you'd like to tell me Mister Dagger?' asked Alphenaar.

Dirk couldn't think for a moment, but then he recalled Frank telling him that Natalie had a twin brother. He'd never been formally introduced to him, until this moment. Alphenaar was keen to speak with Dirk some more regarding Frank's package. However, after seeing Natalie's *brother* naked, Dirk said he was reluctant to discuss anyone's package. This wasn't lost in translation and Alphenaar appreciated the analogy. He drove Dirk back to the hotel and suggested they have a chat in the cigar lounge, if he didn't think that was too weird after his recent experience there. Dirk said it didn't bother him.

'How long do you intend to stay here in the hotel Dirk?' enquired Alphenaar, becoming notably less formal.

'Maybe just one more night or whenever Helena finishes her testimony at the ICC, which should only be another day or two at the most.' said Dirk.

Alphenaar changed the subject. 'We found some diamonds in Jason Sinclair's hotel room. They were inside a Cohiba cigar holder, inside the hotel room safe. There were only the four diamonds you told us about. We searched his room thoroughly and found nothing else.'

'That's too bad Inspector, I thought he might at least have had a few more coins.' said Dirk.

Alphenaar changed the subject again. 'That was a very brave thing you did yesterday. You took a big risk. It took guts.'

Dirk was philosophical. 'Well, we all knew me and Helena were next on the hit list. This seemed like the only way to stop that from happening. Wouldn't you agree Inspector?'

Alphenaar didn't say anything. He seemed a bit circumspect and didn't offer an opinion. The previous evening, Dirk had agreed to give up the name on Frank's cigar safe on one condition: they use him to draw the killer out into the open. The police had warmed to this idea immediately and set up a sting operation. The cigars in Frank's safe were covertly removed by the police and taken away for examination. They had been replaced by an identical box fitted with a concealed electronic tracking device. Dirk's task had been to enter the cigar lounge and wait for the killer to show up. Although it could have gone a lot smoother than it did, the plan had been a success. However, the police were still far from satisfied. He knew the question Alphenaar was waiting for him to ask and he decided not to disappoint. 'Have you recovered anything from the box of cigars in Frank's safe Inspector?'

Alphenaar looked unperturbed, 'Nothing but cigars, like you said. If there ever were any diamonds in the safe, then someone had the foresight to remove them. Who knows, maybe we'll never know. I see you've bought yourself a new hat and coat.'

Right turn Clyde, thought Dirk. 'Yes. I went out this morning and replaced them. You can do what you like with the old ones Inspector. I didn't like the idea of putting on *dead man's clothes.*' He said, referring to the blood soaked garments Jason had died in.

'It makes you look like a cowboy.' Joked Alphenaar.

'Dirk smiled. 'That's what Helena says too.'

Alphenaar paused for a moment. 'Do you like cowboy movies Dirk?'

Left turn Clyde, 'Sure, who doesn't?'

'Who's your favourite cowboy? I'm betting Clint Eastwood, am I right?'

'He's probably one of the best.' said Dirk, nonchalantly.

'In fact I watched a really good Clint Eastwood movie on TV this week: "The Good, the Bad and the Ugly". Did you see it?' asked Alphenaar.

'I can't say I did.' answered Dirk, dryly.

'I've seen it many times myself before, but it never gets old does it?' said Alphenaar.

'They have an excellent vintage port here, can I get you one Inspector?' asked Dirk, when the waitress arrived.

'Just an Americano thanks.'

When the waitress had gone, Alphenaar continued on his Cowboy themed conversation.

'You know it was a really clever ending, how Clint sets up the little bandit in the movie. He knows he can't trust him with the name on the grave where the gold is hidden. So, he gives him another: *Arch Stanton.* This turns out to be the name on the grave next to the grave with the gold in it, a grave marked *Unknown*; an unmarked grave hiding in plain sight. A very simple ploy, but effective, don't you agree?'

Dirk shrugged, 'I can't say I remember.'

Their coffees arrived and Dirk wished he hadn't ordered alcohol with his coffee, but he couldn't very well send it back now. Alphenaar was watching him, waiting for a reaction; anything. Dirk responded by asking if he'd like a cigar with his coffee. Alphenaar declined the offer, but instead turned to look at the cigar safes on the back wall of the lounge and posed a very loaded question. 'Guests of the hotel have the use of those don't they? They call them crypts, did you know that? A crypt is like a grave isn't it? Makes you wonder what secrets are hidden within some of these *unknown crypts.*'

Dirk wasn't taking the bait. 'It makes me wonder about the wisdom of calling it a crypt, since smoking kills. It also makes me wonder about the value people put on their own lives. How much would it have to be to have caused all those killings Inspector?'

Alphenaar smiled ironically at Dirk's philosophical answer and said. 'Hopefully, we'll never have to choose.'

'Supposing there had been diamonds in Frank's crypt, what would have happened to them if you'd found them?' enquired Dirk.

Alphenaar sipped his coffee before giving his reply. 'Well, I suppose they would have to be assessed and examined to see if they had been stolen or if they were conflict diamonds.'

'...and after that? I presume they would have disappeared into a government fund or something equally charitable, but that's only my guess.' added Dirk brazenly.

Alphenaar gave Dirk a slightly disparaging look at his faith in authority, but then shrugged as if to say *c'est la vie*. He drummed his fingers on the table top and glanced again at the wall of cigar safes, then posed another question. 'Have you come to a decision yet?'

'A decision about what Inspector?' asked Dirk.

Alphenaar smiled enigmatically. 'About whether or not you are going to remain in the Netherlands of course; that's quite a woman you have there. How is she by the way?'

'Helena's fine, thanks for asking. But, in answer to your question, no, I haven't made any decisions yet. I need time to think everything through and make the right one. You can understand that right?'

Alphenaar nodded and stood up. He glanced at the cigar safes one last time and then thrust his hand out. Dirk got up and shook it. 'Take good care of her Dirk and yourself too. I hope the decision you make is right for both of you. Goodbye and good luck.'

'You too Inspector...and thanks.'

Dirk stood at the window of the cigar lounge and watched him get into his car and drive away. Neither the police nor Interpol would admit to it, but Dirk knew they were pleased with their overall success: A known international smuggler was dead, although the motive and the killer were still unofficially substantiated, as were the contents of the package they all had coveted with such zeal. However, the overall circumstantial evidence connecting Natalie's brother and Frank, together with all the main players, brokered the missing pieces. Dragan had been officially identified as a Serbian war criminal and the Dutch authorities were getting ready to claim credit for their role in his demise. Maudasi still remained a mystery. The apartment in Amsterdam was not in his name and he was not the owner, as everyone was led to believe. The Bentley was traced to someone in Paris who said he had recently sold it. The new owner could not be traced. No one called Sadim Maudasi actually existed, on paper or anywhere else.

Chapter 80

Dirk flew to Geneva for Frank's funeral the following week. Helena offered to attend with him. He would have been glad of her support, but felt she had been through enough and said it would probably be best if he went by himself. During the service he didn't sense any real emotion coming from the sparse congregation that was in attendance. Frank's banking colleagues and associates, those who'd chosen to turn up, constantly and disrespectfully checked their smart phones and BlackBerrys throughout the service. Dirk stood at the front, alongside Frank's parents. His Mother was very distraught and he'd found that hardest of all to take. Natalie was also in attendance, but was remote and cool towards him when he tried to speak with her. After the funeral, she disappeared faster than the speeding bullet her cross-dressing brother had shot him with, without as much as a goodbye.

When he deemed it timely and appropriate to say his farewells to Frank's parents, Dirk went up to Natalie's house, in a taxi cab, to speak with her on her terms. Both red Porsches stood sentinel in the driveway, but the house had a vacant feel to it. Dirk asked the taxi driver to wait until he had made sure someone was home, as it was quite a way from the centre of town. He rang the doorbell, but just as he suspected no one came to the door. When the taxi drove him away again from the imposing house, Dirk glanced up at the panoramic window. It was impossible to tell if someone was looking out, because the glass was reflective of light.

However, the feeling he had of being watched was tangible.

During his brief stay in Geneva, Interpol seized the opportunity to interview him again. He obliged with their request, but only on the condition that he didn't miss his return flight to Amsterdam. The questions were more of the same and underpinned the fact that nothing more had come to light, regarding the business Frank, Chong and Maudasi had all been connected with and the reason for their deaths. All they had was conjecture and supposition.

They had obtained some information from their Hong Kong counterparts, but these were mostly rumours of a large consignment of gold for sale at time of Chong's death. They had also heard a rumour that the asking price for the gold was diamonds. In light of these rumours, combined with the traditional nature of Chong's business endeavours and the fact Frank had given him a package, it didn't take a genius to work out what they had all been involved in. But without hard evidence, they had nowhere to go. The nature of Frank's death was still inconclusive. However, Interpol and the Geneva police were happy to pin it on the same killer as the others. Dirk suspected Natalie of being involved too. He was sure there was no way Frank would ever have considered screwing over a guy like Maudasi of his own volition. It had to have been someone else pulling his strings. Someone he would have done anything for. He was pretty sure Natalie had planned the whole thing. She had probably coerced Frank before, but this had been the big one.

The police had their suspicions about her too.

However, suspicions don't guarantee convictions. She was interviewed by the Geneva police and by Interpol, but vehemently denied any involvement whatsoever with any business Frank and her brother/sister had been involved in. Natalie's passport had been found among her dead brother's personal effects. It had recently been used to enter Hong Kong, at the same time as Chong and his wife. She claimed he must have stolen it from her. No connection could be made to connect Natalie with any of the deaths or any of the events leading up to them. She had an irrefutable alibi that placed her in Zurich at the time, on business, with dozens of witnesses who, like herself, were mostly lawyers. Consequently, any further questioning was brought to an abrupt halt.

~

By the end of May enquires had ended in a satisfactory conclusion for all those concerned. Helena had moved to a new apartment and Dirk moved in with her. She had been busy covering the continuing Serbian war crimes tribunal and her human interest article, on the atrocities of war in the former Yugoslavia, had evolved into a book. She was something of a tabloid celebrity for a couple of weeks, but now the furore had begun to die down; much to their mutual relief. Dirk too had been bombarded by emails and requests for interviews. He declined all of them.

Melissa had emailed him too, asking when her hero was returning home. He had given a lot of thought to his future and what he should do next, but was in no rush to make any decisions. He was still reflecting on his mortality, after his flirtation with death. The past few weeks with Helena had been bliss, but he was beginning to grow restless. On the morning of May thirty first, as he sat looking out of the window of their apartment he made his decision. Tomorrow was the first of June. It was a new beginning and he knew exactly what he wanted to do.

When Helena returned home in the evening she found a letter waiting for her.

Chapter 81

By the middle of June Dirk had achieved what he'd set out to do. The first thing he did, when he returned to Bristol, was to place his apartment in the hands of an estate agent and get his affairs in order. He visited Melissa in her bar and made his peace with her. She seemed pleased to see him, although her overall demeanour was cool. It *had* been over a month and he hadn't called. He flew up to his birth place of Glasgow, to visit family and friends and get advice on some investments he was considering. One thing his mind was clear on, after his recent experiences, he had no desire to do work of any kind for the near and foreseeable future and certainly never again in an office. First, however, he was taking a long vacation in the sun and had booked a trip to the Dutch Antilles island of Aruba, just off the coast of Venezuela.

The clothes shops were well stocked with summer clothing. Dirk bought himself a few designer linen shirts and a couple of pairs of linen trousers for the tropical heat he was heading into. Anything else he needed he would pick up at the airport or when he reached his destination. He was flying from Glasgow to Schiphol airport, where he would catch a connecting flight. The weather was typically miserable when he flew out and wasn't much better when he touched down in Amsterdam, where he had a three hour stopover until his connection. Fortunately, he didn't have to venture outside. On arrival, he switched on his cellphone and received the customary welcome message from the phone company, informing him how cheap it was to increase their profitability. There was one other message waiting for him, which he read and replied to immediately. He checked the time then strolled around the duty free shops and picked up a few more essentials, before heading up to the executive lounge for some lunch and free drinks.

Inside the secluded lounge, away from the bustling throng, he found a quiet spot and got himself a glass of Champagne. On the table in front of him was a discarded magazine. He picked it up and began flipping through the pages, but soon lost interest. He was too distracted with other thoughts. As he sat there looking out at the rain splashed tarmac, taking a moment of reflection, a familiar voice beside him asked. 'Is this seat taken?'

Looking up, his heart and cares melted away when he gazed into the sparkling blue eyes of Helena. She was a vision in a lovely summer dress. Springing to his feet, he kissed her for such a long moment that the other travellers in the lounge gave them a round of applause. They laughed and hugged and laughed and kissed. She sat down beside him and he just sat there staring at her, stroking her face and hair. He asked her how she was and repeatedly told her how beautiful she looked, although he'd seen and spoken with her every night on Skype.

The war crimes trial was on-going and would be for a long time to come. She had completed her article for her magazine and was now taking an extended leave of absence, before embarking on writing her book. He said he was looking forward to reading it. They left it at that and spoke no more about it. Instead, they talked about the future. Dirk topped up their glasses with more Champagne and then dipped into his pocket and produced a small box. He opened it up and revealed a flawless, two carat, diamond ring. He lifted up her left hand. Without having to be asked, she let him slip it onto her third finger. When they kissed again it earned them another round of applause from their fellow travellers.

They raised their glasses in a toast and she asked. 'What shall we drink to?'

Dirk leaned in close and asked provocatively. 'How do you feel about Arch Stanton?'

Epilogue

Natalie slid elegantly into the back seat of the waiting taxi and closed the door. Things hadn't turned out well. Frank and her brother were dead and the police had made her very uncomfortable. One policeman had even said that she didn't look too upset at losing the two closest men in her life, emphasising the word men as he'd said it. She was angry that all had not gone to plan. Frank's weakness and her crazy brother's fluctuating hormones had blown all her meticulous planning and almost brought her down too. She was lucky to have gotten away without besmirching her solid reputation. But that was all behind her now. The taxi dropped her off in front of Geneva train station, where she was catching the train to Zurich on business. She enjoyed travelling by train. It was clean and efficient and she could appreciate the beautiful Swiss countryside, which wasn't possible on a jet at altitude. Another benefit of train travel was time; none of it was wasted checking in, thus allowing her to effectively get on with some work if she chose to or even just relax. Now, she sat alone in first class and contemplated her future.

She looked up as a well-dressed oriental gentleman entered the carriage and sat down opposite her. He smiled and she politely acknowledged him, her discerning eyes registering the huge solitaire diamond ring he exhibited on the little finger of his right hand. A large Bvlgari watch protruding from under his left cuff was another indicator of his wealth. The gentleman appeared to be all about business and opened his briefcase to remove what looked like a large legal document. However, she knew it was only a matter of time before he struck up a conversation. It was what men did. They always did. They just couldn't help themselves.

Minutes after the train pulled out of the station, a waiter appeared and asked if they would like something to drink. The gentleman turned to Natalie and asked courteously if she would care to join him in a glass of Champagne. There it was; the icebreaker. Seeing no reason to refuse his generous offer, she smiled politely and accepted. Champagne always relaxed her. Men were always offering to buy her things and getting her drinks, like they thought if they did they had a chance. She thrived on the power of her beauty.

The waiter returned with a bottle of Perrier-Jouët and filled two glasses. The smiling oriental gentleman sat back and graciously waited for her to take one. Natalie thanked him again and raised her glass in salutation to his generosity. When he lifted his glass to reciprocate the gesture, she noticed something odd about his hands. At first she couldn't tell what it was because the large diamond solitaire was a distraction. Not wanting to stare she sipped her Champagne, but when he tilted his head back she dared to look. He had no fingernails.

THE END

About the Author

K. J. Warden is based in North Somerset, just outside Bristol, England. He is an IT consultant and writer who lives wherever he finds work or a good story.

Printed in Great Britain
by Amazon.co.uk, Ltd.,
Marston Gate.